Intermagical

TS Davis

For the odd ones, and especially, for Faeryn.

Intermagical

Part 1 - The Valley

She clicked her long, sharp nails on the carved crystal goblet she held in her pale, elegant hand, waiting impatiently. This girl, this problem, this thorn in her, albeit, perfectly formed side, she smoothed the silk gown down along her slim, curved waist, would be here at any moment. She bent forward, peering again at the shallow dish of water reflecting the small, luxurious boudoir, walls dripping with heavy velvet curtains with tassels at the corners, edged with glittering beads. The sparkling chandelier illuminated the tall woman's irritated expression.

Nothing, yet.

Leaning back in the gilded throne of a chair, she shook her artfully coiffed head, and took a sip from the goblet, shuddering as she felt the miraculous liquid suffuse her being with the glow of magical energy. She relaxed, tipping the chair back on its rear legs and letting her eyes drift closed. She must focus. Concentrate on restraint. Her frustration, her supreme irritation at this fly in the ointment, this changeling girl that would complicate her plans, she must take caution and be sure not to let it rule her, and cause her to break her oath to her Lady. But, there were things she could do, within the bounds of her oath, if she got creative.

The door latch clicked and her eyes sprang open. With a twitch of her wrist, she dropped the illusion she had been holding and the room returned to normal. Just in time, the door swung wide, revealing a tall young man. The puppy, she thought irritably, What does he want? He stepped into the box-lined closet, giving a tight-lipped smile to the thin, angular woman in front of him, pitched dangerously backward on an old folding chair.

"Um, hey. I just wanted to let you know that I'm leaving. I don't like what they're doing out there and I don't want to be a part of it. If Father asks, just tell him I went to the Raven, okay?"

She nodded, dropping the chair's front legs back to the cement slab with a click and taking a sip from her paper cup. Just in time, she thought, as the door clicked shut behind the man. The illusion sprang back up around her just as the dish of water grew cloudy and then resolved into the image of a misty tree-lined highway and a lonely minivan. It was time to act.

Chapter 1

"YEEEAAAUUCCHHH!!"

I screamed and wrenched the wheel of my beat-up old van as I swerved off the pavement and onto the gravel that separated the highway from a row of towering evergreens. My tires skidded on the loose stones before lurching to a stop with the tell-tale hiss and sink of a tire losing air quickly.

"Ohmygod, ohmygod, what was that?"

I panted, clutching the wheel and catching my breath. Flipping off the chaotic swiping of the wipers, I closed my eyes and leaned my head back, listening to my heart pounding furiously in my chest. The blazing, multi-colored flash of light that had scared me off the road was seared into my vision, bright against my eyelids. What had that been? Something brilliantly bright, that was all I could see. A big, rainbow flash. I had thought it might have been an oncoming semi for a second, but there was nothing there, now. Could that be what lightning looks like, when it's really, really close up?

I opened the door and peered out through the pouring rain at the dense growth of trees on both sides of the highway, sighing heavily.

"This is gonna be wet, isn't it?" Taking cover under the back hatch of the old minivan, I peered around at the ruined tire and the incongruous angry yellow strip that had stopped it in its tracks. One of those toothy ones like you'd see in a parking lot. That tire was going to need more than a patch. Looking down at my mangled tire, gripped in the gnashing protective jaw, I wondered why anyone would bother to put a thing like that all the way out here. *So far out there isn't even cell reception*, I said to myself, glowering at the X at the corner of my phone's screen and stuffing it back into my pocket. I didn't even know where I was now, really. The last road sign I had read had said *Historic Kalapuya Tribal Land.* How close was that to where I was headed?

As my eyes adjusted to the dimness, I could see a rough track through the trees, and some faint pinpricks of light in the distance. Lights mean people and people are generally nice and want to help each other, right? I reasoned with myself, in my head.

"Finally remembered that talking to yourself is weird, huh?"

The thought ran through my mind in my mom's acerbic voice. Why, though? Mom is hundreds of miles away. I'm an adult and I can do what I want. There's nobody here to think I'm weird for talking to myself, anyway, I thought, defiantly. I looked out again, through the trees. The lights in the distance looked brighter as dusk rolled in. I was alone in these woods. Completely by myself. Get a grip, girl.

"There's nobody here to think I'm weird for talking to myself," I said into the darkness. The thick sound of rain dampened my words and the wind whistled through the trees with a sound like tinkling laughter, as though in answer.

Chapter 2

I grabbed my already-packed bag from the back of the van. Staying at the motel last night had at least prepared me to leave the car in a hurry. "And this," I said, satisfied, stuffing a big manila envelope into the top of my backpack and tugging the zipper mostly closed. Hood up against the drizzle, I slung the bag over my shoulders and pointed my feet toward the lights that I could see peeking through the trees in the distance.

"The Pacific Northwest is home to the only temperate rainforest in the world, " I recited, mocking the soothing voice of the local TV personality that had eventually succeeded in putting me to sleep at the motel last night, "Its lush, green beauty comes with an average rainfall of," I tried to remember, "oh, some just obscene number of inches per- erp!" I made an involuntary noise as a splash of cold rainwater iced down my neck and into my shirt front.

Lush green beauty was right though, I thought wonderingly, as I brushed against a charmingly curled frond of an arching fern, peeking out from the mossy hollow of an old, knotted tree. It was like a scene out of a storybook, or a painting of fairyland. The droplets of rainwater on the tips of leaves and pine needles glistened in what was left of the fading light, almost like magic. One particularly bright flash of a raindrop caught my eye, and I stumbled, tripping over a low root.

"I'd swear that wasn't there a second ago," I said, confused, turning to look at it. As I did, I bumped awkwardly into another tree, closer than I had thought it was, which sent another shower of cold water down onto my head and shoulders. A chilly gust of air whipped through the trees, chilling my exposed skin, and bringing with it that same tinkling, eerie laughing sound that the wind had made before.

"Ugh!" I exclaimed, shivering as more icy rivulets escaped down my ineffective jacket's collar and into my increasingly damp clothing, "I know I'm clumsy, but this is something else!" Gripping my backpack straps with intention, I turned away from the charming ferns and hopped over a mossy little rock-filled stream almost without pausing to look at it, purposefully heading toward the lights, and, hopefully, someone who could help me. It was too wet, and I was too cold.

"Not sleeping in the woods tonight," I said, striding resolutely forward, "That is the goal." I tried to focus on walking without tripping or running into things, but my idle mind wandered, wondering what lay ahead of me. I squinted through the growing dim. The lights were closer now, but I still couldn't tell what I was walking toward, in the rain. "If I'd known I'd be hiking through the woods, I'd have brought some binoculars," I lamented. But, now that I thought about it. . .

I pulled out my cell phone and pointed the camera at the cluster of vague building shapes. Maybe if I zoomed in, I'd be able to tell what I was walking into. The first picture came out blurry. The second one did too, but this was more interesting than continuing to trudge endlessly. By the third try, I could make out some detail in the pool of light surrounding some temporary buildings. Four fuzzy shapes. People! Three people carrying something heavy, toward a box of a truck that looked like an in-town moving van.

"Maybe they'll let me hitch a ride with whatever that thing is," I said, "at least I'd be out of this rain. What is it though?" I wondered aloud, as I picked my way through the trees, taking more photos.

"That's a really weird thing to do," said my Mom's voice in my mind. My ever-present internal critic, once-again piping up with commentary. I rolled my eyes. What did I ever do that wasn't a little weird? But, it was a valid point. What would I tell the men, if they asked why I was sneaking up on them taking photos?

I zoomed in on the most recent picture and smiled. At least the mystery had been solved. It was a large carved stone spotted with green moss, taller than the men attempting to load it and heavier than they were comfortable handling. Two men strained with ropes at the top of the ramp and the other one pushed from the bottom. In the photo, I could see their faces, grim and tense with effort. The men heaved again and the thing slid forward into the truck bed with a loud crash of rock on metal. The whole truck swayed and sank a little lower on its tires to accommodate the new weight.

As I pocketed my phone, glad to have remembered the social convention before being caught, though, I defended myself mentally, entirely unintentionally suspicious-looking, the van's engine turned over, and it drove off leaving two of the men standing in the pool of yellow light that was now all that illuminated the dark, wet woods. I stepped out from between the trees and into the circle of light, raising my hand and calling out to the men.

"HELL-aughth!" Simultaneously, there was another bright flash and a bang like a firecracker, as an enormous splash of icy water drenched my head and shoulders, running into the neck of my raincoat and turning my greeting into a wet splutter. The men turned and gaped at the soaking girl that had just stepped unexpectedly out of the trees. After a moment, the taller man closed his mouth, cleared his throat, and stepped purposefully forward.

"What are you doing here? This is private property. You are trespassing."

Taking a deep breath to explain, I shivered involuntarily in my now-soaking clothing. Instead of answering, I felt my face crack embarrassingly. I sobbed loudly, my breath catching and my shoulders heaving. Blissfully hot, if still irritatingly wet, tears joined the rainwater coursing down my cheeks.

"Oh look at you, little girl," the tall man said, in a deep, resonant voice, "Let's get you out of this rain."

My body continued to wrack with involuntary sobs as the man led me into the nearest temporary building. He flicked on a hanging work light illuminating an office full of bookcases and filing cabinets and filled an empty plastic water bottle from a dispenser, handing it to me. The label on the bottle read *Christian Springs - Natural Oregon Spring Water.* I stared at the bottle in my hands for a moment trying to catch my breath, but didn't drink any. It was nice to have something to hold onto while I collected my thoughts, though. Honestly, although my tears were embarrassing, my emotional reaction had probably been the best thing for me, in this situation, all things considered, I thought to myself as I focused on regulating my breath. They would hardly think I was suspicious now, not after a display like that.

"Now, tell me, child. How did you end up in this part of the woods? We're not near any public hiking trails."

"I... I... I was just driving into town, and my car ran off the road," I spluttered, trying to explain with my face swollen from crying, "and my tire popped and I don't have a spare, and I don't have any phone service, and, and, ohmygod, I just didn't know what I was going to do!" I finished.

The man nodded, understandingly. "These things happen. You've run off the road, and it's by the Grace of our Lord God that you are safe and well. Surely it was His presence in your heart that brought you here to me. Nothing much to be done about your vehicle tonight, though, if you don't have a tire, but I can drive you into town, and you'll have more options in the morning."

"Thank you, Sir." I said and followed the man out. It felt awkward tagging on the honorific, but I figured I had better risk being too formal than not formal enough, especially after he had mistaken my casual blasphemy for being religious. I would really have to stop doing that if I didn't want to give people the wrong idea.

He held the car door open and waited to shut it behind me. I swung my still-dripping backpack into the tall cab of his white, built-tough truck and climbed in after it. We rolled down a dirt track, illuminated by his too-bright headlights, that I hadn't noticed before and might not even have seen in the daylight unless I had known what to look for. In just a few moments, we had crossed the distance that had taken me all evening on foot.

"Uh, Sir?"

"Please, call me Deacon," he said, "And you are?"

"Thanks for the ride Deacon," I said earnestly, "you really didn't have to." Although what else he would have done with me, I really wasn't sure. I chattered on to distract myself from the fact that I hadn't given my name in answer. "I was so worried that there wouldn't be any people with the lights and I would be stuck out in these wet woods all night, or get lost trying to find my car again."

"Yes, praise the Lord. Surely you were held in God's hands tonight, child. It is only my Christian duty to extend you my help in your time of need. I take it as a part of my responsibility as the Elder of the Valley of Christ's Heart Fellowship to shepherd the lost and the wayward in our community into the safety of God's light, whenever and wherever they are found."

Oh, I realized, not named Deacon, after all. He was A Deacon, or maybe The Deacon. Shepherd of the lost and wayward, huh? Yikes. "Mmm," I said, politely. If he could just quietly 'shepherd' me to the closest tire store and leave me alone, I'd appreciate it. But, I thought, glancing warily at his large red face and ramrod straight shoulders in the driver's seat beside me, somehow, I doubted that it would be that easy.

"Well now, as you were saying that you're new in town, might I ask if you have a local church home yet, Miss-?"

"Oh, um, not yet, " I answered, quickly and facetiously, ignoring his interrogative press for my name. In truth, I hadn't been inside a church since my grandma had taken me to youth group once or twice as a kid, but there was no point in telling the Deacon that, while I was stuck in his car with him. It was probably safer than my casual exclamation had made him think I was a Christian, actually. I resolved to try to stop doing that, but those kinds of phrases just roll off the tongue so easily!

"Well, let me earnestly encourage you to come worship with us, this Sunday. Any Sunday! I'll be the one preaching from the pulpit," he said, turning to me and winking. "Let my church family become your church family. A young, pretty girl like you needs a strong guiding hand to help steer her on the right path, don't you agree?"

"Mmm," I said, again, noncommittally. In fact, Mom's strong guiding hand was one of the things I was glad to be leaving behind, in California. I was out of school and ready to make my own way. That kind of control was the last thing I was looking for.

"Youths these days have nothing but temptation. The devil is in all things, waiting and watching. Conniving and tricking us into sin. Tempting and luring us ever farther down the path toward eternal doom and damnation." His voice took on an oratory quality as he picked up steam, his face growing more red in his excitement.

In contrast, I felt the color drain out of mine. Doom and damnation, seriously? Who was this guy?

"Without the Father's guiding hand, how can one help but to fall off the straight and narrow path of righteousness and into the darkness of sin and depravity? The Father tells us plainly what we must avoid if we are to live in the salvation of his light. The desires of the flesh," he intoned, raising one hand from the steering wheel to point aggressively in emphasis, "the desires of the eyes," his own eyes flashed brightly in his passion, "and the pride of life!" His eyes flicked toward me to where I sat, wide-eyed, pressed against the window, as far away from him as possible. His expression changed in an instant. The fearsome orator was gone, replaced by a sickeningly sweet, kindly look that made me even more uncomfortable. "I'm sorry my dear, I didn't mean to scare you like that. All of this talk of sin and the devil is frightening. Eternal damnation, hellfire. But you don't have to worry about that. As long as you listen to your husband and do as you're told, you too can achieve salvation in the Lord."

I did my best to keep my face neutral, and eased back into the center of my seat, now that he had stopped shouting. I just need to keep quiet and get out of this car safely, and then I'll never have to talk to this guy, or even think about him, ever again, I told myself, looking out at the long, empty stretch of road ahead of us.

"It's not really very hard to be a woman, though, is it?" he went on, "Now, men were created to serve God's plan. Men have the heavy lifting to do, to manifest the destiny that God intends for us. Women can just lie there…" he said, "er, lie around and wait until their husband tells them what to do. And I can help you find a good, godly man to help fulfill his mission, don't you worry your pretty little head about that." The Deacon went on and on, as we drove. He told me his thoughts on women, me especially, while I tried my best to keep my expression neutral, clenching my fists into tight balls in my lap, fingernails digging into my palm. "You are all just overgrown children, to be shepherded and brought into the flock. Lost without a husband or father to give direction. See what trouble you've already gotten yourself into?" he scolded, "If a God-fearing, righteous man like myself hadn't found you, who knows what heinous depravity might have befallen you?"

At that, he stopped talking for a moment, although his eyes still flicked busily, as though he were thinking about what those different and varied depravities might have been. The expression on his face made my stomach clench with fright and I thought frantically for anything to say to change the subject.

"Um, the desires of the eyes and of the flesh, I think I get, but what is 'pride of life' supposed to mean?" I asked, purely out of a desire to interrupt his train of thought rather than any genuine interest in what he had to say.

"Pride of life, my dear. That original sin, where Eve did bite the apple that was said to bestow knowledge of good and evil, offering her Godlike qualities so that she might boast in earthly wisdom."

"Oh," I answered, glad to have changed the topic but, if anything, more confused than I had been before. We crossed a bridge over the river and onto a street lined with shops. It seemed as though we had finally gotten to town, and not a minute too soon. He rolled to a stop at a red light, and I mentally cheered when I saw the quaint circular sign for the store on the corner.

"But, if you have biblical questions, my dear, let me offer you a place to stay tonight, where there are many learned and devout minds available to talk with you about—"

"Oh look, Lenny's Tires, right over there. This is me, then!" With a flurry of pleasantries and exaggerated gratitude, I opened the door and jumped out before the truck completely stopped. I hopped over the small river of rainwater in the gutter and onto the sidewalk. With a profound sigh of relief at being safe, and no longer trapped with that odious man, I straightened my backpack on my shoulders, and set off toward Lenny's, to go see a man about a tire.

Chapter 3

Gone Fishin' - Back Monday read the sign taped right below the word *Closed*.

Oh what small-town charm, I thought, as I walked away from the useless, closed tire shop and headed down a likely-looking street lined with awnings and sidewalk tables. The heavy door of the coffee shop on the corner swung open with a push and a warm puff of roasting coffee and burnt caramel air greeted me. This'll work, I thought.

"Your name for the latte?" The barista behind the counter raised her voice to be heard over the screech of milk steaming on the espresso machine, helping the customer in front of me. "What can I get ya, hon?"

I sighed, thinking sweet thoughts about milk foam and flavored syrup. But no, it wouldn't be worth it. "Just a tea? Uh, the mint's fine, thanks." I took my paper cup, teabag, and sleeve over to the self-service counter, and poured a cup full of steaming hot water, having yet again side-stepped my eternal problem.

"You can just give them a fake name if yours bugs you that much," a college friend had once suggested, shrugging off my struggle. But, what name? I could never come up with a chosen name that felt like mine, not even right enough just to get my coffee. Names have always carried a lot of weight for me. Names have power. I had considered so many names over the years, trying to find one that felt like mine. On a shelf of books and sagging board games, I spied a familiar blonde girl with a rabbit and a pocket watch. No, Alice was not my name, I thought to myself, with a little shake of the head. It wasn't quite right.

The cup of tea was nice and warm. It felt good in my cold, stiff fingers as I carried it to a booth in the corner. Hanging my jacket on a hook next to the table, I made myself at home. I stared out at the darkening street outside, and at my own bright reflection in the window. Round face, with soft, high cheeks and a small chin and nose. A baby face, people say. Round eyes, too. A little dark-rimmed and harried-looking after my adventure today.

Would I see my very nose, or my own hazel eyes on the face of some stranger at the park, tomorrow? Anything was possible, now that I was here, the place where I had been born. Where my birth family might still be, now. Or might not, I reminded myself, but I just couldn't make myself believe it. My impulse to come here had been so strong. Something was drawing me here. It must be.

Dragging my backpack toward me, I pulled out my big manila envelope. This packet of papers was why I had come here to this rainy Oregon valley. At least, they had pointed me in this direction. The envelope had arrived a few weeks ago, battered, with a few forwarding addresses on it, the most recent of which had been to my parent's house. Mom had sent it along to my college apartment for me.

Now, I was adopted at birth, and have known for as long as I can remember. It isn't a big deal. A couple of my cousins were adopted, too, so it always felt pretty normal to me. One of them even had an open adoption and knew her birth family, and saw them sometimes. I didn't have any information about my birth family, growing up. Not a single relative's name, or birth parent's picture, or heartfelt letter, just nothing. I fantasized about them occasionally, when I was young, about my birthmother especially, like a lot of adopted kids do, I think. Especially when mom was being extra critical or when I felt like she just didn't understand me. I imagined that she was a magical princess or something, and would come to sweep me away to fantasyland. My Mom had been tough, growing up. She had high standards for her child, and her particular way of being scornfully disappointed made me wither. I'd go a long way to avoid that feeling.

But I hadn't been fixated on my birth family really. Not until a few months ago. The dreams had started a little before my final year of college was about to start. Right after my birthday, maybe, toward the end of the summer. I'd wake up looking for someone. Yearning for something that I didn't know I was missing. I hadn't been sure what to do after college, anyway. As my early graduation date loomed, I didn't have good answers to anyone's questions about my plans. At least, I hadn't until I'd gotten this little packet in the mail. The first thing I pulled out were the hospital records of my birth. I'd taken one look at the address and immediately started planning my drive north. It just felt like the right thing to do.

In fact, it had felt so right that I hadn't even taken the time to go through the rest of the items in the folder before now. That was pretty weird, I realized, in retrospect, now that I was sitting here in Oregon. I liked researching stuff, and it wasn't like me to have ignored such a wealth of information for so long. It was like I had been obsessed with getting here. Well, I was here now, and the first thing to do would be to figure out what I had.

I reached into the envelope and pulled out the first item, laying it out on the worn wooden table. This was clearly a great college-town coffee shop with plenty of room to spread out and study. These were the hospital papers I had seen before. Times, weights, and lengths were all recorded with typewriter precision. Records of a baby girl surrendered at birth to an adoption agency for placement. I drew out another piece of paper and unfolded the small single sheet. It was a black and white photocopy of a picture of a woman. Her face was blurry but she looked young and pretty, smiling at the camera, with one hand on her very long hair. Across the top was written *birth mother*.

"Oh," I said, quietly, "Wow." I had never seen a picture of my birth mother before, and I looked at it for a long moment, although, admittedly, it was hard to tell much about her from the poor-quality photo. I set it down and reached back into the envelope. This time, I pulled out a large hard-back that looked like a children's picture book. The book's title, *Faeries*, was written in large, silver script. As I flipped the book over in my hands, something slipped out of it. A piece of slick yellowed paper, folded in three. A letter. I unfolded the paper and read:

Dearest Estranged Child,

It is with our fondest hopes that we send you out into the world to make your fortune among your father's people. Your begetting mother has listened to reason at last and has agreed that you will be sufficiently well tended to by the hands of guided fate in which we put our indelible trust.

She gives you a true name to carry with you, always, and to resonate with your power. Fiona - fair one. May you bear it with grace.

I looked up, eyes swimming with tears, unable to read on. Blinking the tears away, I held the letter in my hands and looked up at my reflection again. Fiona. A true name to carry with me. Fiona. A name to resonate with my power. I didn't know what that meant, but with the thought came a sensation. A heat blooming at the root of me, near the pit of my stomach, or the base of my back. It grew, tingling with heat and I felt my face spread in an involuntary grin.

A name. A real name of my own.

The name I had been raised with had never felt like mine. I remember being very young and asking my mom about my name, and how she had chosen it. Whether there were any other names she had considered. My mom had pulled out my baby book and showed me the list that they had come up with. First runner up just as strange-sounding and uncomfortable as the name they had given me. I had sighed at that, and given up, defeated, only to try again and again as I grew up. Nothing ever felt right, though. Not until now. I stared into my own eyes in the reflection of the night-darkened window, feeling the warming sensation grow within me, as my soul tried on the new name like a tailored shirt, and found that it fit me perfectly. Fiona! My beautiful, perfect new name.

A bright flash of headlights from outside cut through the night-darkened glass, momentarily blinding me. "Ack!" I yelped, flinching and dropping the letter I was holding. I blinked to clear my spotted vision, and bent down to pick it up. "Oh no!" I exclaimed, seeing the letter face-down in the pool of rainwater collecting under my dripping coat. What awful luck! I held the letter by one sodden corner and watched as the words swirled and ran off the page. Only the bottom edge was dry, I saw as I laid the ruined letter carefully on the table. The signature line was water spotted but still legible.

Her Royal Highness Queen Vivienne of the Faeries of Portal Land and the Twin River Valleys

"Queen?" I said incredulously, leaning over the table to peer more closely at the letter, "Of the Faeries?" Was that who my birth mother was?

No, surely not. It couldn't be. For one thing, I reminded myself, fairies were from fairy tales, and not from real life. And for another, the letter writer, this Queen, had mentioned my birth mother. Had convinced her to give me up for adoption, from the sound of it.

I picked up the photo of my birth mother again, unable to resist. Her face was blurry in the photocopy, but her hair was very long. Smooth and flowing. I looked back up at my reflection in the mirror of the window. My wavy brown hair was getting longer and looked lank and stringy from the rain. It could use a good detangling, too, after that walk in the woods. I did have my backpack with me, after all. Maybe a quick trip to the bathroom to freshen up was what I needed, now that I had dried out a little. I snapped a quick picture of the ruined letter, then scooped up my bag and headed toward the restroom.

The barista called after me. "We're closing up in 5 minutes, hon. You need anything else before I close my till?" I shook my head, feigning a polite smile.

Oh great, now where should I go? I considered my options as I ran a brush through my hair and wiped smeared makeup from under my eyes. I added a coat of mascara and replaced my mud-spattered shirt with a fresh navy v-neck. I remembered the waifish barista at the counter, with too-big earrings to match her too-big eyes, and sighed. That would never be me. I didn't have the body type that was 'in style' but, I smiled at myself in the mirror, tugging my shirt a little lower, I did have curves, and, the farther I got away from my mom and her opinions, the more I thought that maybe they didn't look so bad. I shoved everything back in my bag and gave myself one last appraising look in the mirror. It would have to do, for wherever tonight was going to take me. *Which is apparently anywhere but here*, I thought wryly, remembering the imminent closing time and the fact that I did not, in fact, have anywhere to go. There was that hotel a couple of blocks back, but, I shook my head, it wasn't time to turn in for the night just yet.

Buzzing with the residual energy of my new name, I stepped back out onto the street. A pair of men, shoulders hunched against the renewed drizzle, passed by me on the sidewalk. "What do you do in this town on a Friday night?" I called after them.

One of the men half-turned toward me and grinned, "You go to the Raven," he said, gesturing with his chin back the way he had come.

Chapter 4

After the quiet dark street, the light and sound of the noisy local on Friday night was overwhelming, and I stood frozen in the doorway until someone said, "…'Scuse me," and scooted me out of the entrance and into the swirling mass of bodies.

"Liquid courage would help," I muttered quietly, although in the loud bar the volume hardly mattered. No one could have heard me anyway. I squeezed up to the bar at the other end from where the two bartenders mixed and poured busily. That was good, it gave me time to think about what to order. It still felt like I was breaking the rules by being here at all since I had only turned 21 a few months ago. I had done a little drinking with friends and at parties, but this world was still pretty new to me.

"What can I get ya?" The kindly flannel-clad bartender smiled professionally and warmly.

"A beer," I said, like in the movies.

"Okay, on draft we've got a local Pilsner, an IPA, an Imperial IPA…"

Oh right, this wasn't the movies. "That one sounds good," I lied, having no idea what I had just ordered.

"Coming right up!" he said with a nod and turned back to the wall of bottles and shiny glass.

I felt my anxiety rise for a moment. How was I supposed to know what it cost, with no signs anywhere? I put a $20 bill on the bar. It had to be less than that right? I'd have to see how much change I got back. Yet again, it felt like everyone else had gotten an instruction manual for life and mine had gotten lost in the mail. The bartender was back. He smiled, slipping my change onto the bar.

"Haven't seen you in here before," he said, "what's your name?"

Oh no, not this again. I took a deep breath to say… something, and then remembered. The letter. That name! That new, beautiful, given name. "Fiona," I said. The name felt familiar on my lips, although I had never spoken it aloud before. For the very first time, I truly believed what I was saying. It felt so nice, not recoiling with displeasure at the wrongness of the name I had to say, and then holding stiffly in anticipation of the way others would react once they heard it. For the first time in my life, I was pleased with my answer to that question. "My name is Fiona."

The loud bar seemed to still for a moment. Probably just the song ending, I thought to myself, but the feeling remained that almost imperceptibly, the attention of the entire bar had just shifted, subtly, toward me. I took a sip and made an involuntary noise. "Ehck! Strong!" I remarked, recovering. The first sip had gone straight to my head as the intense alcohol fumes hit my sinuses making me feel like I might sneeze.

"Well, you wanted the Imperial," he shrugged, "9% I think. Better watch out, they'll getcha!" He laughed, turning to the next customer and leaving me to my libations.

"You should sing," said the wizened old broad on the barstool next to me, leaning against my shoulder. I turned to face her, which, conveniently, put a little space between her hot gin breath and my ear.

"What?"

"You should sing, honey. Sing!" She smiled, too slow. Her reaction times had clearly seen better days. "Kara (hic) kara-okie, ya know?"

"Oh, yeah, uh, maybe," I said, realizing that I had been singing along with the music under my breath. There was karaoke tonight, up on the stage. Maybe the drunk old lady was right, maybe I should sing. I stood up, grabbing my mostly empty pint, and swayed a little on my feet. Woah there! I finished that drink pretty fast.

"What's it gonna be, darlin'?" the jolly giant of a man behind the karaoke podium grinned at me.

"Uh, can it be anything?"

"Mostly anything, but you can always look in the books, doll," he said, gesturing to his stacks of binders.

"Uh, how about this one?" I scrawled the name of a song I liked to sing in the car, hoping that I was doing this right.

"Oh, that old one - I got you, girl. Fresh blood, no waiting - go right ahead!" He winked at me and gestured me up onto the stage.

20

"Oh, really, right now? Okay, I guess!" I tugged my shirt a little lower and took a swaying step up onto the stage. The monitor flashed the name of my song and the countdown began. The lights shone bright in my eyes and the faces of the crowd turned toward me, expectantly. My breath caught. It had been a while since I had been on stage, the center of attention. My chest felt tight, that old familiar nervousness, but then the countdown hit zero. With the first note of the song, the bar, the crowd, and the nerves all fell away. It felt so good to sing, it always does.

"Billy Rae was a preacher's son and when his daddy would visit he would come along-"

I started out slow, letting the energy build until I was belting from my chest, and let out a subterranean chuckle as I realized that my awkward car ride into town might have subconsciously impacted my song choice. But, that didn't mean that it wasn't an awfully fun one to sing.

"The only boy who could ever reach me was the sweet talkin' son of a preacher man,"

I pulled back again, using restraint to build tension, working the room.

"Yes he was, he was, oh… yes he was."

As the final notes of the song faded away, the bar fell silent. Then, it erupted in a wave of sound. Had the other karaoke singers gotten this much applause? Maybe it sounded different from the center of it. I felt my face crack involuntarily into an enormous grin as I descended back into the seething crowd. The attention that I had felt on stage was magnified now. I pinged and ponged through the swirling mass of people that filled the boisterous bar room. Now, instead of bumping into people's backs and elbows, bodies turned toward me, interested. I weaved my way toward the wall, looking for a little more breathing room. Faces smiled as I passed and mouths shaped words I couldn't hear over the noise of the crowd.

And hands - ooh! hey! I turned quickly to see who it was whose hands had connected so unerringly with my- hey!

"Mmm- like the way you…" said a big, burly man, thick whisky fumes rising from his straight dark beard. He leaned into me, hands reaching familiarly around my waist, and downward. In the dark corner of the bar, he pressed against me, mumbling drunkenly. He nuzzled into my neck, and I bumped into the wood-paneled wall as he pressed into me.

"Ay, uh… Hey!" I pushed at his shoulders, then shoved against the immovable man-mountain, "Let go of me!"

"Yeah, like that lil' ma," he slurred, tickling my ear with his beard in a swaying attempt at a dance. In his stupor, I don't think he even realized that I was fighting against him with all my strength. With our mismatched size, my struggles didn't make any noticeable impact and I miserably resigned myself, hoping that he would at least notice the end of the song approaching.

Suddenly, I lurched and stumbled, almost falling. The big man whirled around, turning and hauling me with him, in his big hairy arms. "Whu-?" he slurred over his shoulder. I slipped sideways out of his grip, and stumbled, bumping into the chest of a tall man whose hand was on the giant's broad shoulder. The force of his grip must have been what had spun the big man off-balance. With a wink, he gave a little push and sent the burly drunk swaying away from us, careening into the crowd of rowdy dancers and revelers. Now, that same strong grip seized my shoulder. It was not an immovable vice like the burly man's mitt, just a steadying stability in the sway of bodies. I glanced back, up, and over my shoulder at my rescuer.

"Looking for me?" he asked. A friendly, mocking grin spread across his open, startlingly handsome face.

"What? Uh, thanks… for that," I said, spluttering a little in my surprise at the abrupt change in circumstance, and my proximity to his broad, solid chest.

"No problem. It looked like you weren't having much fun."

"I wasn't, thanks again." I moved to step back from him, and out of his strong grip. His hand lingered on my shoulder for just a moment, as though to keep me there. His eyes were bright and intense with something I couldn't quite interpret. "I wasn't sure how I was going to get away, back there," I added quickly, smiling with my lips only, hoping that I hadn't just been pulled out of the pot and into the fire.

"My shining armor is at your service," he said, grinning winfully and making a little mock bow, "You need a drink to recover, I'll get it." He grabbed my hand and I followed as he cut through the crush of bodies, flowing through the crowd easily. A perk of being able to see over most people's heads, unlike me. He flagged down the bartender who appeared almost immediately. "Hey, man, one more, and one for the lady?"

"Sure thing, Bran," he turned to me, "Same thing?"

"Uh…" I hemmed, having suffered through the last strong pint, but not sure what else to ask for.

"She'll have what I'm having," said my companion, whose name was, apparently, Bran. Awfully forward, I thought, but it did solve the problem of what to order. To his credit as a professional, the bartender looked at me for confirmation. At my nod, he turned and spun several brightly colored bottles expertly over a shaker. In moments he had produced two tall, bright blue cocktails garnished with a sunny lemon wheel.

"Here you go," he said, sliding us the glasses, and giving me a look of caution, "This one is strong, also."

I snagged my backpack from underneath the bar stool, and my new friend led me across the bar. As we walked up to some tables by the window, a couple got up to dance and left their seats free. He stepped ahead of me and pulled out the chair for me to sit. How gallant, I thought, especially for a divey bar like this. I resisted my stubborn urge to go sit in the other chair, and just bobbed my head in acknowledgement, instead.

"Thanks," I said, raising my glass, "For the drink, and for earlier. I really didn't have a plan back there."

"Any time," he said, smiling. He locked eyes with me, disarmingly intense.

I scrambled for something to say, to break the tension. "I've never been here before, this bar is, uh, nice," I finished, lamely.

"Yeah," he said, with a laugh, "It's alright. Not very interesting till my friends show up. At least, not until you got on stage," he said, "First time at the Raven, huh? Are you, like, new here or something?"

"You could say that," I said and smiled, "I just drove into town a few hours ago."

"Oh, really? No kidding. Why? It's the middle of the term, so you're not a new student."

"Student? No, I'm not. I just graduated," I answered, then paused, taking another sip of my bright blue beverage. It was good! Strong, maybe, but sour and very sweet which made it easy to drink. "It's funny, you know. That's the first time

I've ever not been a student before when somebody asked me. Ever since I was a little kid, and now I'm a what? Just a human, I guess?" I tacked on a laugh, trying to make my weird observation into a joke.

He looked over his glass at me, intently. "I don't think anyone like you could possibly be 'just a human', do you?" His mouth quirked up at the corner, to show that he was teasing me, and I laughed again, slightly wrong-footed by the odd compliment. "But, you could always go back to school like me, and become a Master of Something or Other."

"Or a Doctor of Something or Other," I teased back. I was surprised to see his face momentarily darken, and then recover.

"Or a Doctor. They don't have a Ph.D. program in water systems management, but…" he trailed off, and I realized my faux pas too late. I was always doing that.

"Water systems management? That sounds interesting," I said, pressing on past the momentary awkwardness.

"It does?" he asked skeptically, leaning back and running a hand through his wavy, light brown hair. It settled back into the same cool, stylish fop. It must just do that naturally, I thought, watching him. Some people have all the luck.

"Well," I hedged, not honestly able to defend against that very basic pressing, "Not really, but I don't know what that is, and I am interested to find out?"

"Fair enough," he chuckled, "It's not very interesting, but it is important. I study the ways that we use water and how it gets extracted, cleaned, processed, and distributed. Water is life, you know. Everybody needs water."

"Everybody does need water," I agreed, sipping again. So tasty!

"But, what about you?" he asked, "You graduated, you're not a student anymore, and you just got into town today." He picked up his drink and leaned back, eyeing me speculatively, "So tell me, what does the rest of your life have in store for you?"

"Uh, well," I hedged, not really knowing what to say. That was a pretty big question. A question that my parents and my college friends had asked me, too. And, one that I didn't really have a great answer for. "I guess I'm here to find that out." He raised his eyebrows at me, over his drink and waited for me to continue. "I'm adopted," I said, not knowing where else to start, "I don't have any information about my birth family. Or, I didn't. I just got this." I pulled the manilla envelope out of my backpack, from where it was tucked between my knees. "It's not a lot. The hospital records from my birth, a copy of a photo," I paused before mentioning the destroyed letter, "but apparently I was born right here, in this valley, so I figured…" I raised my hands in the universal gesture for 'I don't know.'

"So, you just rolled into town today looking for your long-lost family, huh?"

"Yeah, that's pretty much it," I agreed, shrugging, "I guess I'll have to find a place to stay, and, like, a job eventually, but for now, I guess I'm just excited to be… here?" As I drank and talked, I felt myself getting looser, and by now I was animatedly talking with my hands, elbows on the table, leaning into my new friend. At this last comment, he reached across the table and took both my hands in his, bringing them down to rest on the manila envelope between us.

"Well, let me be the first to officially welcome you… er, what's your name?"

"Fiona." It got easier every time.

"Welcome, Fiona. I'm Brandon." He stood, pulling me to my feet. "Let's go dance."

I hadn't realized that the bar had an upstairs. Sure, some people had been dancing in the karaoke crowd, but once we headed up the steep back staircase, I realized that the party had been up here the whole time. Bright lights stung my eyes and then darted away to play over the seething masses of young people writhing on the dance floor to the latest, loudest club remix, and crowded three-deep around a second large bar.

Brandon let go of me and I rocked back, unmoored, taking a moment to get my balance. He dove into the press of bodies around the bar and emerged much quicker than I expected with two more of the tall blue drinks that we had just finished downstairs. I followed his lead, setting my new beverage on a big round table by the dance floor, and let him pull me into the press of dancers. He drew me close with a practiced movement.

This was pretty fun, actually. There weren't a lot of bars like this in my college town. At least not that I had been to, anyway. In fact, I hadn't gone out much in college, really. In High School, I had a couple of boyfriends. I'd expected to date more in college, but I never really did. I ended up staying pretty isolated with a small group of interesting, kind women and a couple of their high-quality long-term boyfriends. There just hadn't been a lot of prospects for love interests for myself. Maybe that's because I didn't do things like actually go out and try to meet new people, I thought wryly to myself, as my body warmed with the exertion of dancing.

The drinks from downstairs were working their intoxicating magic. Brandon's larger body encircled mine and controlled so much of my motion that I really didn't need to make decisions at all, just lean into him and let him move me. I guess this is the modern form of partner dance, I mused, as his strong arms physically turned me into him. Then I was in his biome, crushed into his humid chest, and I looked up at his chin and long, straight nose. Our gazes locked, and his face closed in on mine, coming in for a kiss.

I lurched, pulling back, awkwardly. His big green eyes were close to mine and looked confused and concerned by my surprising reaction. And why had I reacted like that, I asked myself. It wasn't like I hadn't given him every indication. In fact, I had always wondered how to signal to strange men that they should kiss me. Maybe that accidental chin lift was the answer I had been looking for. It had certainly worked here, on this charming, attractive man who I had just rebuffed. Good grief girl, get a grip! If not him, who? If not now, when?

"Nothing," I said, and smiled reassuringly. I reached my hands around his neck, which seemed like something people did in moments like this. It worked. He bent down again, and kissed me firmly and a little toothily. The sensation of heat and the dampness of his body pressed against mine, along with the thump of the music in my skull was overwhelming, but I didn't really need to do anything except go with the flow. The large amount of alcohol in my system seemed to be doing a good job of keeping me loose. As the song ended, he loosened his grip and we drifted a couple feet apart on the crowded dance floor.

"Drink?" he mouthed, over the resumed thumping of the DJ. The table where we had left our drinks was now crowded with a group of laughing strangers. As we approached, their laughter turned into overlapping shouts of greeting, mostly lost in the bar noise.

"B-man! Where ya been?"

"Who's the girl, Bran?" Apparently, this was his regular table, and his friends had now arrived. People shuffled to make room for us in the overstuffed oval booth. Brandon scooted in behind me until I was pressed snugly into the shoulder of a pretty blonde girl. She turned to me, grimaced once, and flipped her hair back, resuming her conversation with a girl who might have been her twin.

"Shots! Shots! Shots!" They passed around a tray of narrow glasses. Brandon made sure I got one before upending his own and swallowing it with a shudder. I took a few sips, trying to down mine quickly before anyone noticed that I hadn't even tried to shoot it. As soon as I set my glass down, a little behind everyone else, a rumble started again from the far end of the table, and another, shorter glass was in front of me. That one went down easier, like a juicy green melon. Barely even tasted like alcohol at all, I thought, and that was a good thing because at this point...

My memories of the night were in loud, bright glimpses, like moving pictures. Brandon's face leaned close to mine, laughing. Two smiling red-faced boys assured me that I could stay in the extra room at the frat house. The shock of cold air as we headed outside, and the loud country western music of a second bar. My stomach turned over, as I was swung around and around. An icy glass pressed into my hand, and cool relief sliced down my throat.

Cold air again, as the wind blew my hair back, and the group piled out of the second spot. They stumbled down the sidewalk, joking and bumping into each other. I let myself bop and drift along with the group drowsily, conversation swirling around me. The cold air and the water had helped to clear my head and I felt more alert as we ambled past mostly closed storefronts and a few bright, inviting windows. Partiers peeled off in groups of two or three, and the group dwindled down to a handful.

The residential street was dim with far-set street lights. I tuned back into the voices around me and noticed that they were all deep and low, without the high-pitched laughs and squeals that had punctuated the conversation a few minutes ago. A tingle of alertness ran down my spine and cleared the remainder of my drunken fog. The tone of the voices, and the motion of the bodies of these men, yes the group was all men now, I realized, had shifted and my instincts alerted me to present danger.

Four men. No, five.

Brandon, of course, was not among them. Had he been with us when we had left the bar? It was hard to say. I didn't think so. What about those two frat boys? The gentle ones, with the round cheeks who had promised a safe bed for the night? I glanced over my shoulder and caught a glint from the eye of the man behind me. It made me shudder again. No, there was no one in this group that I recognized.

One man leaned in to tell his friend a joke. The friend laughed loudly, harsh and joyless, and let his gaze linger on me with a sneer. We had walked out of the downtown area and into a neighborhood, still bordered by the river to the right, where the manicured riverside park of the downtown promenade transitioned into a scrubby wooded area. The leader of the group turned at the upcoming intersection, heading deeper into the neighborhood. This procession was not heading anywhere that I wanted to go.

Chapter 5

I tried not to change my body language as I let my pace slow subtly and drifted to the back of the group. I leaned down as though to tie my slip-on shoe, and when the men's backs were all pointed down the side street, I darted across the road and into the brush and the trees. When I hit the tree line, I stumbled over a thick root, making a big rustling commotion as I scrambled back up.

"Hey!" one of the men shouted, and the group turned as I hurried into the underbrush, looking for somewhere to hide. I heard the sound of running feet hitting the pavement behind me. At least two people had followed after me, but not the whole group, I didn't think. Finding a shadowed spot where two trees twined into each other, I crouched as low as I could and thought tree-like thoughts.

"Hey, come on now, we weren't tryna' hurt ya," one of them called out into the dark, cajolingly.

"Wouldn't wanna hurt ya," his buddy mocked him with an exaggerated earnestness, "Yeah, that's right, what I'm thinking won't hurt a bit - hey!" he exclaimed as his buddy cuffed him on the arm.

I'm a tree, just a tree. I'm just a little tree, I thought, forcing myself to take silent, shallow breaths as the men passed beside the two entwined trunks within inches of my hiding place.

"She was pretty far gone, we better make sure she didn't fall in the river," I heard the first man say. It sounded like they were going to keep looking for me if they didn't find me. I was in for a long wait.

Staying motionless in the shadows, I looked out from my hiding place. Through a gap in the brush, a circular moon and halo were reflected in the shifting surface of the river. The full moon's light illuminated the area and glinted off the caps of a row of spindly white mushrooms. I turned my head slowly to see whether the line continued all the way around the tree. I couldn't tell, but it looked like it might. The rain had stopped hours before, and the ground under the trees was cool and fairly dry. In my big weatherproof jacket, with the hood up, and quite so much liquor still flowing through my veins, I was almost comfortable.

"The goal," I murmured, as I leaned against the tree and curled in on myself, letting my eyes drift closed, "was *not* to have to sleep in the woods." The dreams came on quickly that night. As soon as my eyes closed, it felt like I had opened them into dreamland, from dark, cold night to bright, gay revelry. I was whisked away into a beautiful vision of glittering colors, tinkling sounds, and whirling motion.

Dancing, we were dancing. The word drifted, unmoored by other thoughts as I spun and whirled. In the dream, of course, I knew the steps to the dance. I twined in and out, weaving through the other dancers, joining in with their tinkling laughter and answering smiles that showed bright, tiny teeth. In this dream, there was no self-doubt, no endless internal analysis, only joyful motion. The music picked up the pace, and so too did the dancing. Graceful long leaps became quick jumps and then frantic hops. Bright smiles widened into fierce grins and wide eyes widened still further, as the tempo continued to build and build, the tinkling music coming from nowhere and everywhere, until, in a great cataclysm, the dancers, as one, threw themselves to the floor in a tangle of limbs, flowing silks and billowing skirts.

Having known, dreamlike, when to fall with the rest, I lay panting, head resting beside the row of spindly white mushrooms. Next to me was the face of a pretty bright-eyed girl with long, flowing copper-golden hair and lips that looked petal pink even as the moonlight made everything gray and muted. She was perhaps the single most beautiful thing I had ever seen. Not like a supermodel was beautiful, but like a flower or a sunrise, or a dewdrop was beautiful.

"Are you a fairy?" I heard myself ask, without intending to do so.

She smiled and laughed, making her glinting hair bounce mesmerizingly. "Fairy's all fair, but aye's the ae makes fae an we're as fae as we are faerie."

"Oh," I said, nodding, this making perfect sense, in the dream.

Blop. The big water droplet splashed onto my forehead and ran down my nose, waking me with a jolt. "Huh?" I shook my head to clear it. Reoriented, I remembered why I was sore, dew-damp, and curled against a tree. I yawned and stretched, glad that the sun was up, and I had made it through the night in one piece. "And with a hell of a story to tell," I said, as I picked myself up off the ground, then bent back down to pick up a beautiful silken scarf that had been pinned underneath me. Its blues, purples, and greens all blended together in a flowing gradient, and the fabric felt incredibly smooth and light as I ran it through my fingers.

A sudden flash of sparkling light glinted off the water, which caught my eye and startled me. The scarf whipped out of my fingers, caught by what must have been a gust of wind, and flew away, toward the river. I lunged after the pretty thing, but it had already drifted down to the water and was gone, carried off on the fast current. I felt a pang of loss for the beautiful item, but, I chided myself, it hadn't ever been mine in the first place.

How had I ended up with it, anyway? It had probably been one of the girls from the bar last night. I sifted through my fragmented memories, not remembering the colorful thing, but there had been so many people wearing so many things, and there were large parts of the evening I struggled to remember. As I picked myself off the ground and dusted off my jacket and pants, I strained to recall through the fog, and found myself thinking instead about my dream, and the colors of the dresses of the fairy dancers. No, I reminded myself, remembering what the red-haired girl had told me. Not fairy, but faerie. The difference in spelling had been clear when she said it, even though the two words sounded the same. What an intense dream that had been!

I sat back down and looked out at the glittering morning sun hitting the river. Through the trees to my left, I could see that the riverside park was full of people and the bustle of a busy Saturday morning. I slowly woke up and prepared to face a new day, running on the few hours of sleep I had managed to get, outside on the ground, in the cold, and the damp. This had certainly been an inauspicious way to spend my first real night of post-college adult life- effectively homeless!

I shook my head to clear it and ran my fingers through my hair, working out some of last night's tangles. There was no use wallowing in that kind of negative self-talk, and anyway, it was true that I had spent the night outside, but what had the options been? I had gotten out of a very precarious situation, and now here it was, morning, and I was safe and whole, if a little dingy and rumpled.

And the night hadn't been all bad, had it? I thought about Brandon. About how gallant and gracious he had been, welcoming me to town like that. And so considerate, pulling out chairs and ordering my drinks for me. He even made sure I kept track of my- my backpack!

I scrambled to my feet, patting the ground behind and underneath me, as though I would lay my hands on the bag that was clearly not there. This was not good! My backpack had my car keys in it, and, oh no! My frantic patting resumed, as I searched my coat. Feeling the hard rectangular outline of my phone, debit card, and ID, I let out a sigh of relief. I wasn't totally out of resources.

"Well," I said, straightening my shoulders and preparing to meet the day, "at least now I have something specific to do with myself, instead of wandering aimlessly and hoping I run into my birth family." And, of course, my important birth family records were also in the backpack, I reminded myself ruefully. I had to get it back. That was all there was to it. Brandon had made sure that I had left the Raven, the first bar, with it. Where had we gone after that? I had no idea, but there couldn't be that many bars within walking distance, could there?

I stayed within the tree line, heading toward the bustle of the downtown riverside promenade. As I got closer, I could see that it wasn't just townspeople out at the park on a weekend. The square was bustling with a charming farmers market, stalls piled high with fruits and vegetables, and shoppers swarming with baskets of local produce. White-roofed tents lined the sidewalk, and in the grassy areas, children ran around, shouting as families picnicked on blankets.

At the far side of the park, raised on a grassy hillock, I noticed a group of people whirling and dancing. I paused to watch the dancers, mesmerized, as they spun and twisted with some sort of a prop, but from this distance, and with the speed they moved, it was hard to tell exactly what I was seeing. Then, one of the dancers slowed, their arm came forward, and they traced a circle in front of them making the item appear to hover in the air. It was a hula hoop or something like it, but I had never seen a hula hoop move like that!

I watched on, entranced. One figure, in particular, caught my eye. She was very tiny, smaller than any of the others, with long hair that caught and blew in the wind, twisting and twining with the hoop as she spun. Mine would get all tangled if I tried to do that, I thought. Hers seemed to curl and untwist in the breeze like liquid magic. A little girl walked up to her, and right away the small, lovely woman popped her hoop up in a graceful arc and offered it to the girl who began, awkwardly, to copy some of the movements of the other dancers.

At that moment, a woman on a shiny new bicycle winged past with a flash of brilliant chrome, so close that it made me step back off the path and out of her way with an exclamation of surprise. This interruption snapped me out of my reverie, and I continued walking down the path toward the center of town.

It seemed like that dancing group had been welcoming. If I had just walked over there and said I was interested, I probably could have joined them, I thought, gazing longingly back over the lawn at the spinners' unchoreographed performance, and especially at that long-haired woman with the almost magnetic pull that made me want to go talk to her and learn more.

No, I needed to stay on task. That was hardly the way to go about finding my long-lost family. I was my mother's daughter and if there was one thing she had taught me, it was to put first things first. Getting my backpack back had to be the priority. If I lost it, I wouldn't have any clues to follow at all! I headed onward through the market, stopping to buy a wild mushroom tart. It was flakey and delicious and I felt much better by the time I reached the Raven.

I was relieved to see that it was open. I hadn't been sure, early in the morning, but there was a sign on the window that I hadn't noticed before advertising 'Bacon & Eggs, Coffee, Saturdays, and Sundays; and the door was propped open, letting in the morning sunshine. Behind the counter was the karaoke DJ from last night, rag slung over his broad-sloping shoulder, grinning at me with most of his teeth.

"Morning, darlin'! Long night?" he asked, polishing a glass with his rag, and filling it with water, "How about you start with a big tall one of these?" I reached for the glass and took several deep swallows, not having realized quite how thirsty I was. "You sure do look familiar, girl," he said, eyeing me speculatively as I drank.

"I was here last night," I said, when I paused to catch my breath, "Thanks for the water." He reached over and filled the cup back up to the brim with his beverage gun, and I smiled, gratefully.

"Now, what else can I get ya? Bacon and eggs? Bloody Mary, hair of the dog?"

"Just some information, if you've got it," I explained my situation, and he pointed me toward a few likely establishments up the road.

At the first place, I inquired, a gruff barman retrieved my dusty black bag from behind the counter, and I grabbed it, hugging it to my chest with a sigh of relief. I stepped out into the morning sunshine with a satisfied smile. For once in the last couple of days, something had gone smoothly.

A block down, a car turned hard onto the one-way street, accelerating in my direction. I was probably safe here on the sidewalk, but reckless driving made me nervous, so I was already taking a big, quick step away from the road when a bright shine from the car window momentarily blinded me. The car drove straight through the rainwater-filled gutter, thoroughly soaking the area that I had been standing in moments before. I gasped in surprise and caught my breath, leaning against the brick wall behind me, glad that I had not just been soaked from head to toe in cold, mucky water. My shoes and ankles were spotted with some wet brown droplets, but I had managed to avoid the worst of it. That would have been an incredibly irritating new complication, since my jacket was wide open in the warm morning sun, and I was already wearing the extra set of clothes from my backpack. What an unfortunate coincidence that would have been, for the car to splash right where I was standing. And that flash had just happened to blind me right before it had happened… Maybe it was all this Oregon rain making things wet and shiny, but these flashes were starting to feel awfully familiar. Almost predictable.

A quaint little signpost pointed the way to the City Hall, Courthouse, and Library. Well, the Library seemed like a good place to search for information, even if I was already carrying the book I wanted to read. Inside the big building, airy with an open, second-story balcony and wide windows, I gravitated toward a cozy dark back corner and found a spot in a nook between shelves to sit and read.

I reached into my now somewhat tattered manilla envelope and took out just the book, *Faeries*. Why had this children's book been included with the things I had been sent? It was a sweet idea to send an adopted kid a book of fairy, er *faerie*, stories from their family, though. I would have really enjoyed this, if I had gotten it when I was young, I thought, opening it.

I expected to see a familiar, illustrated fairytale inside, but it actually didn't seem to be a storybook at all. More like an art book mixed with an encyclopedia, with all sorts of information about the folk of faerie. Craggy, twisted impish smiles peered back at me from illustrations on the page, and in the dimness of the library corner, the bright little eyes almost seemed to dart and twinkle. The section of the book I had opened to provided descriptions of a variety of magical creatures including Pixies, which, the book noted, would sometimes take on the appearance of hedgehogs, and Bogles, evil-natured little Goblins who particularly enjoy finding ways to do harm to liars and murderers.

As I flipped through the book, reading passages here and there, I found myself becoming lost in thought, or maybe lost beyond thought, gazing at the faces in the illustrations. They had so much personality and life to them that I felt as though I knew what several of the faeries and pixies on the pages were thinking, and their thoughts made me giggle. I paged through the book quickly once, and then started on a second pass, stopping to examine each of the illustrations, and read the curious passages.

"Ahem." An obviously affected throat-clearing sound from directly above me broke my trance and startled me, causing me to almost drop my book. I hugged it, open, to my chest and looked straight up at the man looming over me. He wore a brown leather coat and carried a gnarled walking stick with a number of bangles and charms tied to it. From my vantage underneath him, looking up, this made him look very much like a crooked old oak tree in the dead of winter that someone had tried to decorate for the holidays.

"Er, yeah?" I said when it became clear that he was waiting for my response.

"Ah, yes, well, I happened to notice your choice of reading material." He used his big stick to gesture toward the tome held flat against my chest. "It is a good one, in many ways. Not one carried by this library, though, unless I am very much mistaken."

"No, or, well, I don't know. This one is mine, I just came in here for a quiet place to read." I wasn't sure what to think of this strange man, with his funny little flat hat and curious lumpy nose. I certainly wasn't afraid of him. If anything, I found him quite charming. I eyed the curious collection of charms on his staff and wondered if it might be one of those that was doing it.

"Ah well, I can see how that might be, but I'd say there are a few safer places to read a thing like that than in a place like this," he said, glancing over his shoulder at the librarian, "This is the city library." He leaned in, conspiratorially. "Government funded. You'll find more scholarly types, willing to talk about the more… esoteric sides of life, if you head toward the university, uptown." He gestured up the street, away from the river.

"Oh, thanks, I, uh, didn't know," I said as I stuffed the book back into my backpack and slowly unfolded my stiff legs to get up from the nest I had made on the floor. I looked to my left, at the big central library desk. Had that librarian just shot me a nasty look? I hadn't noticed before, but now that he mentioned it, the library employees did seem to be glancing my way more frequently than I would have expected. I was surprised I hadn't noticed. I tended to be quick to perceive things like that. I must really have been lost in that book.

The man offered me a hand, as I prepared to stand. I seized his papery, age-spotted hand with mine, and was surprised by the tingling flow of energy between us, a tickling ephemeral heat that faded as he let me go. I took a rocking step away from him, not upset but very surprised. The not-unpleasant sensation of energized particles made my fingers tingle, and I shook and flexed my hand in response.

"What was that?" I asked in a loud whisper, not wanting to call any extra attention to myself.

"Like recognizing like," he said with a crooked grin, looking ruefully at his own hand, "though I didn't expect there to be quite so much. Apologies for the…" He wiggled his fingers in explanation.

"That's okay, I just- what do you mean, like recognizing like?"

"Oh!" he said, as though a thought had just come to him. He opened his heavy coat and began to rummage through a number of small inside pockets. After a few moments he drew out a worn scrap of paper and unfolded it, handing it to me. The paper was old but high quality, and felt good in my hands, with a neat, hand-written address in a dark purple ink with specs of mica in it, making it glitter, and an ink dot blooming at the corner.

"Come," he said, "If these are the kinds of things you are reading," he leaned in, conspiratorially, "in public, you really must come for the party."

"Okay," I agreed, liking this curious man, "when is it?"

"Oh, tonight," he said, dreamily, "or perhaps it could be tomorrow?"

"Oh, uh, okay," I nodded, confused but not wanting to press the matter. It was probably tonight since tonight was a Saturday. Maybe the old man was a bit addled.

"Yes, yes. Yes, yes," he said, nodding nervously and backing away, eyes darting at the two librarians who had started to move purposely in this direction, "be seeing you then, be seeing you." The two staff members' shoulders turned to track the little man as he headed for the wide bay of doors. I didn't want to wait to see if they would approach me, so I gathered my things and followed him out.

On the sidewalk, I paused and unfolded the little scrap of paper tucked in my palm, reading it again. Across the street, the shiny courthouse steeple caught the sun and sent a glinting ray right into my eyes. I felt a gust of wind rip at the paper I was holding, but this time I was ready! I lurched forward and grabbed the little scrap before it could fly off with the breeze, lost forever.

"HaHa! Gotcha!" I shouted, triumphantly, crumpling the little scrap in my fist.

With all the stress that I had been under since yesterday, it had taken me longer than I liked to recognize the pattern, but these blinding flashes and the immediate bad luck that followed had started to feel just a little too convenient. And now, here, I had proved it, predicting the gust of wind that had tried to blow away my party invitation. This bad luck, whatever it was, had been following me ever since I arrived in town. In fact, I realized, that flash of light that had run me off the road had been the same flash, hadn't it? And the flash before the letter had been ruined, and certainly when the scarf had flown away this morning.

This isn't random bad luck, I decided, with conviction. Whatever this 'ill will' is, I think it's intelligent, and looking for opportunities to mess with me. How was it happening, though? I thought about whether a stage magician could manage these tricks with mirrors and fishing line. But, this morning, in the middle of the woods, a scarf that I hadn't even known existed had picked itself up and flown into the river as soon as I had looked at it. No one could have set that up.

A tingle ran down my spine and I shuddered, glancing over my shoulder nervously, but there was nothing there. My mind flicked busily over all of the unexpected stumbles, improbable accidents, and strange happenings of the last two days, trying to find an explanation, any explanation for what I had been experiencing. The only thing that seemed to make sense, I thought, rubbing my hand as the memory of the electric sensation of that old man's touch still lingered, was that it was some kind of real magic, doing it. But, magic wasn't real, was it?

I pocketed the scrap of paper with conviction. Well, at least this 'ill will' had done one thing for me, I thought, with a determined grimace. Losing that address would have been bad luck, apparently. Now, there was absolutely no way I was going to miss this party.

Part 2 - The Party

The tall, angry woman paced back and forth, her long, flowing dress trailing behind her. This room also sported her signature thick, luxurious curtains, but here, the walls were lined with long shelves filled with bottles of all shapes and sizes, glinting invitingly.

This child is irritating me, she thought, clenching her narrow hands into tight fists. Her natural luck makes it seem as though she can almost predict my little trips and jabs, sidestepping or slipping away into the safety of the shadows.

The woman paused her pacing to stare out a small leaded glass window. She had gotten far too close this morning. Far too close. Close enough to see her. Close enough to break my Lady's spell, drawing her here. At least that might end up working in my favor, she thought, her mouth turning up into a cold smile. Perhaps the little bird will just fly away again, now that my Lady's geas has been broken.

She reached up and seized a small bottle from a high shelf, turning it over once, setting the iridescent liquid spinning and whirling in hypnotizing swirls. I'll need to get closer, though. Get hands-on with the situation. I do have a few more tricks up my sleeve after all. She nodded, satisfied. Pocketing the bottle and wrinkling her pale forehead in concentration, she stamped her foot once, and with a sharp crack and a flash of light, she was gone.

Chapter 6

The address I had been given led me to a large stone house near the river. It reminded me of the impressive halls of the university uptown, where I had walked this afternoon, following the funny old man's other suggestion. I hadn't found any leads on the 'more esoteric side of life' there, but I had enjoyed the architecture, and, other than the need to sidestep a few more coincidences and close-calls, it had been a relaxing afternoon.

Other than the few words necessary to check into a hotel, so that I had a safe place to leave my backpack, and to sleep tonight, I hadn't talked to a single person since being invited to this party. Social battery fully charged, I was as ready as I would ever be. At my knock, the heavy wooden door swung open just a little, on silent, well-oiled hinges. A sliver of light illuminated a golden slice of the dusky entryway, letting out a rumble of voices from within.

"Hello?" I called through the crack. No one answered, so I pushed the door open a bit wider, and stepped into the back of a large room. It was dominated by a looming stone fireplace surrounded by wingback armchairs, overstuffed loveseats, and dark wood benches, many of which were occupied by people talking, laughing and drinking. Thick wooden beams supported low ceiling, and the effect, with the crackling warm fire and dripping candles providing flickering light, was of supreme coziness and comfortability. As I stepped further into the room the door swung shut behind me with a loud metallic clunk, and as one, the room fell silent, and all eyes turned on me. Like a deer in the headlights, I stared at the group, frozen.

Slowly I raised my open palm. "Hi… uh…"

Interrupting this incredibly awkward moment, the door abruptly opened again behind me. I stepped out of the way, as a tall, stately woman ducked through the low doorway in a practiced way. Her dark red hair was piled so intricately high that it nearly brushed the ceiling. She spread her arms wide in greeting, long flowing sleeves emphasizing the graceful motion. The faces around the fire alit with recognition and surprise.

"Velia!"

"Lady, welcome!"

"What brings you down from the hill?"

"Ah, my friends, it has been too long!" She smiled beatifically as though in benediction before turning to me. "Oh!" she said, with a look of too-practiced surprise, "And who, do tell, are you?"

The crowd around the fire returned to their conversations, leaving me effectively alone with this elegant stranger. Her simpering smile invited my answer, and she blinked large, intensely green and smokey eyes at me. My mind remained conspicuously and awkwardly blank. I hadn't considered what would happen if the man from this morning wasn't here to greet me. I had assumed that it was his party, but now that I was here, I found myself wondering what exactly it was that I had just walked into. The old man, with his funny hat and bedecked walking stick would be one of the more ordinary looking people in this group.

"Um, well, my name is Fiona," I said, glad to have a place to start at least, "and I was invited by," I paused awkwardly, realizing that I didn't know the strange man's name, "well, I was reading a book about faeries. Wait," I backpedaled, starting again, "I'm here because I'm looking for my family. I have, well, I did have a letter from the Queen of the Faeries, and I thought, maybe…" I trailed off, realizing that I was rambling.

The beautiful woman chuckled musically and intertwined her long fingers, a picture of amused elegance. "Oh, you're a seeker, my dear. Of course, of course. Many do come to this part of the world with an interest in the folk," she gestured behind me, and I turned, seeing a row of progressively faded posters featuring illustrations of winged maidens for what must have been almost 20 years of themed festivals. "But, perhaps a bit of a novice, to look only at faerie, when you say you seek the fae," she said with a teasing lilt. She placed her cool hand on my shoulder and led me to a vacant seat by the fire. "Godrin, here, can surely educate you on the difference between faerie and the fae, can you not, my dear old friend?"

"Oh, aye, Lady Velia, surely I can," said a squat brown man whose thick beard was braided into three long beaded plaits, one of which was soaking in the large flagon of foamy beer resting next to him on a small side table. He leaned forward toward me, causing the braid to flop out of the tankard and slap wetly against his broad chest, and began. "In the old countries, aye, there are the Faeries, High Sidhe, the fae as you would say, and there are the Piskies and the Brownies, and among the Brownies, there are the Bouka, and the Fenoderee, and the Killmoulis, an' they mostly keep to themselves, gang together in their age-old hills, an' dance the same dances they've worn into the same hill circles for a half-dozen centuries or more,"

A voice called out from behind me, interrupting, "An' war with each other, an' dwindle even farther!"

"Aye, aye." said Godrin, resuming his speech, "An' that's just in England and Isles, and there's magical folk from all over, with names, an' without names both. But we've been here a long time, and we've mixed together, or mixed with humans and we've changed or we've forgotten who we once were."

"An' there's not enough o' us who knows what he is, or who has enough o' one thing in 'em to make a big enough troupe to matter any ways," put in the wizened old man next to the fire, a thin trickle of smoke rising from his long curved pipe.

"There are some as still do," countered Godrin, " Mostly up in Portal Land, closer to the source, sure. One o' them city fae told me once, but, well… Blast, now I've forgotten." He scratched his beard and took another long drink from his flagon, then turned his round face back to me and smiled warmly. So, we're all just fae, or the fair folk, for a lack of a better. An' let's just say we fae live long lives, but our memories, well… an' our attention, too…" He trailed off with a rueful expression. He waved this off with a sharp shrug of his chin that sent one of the braids of his beard back into his drink, and continued. "If you're like me an', well, most are," he gestured to include his fellows, "it does nae matter whether yer Awakkule or Cagn-Cagn." He turned to a pair of men who must have been brothers. They looked almost identical except that one was blond and fair and the other was darkly olive. "Though sometimes, ye'll know who's Ljosalfar and who's Dokkalfar." He raised his glass to the folks gathered around the fire, and they roared with laughter. This last statement had clearly been a joke that I didn't understand.

While the gathered folk laughed, I looked from one to another. Some of them, okay, most of them, were unusual looking and upon first glance I had even found some aspects to be frightening, while they were talking seriously, or listening, leaned over their mugs. But now, in laughter their faces twisted into impish joyful, expressive grins, with bright eyes that sparkled far more than the reflected firelight could naturally account for. Their gnarled, expressive faces reminded me of… well, of trees, more than anything else. Others, like craggy boulders or sea-cut cliffs. A few like lumpy, woodland mushrooms. And they looked like the illustrations in the faerie book, I realized, remembering the way those illustrated expressions had felt familiar, as though they hid curious and entrancing thoughts behind their eyes. These people were fascinating, and, as my gaze lingered, unable to look away, I realized that they were incredibly beautiful. These were magical creatures surrounding me.

I desperately wanted to ask Godrin an insightful question. I wanted to keep him talking, to encourage him to tell me more. But to my chagrin, when I opened my mouth, I spoke in my mom's voice and not my own. As my mouth formed the words, I could feel the wrongness of them, in direct contradiction of my own recent experiences and new convictions, but the beliefs of our childhood run deep, and the declaration was out before I could stop it.

"But… Faeries aren't real. Magic isn't real!" All around, the laughing faces fell silent, and their wide, open expressions closed into something harder and colder.

"Aye, she said ye were a newcomer, a novice, aye," he said. Heads nodded, and low voices grumbled. "But, to say summat like that, in a place like this…" He trailed off, and raised his mug to take a drink. He scowled cross-eyed at the braid dangling in it. At his withering gaze the thing slithered out of the mug and fell, swinging wetly from his chin. With a satisfied grunt, he took a long foamy drink, belched and continued. "Well'en how'd ye find yerself here, then, miss? How 'bout that?"

"Oh, well, a man gave me this." I held out the scrap of paper with the address written on it.

Godrin seized the thing and squinted at it. "Oh, aye. Haven't seen one of these in a long time." He leaned over and clapped my shoulder with a huge, tough, rounded hand like a baseball mitt. "Well, miss, if ye truly read this here missive, in this sparkly ol' ink, an' walked right up to this door clear as day, well, believe in it or no, you've got enough magic in ye to bide."

This time, the murmurs from the surrounding crowd were less sinister and more curious, but they still made me feel uneasy, as I looked from one strange face to another. "I have magic in me? What is that supposed to mean?"

"It means a lil' fae slipped a lil' magic in a lil' human!" piped up a high-pitched voice from the back, and the crowd roared with laughter again.

"Or'n it's the other way around," said Godrin, "Our fae lasses can be terrible charmin', you know. But, then, those children don't come seekin', all grown, not knowing anything about magic, though, do they?" He smiled at me in a kindly way, "But seekin' ye are, and now ye know, though if it were me, not knowin' nothin' I'd head straight on up into Portal Land. More to see there, than in a sleepy ol' valley like this.

"Portal Land?" I asked, confused.

"Aye, the big city. Up to the north a ways. Met a lass up there once, at the Faire Isle. Best pub you could 'ope to find, that one is, if an' you're wantin' to meet with the fair folk." He leaned back and took a drag on a long curved pipe I hadn't seen him holding a moment before. "She could tell a body just how much o' this an' that they were made of just by looking at 'em. Daughter o' the Faerie Queen said she was. Big bunch o' them faeries up there near the source. He paused and looked at me critically, cocking his head as though really seeing me for the first time. "Uncanny. Well, but if you're looking for faeries, though, there's them's up on the hill that-"

At that moment, the elegant woman re-appeared at my elbow. With a loud peel of laughter and a flurry of richly dyed silks, she rolled over the previous conversation and immediately became the focus of the room. "Still got a bug in your bonnet about the faeries, hmm?" she said in a high, teasing lilt. "Well, you certainly have a one track mind, don't you? Luckily for you, there are some lovely faerie lads here tonight who'd just love to meet you." She pressed a small glass of a mesmerizingly swirling liquid into my hands, and looked deeply into my eyes. "Here, child, drink. It's delicious."

The large crystal in her necklace glinted in the firelight, and I sipped before I had consciously made the choice to do so. It was delicious. The drink was sweet, and sparkling. Not like carbonation but like liquid glitter on my tongue, coating it with the same iridescent shimmer making hypnotizing whorls in the glass. As I drank, the effect of the liquid spread through me, warming like alcohol but different. Unlike liquor which warmed me from the pit of my stomach, this drink, this potion maybe, made me glow from the outside in, igniting my fingers and toes with a pleasant tingling warmth that spread until my whole body was alight with it.

My thoughts became wide spaced and airy, and my eyes drifted. What was this lovely thing, I wondered lazily, watching the firelight sparkle through the viscous liquid. The glass itself now glowed, its halo taking on the same swirling effect of the liquid in the glass. I opened up my mouth to ask about it. "Haaah…"

"Yes, it is nice, isn't it?" said the elegant woman, Veilia, at my sound, "Now, how about you let me introduce you to some nice faerie boys, hmm?" The elegant lady Velia took my hand and I moved with her as though I were floating. Every surface glowed with the same swirling iridescence as the cup, making me pleasantly dizzy. She led me down a long passage and out into the darkness of the night.

The back of the house was absolutely magical in my altered eyesight, with a mossy, tree-canopied garden that blended seamlessly into a wooded area, lit by richly colored hanging lanterns in a variety of styles. Beyond the hypnotizing swirls of light cast by the lanterns, I could see at least two other distant fires. The sweet smell of early spring must be drawing everyone outdoors tonight.

"Ah yes, here they are," said Velia. She gestured to a group of young men sprawled on pillows and mats in an open-sided tent to one side of the yard. Some were angular and strange, others delicate and fine-featured. A few of the men were shirtless in the cool night air, and others wore incongruously warm-looking fur pants, though it was hard to see many details through the distracting effects of the drink. "This is Fiona," said Lady Velia.

She really was so elegant and charming, I thought, dreamily.

"She has a *particular* interest in faeries, boys," she said, then turned toward something I didn't hear. "Oh! Be right back, darling!" She whirled, and left me standing there, dazed in the lamplight.

One of the men stood up. His broad naked chest glinted in the near-full moonlight. He smiled a crooked smile at me and cocked his chin to the side, questioning. I opened my mouth to speak, but the only thing that came out was a breathy "Aaaah-"

Ouch! I felt a sharp sting of pain on my backside, as though something had just cruelly nipped my cheek from behind, and another familiar bright flash seared my already-swirling vision. I lurched forward, stumbling into the man, and my hands raised between us, pressing flat to his broad chest. He reached up and ran cool, strong fingers up and down the outsides of my arms. It made me tingle and a shudder ran through me. He chuckled and drew me back toward the pavilion, the pillows, and his friends.

Chapter 7

"Ah… Ah…" I babbled, as I floated along with the man and the potion, not able to find the words to resist. I found myself flowing onto a pile of pillows, as intricate lamps swung mesmerizingly above me, and a tall, lean male silhouette, slimmer than the one who had greeted me, loomed overhead, blocking the light. In outline, I could see thin curving horns emerging from his curls. Two more masculine shapes moved in on either side of me. Sensuously and languidly, hands started to move along the backs of my arms, and the outsides of my thighs. Another figure appeared behind my shoulder, and something gently tickled my ear. Was that a tongue?

"Uh…" I turned, surprised, and a pretty, impish face grin playfully at me before seizing the opportunity and planting a deep, skillful kiss on my surprised, open mouth. While I was being kissed, roaming fingers searched underneath the hemline of my shirt and into the waistband of my pants, while still more were caressing my neck and hair. How many hands was that now? The haze of the drink clouded my mind, and invited me to lean into the sensation.

The sensations, all the sensations. So many sensations. Too many. Hands, lips, tongues, everywhere. Tugging at my clothes, my hair. What had been almost pleasant in my stupor was now completely overwhelming. Claustrophobic, at the center of so many bodies. Hot, too hot.

Need to get out. Now!

"Eh! Eh! Uh…" wordless, I tried to disentangle myself, but my efforts were interpreted as enthusiasm, and the crush of bodies intensified. One of my hands waved wildly, punching through the mass of writhing faerie men, and to my relief I felt it seized in a cool, strong feminine grasp.

"Boys, I think she's had enough," came the lilting sing-song of the beautiful Lady Velia, cutting through the feral energy of the throng like a knife. Like petals on a dying rose, the men fell away, leaving me a little cold, though grateful for my rescue and for the easing of the overwhelming sensations. "You must have really come on strong, to get them going like that," she said to me, conspiratorially, helping me up and away from the tent, "I was only gone for a minute. You really do like faeries, don't you? Although you don't seem to mind a nice satyr, either."

"Uh, Ah…" I tried to answer, but couldn't seem to find the words. I hadn't come on strong, or done anything at all, I thought blearily, trying and failing to communicate through the fog of that strange drink.

"Oh, was our house specialty a little strong for you? Shame. But, I did want you to have the full experience. You just never quite know how one will react, the first time, though, do you?" She cupped her slim hand around my chin and patted my cheek with a sad little sigh. "Some just haven't the strength of character. Ah, well. You look just bedraggled now. Lucky I came upon you when I did. If you're not accustomed to our ways, you're apt to just be eaten alive, you know. But, you did ask for faeries, and you certainly got what you asked for." She laughed her tinkling laugh again, drawing me back into the house through a different entrance than we had exited.

"Ah, look, see? This is what you need. A nice bath, to relax and, well…" She picked up a section of scraggly hair, and let it fall back with an air of politely contained disgust. We walked into an elegantly appointed bedroom. I wondered again what this odd house was. Was this room someone's personal bedroom, or was this place like a tavern, with rooms available to rent? In either case, a huge steaming tub was visible through the door to the attached en suite, and the potion made such inviting curls and swirls out of the tub's rising steam.

"Ahh…" I started again, trying and failing to ask more questions. Why was I being drawn a bath, of all things? And why… my thoughts trailed off, mesmerized by the lady's beautiful, shining necklace. "Uh? Wha-" I snapped back to myself as my shirt was pulled over my head.

"Talking to yourself again? You silly thing," the Lady Velia said, chattering as she continued to undress me. "…just such an unusual look for the fae, you know. Nobody really thinks, but, well… it does take all sorts. Perhaps you're actually a dwarf or some sort of round little gnome or goblin or something," she pinched the soft flesh around my waist critically, and prodded my fleshy backside as I turned around, "Faerie, though, really, I think not." When had she taken off my pants? "Now, off you pop," she said, ushering me into the bathroom and helping me up the stone steps and into the deep, steaming tub.

The door closed behind me with a click, and I sighed, my muscles beginning to relax in the hot water. The steam rose around me in curling, twisting spirals, and as I watched them, I imagined the steam curls taking on the twisted little grins of the imps in the faerie book. Was it my imagination, or were the faces really there? Did that one just laugh? The steam imps jumped and danced above the surface of the water, and I watched them, entranced.

Wide glass doors made up one wall of the room. The lower half was frosted but in the top, I could see the near-full moon peeking between tree branches. As I gazed out at the moon, I noticed that the ambient light in the room around me had dimmed. The candles at the corner of the tub were still lit but somehow their circle of light didn't extend as far. My chest tightened, suddenly nervous in the newly darkened space. From the corners of the room, twisting tendrils reached from the shadows. To my altered vision they looked like grasping, scraping claws. It's just a shadow, I told myself, and shivered, a sensation of ice going down my spine in the piping hot water.

The playful imps had evolved into creatures with cruel little faces, twisting out of the steam to flash malicious sharp-toothed grins and roll their eyes at me. Out the huge window the dark shapes of the trees now looked like sinister, gnarled, grasping hands. The sound of scraping nails on glass made me jump, my splash dissipating the menacing faces in the whorls of steam. I looked up toward a skittering noise coming from the dim ceiling, and as I watched, tiny shadowy creatures poured from the dark corners, disappearing as they hit the circles of glowing candlelight.

Something fell from the ceiling, and landed in the bath with a 'plop!' I shot out of the tub, with a shriek. I stood shivering and naked in the dim, wavering light of the candle, and spied a big fluffy towel gratefully. As I turned to grab it, a great, shadowy shape rose out of the tub behind me. Screaming, I shoved the frosted glass door of the bathroom open wide, and ran, terrified, out into the night. Mindless with terror, I streaked across the manicured back lawn, and off into the trees, towel clutched to my bare chest.

Chapter 8

Fear mixed with whatever else was coursing through my system, I tore naked through the dark woods, branches scraping against my exposed skin. In my fright, they felt like grasping hands. Terror kept me moving fast for maybe a hundred yards, before, panting and freezing, I tripped over a root, and sprawled onto the pine-needle padded ground. I scrambled to a seat and wrapped the now-filthy towel around my shoulders. It was large and wrapped around me completely, if I curled into a ball around my knees. I clutched the towel to me, the only thing separating my naked body from the night, and huddled next to a big tree, shivering, as I collected myself and got my bearings.

My eyes had adjusted first to the candlelight and now to the woods-dark night, so when I looked around, I was surprised by how much detail I could see. Individual trees were illuminated in the filtered moonlight, and through them, a sliver of river, and the reflection of the near-full moon shining in its shifting waters. The river helped me orient myself, and once I had stopped panting, I stood up, slowly. If I kept the river on my left, I would eventually get back into town, and to the hotel room that I had rented. I could worry about the fact that I didn't have a key card or an ID, or any clothing on, when I got there.

Shivering, I picked carefully across the twiggy, rocky ground with tender bare feet, making slow, painful progress toward my goal of not spending another night in these terrible, dripping woods. The adrenaline and the cold seemed to have burned off most of the effects of the strange, swirling drink. More questions surfaced in my mind as I walked, again, through the cold, wet Oregon woods. How far away from town was I? How much of the night was left? Would I even get back to the hotel before morning?

I had shown up at the River House a little after 9. Remembering how it had been at college parties, I didn't want to risk showing up too early and being the awkward first guest who couldn't pick up on social cues. How long had I been there? Maybe two hours. I couldn't imagine that I had stayed there longer than that. Which means that it's probably not even midnight, now, I thought, gazing up at the high, bright moon. I walked on, staring up at the luminous orb above me.

"Ow!" I yelped, stubbing my toe on a thick root, "That really hurts!" Except, to my surprise, what came out of my mouth sounded more like 'Owaah' the words fading into one long syllable, as though they were flowing from my brain and directly out of my mouth, missing my tongue entirely. "Thiihhh" I said again, my eyebrows knitting together in concern. I had intended to say, "This is weird" but again, the thought got stuck on the first syllable and a single, long sound was the only thing to come out of my mouth. "Waahh" I said, making a further attempt to ascertain what was happening. Had this been going on at the party as well? I thought now that it had, but with all the other effects, I hadn't entirely realized. The intoxication of that strange drink had mostly dissipated in the cold of the night, but apparently some of the more unusual effects had lingered.

I looked down at the once-white towel wrapped around my shoulders and saw that the edges of the shape against the dark still swirled faintly with those same strange iridescent whorls. The bonfires that I could occasionally see peeking through the trees in front of me danced with glowing swirls as well. In ten more minutes, my feet were numb. On the one hand, now that I couldn't feel them they didn't hurt, but on the other-

I tripped, hard, sprawling onto the ground. In reflex, I spread my hands wide to catch my fall, letting go of the towel around my shoulders. My naked chest scraped along the gritty, damp ground painfully, smearing my torso with mud, gravel, pine needles and other forest detritus. I lay stunned for a moment, trying to recover the wind that had been knocked out of me. As I did, a bright flash lit the trees in stark relief, searing my eyes and making the night look black.

Oh no, I thought to myself. Bad luck headed my way. But, that flash had definitely happened after I had already fallen down. Whatever it was hadn't tripped me. So what, then? I slowly got to my knees and brushed at some of the grime that I could feel but couldn't see, since my eyes were no longer adjusted to the dark. This would be easier with the towel.

I turned around to see where it had fallen. I kept turning, seeing the moon again and realizing that I had made a full rotation. Where was it? I felt around, not trusting my blotchy light-seared vision, but all I could feel were dirt and cold rocks. *Oh no. Oh no. Where is it?* I searched frantically, looking behind trees and under thin fern fronds that couldn't possibly be hiding a plush, off-white oversized cotton bath sheet. Of course, it was nowhere to be found. This time, the bad luck had me so far on the ropes that I didn't even know where my towel was. I shivered and wrapped my arms around myself against the chill of the night.

"What was that?" a voice sounded, off in the trees to my right.

"Hey, over here, man." They were coming from the direction of the campfire.

"I dunno, but it was right behind that-" A tall figure stepped into view, right in front of me. "Woah! Naked girl!" he said, as he skidded to a stop, round face gaping at me, cheerfully drunk. His jaw hung open for a second before he snapped it shut and took several steps toward me. "Can I touch your boobs?" he asked.

"Aah-" I started, physically unable to finish the thought aloud.

"Thanks!" he said, and reached out, grasping and squeezing, then rocked back, unsteadily. He belched, and pounded his chest, releasing a thick scent of beer into the air. "I had to ask because I'm a Christian," he said with an earnestly proud, drunken smile. His eyebrows furrowed and his expression slowly changed to one of confusion. "Why are you naked?" he asked, puzzled. It was as if he had just now realized the oddity of my situation.

"Uh-" I started and trailed off. I tried again, "Iii- ," with no more success.

"Hey bro, come here!" Another similar looking guy loped out of the trees. His mouth and eyes fell open at the sight of all of my glowing white skin in the moonlight.

"Woah! Hey…" As his shock faded, the second man's eyes narrowed and he smiled in a way that made me wrap my arms even tighter around myself. He took one step toward me, and another.

"Eeh!" I said, in warning, stepping back and wrinkling my face defensively. Without clothing or words, though, I really didn't really have anything to defend myself with.

"Hey, what are you doing, man? She's a good Christian girl," the first guy said.

The second man startled and turned on his friend, as though he had forgotten the other man was there."How do you know? Do good Christian girls walk around in the woods naked like that?" he pointed at me, accusingly.

"Well…" the first man seemed to consider, "Are you a good Christian girl?"

What a question, at a time like this! What was I supposed to say? I was not, in fact, a good Christian girl. I wasn't a Christian at all. In actuality, my entire religious upbringing could be summarized in one short sentence. As a child, I had asked my mom about this 'God' thing that I kept hearing about. She pursed her lips, rolled her eyes and said, "Well, *some* people believe that." But, then again, this was the same woman who overheard my little cousin ask her mother whether fairies really lived in the garden gate and interrupted my Aunt's lovely answer about the mysteries of the undiscovered unknown to shout at the little girl that, "Fairies are NOT REAL." That was the firm, unyielding stance of the woman who had raised me. One that, after the last several hours, I was finding myself seriously beginning to question. Deciding it would be foolish to risk my personal safety by refusing to misrepresent myself, I made an affirmative noise and nodded.

The first man broke into a grin. "See, I told ya! I think I've seen her at the big church on Sundays, too. She looks real familiar."

"Hmm…" his friend looked unconvinced, "Well, come on back to the fire anyway." He looked me up and down, uncomfortably. "Enough meat on your bones you won't freeze. You want me to warm you up, anyway?"

I shook my head violently, not wanting this sinister man to get any closer, and tucked my arms deeper into my armpits, walking toward the closest spot of firelight in the darkness. I didn't wait to see whether or not the men followed after me. The fire would be warm, at least, I thought, glancing down at my goose-pimpled flesh. I had hoped to make it back into town by myself, but without the towel, I was going to need some help. But, as I got close enough to hear the low, rowdy rumbles, and see firelight shining off the tops of quite so many broad shoulders and close-cropped haircuts, I began to wonder whether I would have been better to run back into the woods and try to hide again.

I tried to say "Oh no" but all that I managed was a strangled little moan. The protection of being a 'Good Christian Girl' would be pretty flimsy, if I really was walking into the middle of a frat party with no clothes on. This was not good at all. Had I just hopped out of the pot, and into the bonfire?

Chapter 9

"Hey guys! Look what we found out in the woods!" shouted the slow, earnest first guy. He probably didn't even realize how much that made me sound like an object. "It's a Naked Girl!" He seemed to like the sound of that, and started chanting, "Naked Girl! Naked Girl!"

More bodies started to filter through the trees, pumping their fists and joining in. "Naked Girl! Naked Girl!"

As I reached the fire, the group of men swarmed around, encircling me, with the bonfire at the center. With wide nervous eyes, I looked out at the gathered crowd and tried not to look too much like a victim, although the reality was that I was at the mercy of this throng. I kept my arms wrapped tightly around my chest, as the hot fire started to toast my now-not-freezing naked backside.

The chanting continued, "Naked Girl! Naked Girl!"

Then someone creative switched it up, inspiring half of the men to join a counterpoint of "Show your Boobs! Show your Boobs!"

I looked from face to grinning, sneering, shouting face. In the tavern earlier, all the faces had been so unique and intriguing in their laughter. Here, around the fire, all of the faces, to a man, looked exactly, and horribly the same. Except…

"Fiona! Is that you?" Pushing through the crush of men around the fire came a familiar face looking surprised and concerned.

It was Brandon! My knight in shining armor from last night, here to save the day again! Oh what incredible luck. "Baa-" I tried to call out, reaching my arms forward toward him. As my arms left my chest a cheer went up from the men.

"BOOBS!"

I launched myself forward into the protection of Brandon's arms, but he held me at arms length. "You okay? I've got you," he said, slipping out of his light rain jacket and pulling it around my shoulders, "Here, wear this." Oversized, it went down almost to my knees. I wriggled into the arm holes and zipped the coat up to my neck. The plasticky thing felt like a bag around me, and the fabric stung where it touched the welts that the branches had cut into me, but I had never been more glad for an item of clothing.

"Tah…" I started, then remembered that I couldn't actually manage the words. Instead, I looked up at him with apologetic eyes and smiled a grateful smile that said what I could not.

"Come on, let's get you out of here," he said, putting an arm around my shoulder possessively, and walking me through the crowd and back out into the darkness. A low, hooting noise rose from the group and followed us as we walked away from the fire. Were they booing? We left the light of the fire behind us, and in the darkness the night felt cold again, but now that I had Brandon's jacket around me, it wasn't so bad. I let out a sigh of relief.

Brandon's grip around my shoulders tightened. I glanced up at him, but his face didn't show the caring concern I expected. He looked angry. "What are you doing out here, like that?" he asked, not waiting for my answer, "Anything could have happened to you! If I hadn't known you, if I hadn't recognized you back there, all naked and muddy and bedraggled. I almost didn't, through all that grime, distracted by all your…" he trailed off, "A naked woman in the woods? Jesus- I mean, uh…" he cut himself off, embarrassed. We walked in silence for a moment before he continued. "And what happened to you last night? One minute you were there, and the next…" He looked down at me, and shook me, from his hold on my shoulder. "You could have really gotten hurt, you know? Some of the guys said they thought you might have run off into the woods…" He turned to look at me, shocked. "Wait! Are you still out here? Fiona, have you been lost in the woods for two nights?"

"Ehh-" I tried to deny it, forgetting that I couldn't speak, but he had already continued on, over me.

"This is always what happens to women, when they go off on their own, isn't it? You're all foolish creatures. Running off, getting lost and hurt. Worse! Careless, that's what you are. No common sense." His hold on my shoulder ached as he gripped me tightly, shaking me for emphasis. "This is why women need men to take care of them, to shepherd them and protect them. I was the savior of your virtue last night too, wasn't I? Wasn't I?"

Ouch, that shaking really hurt.

"Where would you even be without me, Fiona? I'll tell you where." He glanced over his shoulder, back the way we had come, then down at me, his face a mask of anger. "Well? Don't you have anything to say for yourself?"

I did not. Or, at least, I could not, so I just opened my eyes wide and fluttered my lashes apologetically. He was right, he had saved me. Of course, the things he was saying about women were backward to the point of being nonsense. But it was true that I had been completely helpless, and he had rescued me, twice. Where would I be, without him?

We reached the treeline and Brandon pulled a fob from his pocket, making a big SUV blink and honk. He walked me around to the passenger's side and boosted me unnecessarily into the cab and as he went back around to the driver's side, I noticed several unopened water bottles on the floor. I grabbed one and took a long drink. The relief was intense and immediate. I had not realized how thirsty I was! But, the water seemed to refresh me beyond simple thirst. As soon as the liquid hit my throat, an energizing, and clarifying coolness washed over me, making everything look sharper and clearer than it had a moment before.

Brandon climbed in and settled himself, fumbling with his keys and not looking at me. I took the opportunity to take a long look at him. A minute ago, in the moonlight, the curls of his hair had twined with smokey ethereal tendrils. Now they lay still, which was a relief. I hadn't realized how much the constant motion had been making me queasy until it stopped. In fact, after that sip of water, I felt much better, all around. My vision had cleared, and my stomach stopped rolling. My cold, sore muscles also felt better, and the stinging from the scrapes of branches had eased as well.

"Brandon," I said, marveling, "What is with this water?"

He turned. "What? Why did you-" he started, shocked to see me holding the bottle, but collected himself quickly. "Of course. You were thirsty. Sorry. It's just that that's water from my new extraction project. It's not exactly cleared for public consumption yet."

As he talked I realized that I had spoken, as well. The water seemed to have washed away the effects of that problematic potion entirely. Grateful to be able to communicate again, I focused on the most important thing I wanted to express. "Thank you, Brandon. Thank you so much for saving me back there. I really don't know what would have happened if you hadn't stepped in."

"You sure looked like you needed it." He shot me a look full of speculation. "Glad you seem to have found your voice again," he continued wryly.

"Me too. Thanks, again." I took another sip, and felt the water flow into me like liquid energy. "Seriously, though. This stuff is incredible. It's not like any water I've ever had."

"Yeah, it's great, huh? A real, natural mineral spring. Some pretty special minerals, too. We're still analyzing but as soon as we get final approval from the city council next Monday, we-" he cut himself off abruptly, "Sorry, I get excited about this stuff, but I'm not really supposed to talk about it. Industry secrets!" He held up a finger to his lips, in a playful 'shh'.

"Well, whatever it is, I'm grateful for it. I'm feeling a lot better now," I said, nestling more comfortably into the plush leather seat, "It's been a rough night."

"Seems like it." He looked at me, with a raised eyebrow, inviting me to explain.

I thought about how to answer, and while I did, he turned the key and the engine started with a rumble. "Can you take me to the Oak Tree Motel, please?" I asked him, "It's near the center of town."

"Okay," he replied, "Well?"

I just couldn't bring myself to tell Brandon about faeries or potions or magic. It all just seemed too strange, especially here in this big, solid normal car, away from the crackling fireplace and the curious fae folk. "I was at a party," I answered truthfully, "and I got scared. I ran away into the woods and I-" I wrung my hands, not looking at him, "I got lost."

"Naked?" he asked, incredulously.

"I had a towel," I said, "but-" I finished lamely, "it got lost."

"Huh. Well, you do seem to have a talent for getting yourself into trouble," he said, scowling at me, accusingly, "You should really try harder not to put yourself in situations like that. You were lucky to get out of there safely, tonight. One of these days, you're going to get yourself hurt."

"Do you think I like being naked with frat boys in the woods?"

"I don't know. Do you? You didn't look all that upset to me. Maybe that was the kind of attention you were looking for. Maybe I should have left you there."

"Not that upset? Brandon, I was terrified! I've never been more terrified. I didn't mean to end up in the woods like that, again. I hate these terrible dripping woods!"

"Well you certainly have a funny way of showing it," he shot back, "running away from my friends last night. Scaring everyone. They looked for you for an hour!"

"Last night? When I was all alone with those men? I don't think they were looking for me so they could help me get home safely, Brandon. You saw those guys tonight. Your so-called friends last night were just the same."

"What are you talking about? They're good guys."

"Unlike the guys tonight?"

"No, they're good guys too. That's my old fraternity. We're all getting ready to go camping tomorrow."

I had been right. That whole party had just smelled like a frat. "Well what did you mean, 'I was lucky to get out of there safely,' then?" I asked, accusingly.

"Come on, Fiona! You were naked. You know how men are. What did you think would happen? A defenseless woman without a man to protect her, and then to top it off, she's totally naked? Seriously! *Come on!*"

"What? So it's just okay, then? To assault women, just because they're defenseless?"

"*Naked!* You were basically asking for it!"

"I couldn't talk, Brandon! How could I possibly have been asking for it?"

"Well, you just can't walk through the world like it's a safe place, Fiona. People sin, okay. All people sin. It's just what they do. Good Christian men do their best, but we're just men. We are how God created us. There's only so much we can do!"

"That's crazy, Brandon."

"It's not crazy, it's human nature. You're weak and vulnerable. You need a man to protect you and keep you safe. You're just a woman, Fiona, you wouldn't understand."

"Just a woman? What is that supposed to mean? Why wouldn't I be able to understand?"

"See, you're getting hysterical, just like a typical female," he said, raising a hand, dismissively, "small brains, small bodies, small understanding." He smiled at me, in a pitying way. "Women are just overgrown children. They need to be shepherded and brought safely into the flock."

"What?" I shrieked, my shrill voice making me sound like I might, in fact, be hysterical, "What is with this valley, I swear! The guy who drove me into town said almost the exact same ridiculous thing to me. This Deacon guy."

"You were the wayward girl that Father found?" he asked, incredulously.

"Father?" I asked, confused, "I thought only Catholics call people stuff like that."

"We don't," said Brandon, shaking his head, "Most people call him the Deacon, or Elder, now that he leads the whole church, but Deacon's kind of stuck. I just call him that because he's my father."

"What? Really?" I did a double take, looking for echoes of the Deacon in the younger, handsome man. "Like, he's your dad? You don't look anything like him," I said, distracted by this unexpected information.

"I'm adopted, like you" he said, flushing red in the dim light of the streetlamp, "I should have told you last night. I just don't usually talk about it too much. The Deacon raised me, but technically I'm one of 'God's Children'," he continued, "We belong to the church."

"To the church?" I echoed, not understanding what he meant.

"Valley of Christ's Heart Fellowship," he explained, "we're the fastest growing Christian congregation in the world," he took his eyes off the road to look at me and grin, "because we're the best."

"Oh yeah?" I asked, unconvinced.

60

"Oh yeah," he said, "I was raised in the church, but all those guys tonight are members too. They're mostly converts. We love converts!" he looked over and smiled again, his eyes excitedly wide, and went on. "You've gotta come with me tomorrow, on Sunday. You'll see. The church knows everything. They'll teach you how to live, how to act, how to do right and be good. You don't know what you don't know till you come, I promise. And if you're part of the church, we can all keep you safe, and protected. I really like you, Fiona. I don't want to see you get hurt, or let you get lost down the devil's path."

"I don't know," I hedged, not wanting to offend him, "I don't think I'll have time. I was thinking about trying to head up to Portal Land tomorrow."

"Portal Land? Oh, Portland? Okay, yeah," he nodded, drumming his fingers on the steering wheel, "I can take you! Yeah, that'll be perfect. I'm heading up to the mountains after church, for the retreat with the boys, and Portland is on the way. You can even stay at the fraternity tonight if you want. We have extra rooms," he grinned that wide, winning grin again, "I'll make sure everyone knows I'm looking out for you."

I shook my head. "No, that's okay, just take me to the hotel, please."

"Okay, I'll pick you up in the morning, then. Nine am okay?" he asked, misunderstanding.

"No, I don't need a ride," I said, "I'll figure it out."

"What are you talking about? Father told me about your car. How are you trying to get there? At this rate I bet you'd just try to hitchhike, huh? At least don't try to do it naked, okay?" he laughed a humorless little laugh and continued, "Don't be weird. Just let me take you to church, and then we can go to Portland. Or we can just go out for breakfast after, okay?"

"No, Brandon. I don't want to go with you. I'm not interested in your church, okay?"

"What are you talking about? Why?"

"It's just not my thing."

"You don't know until you try it. There's music, everybody's shouting and clapping. It's exciting. You'll see."

"Look, I'm not going to go to church. It's just not the way I was raised. That's something other people believe in, not me," I said, remembering my mom's words to me as a child.

"Bad breeding doesn't have to stop anyone from seeking entrance to the glory of Heaven, Fiona. I can see that you're headed down a dark path, but God can still save you."

"I don't think so, Brandon. This is my hotel up here, okay? I'm just going to say good night." I looked down and realized that I was still wearing his jacket, but there was nothing I could do. It wasn't like I could give it back and walk into the hotel naked.

"Come on, Fiona. You're really making me mad, now. After all the nice things I've done for you, and now you're just going to refuse my kindness and generosity like that? Refuse the help of the church? Who do you even think you are? You just ruined my night. No, you ruined my whole week." He was upset now, rage burning hot, then cold again as he ranted at me and jerked the big car around. "I might just get back to work on Monday, like Father wants to. Skip camping and get an early start on testing. I don't even want to go on the trip now and have to tell those guys that the naked bitch in the woods that I saved was just some worthless," he punctuated his yelling by hitting the steering wheel, "wretched, Godless, no good SLUT!" He hit the last word hard, making the car lurch dangerously.

My breath came fast as he careened down the blessedly empty road into the center of town. He screeched to a stop near my motel, and I bailed from the car as quickly as I could, stumbling on the curb as I jumped down from the tall vehicle. I scampered into the little motel lobby, even more glad to be escaping the son's car than I had been to leave his father's.

"Hi, uh, sorry. I have a room here but I lost my key card."

"Okay, got yer ID?" the tired looking man behind the counter asked.

"No," I answered, "It was in the wallet with my key card. The whole thing got lost," I gestured at my unusual attire, "along with my clothes."

"Huh, well, I dunno then, miss." He thought for a minute and then, slowly a dim light bulb seemed to turn on. "Oh, wait, are these yer clothes?" He set a neatly folded stack of clothing on the peeling desk, with my wallet and phone stacked on top.

"Yes! Yes they are. How- uh, never mind." I thanked him and scooped the pile off the desk. I had never been more eager to get inside a shabby motel room.

Inside the room, I re-dressed myself. It felt like an eternity since I had worn real clothing. Even longer since I had had a private space of my own where I could relax. Or, I thought with a sigh of contentment as I flopped blissfully, an actual bed. Finally, after two solid days of being on the move, I had a moment to sit still and think about what had happened since I had crashed so ignominiously into this valley.

I was physically and emotionally exhausted. The amount of adrenaline that had been coursing through my body in the car just now, and earlier tonight in the woods with the frat boys and before that at the party was enough to leave me completely drained. And, I thought ruefully, yesterday had hardly been better. I had crashed my car, slogged through the rainy forest, had far too much to drink, narrowly escaped yet more dangerous men, and ended up sleeping under a tree, again in the woods. The last two days had been utterly exhausting, it was true, but they hadn't been all bad.

My thoughts drifted back to the group by the crackling fire, and that funny old man, Godrin. All those fantastical things he had said! Magic was real, and faeries and all those other funny folk he had mentioned were real too. It made me tingle just thinking about it. How electrifying it had felt, with all of those strange, wonderful people gathered around me. "Enough magic in me to bide," he had said. I wondered what he had meant by that. It sounded like he thought I was like them, which that letter from the faerie queen seemed to corroborate.

Growing up, I had always felt different. A little apart from everybody. Like everyone else got a rulebook for life and I just never got my copy. Maybe this was why. Maybe I had always felt different because I was different. Maybe that feeling of belonging that I had always yearned for could be found among the fae.

I unzipped my backpack, which I had left safely in the hotel room, and reached for the faerie book, wanting to look at those curious faces again. Instead of the hard paper bundle I expected to find, I felt only dirty clothes. My fingers yielding nothing, I peered into the top of the backpack. It was gone! The whole manila envelope with the book and all my papers, all gone! I dumped the bag out just in case, rifling through clothes and toiletries, looking for something that was obviously not there.

Then I looked under the bed and behind the single faded armchair in the corner. In the sparse hotel room I quickly confirmed that the book and the paperwork were gone. I dashed back to the front desk.

"Hi, hello. Um, do you know, has anyone been in my room?" I asked the man behind the front desk.

"Oh, I dunno," the night shift clerk answered dully.

"Okay, well, can you tell me who dropped these clothes and my wallet off earlier?"

"Dunno about that either," he said.

Fists balled with frustration, I stamped the tile floor of the motel lobby. I had zero leads on the thief. There was nothing I could do. My documents were irretrievably gone. Not a single thing had gone right in this terrible valley, since the moment I got here! Even the nice guy I had met turned out to be a pushy judgemental churchy jerk. Maybe I should just give up and go already. What had I expected, coming here? To run into my birth mother at that farmers market, and recognize her instantly? That was crazy. Impossible. A child's fairytale dream.

Even if she did still live in this area, if she was even still alive, how would she recognize me? Or me her? This whole plan had been foolish from the start. If only I could just get in my car and drive away from here, but of course, my car was still out of commission.

"UGH!" I vented at the man behind the counter, "I just want to leave this awful place. Why does the tire store have to be closed until Monday?"

"Oh," he said slowly, "I dunno about that, but if ya need a tire I can sell ya one. Lenny's my brother."

"Really?" I looked at the man, incredulously. These small towns, everybody really did know everybody. "That would be amazing." I worked out the logistics with the helpful man, then headed back to my room to get a good night's sleep. I'd go to the tire shop in the morning, then I'd be away from here, as fast as my mom's old minivan would carry me.

Part 3 - Portal Land

Leaning over the shallow scrying bowl, she peered intensely at the picture within, clutching the bowl with both hands and grinning maniacally. Yes, yes, just a little further, now.

"Velia, Velia, Velia!" her lady's voice rang inside her like a bell, pulling her to come. To obey. With a flash and a crack, she was there. No longer in the shadowy boudoir, now she stood in the center of a bright, vine-filled room, at the end of a very small woman's imperious gaze. "Velia, what is going on?"

"My lady?" the taller woman feigned confusion, "whatever do you mean?"

"My daughter, I felt her. Right here. Close to me, getting closer all the time, and yet, you say you can not locate her. And now, I feel her presence retreating!

"I assure you my lady, I am using all the powers at my disposal, " Velia simpered.

Chapter 10

"'Appreciate it!" I called, waving my thanks to the kindly man from the hotel, as I pulled out onto the highway with my brand new tire. I was more than ready to get out of this valley. It was funny, I thought, how excited I had been to get here, just a couple days ago. The place where I had been born and where my birth family might still be.

The sudden pull to come here and find them had been so strong that I had surprised everyone around me with my sudden decision to move to Oregon, but it was all that I had been able to think about, and I had dived into the work of packing my things with, now that I was looking back at it, an extremely unusual amount of intensity.

Driving away from this valley now, though, I felt nothing but relief. The last couple days had been harrowing, with more terrifying experiences and near-misses than I had ever experienced before. Men at home didn't act like that. Neither did drinks, or towels, for that matter. But, it was more than that. Sure, my time in this valley had been both scary and unpleasant, but I wasn't running away out of fear. I just didn't feel that tug in my gut drawing me to it, anymore. It was strange, the way I had been drawn, almost magnetically to Oregon. The dreams, which had started right around my birthday last summer, had come with an intense feeling of yearning and of being incomplete, after a lifetime of being pretty much okay with my adoption and my family.

It must have been magic, I said to myself, tapping the steering wheel rhythmically, Something was drawing me here. Something that isn't doing it, now. I thought about the way I had felt after I had drunk that swirling potion, last night. After I had, essentially, been drugged by that Velia woman. Loopy and senseless, unable to speak. Thinking about it, my tapping fingers got faster, lips tightening and eyes narrowing. Maybe that had done it. I mean, it could have. It was a magic potion. It had to have been, to have affected me like it did. And, if there was some magic pulling me here, the magic potion could have canceled it out, because they're both magic, right? Magic cancels out magic. Really? That's the theory I'm going with? I shook my head. That was nonsense. I had no idea how magic worked. After all, I had only become convinced that magic worked at all, yesterday.

The faded upholstery of the old van's seat felt incredibly homey and familiar, and I nestled into it comfortably. It was good to be back inside this big tin can.

There's an awful lot more freedom and security with a car than without one, I thought, checking my rear-view mirror and merging into the fast lane toward Portal Land. It was the first excuse I had come up with for why I couldn't go to church with Brandon, but the more I thought about it, the better the idea sounded.

I had one piece of information that hadn't gotten lost, or stolen. One big thing that I knew today that I had not known yesterday. That funny old man, Godrin, he had said something. The Faire Isle Pub in Portal Land. That was the best place to go, if I was looking for the fae. And so, I thought, that was where I would head, because now that I had discovered this secret new world, I just had to find out more.

I had all the time in the world to find my family, now that I was here in Oregon. "I'm an adult with my own priorities and agenda," I said into the breeze, as I rolled down the window and took a deep breath of the fresh spring air, "and I want to go find out about magic."

As I drove away from town, I had been glad to leave the river, and its now too-familiar bank of trees, behind me. Now though, as the interstate criss-crossed its winding path, I watched the water twinkle in a friendly sort of way. I had always loved water. It wasn't the river's fault that I had kept getting so uncomfortably stranded in its adjacent woods.

I glanced at the clock. 10 a.m. And what of it? There was no one in the world who expected me to be anywhere at any particular time. I pulled off the interstate and found a place to park alongside the wide, sparkling river. Large and larger boulders formed the bank of the river here, and by scrambling out onto one of them, I surrounded myself on all sides by the rushing burble of the water. I dipped a toe in. "Ack! Cold!" I exclaimed, and pulled the foot out like a snail retreating back into its shell.

I sat cross-legged on the sun-warmed rock and let my thoughts wander on the breeze. Mom would never believe what I was uncovering, here. What I seemed to be discovering. She would think this was absolute nonsense. But, she didn't have to believe it, did she? I didn't technically even have to tell her. And, I probably wouldn't, I thought with a half smile. Eventually, I spoke, my voice drowned in the roar of the river.

"I'm an adult now," I told myself firmly, "I can do whatever I want." The affirmation blew down the river on the wind. "I can be whoever I want, I can believe whatever I want," I said, gaining momentum. I had come here looking for something.

For my family, yes. But, more than that. I was looking for a community. For belonging. For understanding, and for people who saw the world like me.

Looking down at the shifting water, my fractured reflection stared back at me. What a strange little girl I had been. Always a little different, a little apart from everyone else. Thoughtful, off in my own little world, with peculiar interests that no one else shared or understood. Every now and then there had been someone, a good friend or a teacher, who had seemed to cut through the static and connect with the real me. The real person behind the mask. But more often than not, when I was around other people I felt like an alien in a human costume, just trying to fit in well enough that no one would notice that I was pretending.

In the Raven that first night, I had felt that way. Like an explorer on a human safari, trying as hard as I could to blend in and act like everybody else. A constant, exhausting effort. It always got easier after a drink or two, or, at least I found myself worrying about it less. Last night at the River House had been different, though. If the Raven had felt like a safari, the group around the fire at the River House had felt, well, if I had to guess, it felt like a family reunion, although I had never been to one. I hadn't believed it at first, when Godrin told me that I had magic in me. It had sounded so unbelievable, in fact, that my first reaction had been that embarrassing public outburst. But, having digested the idea overnight, and remembering how at-home I had felt among the, albeit very strange, folk gathered there, I had to admit that, whatever it was, that ineffable thing that made it possible for me to connect with someone, every single person in that room had had it.

Was that the magic that I was feeling? Maybe. The feeling of hope welled up inside of me. It would be so amazing if that was true. If I had really found my community here, among these wonderful magical creatures. Among the fae. A place where I could truly be myself with everyone around me, and not just those rare, special people that I happened across only occasionally.

Brandon had seemed like one of the real ones. One of the ones who got it. One of those rare people that I could just talk to. What a shame that his views on life ended up being so misogynistic and backward! It hadn't just been Brandon, though, had it? That whole town had been full of aggressive men. That kind of thing had never happened to me, back in California, not once, and here, I had narrowly avoided assault multiple times in the span of 48 hours. I felt my face grow hot as tears welled behind my eyes. I had been running on adrenaline since I first crashed my car, careening from crisis to crisis.

Last night at the hotel, I had been too exhausted to think or to feel, and I'd fallen asleep as soon as my head hit the pillow. Now, though, the reality of the last couple days came crashing down around me. My tears overflowed, running down my face as I sobbed. All of those contemptible men. All of those terrible experiences, which, but for my extraordinary luck could have been much worse. My shoulders heaved with my gasping breath as my body released all of that pent-up emotion. Eventually, my sobbing quieted and my breathing slowed. I wiped my hand across my soggy face, then dipped it into the river and let the water wash away the tears before unfolding myself and climbing down from the rocks, ready to get back on the road.

As I approached the car, I scowled at my reflection in the window, wearing the same functional pants and dark blue shirt that I had put on at the coffee shop two days ago. The clothing itself was perfectly fresh, having been returned pressed and clean last night, but I was unbelievably tired of this outfit and the memories it held. I was fresh and clean, too, after a long shower at the motel this morning, and now that I had my car back with all of my clothing in it, I was more than ready for a change.

Climbing deep into the van, I dug a duffel bag out of the pile of pillows and blankets on the third row seat. "This is actually pretty cozy," I said, as I clawed my way back out from underneath every bit of soft bedding that I owned. Sleeping in my car would certainly be preferable to another night under a tree. From the bag, I pulled out a light cotton dress that would feel nice in the mid-morning sunshine. The rich colors and intricate paisley fabric reminded me of some of the designs on the hanging lanterns and the throw pillows that I had seen scattered around the River House last night. To my eye, the patterns looked like something fantastically magical. *Made in India* I read from the tag. Well, fantastically foreign, anyway. I pulled the new dress over my head and admired my reflection in the window. Much better.

I climbed back into the driver's seat, then paused. Until now, I had just been following signs to Portland and hoping that they would also take me to the Portal Land that Godrin had mentioned. Brandon hadn't seemed to know what I was talking about, and it seemed likely that the old man had just been pronouncing the name in that funny dialect that some of the fae folk seemed to have. And, as the largest city in Oregon, Portland was at least a place I had heard of before. Now that I was getting closer, though, I was going to need a more specific destination.

I pulled out my phone and sounded out the name I had heard last night. "Faire Aisle Pub Portland," I said aloud into the tiny microphone. The search returned plenty of pubs with distances of 30 or 40 miles. I scrolled down the list, scanning quickly, and felt my heart rate increase. It wasn't here. None of the names even started with an F. I had assumed that I would just be able to search and find it, but it wasn't here.

But, why would I have assumed that? This was a fae place that I was looking for. A magic place. Why would I have thought I could just search it up and find it on the internet? I set my phone down hard and pressed my fingertips to my eyelids, breathing through my frustration. I had only one clue to go on. Just this one. I had thought it would be straightforward. A public house. I had assumed something public would be easy to find. But, nothing about this was going to be easy, was it?

Taking a few more deep breaths, I tried to think. I realized that I didn't actually know what the pub was called, only what I remembered hearing. There had to be a way to find this place online, if I could figure out what to search for. But, I considered, maybe technology could help with that. I opened up the phone's voice command again.

"Faire isle" I said, quickly.

"Sure," said my phone's pleasant robotic voice, "searching for 'feral.' Feral, *adjective*, An animal in a wild state, especially after escape from captivity or domestication."

No, that wasn't it. I tried again. "Faire isle,"

"Sure, Ferrel, *noun*, a ring or cap, typically a metal one, which strengthens the end of a handle, stick, or tube and prevents it from splitting or wearing."

"Ugh! No!" I shook my hands from the wrists to release some of my pent up frustration, and tried again. This time, I let myself drift back to last night by the fireside, and tried to channel Godrin's slow, richly accented speech. "Faire isle" I said, slowly, into the little speaker.

"Okay, Fair Isle is a traditional knitting technique used to create patterns with multiple colors. Named for the Fair Isle, one of the Shetland Islands, in Scotland."

Fair Isle. A Fair Island. In Scotland! Godrin had mentioned faerie isles, hadn't he? An island for the fair folk - this must be it! And, what else did the definition say? A type of colorful knitting pattern? I looked at the examples. Geometric designs and little boxy animals. They looked like the patterns my crafty college roommate had added to her knit hats. Hadn't she called those Fair Isle? She might have done, now that I thought about it. They reminded me of some of the sweaters I had seen around the fire last night, too. Old world, and cozy. My legs bouncing with excitement and anticipation, I searched again.

"Fair Isle Pub, Portland." Nothing. "Fair Isle Pub, Portal Land" No local business listings. Yet again thrown into the depths of frustration, I almost closed the window, before I noticed that there was a single search result returned, with some pertinent text highlighted.

"...before heading to the infamous **Fair Isle Pub** of **Portal Land**, to interview..."

Tingling with excitement at my success, I clicked and navigated to an old-style, boxy-looking website. "PNW Bigfoot Hunter" read the title, with the tagline, "Paranormal Investigation in the Pacific Northwest". The website looked like some guy's blog documenting his personal experiences with the supernatural. Mom would say that this guy was a nutcase, I thought, with a quiet chuckle, as I skimmed quickly over the text, searching for the reference to the Fair Isle from the search preview. I found the quote and scanned quickly to the end. It had been just a casual mention of Fair Isle as the location where he had met with a potential source for his article on local cryptid sightings. No mention of where the Fair Isle was. Certainly, no address to put into my GPS. I scrolled back up to the top of the page and started to read, word by word.

Today, my search for the legendary bigfoot continues. If this new information turns out to be genuine, I plan to be out searching all afternoon, so I stopped at the nearby Gardener Market to resupply before heading to the infamous Fair Isle Pub of Portal Land to interview the latest source in my investigation.

Nearby Gardener Market, huh? Well, that would at least get me to the right part of town. I typed in the name, hoping that this wouldn't be another dead end. Luckily there was only one Gardener Market in Portland, and I would be there within the hour.

Chapter 11

Okay, so it's a grocery store, I said to myself as I pulled into the small parking lot. I didn't know what I had expected, but this charming market festooned with leafy plants hanging from sloping green awnings seemed as good a place as any to search for faeries. Inside, the light misting of the garden section made it feel like a cool grotto. The expensive houseplants and artistic florals on display at this chic little grocery gave me a taste of Oregon's biggest city's particular aesthetic. I walked around the outside edge of the store, slowly. Once, then again.

As I passed the other shoppers, I looked at each one, carefully, searching for signs of that unusual impishness that I had seen in my faerie book, and on so many of the faces last night. Or else, for that otherworldly-strange beauty. The uncanny, too-wide eyes of some of the young men, or the craggy rock-like curves and wrinkled jaws of some of the impossibly old-looking women. Everyone I peered at looked ordinary, like any urban shopper buying organic cold pressed carrot juice. I looked twice at a pair of teenagers dressed all in black, buying sweet Japanese snacks, but their unusualness was of an extremely ordinary kind. I lingered in the produce section next to a display of seasonal local rhubarb, watching the shoppers. A short exhalation of breath behind me, which I felt more than heard, made me turn my head. There was a man behind my shoulder and, having gotten my attention, he gave me a sly smile.

"Something tells me that whatever you're looking for, it's not apples or oranges," he said, selecting a few mottled, rusty-looking citrus for his black cloth shopping bag, "You might want to try a little harder to pretend you're shopping." He winked at me and moved off toward the next produce display.

"What? I, uh-" I turned to look, but the man had moved away. I followed him as he wandered off toward the store's curated selection of wines. The tall, lean man was dressed all in black, and his mahogany skin looked bright against his dark clothing. When he reached up to take a bottle of red from a high shelf, his long, dark coat fell open, revealing an intriguing collection of talismans hanging from his belt. Of all the people I had seen in this store, he seemed by far the most likely to be who I was searching for.

I followed him into the wine section and lurked awkwardly behind him until he turned. "Um, hi," I said, nervously.

"Hello," he replied.

"You're right, I'm not grocery shopping," I said, hanging my head a little at the admission.

"You don't say," he replied, with a crooked smile and a long, arched brow.

"No," I said hesitantly, not quite sure how to broach the subject of my interest now that he was in front of me to ask. I might as well just dive in, I decided. "I'd like to go to the Faire Isle Pub. Do you know it? I've heard that it's near here."

"Where did you hear that?" he asked, his expression concerned.

"I read it online," I said, a little defensively.

"You did? On the internet, it says that the Fair Isle Pub is near here?" he asked, with a lot more intensity than I had anticipated.

"Well, not exactly," I hedged, "I had to put it together myself, but after this guy Godrin told me about it. I just had to try and find it."

"Hmm," the man said, looking dissatisfied, "Well, if you put it together, other people could. I'll have to see about fixing that. These are not the times-" he paused and refocused his eyes on me, "Godrin told you about the Fair Isle, huh? Well. Many are the pints I've shared with ol' Godrin when he sees fit to visit the city, aye." His unaccented voice broadened, becoming a fair copy of Godrin's old-country-sounding speech. The imitation made me smile and he returned the expression.

"He made it sound like the place I needed to be," I said, with a shrug.

"Well, you're in luck, I'm headed that way now and you can walk with me." He turned, his coat swishing behind him, and headed for the bank of cash registers by the door. I followed behind him, grabbing a fermented tea from a cooler so that I had something to buy.

Waiting in line behind my new companion, I said, "I'm a little surprised I didn't notice you first. I was looking for anyone that looked-" I trailed off awkwardly, not liking any of the options I had in mind for finishing that sentence. "Weird" and "Strange" didn't seem like nice words to call him, and "Magical" just wasn't something I was ready to say, out loud, in public.

"I was behind you," he said.

"I mean, sure, but I looped the store a couple of times and I didn't-"

"I was *behind* you," he said again, with emphasis.

"What- wait, were you following me?" I asked incredulously.

"You didn't look like you were shopping," he said, turning to look at a large display of ethically sourced chocolate.

"Are you, like, security or something?" That would explain the all-black, efficient-looking outfit. It was a decent security uniform.

He shrugged, noncommittally. "I look out for my neighborhood."

The register was clear, and he gestured for me to go ahead. I paid for my drink and we left the store together. I didn't mention my car waiting in the parking lot and fell naturally into step beside the man. We walked along in comfortable silence. Under the open sky, his stride widened, and his gate, beside me, took on a strange syncopation, almost like he had an extra joint at the end of his long limbs. The lilting cadence made the walk feel almost like a rhythmic dance.

The day was beautiful. A clear blue sky promised a rain-free afternoon, and the fresh spring-green leaves of the trees glowed where they were backlit by the afternoon sun. Occasional cars broke the silence, but between them, the loudest sounds were the birdsong and the rustle of the leaves in the breeze. A screech of tires cut through the silence. The man next to me grabbed my arm, jerking me to the side. In the same fluid motion, he pulled me with him over a low stone wall covered in moss. He crouched, one arm over my shoulder, keeping me low.

"What-" I started to ask.

"Shh," he squeezed my shoulder and warned me with his eyes to be quiet.

A moment later, a giant white truck careened down the road we had been walking down, tires screeching. Peering through the open brickwork of the wall, I could see that the cab and the bed were both crammed full of hollering, yowling men waving banners featuring a popular hate symbol. The men in the back sat on large cases that could have been coolers, but their padlocks suggested they were holding something more sinister than beer.

The truck grazed the sidewalk near where we crouched, and the tires made sparks on the pavement. It course corrected and swerved, heading back the other way, and in another moment was out of our sight. Heart pounding with adrenaline, I turned to look up at the face of the man next to me. He crouched, perfectly still, head raised, looking down the road after the truck that had now disappeared. After a long moment, he nodded, satisfied, and we both moved to stand and climb back over the wall. He offered me a hand, and I took it, glad for the gentler assistance over the wall, the second time. Back on the sidewalk, with two feet underneath me, my pounding heart slowed enough that I could speak.

"What was- How did you- Who were those guys?" I asked, wide-eyed.

"Corpsos," he said, with a grimace. At my confused expression, he elaborated. "They call themselves the Corps. The CCC's unofficial army."

I nodded, recognizing the name from some scare-tactic news programs that I had seen back in California. If our state government didn't remain strong in controlling local troublemakers and dissidents, it warned, The CCC would step in to ensure a peaceful and harmonious international civilization. "Here? Really? I mean, I've heard on TV that the CCC was taking strong necessary action to help citizens in, um, less developed nations overseas, but right here? In Oregon?"

He looked sideways, and down his nose at me. "There are some things you should understand, before you head into a place like the Fair Isle, talking about the CCC's 'strong necessary actions to help.'"

"Okay, tell me," I said earnestly. "I don't know…" I paused to reflect, then said, "…anything, really. I really don't know anything."

That made him smile, splitting his expressive face into a wide grin that showed several large, square teeth. I thought I might even see the shadow of a dimple under his short-cropped, pointed beard. "Well, that's not a bad place to be starting, all things considered. You say you don't know anything, which is true, but you've heard a few things, apparently. Tell me what you thought you knew."

As we walked, I tried to remember everything I had heard about the international governing organization, The CCC, that had entered the world's political scene so recently and become such a global superpower. "Well, we all agree that the world has been going bad for a long time," I started slowly, thinking aloud, "The climate is being destroyed, for one thing." The man nodded in agreement, encouraging me to go on. "Corporate greed makes the rich richer, while poor people suffer, even though there's enough to go around. And, um, it seems like people's rights are being taken away, left and right. What we're allowed to do with our bodies. All kinds of stuff. It's like we're regressing. All these old-fashioned rules and traditions cropping back up, that it seemed like society had grown out of, controlling what people can and can't do." There had been protests at my college for all sorts of things like that. Some I had gone to, and others I hadn't. "And, just a whole lot of hatred. Sexism. Prejudice against all sorts of people," I glanced at my companion, acknowledging in my look that he was one sort of person that the men in that awful truck would have been prejudiced against.

"True, all true."

"And so a bunch of countries all got together and formed a council, the Calamity Control Council, to help fix all the things that were going wrong and keep people in line, and they have a lot of, uh, flexibility and power so that they can do that," I finished.

"And, how do you think they have been doing with controlling this calamity?" the man asked.

"I don't know. It doesn't seem like things are getting better, but The CCC hasn't existed for very long. Maybe it just needs more time?"

He chucked humorlessly. "They've been around for longer than you think. Just because they've finally moved into the open… But no, these players have been in control of this calamity for a long time."

"They have? But, if they have it under control, why-"

"Not under control," he laughed again, this time with somewhat more warmth.

"But what… in control of the calamity? That sounds like you're saying that The CCC started all this trouble. That's cr-" I had started to say, "That's crazy" but the expression on the man's face made me stop. "Really? You think The CCC-?"

"I don't think so, I know," he said, his face deadly serious, "We have been standing against this force we call The CCC, for a long, long time. This 'Calamity Control Council' is the newest head on an ancient hydra. They're barely trying to disguise themselves at this point," he shook his head, "No, this enemy is old. Like you said, they're resurrecting a lot of the old rules that worked for them in the past.

Preparing for their next great stand. Another bid for world control. We can see what they're doing, clearly enough. Who they really are. Whether that'll be enough to stop them…" He looked in the direction that the Corpsos had driven off in. "Their foot soldiers see the battle lines being drawn just as clearly as I do."

"World control? Foot soldiers? Come on, that's a bit of an exaggeration, don't you think?"

"I don't know, is it?" he asked, "You said it yourself, an international controlling body, in charge of making the rules and keeping people in line. That sounds like world domination to me."

"And this shadowy international superpower, you're telling me that they're also sending people around in big ugly trucks to terrorize people?"

"Of course not. The shadowy international superpower gives them ideas and infiltrates their minds, poisoning them from the inside. Then they buy the guns and flags and get in the trucks all by themselves." A crashing sound made us both raise our heads and look in the direction that the truck sped off in. "Come on," he said, "We're almost there, and we should get off the street. It's not usually this bad around here, but these last few weeks have been," he paused, looking left and right, before cutting between some trees and into a vacant lot between buildings, "unsafe. It's probably the same information that brought you here that's drawing the extra patrols to the area. When we get there, can you show me what you saw online?"

"Yeah, sure. I can show you. It was somebody's blog. A bigfoot investigator guy."

"Oh, that moron." He looked back at me and rolled his eyes, holding a big branch so that it wouldn't snap back and hit me. "He comes into the Fair Isle now and again. Got enough in him to get through the front door, but not enough to understand much of anything. Runs around the woods trying to snap pictures of old nature spirits who never did anything to anybody except ask to be left alone. And now this. Honestly, some people. Here-" He motioned me into a nondescript door in the side of a building and into a cramped wood-paneled hallway with a narrow twisting staircase. It seemed like we had come in through the back. My new friend stepped forward and opened a heavy wooden door into a dimly lit drinking establishment and gestured grandly, sending me through. "You wanted it, you've got it. Welcome to the Fair Isle."

Chapter 12

I stepped through the door and it swung closed behind me, leaving my new friend on the other side. Alright, I guess I'm on my own then, I thought, as I stepped down into the sunken main floor of the room. I made my way through the sea of mostly empty tables toward the bar, raised on a dais at the other end of the hall, a bit higher than the door I had entered. Across from the bar was a large, round stone fireplace, crackling with a low, warm fire.

As I walked across the room, I stared, enchanted, at the walls around me, which were painted with marvelously complex designs like giant knitting patterns. These elaborate geometric pictures wove in and around the pillars and archways that created cozy nooks at the edges of the large dim room. At the bar, I sat down on one of the high-backed, studded leather stools. The wall space above the shining bottles was covered in posters and signs, some new and some bleached and faded with age. I read one elaborately carved sign, sounding out the strange word, "sess…qui…centennial."

Appearing from the bar's backstage, or from out of thin air, I couldn't tell which, the barman who now approached me was one of the stranger-looking creatures I had seen, and after last night, that was saying something. He was bald, bat-eared, and long-nosed, with long, spindly fingers twisting a cloth in a cup.

"Welcome to the Fair Isle," he said, "Sesquicentennial. It means we've been here for a hundred and fifty years, as a safe resting place for our kind of folk. A few more, now, I suppose," he said, smiling thoughtfully, then went on, "And what can I get for you this afternoon, miss?" His polite, professional speech surprised me with its contrast to his strange appearance. "Unless you're satisfied already?" He nodded toward the glass bottle of tea that I had forgotten I was holding.

"Oh, uh, would that be okay, if I just drink this?" I asked since he had mentioned it. It was a little early to start drinking alcohol, especially after the last couple of nights I had had.

"Of course, miss. This is a public house. I'm a ghoul, not a capitalist." He gave me a short nod and returned to fussing with the glasses.

Well, alright then. For a bar in the early afternoon, it was busier than I expected. A public house, I corrected myself. Similar, but not the same. And better yet a magical public house, full of the fae folk. Involuntarily, I felt the corners of my mouth turn up in a smile. I found it! This was a place where I could get some real answers. I eyed two burly men laughing as they played a game at a table near the bar. They shook a collection of stones, and tossed them out onto the table, exclaiming in joy or defeat. Soon, the game devolved into jocular shouting.

"I'll have you know I'm more'n half human, an' I'll have you respect it," said one man to the other, slamming his flagon down onto the thick table so that his drink sloshed out the side.

"Oh, aye, sure ye are. An' if that's true, then I'm the great faerie queen's own personal lapdog, I am."

"Oh come off it an' I'll show ye. I'll walk right out that door, clear as day, an' jus', an' jus' hail me a cab."

"Do it, then. I'd see that."

"I will, then and you'll watch me."

"Like I watched you romance that human girl the other night, aye."

"Like I did, like I did!"

"An' did ye wake up in the mornin' with a bed full of yellow and sunflower knorls, or did her pretty petals all stay in place?"

"Wasn' a sunflower. Was a human girl, that was."

"Wasnnae! Wasnae neither!"

"Now, I know a girl from a sunflower. Look, that girl there. She's nae a sunflower is she? Are you?" The two men turned and looked directly at me. Surprised by the sudden attention, I gaped at them, mouth and eyes wide open.

"No, I'm not a sunflower," I said after a moment, hoping that the obvious answer would work.

"See?" said the man on the defensive.

"But is she a more'n half human girl?" asked his companion, "What is it then, girl, over or under?"

I didn't have any idea what he meant. Over or under? I felt, at that moment, like Alice about to step foot into Wonderland. But, Alice had not gone over or under the looking glass, had she? She had gone through it. All my life, I had tried my best to fake it and fit in. To pretend like I knew what was going on, or why people acted a certain way. Not to ask too many questions. But, that habit would not serve me well here. To find out what I wanted to know, I was going to have to set my old insecurities aside and just ask.

"What does that mean, over or under?" I asked, leaning toward them with interest.

"How much magic, o' course. Are you more'n half fae, or more'n half human?" he clarified.

"Oh," I said, "Um, human, I think? I, er-" I hesitated, then plunged ahead. "I just found out about the fae yesterday, actually. So, I don't know how magical I am, or much of anything really. Probably not very much though, I'd figure." I shrugged, apologetically. "But, now that I do know about it all, I just want to learn more."

"Yesterday, eh? Well, you've made fast work of it coming here then. The best place you could happen to find, for all that, I'd say." He raised his glass in salute to the pub around him. "If you'd care to have a drink with us, we'll tell you what we can."

"Thanks, that's very kind of you," I said, picking myself up and moving to sit with the two large men.

"Eudo," he said, extending his hand to me, "And this is my brother, Odo."

"Charmed," said Eudo's brother, who had definitely not gone home with a sunflower.

I smiled and bobbed my head, in greeting. "I'm Fiona." It got easier every time.

"So, what's brought you so suddenly to the notion that magic's real, then, Miss Fiona?" asked Eudo.

"Well, I'm looking for information on my family," I explained, "I'm adopted and I don't have much to go on." I frowned, thinking about the missing papers. I had so much less today than I had yesterday. Suddenly, I lost my train of thought, distracted by something over the man's shoulder.

A pretty girl had just come in the back door, and I watched her as she glided gracefully from here to there, the airy garment she wore floating behind her unnaturally like she was underwater. When she touched a cup at the center of a table, it blossomed out with a delicate collection of curling fiddlehead ferns, buttercups, and long green stalks of sweet grass. Wide-eyed with amazement at this evidence of actual magic that I was seeing with my own two eyes, I kept staring until Eudo cleared his throat, bringing my attention back to the table and my companions.

"Sorry, I- what is she doing?"

"Oh, Isla? She'll just be setting up for the evening crowd."

"Oh. Okay." I accepted the non-answer and tried to remember what I had been talking about.

Right, I had been telling them that I was searching for my family without many leads. Which was true, I thought, as I watched the graceful girl float from table to table in my periphery, but I knew so much more today than I had a week ago. "I had some clues about my family. Just a few things. Some papers, but-" I didn't want to sound overdramatic, saying they had been stolen when I really didn't have any evidence. "But I lost them. And I had a book about faeries, but I lost that, too. That's what got me here, I guess. That book. And the letter. Oh!" I dug into my pocket and pulled out my phone. I had forgotten. There was one thing that I hadn't lost when my papers had been stolen. There, safe in my camera roll, was the letter that had fallen out of the book, or at least, what was left of it, after it had gotten wet. I held the little computer out to the brothers, to show them. To my surprise, the two burly men shrank back as though I were holding a viper and not a cell phone.

"Er, not sure that I'd be wanting to get too close to a thing like that, miss," said Eudo, with a perplexing mix of fear, confusion and disgust on his face.

"Right dangerous, those are. Right dangerous," said Odo in agreement, nodding his head.

"Oh, sorry," I said, pulling the phone back, "I didn't realize. Is it-" I searched for the words to navigate this unexpected social faux pas, "is it okay if I use it? You wouldn't have to touch it."

"Oh, aye, fine."

"Certainly fine, aye"

"If you know what you're up to, with those things."

"Never did have much notion,"

"Never did have the knack,"

"That human magic,"

"That real powerful human stuff, you know."

The brothers' speeches overlapped, tumbling over one another as they reassured me and eyed my device suspiciously.

"Well…" I scanned the letter again, but most of the words were smeared or blurry. The only real piece of tangible information was the dry signature line at the bottom. "Do you know anything about *Queen Vivienne of the Fae Folk of the Eternal Realm of Portal Land and the Twin River Valleys,*" I read, "I think she had something to do with arranging my adoption."

"Oh aye, but if you'd be wanting to find the faeries o'er in the faerie city, them's who gang around the queen, well, then you'd just head on o'er to the gorge and visit, wouldn't you?" asked Odo incredulously.

"I would?"

"Well, you might, and they'll likely have a few things to tell you," agreed Eudo, "but there's no rush to be off to them right away, now is there? You just found yourself to the Fair Isle, and tonight," he clapped a hand on my shoulder companionably, "ye'll raise a glass with the fair folk o' Portal Land!" Odo and Eudo raised their large mugs to toast, and I picked up my little bottle and went to unscrew the cap to sip, but before I could, Odo snatched it out of my hand. "This'll never do for a slainte. Barkeep! Get the lass a pint of the house, aye?" The goblin bartender appeared and slid me a tankard just like the men's. I raised my glass and toasted.

"Skaal!" they cried and drank deeply.

I sipped, and the sweet, light, bubbly taste of the beverage in my mug surprised me. "What is this?"

"Mead, of course. What else?"

What else, indeed? I took a second sip, tasting the delicate floral flavor of the honey. It was like sunshine-warmed daisies on a bright summer day.

"So, lass, you've found us out and you've got questions for our fair queen when you find her, but for tonight," he reached long arms around and grasped both my shoulder and his brothers, "you've got me, and you've got Odo. What secrets of the fair folk can we be spilling for you first?

"Well, you asked me if I was more human or more fae, and I don't know for myself, but what about you?"

"Oh, um, er-" the brothers looked around shiftily, and Eudo replied, "Well, we don't rightly know either. An' it's not particularly polite to ask. Shouldn't have asked you. Impudent, really. But, if I had to say, well, we don' get out in the human world much, so I'd have to say we're likely fairly unalloyed."

"Unalloyed?" I pronounced the unfamiliar word slowly.

"Aye, unalloyed. Near pure, mostly fae. Very little human. Maybe none at all."

"Unalloyed, like an alloy? Like metal?" I clarified, wanting to confirm that I was hearing the word right through his particular way of speaking, that mannerism I was beginning to think of as the 'fae accent.'

"Like metal, aye," said Odo gruffly, "pure fae, no iron."

"And, uh, what difference does it make? Being pure fae, or part fae? Being more human or less human? I heard someone say that somebody who was 'just a little' wouldn't understand, but, understand what?" I looked from one brother to the other, nervously. What if there wasn't enough in me to be able to understand?

"Ah well, It's all a matter of perception you see," answered Eudo. He sat back and drank deeply as he prepared to explain. "Those who are fae can access the magic. Can experience it. And those who aren't, well, they can't." My confusion showed on my face, so he went on. "Like, when a dandelion springs up all golden and bright when there was nothin' but green the day before, and then blows off to dance ceili on the breeze," he pantomimed a floating seed's spin, "is that magic?"

"Um, well, I guess I always sort of thought so," I answered, slowly and thoughtfully. As a child, I had been mesmerized by the small natural miracles of springtime. The way that bulbs bloomed, and tiny leaves unfurled on tree branches, suddenly green after the long, brown winter.

"Right. And so it is. But someone who was entirely human, and they do exist, although I admit it's been a while since I've personally laid eyes on one, well they would look at that entirely without wonder, and see it as a perfectly mundane happenstance. Not magical at all."

Odo rumbled his displeasure at this idea, and Eudo continued.

"And just so, if the great faerie queen herself were to materialize right in front of them, chances are, they wouldn't see that as magic either, and being as she's entirely magic, well they likely just won't see anything at all."

"Just… nothing? Empty space?" I asked.

"A completely non-magical human? I'd expect so. What else would you think they'd see? But we keep to ourselves and let them keep to themselves. Not much chance of the faerie queen materializing in front o' a bunch of humans anyway. What would be the point?"

"I don't know," I answered honestly.

"So, if you've got no magic, you just can't see it at all. Just a little bit o' magic, and maybe you'd think it was a trick o' the light, or maybe what they call stage magic. But, the more magic you have, the more real it all becomes."

"The more real what becomes?"

"The fae magic, of course. The glamour. The illusion. First thing's the sight, o'course. What good's an illusion if you can't see it?"

Odo nodded vigorously in agreement. "Little more magic in ye, and you can smell 'em, taste 'em, touch 'em." He made a move like snatching something out of thin air and grinned at me slyly.

The distractingly pretty girl had made her way to our side of the bar now. She glided up to our table and leaned over the tiny empty cup at the center. "And, create them," she said, dreamily. She touched the cup with one long finger, and out of it sprouted a delicate bouquet of tiny purple pansies, clovers, and a few tall spindly mushrooms.

"Or destroy them," said Odo gruffly. He slammed a fist down on the table, and a slice of air like an invisible knife sheared off all of the plants right above the top of the cup. As soon as the tops of the plants fell, the entire display dissolved into a puddle of mist that immediately dispersed and evaporated. The pretty girl walked off with a "humph" and a moue.

A moment later, something unexpected caught my eye. A tiny flower bud had sprouted low down on Odo's beard, where he couldn't see it. Its stem grew at a rapid pace until it was tall enough to nestle right under his large red nose. I watched as the tiny flower opened and bloomed, tickling his long, curling nose hairs.

"Hah-choo!" sneezed Odo, wetly. Isla tittered in a high trill, and I joined her in laughing, unable to help myself.

Eudo nodded to Isla in acknowledgment of her humor and talent. "But then, if you can do all that, then you can't do all that powerful human magic, so that's the trade-off. Course, the theory is that someone who was half and half, or near enough so, might be able to do both," Eudo said speculatively, "But that would mean an unalloyed fae progeneratin' with a completely mundane human, and there are things a sight more likely than that."

"Or," I considered, thinking about those pea flower graphs in the genetics section of my textbook, "couldn't you have a three-quarter fae and a one-quarter human? Wouldn't their child be fifty percent?"

"Well…" said Eudo, "well, maybe that's so. Never thought about it that way, but-"

Odo interrupted, gruffly. "Nae, nae, it's the most power as comes from one who's half one and a half t'other, and all the fae comin' from one source. Straddling the two worlds, like. That's what they say, aye."

"What do-" I started to ask another question but was forestalled by a hand on my shoulder. I turned to see the man who had led me here, his expression concerned.

"Ah, you know the Gullah," said Eudo, raising a glass in salute to the tall, dark man, who nodded in reply.

"Who doesn't?" replied Odo, who had saluted as well, and now drank deeply from his tankard of mead, punctuating his comment with a loud belch.

"Would you show me what you saw online that sent you to the market?"

"Sure, okay," I said, excusing myself from the brothers' table and following the man they had called 'The Gullah' back across the open floor and through the same door I had come in by.

Chapter 13

In the door-lined hallway, we passed the bat-like bartender, his arms laden with boxes of supplies. "Hey Kep, can you let me know if that bigfoot guy comes back in? I'd like a word," said my companion. The ghoul grimaced and nodded, heading back into the bar.

The Gullah led us up a long, narrow flight of stairs, and into a small set of rooms with the steep pitch of an attic. Light poured in through the leaded glass of the large, arched window that followed the slope of the low ceiling. He opened it wide, letting in the spring breeze, and I followed him, leaning out the window a little to see the front of the pub on a street full of charming-looking boutiques and restaurants.

"What name's on the door, then, if not the Fair Isle?" I asked, watching the shoppers below.

"Nothing. We just leave it off. Anyone who comes through the door can see it's a pub. What more do they need to know?" I shrugged, failing to find fault with the logic.

Turning away from the view, I saw that the man now had a laptop open on the single high table. He turned the screen toward me, showing the old-school stylings of the "Paranormal Investigations" blog. "This here? Just this?" He highlighted the text that mentioned the Fair Isle and the Gardener Market.

"Yeah, it was that," I said, impressed that he had found it so quickly. But, I speculated, if that really was the only reference to the Fair Isle on the internet, this man might be the reason.

"Alright, thanks," he said, switching to a command line, and tapping quickly on the keyboard. He pulled up the window with the website again and reloaded it. This time, the page defaulted to a bold message. **404 Page Not Found.**

"Did you just delete that website from the internet?" I asked.

"No," he said, his face splitting into a wide smile, "I just re-routed the traffic to somewhere that doesn't exist. He could fix it if he knew how, but with the outdated HTML and the total lack of security, I doubt it'll be back up any time soon."

"That's amazing. How do you know how to do all that stuff? I thought, um, I thought fae folk couldn't really use computers."

"I'm a technomage," he said, grinning again, "wouldn't be a very good one if I couldn't use computers." He crossed the room to a shelf full of interesting artifacts, books, and devices. Many of them looked to be of African origin. "And, I wouldn't say that I was one of the fae folk, exactly, anyway. It's generic, sure, but it's a pretty Euro-centric way of looking at things. My family line goes back a little farther to something quite a bit older," he said, smiling again, slowly and languidly this time.

"What family line would that be? Is that okay to ask? I'm learning so much and there's so much I don't know," I inquired, not wanting to pry, but interested to learn more about the strange man.

"Well, Mom's a human-enough nurse down South, and Dad's a minor African fertility deity. I like to think it was some kind of big, elaborate ritual that they did to make me, you know, but Mom's real private. Could have been a run-of-the-mill one night stand all I know," he chuckled, good-humoredly.

"An African… fertility deity?" I asked, now nervous for a different reason, although my sense of the man's presence gave me no reason to be.

"Well, I don't actually know all that much," he confessed, "but I've been able to trace his line back to the Gullah Islands off the coast of South Carolina, at least."

"Ah, The Gullah," I said, understanding.

He nodded. "And," he raised his hands as though to demonstrate something, "of course, I know him because of what he passed on to me."

"What, uh-" I asked, curious, but a little wary.

"It's easier if I show you. May I?" He held out his palms, facing me.

"Uh, I- I just met you and I'm not that kind of girl, I-" I stammered nervously.

He laughed, breaking the tension. "Nothing," he waved his hands in circles, searching for a word, "Inappropriate. Just a touch of the hand."

"Okay," I stepped forward and raised my palms to mirror him. He stepped into me, his larger presence overwhelming all of my senses. As he brought his hands forward to touch mine, a spark like an electric shock rose between us. Our palms touched, and my entire universe was reduced to a single point, focused on that connection. Waves of sensation coursed up my body from my toes, flowing upward toward that central point. I felt my heart rate speed up, and my body echoed with an electric buzz.

He stepped back, and the feeling ebbed, energy draining out of me. I sat down hard on the couch behind me, not trusting my knees to keep me upright. He flopped down next to me, a respectful distance away, with an expression like a plump, well-fed cat. "Have you felt anything like that before?" he asked, after a few long moments of silence.

"Yeah, actually, I have," I said, surprised by my own answer, "Most of the time, at least the first time or two, with, you know, with someone new." I shrugged, embarrassed. "When everything is tingly and exciting when you've been anticipating it. That first touch, first kiss, it usually feels kind of like that. Maybe not so strong, but those same almost painful electric tingles…" I looked at him, quizzically, realizing I was rambling. "Is that not the way it is for everyone?"

The Gullah laughed, a nice low comfortable sound. "No, no it is not. You have quite a bit of inherent magical power in you, it seems. My particular magic heightens physical connections. It's my father's legacy. That, and a few other things. For you, it just seems to be," he paused, stroking his short pointed beard contemplatively, "a natural extension of a very powerful magical aura. For me, the touch sensation usually only goes one way, though." He looked thoughtfully at me, slowly wiggling the fingers that had touched mine. "That was something else," he said, "The two of us could raise some energy, like some serious energy if we wanted to."

I thought he was probably right. We sat in silence for a moment, while he continued to roll his wrist and fingers contemplatively. I thought about what I had learned in the last hour. So much information that it was overwhelming. My brain felt like an inflating balloon with the potential to burst out of my head, it was so full of new thoughts that were pressing uncomfortably against the ideas that I had previously held about reality. But here I was, seeing it with my own two eyes, and I believed what I saw happening in front of me.

Magic was real. Magic like I had seen in the bar, flowers appearing and blooming out of thin air. But, not real flowers, I reminded myself. The brothers had called it fae glamour. An illusion. She hadn't been creating actual flowers out of thin air, just their appearance. The semblance of flowers. That made more sense to me, logically. But, if someone had enough magic, Eudo had said, they could interact with the illusion like it was real. Hadn't he even said that they could taste it? That was very interesting. And, just now the Gullah had said that he felt a lot of magic and power in me. Could that be true? I didn't know anything about my birth mother or father. Anything could be true, really.

Interesting too, what Eudo had said, about magical people finding the world to be magic. Seeing it in the blooming flowers of the springtime. I could identify with that, I thought. My life has always been full of magic. In picking through the sand for lucky talismans at the beach and making witches' potions out of leaves in the backyard. At sleepovers, we would recite lines into mirrors and draw circles in salt when we got scared. I devoured any fantasy book I could get my hands on. My whole life had been full of make-believe magic.

Maybe not as make-believe as I had assumed. Certainly, the things I focused on tended to work out in my favor. I had credited my hard work and persistence, certainly, but also, my unusually good luck. Maybe my luck wasn't luck, after all. Or maybe, I thought with the feeling of realizing something obvious, luck and magic are just two words for the same thing. Looking back at my life now it felt a little silly that I had missed it. Of course, there was magic in me. Why else would I have been so drawn to it?

I wondered how many other people felt this way, who didn't have letters from mysterious faerie queens to lead them here, who just lived life feeling different, without knowing why. How close I had been to being one of them. It would have been so easy just to stay in my college town with my friends, or to move back and take over my mom's store. To stay in the world that I knew, and be the same person that everyone expected me to be. But I hadn't done that, had I? I hadn't stayed in the safe and the known. I had felt drawn to come here, and now I was on a new path. And what an exciting one it was!

I needed to find out more about real magic. As much as I could. I eyed the Gullah speculatively. He was a very good-looking man, I thought, remembering that incredible feeling of power that had passed between us. The memory made me tingle and I gave an involuntary little shudder. And he said he was a technomage. That was something I would like to know more about. I asked him about it and resettled myself on the couch to listen, body pitched forward with interest.

"Technology is one of the most potent forms of human magic," he said, with the air of a passionate academic, "Hiding that fact has been one of The CCC's most pervasive global successes, but it still shocks me that more humans aren't able to see it." He stood up, and walked across the room to the shelf of artifacts on the wall, taking a shallow, painted hand drum and giving it a few taps. A complex rhythm, something quite different than what he had played, flowed out of it.

"Nice, huh? And take a look at this…" He took a glass lens and held it up to the light of the window, so that it cast a shadow of blurry human shapes on the far wall, then squinted at it and moved it to and fro, trying to get a clearer image. "In the right light," he said, giving up and setting the thing carefully on the window sill, "it'll show the steps to a powerful, ancient dance. These are important and old magics that have been entrusted to me," he said, gesturing to the shelf which held many other curious artifacts, "But, I have a much more potent magic than any one of these, right here in my pocket." He pulled out his cell phone, a regular smartphone in a plain, durable black case. He reached out with it and touched my phone, which was sitting on the couch next to me.

A second later, my phone buzzed to life, and I picked it up. It seemed that he had dropped me a file. It was just a video clip of me, sitting on the couch, right here, that he must have taken a moment ago. Three seconds of my interested expression, from his perspective. I looked prettier than I would have expected, I thought, looking at it. It was as though the Gullah viewed me from a particularly flattering angle.

"Magic," he said, spinning his phone in his hand, with a little flourish.

"Your phone, seriously?" I asked incredulously, "I mean, they're awesome and I wouldn't want to live without one now that I've got it, but magic? I just don't really believe that."

He smiled as though this was exactly what he had expected me to say. "Their propaganda is thorough," he said with a little laugh, "of course you don't, but it's a matter of perception. Magic, technology. In English the words are different, but what if they weren't?"

"What do you mean?"

"I call these things," he gestured to the shelf and its contents, "*msaada*, which is a word in one of the many languages of Africa that means helper, or aid, and when I use them," he shined the light through the lens again in a demonstration, "I call that *matumizi*, to use." This time, the angle was right, and the abstract shapes on the wall resolved into tiny human dancers. "When I use these words, I do it with a mystical connotation. They are the words I use for my magic. They mean that whatever I do,

I don't do it by myself. I rely on the wisdom and power of my wise ancestors, the ones who built the tool, who have the skills and know the way. With *msaada*, I do not need to understand how to do a thing by myself, to *matumizi*, and to bend the forces of nature, and even reality itself, to my will."

"Miss- uh, massa-," I tried to repeat the unfamiliar syllables, unsuccessfully, "uh, can you spell those out for me, or something?"

"Don't even worry about it," the Gullah said, shaking his head, "You'll find your own words for your own magic, and I bet they won't be borrowed from Swahili. I just want you to understand the concept." I nodded, and he picked up his phone, playing the video clip again. "By my definition," he continued, "this would also be *msaada*. A helper or an aid. A tool to *matumizi*, to allow me to do incredible things that I have no ability to do without it. Do you see?"

"Yes, I guess I do," I said, thoughtfully, "But, we know how to make phones. We don't know how to make magic. Isn't that the difference?"

"Do we?" he asked, "I don't know how to make a phone. Do you?"

"Well, no," I admitted.

"And someone knows how to make these artifacts and tools. Someone with magic running through their veins, certainly, but someone. Some of my own ancestors, even. I am much farther removed than that from being able to make a phone."

"But, a phone isn't magic," I insisted, not being able to help myself.

"The smartphone is an incredibly potent human magic," he said, patiently, "A kind of magic that humans love to disregard, just because they can do it, and if they can do it, they think that it must not be particularly special." He chuckled at this absurd notion.

"Incredibly potent, huh?" I asked, my look making the question a challenge.

"Yes," he answered, meeting my gaze levelly, "First, and perhaps most powerfully, it can light the darkness." He turned on the camera's flashlight and pointed it at the wall, where it wiped out the lens' shadowy image instantly. Looking affectionately at the small black bar in his hand, he went on. "That is something that humans have dreamed of for centuries, and now we carry it in our back pocket.

94

What else? Communicate with anyone anywhere, instantly, with the touch of a button? Capture anything you can see or hear, and share it just like the moment you experienced it? Access any information from the largest repository of human knowledge in history? All this, instantly, at your fingertips, running on the extracted and concentrated lifeblood of the very universe itself, which we leech into it, every night. Pure power coursing and sparking through its elemental metallics, to suffuse this immeasurably potent artifact and fill it to capacity with energetic charge."

"Okay, um, well, when you put it that way," I said, quietly, as he went on.

"And that is just this single, small technological artifact that each of us carries around in our pocket all day. There is so much more that almost everyone takes for granted, that so many people just don't see. We build giant sky-scraping monstrosities and strip resources from the Earth and leave it barren. We manipulate the characteristics of plants and animals to suit our needs. We've unlocked the keys of the very genome of human life itself to tinker with. These are the kinds of things that human magic is capable of, these days," He punctuated his speech with a dramatic raised finger point. "And somehow the humans remain unimpressed! Un-awed by their own fearsome power…" He sighed, exasperated. "I don't understand, but I know it's not their fault. There are forces at work to control and subvert that magic, and it is much easier to do that if people don't notice that they have the power in the first place."

"I guess-" I started, before being interrupted by a voice coming from a metal pipe in the wall that I hadn't noticed before.

"Gullah." The man stood up and walked quickly to the pipe, making a noise of acknowledgment. "You asked me to say if that bigfoot fella ever came back. Well, he's here now."

The Gullah made a grumble from deep in his chest. "Be right down."

Chapter 14

Derailed entirely from his previous train of thought, the Gullah slipped on the big overcoat he had been wearing and loaded several wicked-looking knives as well, as a number of items from his shelf, into what must be cavernous interior pockets. Noticing me eyeing a particularly large, curved blade, he smiled mischievously at me. "I'm sure I won't need to use them, but if I'm trying to make my point clearly," he turned one intense eye on me in demonstration, "it helps to have props."

Making our way back down the steep, narrow stairs, I found I was curious to see how the Gullah communicated his displeasure to this bigfoot-hunting stranger. He opened the door to the bar, and I saw that it had filled up considerably while we were upstairs. Now, most of the tables were filled with talking, laughing people of all shapes, colors, and sizes I noted as I eyed a group of impossibly small men sitting on thick books that doubled as benches and swilling from miniature glasses. Tall women and tiny women, many in the same airy flowing silks as the barmaid, were interspersed with the thick, rough-looking, bearded men. The ladies looked to me like blooming flowers, and the men like craggy rocks and various types of trees.

I recognized Eudo and Odo at a different, larger table, drinking and laughing with a group of burly male friends. Wait, that's wrong, I realized, looking closer. That one, I thought, noting the long braids starting behind her ears rather than at her chin, and the roundness of her chest which extended well beyond the barrel-chestedness of the two brothers, was certainly a woman. And him, I thought, eyeing a particularly beautiful, tiny person with long white-blond hair and ice-blue silk robes that I had initially read as a woman. And that particularly thick, muscular woman near the bar, too.

I realized that my preconceived notions about gender were being thrown out of the window here. There were all combinations of physicality and self-expression at the Fair Isle. Everyone here seemed to be expressing their truest nature, out loud, without trying to hide it. It was unlike any human gathering I had ever been a part of, or even imagined. This was a real fae bar, and it was teeming with real fae folk. I had really found them, I thought, looking around me with amazement. Now what?

While I stood just inside the door, looking from table to table, from face to face, amazed at the varieties and peculiarities of the denizens, the Gullah had moved purposefully across the room and now stood behind a man in a bright-colored windbreaker sitting at the bar. As I watched, he tapped the seated man on the shoulder, and he turned around. I couldn't hear what they were saying, but I could read their body language clearly.

The Gullah leaned down with exaggerated patience and began to lecture the shorter man on the barstool. At first, the blogger's face looked abashed, but at a word from the Gullah, his expression changed to one of extreme indignation. He threw his hands in the air, and his eyebrows furrowed as he gave back as good as he got. The Gullah looked on calmly as the small man raged, and watched placidly too when the bigfoot blogger rolled his eyes and flapped his hands at him dismissively, turning away. Then he looked back over his shoulder at the Gullah and made one final comment. All of a sudden, the mood shifted.

The Gullah's mouth, a serene line the moment before, dropped open with shock and horror. In a swift motion, he reached a long hand into his coat and whipped out the long curved knife, pinning the blogger's bright-colored sleeve to the bar with a violent, practiced grace. Getting close to his face, he hissed at the man. Even if I were next to them, I doubted I could have heard what words he said but, even from across the bar, I could feel their intensity. The blogger's face paled to a deathly white. His eyes grew wide, and he scrambled out of his seat, coat arm ripping where it was pinned to the wood. Slipping out of the jacket, he left the gaudy heap behind as he sprinted out of the bar and into the night. Looking like he was on a warpath, the Gullah cut through the crowd like a hot knife. A moment later, he swung back through the door next to me, and I followed.

"What was he, uh-" I started to ask.

"He didn't like that I took down his website," the Gullah said as he started back up the stairs, "Seemed to think I was being unreasonable. Overcautious about security." He paused, halfway up, and turned to look back down at me over the wooden banister. "Said he told some cool guys about this place, guys who would 'liven it up a little'. Told them how to find it. Said they would be by later." He spit the words, clearly seething with barely contained rage. "I bet they'll be here any minute. I told you the neighborhood's been swarming with Corpsos, just waiting for a chance."

As he spoke, the noise from the bar changed. The jovial laughter and shrieks of delight turned into screams of surprise and fear, and the sound of loud, shouting male voices. A bang of what might have been gunfire was followed by a moment of silence.

"Blast it all! They're here!" The Gullah ran up the stairs at a full gallop, taking three steps at a time. I thought about his room's wide window and pictured him climbing out of it and onto the sky-light spotted roof, or leaping down on top of an unsuspecting attacker on the street below. He shouted to me over his shoulder, "Go. Out the way you came. Go find the faeries. They'll tell you what you want to know. Vista House, circle it nine times." With these last words he disappeared behind the door at the top of the stairs.

I didn't wait for the invaders in the bar to burst in and dashed out the back door into the night. In the alleyway, in the dark, I resisted the urge to run. Anyone watching the bar would be on the lookout for people running away. As quickly as I felt I could, I made my way through the overgrown bushes of the vacant lot I had come through earlier. Behind me, I heard more gunshots, screams, the breaking of glass, and the screeching of car tires that could have been more assailants arriving, or the pub's occupants fleeing. Everything sounded like chaos. If I imagined what a war would sound like, it would be a lot like this.

I continued walking robotically without pausing or slowing until I was out of the immediate vicinity of the bar, and all the way up the long curving road we had walked down this afternoon, back to the safety and security of my car. I got back to my van, and heaved a grateful sigh for the safety and security that it offered. Locking the door with a satisfying click, I drove away from the harsh brightness of the little shopping center, and into a dark, residential road with no streetlights.

Only after I had double-checked the door locks and crawled into the back seat and under the pile of blankets and pillows did the adrenaline finally wear off enough to allow me to cry. My face cracked, spilling over with tears, and I shook violently, shuddering like I was freezing even though the thick covers were already making me too warm. I gasped shuddering breaths as I sobbed in the release of my suppressed terror. After a few minutes, I was able to catch my breath and curled up, cocooned on the back bench seat, quaking a little from the overflow of emotions, but now at least able to form rational thought.

The poor Fair Isle! I had only spent a couple of hours there, but already it was one of my favorite places in the world. And now, based on what I had seen and heard tonight, it might not exist anymore at all. All that breaking glass and those screams… I couldn't imagine what kind of damage had been done.

Out of the corner of my eye, I had seen several of those awful flags and symbols on big trucks and SUVs that were parked illegally, one tire up on sidewalks, arrowed in toward the bar. How many people had been in this invasion force? I had no idea.

The unsuspecting drinkers hadn't stood a chance. Those fascinating characters I had seen, what had become of them? Well, there was nothing I could do, was there? The Gullah had told me to go, and I had done what he said. I would just have been in the way, and in even more danger, if I had stayed.

What a wild coincidence that I had happened to be here on the one night in, what, a hundred years when the Fair Isle had not been a safe refuge for the fair folk? But, I supposed, those evil men had been sniffing around the neighborhood using the same information I had used. It had been incredible luck that I had been able to find a reference to the pub on the internet, apparently. From the sound of it, The Gullah worked hard to keep that information out of the public eye.

Part of me wanted to go back to the pub and check-in. If I just drove by, I thought, that would be safe enough, right? But I had walked the better part of a mile back to my car, and had no idea how things were there. The Gullah had told me to go, and I should stay gone. Even if I did go back, I would just be a spectator and not a help to anyone. He had also told me to go to the faeries, and so had the Eudo and Odo. They had said a lot of things, I thought, mind drifting back to the conversation with the two brothers. Glamours. Illusion magic. Incredible!

The lovely flowers that the girl, Isla, had created out of thin air. I longed to be able to do something like that. Even if it was only an illusion, it was instant, beautiful, natural art. Art that I might even be able to smell or taste if I really had enough magic. As I imagined the tantalizing possibilities, I realized how hungry I was. Neither the bottle of tea nor the tankard of mead had been food, and now that I was paying attention, I realized that my fingers and toes were tingling in that particular way that meant I had better get some calories fast, unless I wanted to feel worse, soon. "Something to eat before I go to sleep," I said to myself, deciding.

This nest of blankets was incredibly cozy, I thought, as I struggled to hoist myself out of my wrappings and back into the driver's seat, feeling dizzy and a little woozy from my hunger. I would just come back and sleep in the car tonight after dinner, I decided. And then, tomorrow morning, I would follow the Gullah's directions. What was it that he had told me, right as I had left?

"Go find the faeries. Vista House, circle it nine times."

Well, it was worth a try. Tomorrow, I'd pay a visit to the faeries.

Part 4 - The Silent City

Velia leaned back in her gilded chair and twisted a crystal goblet in her hands, considering. The pup had been back, again, wanting to talk about the girl and lick his wounds some more. How she had managed to get mixed up with him, Velia could not guess. That abominable faerie luck again, surely. Now Velia had to deal with the irritating chit on both sides of her dual existence.

Finishing the drink with a pleasurable shudder, she set down the beautiful vessel and enjoyed the way it sparkled in the low light of her sanctuary. Now that she thought about it, this newfound closeness with the puppy might be used to her advantage. There was some power certainly, in using basic glamour to make her mediocre minute-taking appear to be a critical and essential part of the business. The secretary with whom they simply could not do without. But, she speculated, stroking one long finger contemplatively along her sharp, white jawline, much more power, certainly, in being amorously tied to the heir, and, she suspected, the brains behind the throne.

Chapter 15

"Vista House was built in 1917 on one of the most beautiful scenic stretches of this historic highway," I read from my phone screen, over the top of an excellent latte with 'Fiona' scrawled on the side of it in black. I was pleased and a bit surprised to find that, unlike the Fair Isle, the address of this Vista House seemed to be common knowledge. And open daily from sunrise to sunset, I noted. Its description on the website made it sound like a common tourist attraction.

The morning sun sparkled down the wide, curving river next to me, as I drove down the highway toward Vista House. This wasn't the river I had followed up from the valley, this was its much wider twin sister, winding down from the mountains to form the northern border of the state, between Oregon and Washington. Grinding to a stop on the rough gravel of the hillside, I stepped out of the van onto the top of the gorge. "Guess early Monday morning isn't a busy time for tourist attractions," I said into the empty parking lot, but I was glad that I was the only one there. After what had happened last night at the Fair Isle, I didn't want to risk inadvertently sharing faerie secrets with the wrong people by accident.

"This isn't gonna work," I muttered under my breath as I passed the front entrance of the small octagonal building for the third time, "This is ridiculous. There's no way this is going to do anything." By the seventh go around, I was getting very tired of walking in circles, and by the ninth pass, I was so bored and distracted that when the tiny door appeared in the stonework, I almost missed it. "Oh!" I exclaimed, stumbling as I abruptly reversed my momentum.

The entrance was small. No bigger than the door of a child's playhouse. It was wooden and old, with large dark hinges and a thick metal ring in place of a doorknob. There was no keyhole. Ideal, I thought, since I didn't have a key. Well, there was only one thing to do now, and no point in delaying further.

"Here we go, into Faerieland," I said with resolve. I strode forward, seized the ring, and pulled hard. Nothing happened. The door was solidly locked. Immovable and secure. It didn't rattle when I pulled or pushed, and after a few minutes of straining, my arms were getting sore, so I turned my back on it and stamped off, fists in tight balls of frustration.

Across the parking lot, I climbed onto a low stone wall that surrounded the outlook point. I had been so close to success, and now what? Another immovable obstacle. I stewed, in my frustration, not seeing past my own irritated nose. But, after a moment, I looked out and saw what was in front of my eyes. Before me spread the sweeping panorama of the river gorge, where beams of golden morning sunshine cut through high, fluffy clouds, and blue sky reflected off the sparkling river. I breathed in deeply, tasting the cool crispness of the mountains and the fresh tang of pine. As I breathed out, my frustration left me with my breath, dissipating into the vastness.

"Vista House," I breathed, understanding the need to erect a monument to this particular view. Enjoying the feeling of the sun on my shoulders, I relaxed and let my eyes drift closed, listening to the sound of the birds and the rustling of the trees, allowing my brain to become quiet. After an eternal moment, a tiny thought drifted through my mind, twining like a breeze-blown ribbon. I reached out and snatched it.

You know, it's always more polite to knock first.

It wasn't much of an idea, but it was better than nothing. The door had, it seemed, taken this opportunity to disappear, and I resignedly started the nine-times march around, once again. This time I was ready, and as I rounded my 72nd octagonal corner, I saw it immediately. My door to faerie land, if only I could get inside.

"More polite to knock," I said, quietly, contemplating the curious little door. Well, if politeness was the idea, what was the old saying, 'in for a penny, in for a pound'? "Hello door," I said with my brightest customer service smile, "May I please come in?" Then I tapped three times with the heavy round ring and waited. Nothing happened.

"Obviously," I said, rolling my eyes at my own foolishness, "Why had I actually thought that would- Oh!" I was interrupted by an audible 'click' from the door. It swung backward on its thick metal hinges with a creak like a pleased little sigh. "Seriously?" I asked, peering through the open doorway. It was dark and I couldn't see very far with the bright sunshine outside.

Pausing for a moment, I regretted leaving my nearly-dead cell phone in the car, but I wasn't trying to circle the building again, and there probably wouldn't be any reception this high in the mountains anyway. I squared my shoulders and hiked up the stretchy athletic pants I had put on under my dress. Steeling myself, I took a deep breath and stepped through the door into faerie land.

Chapter 16

"Hello?" I called, stepping gingerly onto the bumpy cobblestoned floor of a wide tunnel-like hallway, dimly illuminated by the light of the open doorway. My voice was swallowed by the darkness of the passageway, and I took a few steps forward, following it. Behind me, the door creaked again, and with a heavy thud, it settled into place, filling in every crack and casting the hallway into absolute, pitch blackness.

"Oh no. Okay. Oh no. Okay. Oh no," I repeated, feeling along the wall back toward the door and beginning to hyperventilate. In a few seconds I had found it, and my hand scraped and scratched at the age-smoothed edges of the thick door. I could feel heavy brackets of the hinges but no ring or knob on this side. There was nothing I could pull or grab ahold of. "Door?" I asked, cautiously, "Could you let me back out, please?" I knocked thrice, just like I had when I entered and waited. This time, truly, nothing happened.

I knocked again, then banged both fists hard, wailing on the smooth boards until my hands were sore. It was hopeless. The thing was immovable. I closed my eyes, and turned my back to the frustratingly solid planks, letting gravity take me. I slid down to sit on the ground, hands around my knees, and let out a single pitiful little moan.

"What good is sitting there feeling sorry for yourself supposed to do?" my Mom's voice asked in my mind.

None particularly, I answered, also in my head.

"Good grief girl, get a grip," I mouthed silently, taking slow, intentional breaths until the exercise lowered my heart rate enough that I could think. I couldn't get back out, that was true, but, hadn't I wanted to go in, anyway? That had been the point of opening the door, hadn't it? Not in the pitch-black dark, though! My heart rate sped up again at the thought. True, I did not particularly like to be in the dark. And who did, really? Things are scarier when you can't see them. That's just human nature. It's so pitch black in here that it doesn't matter whether my eyes are open or shut, I thought. Probably.

Testing the theory I opened one eye and then the other. The blackness was thick and dark, but there was a subtle difference and I realized that I could make out the faintest outline of the passageway. I headed toward the faint illumination. As I walked onward the light grew brighter, and a sound that had been barely audible built into a thundering roar.

I rounded a final corner and the hallway opened up into an airy chamber that had been carved by nature into the heart of the mountain. Light poured into it from natural holes high up on the wall, and through them poured the misting spray of a waterfall thundering down the face of the mountain outside. Stalactites hung from the ceiling and were reflected in the dark water that seeped under the rocks and pooled on the chamber's sunken floor.

I stood, entranced by the great thing, with its cool mist and deafening noise, for a long moment, then shook myself from my reverie and skirted along the outside of the chamber looking for a way onward. I found it behind an outcropping of rock, its gaps erupting with clusters of natural crystal. Acquisitively, I reached out and wiggled one sparkling outcropping. It didn't budge, being firmly attached to the rock shelf. That was probably for the best. It just wouldn't do, to be taking things from the faeries, I thought. Turning back for a last look at the thundering falls, I headed deeper into the mountain.

Here, the faint illumination of the passage took on a subtle green cast. Maybe a bioluminescence, I thought as I bumped the wall, and the green glow transferred to the leg of my pants briefly, before fading. The clusters of crystal points grew larger and larger as I walked, glinting green in the low light, and before long, there seemed to be more crystal than rock. Icy blues and shifting purples emanated from deep within the clusters of clear crystal that formed the arching walls and ceiling and mixed with the pale glowing greens to form mesmerizing cool rainbows. The quality of the light continued to change as the flat gray rocks grew fewer and farther between, and I realized that the light of the bioluminescence was being replaced by an ethereal glow from within the crystals themselves. I almost missed it.

Walking quickly with my eyes to the front, it might have slipped by my notice, but some motion had caught my eye, and I stopped to peer at a curious little rectangle, not even six inches tall, about halfway up the wall. It was conspicuously flat amongst the jutting clusters, and with a tiny, perfectly formed crystal doorknob. Curious, I reached out my thumb and pointer finger and delicately seized the handle. It turned easily, and the tiny door opened inward. I leaned down to peer inside and found myself eye-to-eye with someone very small. The door slammed closed with a bang.

I stumbled back a couple of steps with a surprised "Eek!" Ahead of me, there was a flurry of motion and the clicks of a score more crystal doors slamming shut.

Well then! Apparently, I had found the faeries. After the initial flurry, everything fell silent again.

I wandered on, undisturbed, past increasingly larger and larger doors. Hallways wended outward from this wide central corridor, growing larger along with the doors. As I approached the end of the passage, an opening into what appeared to be another large cavern, the largest of the doors came almost to my chest, nearly the size of the entrance at the Vista House. The thundering sound of the waterfall had retreated as I walked farther onward and then had increased again, building to a roar of bone-rattling thunder that far surpassed the sound of the first falls. I reached the end of the tunnel and looked out at the enormous cavern that spread before me. The spray of a much larger second waterfall thundered down outside, and poured in through gaps in the stones, letting in shafts of ever-changing light and bathing the city in an ethereal mist.

For a city it was. Inside the mountain, and essentially backstage to this magnificent waterfall, rose the myriad twisting towers of a glittering, jeweled metropolis. The architecture was a marvelous hodgepodge of styles, with towers topped with colorful mushroom-shaped domes and sweeping curved staircases peeking through incongruous archways and behind gilded pavilions, as though taking all of the most fanciful bits of the world's building styles and combining them to create something completely chaotic but nonetheless magnificent.

At the end of the crystal-studded tunnel was an enormous staircase made out of smooth white stone and inlaid with sparkling gems in patterns of leaves and flowers. I descended it slowly, turning my head this way and that way, taking it all in. As I passed close to some of the artfully decorated towers, I noted that some of the details appeared to be functional, like the larger and smaller staircases that wound together to create an effect like the helix of a DNA strand, while some were clearly purely artistic. I admired a glittering faux garden made entirely out of jewels and gemstones set in gold and silver. As I walked through the city, I was struck by the overwhelming opulence in material and artistic detail of every one of the intricate twining palaces, and in the carved stone lattice work that decorated some of the larger openings to the thundering falls. Every corner of the city was festooned with statuary, floral design, or other sparkling frippery.

I paused and closed my eyes, blinking against the glints and shines of a thousand glittering surfaces, twinkling in the ever-changing light filtering through the massive waterfall. With my eyes closed, the eerie sensation of stillness was even more amplified. Apart from the thundering of the falls outside, this city was completely silent, and I appeared to be entirely on my own.

As I walked, I realized that every pathway seemed to be leading to one place, and it wasn't long before I found myself walking up a set of sweeping marble steps to the wide plinth at the very center of the city. At the crest of the plinth, I could see that it was not, in fact, a plateau, as I had assumed. This structure was a sloping step-well with a network of different sizes of stairs all leading downward. To match the doors, I thought, eyeing the tiniest of them. Far down below, at the base of the well, ran a burbling stream. The tiny rivulet sparkled in rainbows, reflecting the bejeweled city surrounding it, or, perhaps simply full of faceted, river rock-sized gemstones.

At the bottom of the stream was a girl, just a bit small for a human, lying perfectly still in the water with her long red hair flowing out behind her. She was beautiful, with nearly translucent skin and faintly red lips, contrasted by the rich auburn of her hair which swirled around in the eddies of the river like so many twirling dancers. I wondered how she could be alive, lying at the bottom of the creek like that, but, I realized, I didn't actually know whether faeries needed to breathe like humans do. Watching her hair twist in the river, mesmerized, I drifted all the way down the long flight of stairs without thought, and found myself at the bank of the glittering river, steps away from the clear, sparkling stream.

Yes, the river rocks were actually gemstones. I bent down and picked one up. It was an amethyst. Clear as a crystal goblet, with straight, perfect facets and clear, even coloring. Just one of these would be worth thousands of dollars, I thought and smiled wryly. Or, it was a fake. That's what I would think, if I saw a big shiny gem like this at a store, anyway, I thought, gently dropping the stone back down on the bank. It rolled and splashed into the water at the stream's edge.

The girl's eyes blinked open.

Chapter 17

I froze, unsure what to do. It was a relief that the girl wasn't dead but now I was faced with the reality of her being alive and, it seemed, increasingly awake. Sitting part way up, she propped herself on her elbows so that the river still ran over her shoulders. The girl turned toward me and I was surprised to find that outside the distortion of the water she looked familiar.

"Oh!" I said, recognizing her from my dream. She was the one who had fallen down next to me and told me the proper spelling of faerie. "It's you!" I said, eyes and smile both widening. She had felt so familiar in the dream, and now even more so. Had it really been a dream? I supposed that it likely hadn't, since she was here in front of me now.

"Oh," she said and smiled, sadly, "I suppose it is." As she sat, propped on her forearms in the flowing water, silver rivulets of liquid ran off of her hair and down her back like glittering snakes, and within a few moments she appeared to be dry. With a painterly gesture of her hand, the bejeweled riverbank rose up to meet the new angle of her back, and she leaned back against the bank with a pained little sigh.

"What, uh-" I paused, not sure where to start, after all the myriad things I had wondered about while wandering through the beautiful, silent city, "What is this place?"

"Oh this? Nothing soon, I suppose, now that everyone else has left, and we'll be leaving any time. Shame really, it is quite pretty." She drew a hand through the pool of still water that formed in her lap, shielded from the current by her narrow back. An image of the sparkling mushroom cap domes of the city appeared in the water and dissipated as she drew her hand back the other way. "I will miss it." She closed her eyes and sunk a few inches lower into the water.

"But wait, who are you?" I asked as she sank lower, worried that she might be going back under without giving me anything more than this frustrating riddle of an answer.

"Mmm?" she replied, dreamily, hair floating in the stream again, and just her face and ears suspended over the water, "Oh, right now I suppose that I'm Faeryn, but most people just refer to me as the Broken Hearted Girl. Not very nice, really, if you think about it."

"Broken… Hearted?" I asked, not understanding but also not sure that it was polite to inquire.

"Yes, the Broken Hearted Girl, they say. Poor thing born with a heart that's broken. The heart, the heart, they say, but what of the girl? The girl who has to lie, day in and day out, in this," she flicked the water with her hand, and sent shining droplets scattering onto the marble steps across from me, "eternal watery internment."

"Why do you-" I started to ask, but she was already nodding, anticipating my question.

"The water of the spring goes around, you see," she gestured, stroking the water as it flowed by. She resettled herself, sitting up straighter, the riverbank shifting again to accommodate her. "But the magic," she raised her hand, and little motes of light rose with it, some dripping off back into the water, most still clinging to her fingers like static electricity, "it flows right through, and keeps my broken human heart beating with the pace of the current." She flicked her finger and little light motes flew off like water droplets, back into the stream. "I'm nearly half-human, would you believe it? I do actually need a beating heart to stay alive. Now, some-fae like you," she turned her gaze on me, taking the time to look at me properly for the first time.

Her eyes widened, and a narrow hand rose to cover her mouth and it's round' 'oh' of surprise. "But, you!" she said and turned to climb out of the low pool. Her face turned up to stare in wonderment at me, peering close. "But, if anything, you're even more human than I am. And yet, you are here! Wait, how are you here?" She turned and shouted over her shoulder in a high-trilling voice. "Arlee? Arlee!" Then she turned back to me, taking my face in her cool hands and pulling it down toward her own. She peered into one eye and then the other, quizzically. Turning my head, she eyed my ears and used a single imperious finger to raise my chin and look into my small round nose.

"Hey, uh, wait a minute," I said, having had enough of this unexplained prodding.

"Sorry," she said, stepping back, and smiling apologetically. "I like the fae. It's a bit of a special interest of mine, and I've never seen one quite so much, well, quite so much like me, really." She blushed and ducked her head, charmingly, and I shrugged, letting her go on.

While Faeryn poked at me, a tall blonde woman appeared in a doorway high above us. She bustled down the curving faerie tower, disappearing as she climbed the plinth, then hurried down the steps to join us. Her voluminous, many-layered skirts seemed like they ought to have gotten in the way as she scurried down the steep steps, but they flounced behind her in a train of pale blues. Behind her, I could see the thundering waterfall and saw that the shifting colors matched her dress exactly. I wondered if it was intentional. The blonde woman skipped down the last few steps to join us, panting and flushed. She had appeared tall as she approached, and still did, standing in front of me, stately and statuesque, but now that we were on the level, she came up no higher than my breastbone.

"What is it, my lady?" she asked, breathless, "And what in all Faerieland, are you doing out of your spring?"

"Look, Arlee, see?" asked the girl, face alight with interest, darting glances between me and her friend.

Arlee stroked her pointed chin quizzically, and frowned at me, considering. "No, I don't."

"She's, she's-" the girl repeated, flapping her small hands in excitement, "she's just like me. I've never met one so similar. All the signs. The eyes, the cheeks-" she opened her own eyes wide and as though in demonstration grinned widely, drawing her lips back, "the teeth!"

"Ah, I see," said Arlee, who, looking unconvinced, turned to address me, "And who might you be?" She eyed me speculatively. "Awfully tall for a faerie, aren't you? But, here you are, in the middle of our city, uninvited, without having set off any-" she turned to the girl, suddenly urgent, "Faeryn, are the protections still in place?"

"Yes, Arlee," Faeryn said, rolling her eyes, "I told you. She's like me. Nearly half human."

She squinted, considering.

"Maybe even a little more human than I am, though that hardly seems possible."

"How did you find your way here?" Arlee asked me accusingly, "At a time like this when we two are the only high Sidhe for leagues around? What, do you seek to plunder our source of power, at this, our darkest hour? Who sent you? What court in the world has such excess power that they would consign a being such as you to a task such as this? A female, and more human than my lady?" She shook her head, wonderingly.

"If she hadn't just said it was so, I would hardly believe it possible."

"The courts? No, I wasn't sent by-" I was interrupted, as the imperious woman's frustration intensified.

"Oh! Oh!" she said, hopping comically, "I see it now. Not of the fae courts at all. You are of the Enemy! I have heard the tales, stories of faerie children captured and conscripted to their fanatical purposes." I found her outrage less comedic, though, when she drew a thin but wickedly sharp-looking blade from a narrow scabbard hidden in her voluminous dress and advanced on me, sword raised aggressively.

"No, no, nope I'm not. Not me. Not the Enemy," I said, putting my hands up in front of me and backing awkwardly back up the slippery marble stairs away from her, "I'm here because I got a letter, okay? A letter from the queen of, um-" I tried to remember the long list of titles, "Queen Vivienne of the Faeries of Portal Land," I finished, thinking that at least that part was mostly right.

"Is that so?" said Arlee, eyeing me down the point of her sharp blade suspiciously.

"Yes! I can show you, wait…" I patted my pockets, looking for the phone I had left in the car as Faeryn stepped between the sword and my chest.

"Arlee, I really don't think she's the Enemy," she said to the woman in the water beseechingly, "Can we please talk to her and find out more, before we throw her off the top of the falls?" She looked over her shoulder and winked at me, letting me in on the dark joke.

"Well, if you think so," Arlee said, looking unconvinced, "I really think you ought to get back in your spring, Faeryn," she cajoled, "You should be recovering after the full moon. Conserving your energy, lest we need to flee."

"I know, I know, but-" Faeryn turned and flashed her wide grin at me again, "she's just so interesting!" She turned back to her companion. "Arlee, can you do the meeting glade, please?"

"Of course, Lady, if you will get back in the spring. Now," Arlee said, with emphasis. The girl lowered herself back down into the little river as the stepwell

112

around us melted into mist. A moment later the mist cleared and the scene around us had changed.

The city looming above us looked the same, but the steep white walls of the stepwell were now a forested glade in the springtime, overhung with bright green leaves and blooming flowers. The brilliant sparkling gemstones of the creekbed had faded into the soft earthy glimmer of natural wet river stones and the water itself reflected a blue sky and white fluffy clouds. I looked up to check, and saw that the cave's ceiling was still covered in long stalactites.

Soft moss covered the rocks that lined the bank, making logical and surprisingly comfortable seats. I settled myself onto the mossy stone closest to Faeryn's spot in the stream. Now that I was seated, I realized how tired I was, and as my head spun with the change in elevation, I remembered that my breakfast had been that latte. I wondered idly what it was that faeries liked to eat.

Faeryn also took a moment to settle herself and sighed again in obvious relief at being back in the water. Her eyes resting closed and her hair once again pooling around her and swirling in the eddies, face just barely out of the stream, I thought she might have fallen back asleep, and it surprised me when she started to speak. "So, you have a letter from my mother," she said with a deep, sorrowful slowness. It was a sharp contrast from her previously energetic chatter.

"Yes, I do. I, uh-" I paused, then asked, "Did something happen, just now? You were so excited, and then-" I trailed off, not wanting to say the wrong thing.

"Oh, no, it's alright, it's just me, that's all. I am still very interested to learn about you, you know. It's my broken heart. How else is a broken-hearted girl supposed to be, except dolorous?" she asked, with a sad smile, "It's not so bad when I'm out of the water. The residual magic keeps me alive and keeps my heart beating, at least for a while. It makes me feel like a whole girl, or even like a whole- well, anyway. But it's easy to feel my heartbreak in the water, with the tears of the world trickling through it." She stroked the water next to her, creating a vision of beautiful faeries dancing in a circle next to a star-filled river, which appeared and immediately began to dissipate before my eyes.

"Wow, that's beautiful. Wait," I started, recognizing the incongruous block of my solid navy blue shirt among the shifting rainbow hues, "is that me?"

"Mmm…" She sighed and stroked the water again, and the image zoomed in on my brightly smiling face as I danced on a moonlit riverbank in the clothes I had been wearing on my first night in Oregon. "You reveled well that evening. I don't often come down to the valley to dance the full moon, but," she gestured up at the empty city surrounding us, "it is hard to drum up the proper enthusiasm, all alone."

"I had thought that was all a dream," I said, wonderingly.

"It is a dream," she said, sadly, "A wonderful dream."

As I watched her beautiful, sad face, sparkling silver tears began to stream from her large eyes and run down her face, mixing with the spring water and flowing off into the stream. She lifted a small white hand expectantly, and Arlee strode forward, grasping it in both of her own. She brought the cool little hand to her lips and kissed it affectionately.

"I know, darling. It'll be alright. We will dance again at the next moon."

"Will we, Arlee? Do you promise?" She raised her streaming eyes to the woman.

"Of course, my love. We will find a way. There is still time, and therefore there is still hope."

"What do you know of hope? You're a faerie. You don't have the capacity for hope," she said bitterly, turning her face away from the woman.

"You know very well that I am 7.7% human. You told me so yourself," said the blonde woman, smiling softly, clearly repeating a well-tread argument between close companions, "and loving one as unique and thoroughly human as you, my dear, has brought out my own human capacities in spades." She leaned down and kissed the smaller woman tenderly on her forehead, then looked back up at me. "Didn't you have some things you wanted to ask your new friend, here, love?"

"Oh!" Faeryn turned back to me, apparently having forgotten I was there. "Yes, you're right I do." She peered at me quizzically for a moment and then asked simply, "Who are you?"

"Oh!" I replied, in much the same tone as the girl, "Well, honestly, I'm not entirely sure. I had sort of hoped that someone here would be able to tell me, but…" I gestured to the deserted city around us.

Arlee laughed, a high tinkling sound like a fine silver bell. In the vast silent emptiness it echoed off the stone walls before being swallowed by the ever-present roar of the great falls. "If anyone here could tell you anything, it would be my lady," said Arlee, with a loving smile for the girl.

"Oh, really?" I asked.

"Oh yes," said Arlee with a proud look, "Won't you show her, darling?"

Faeryn shot her a glance. "Of course I will, Arlee. I was just getting to that. Put your hand here, please," she said to me, gesturing to the spring which glittered invitingly in the peaceful green glade.

Cautiously, and admittedly a bit nervously, I reached out and dipped my fingers into the water. It was cool and wonderfully refreshing, not just on my fingers, but as though the spring were washing immaterially over me, soothing my sore muscles and erasing the long, uneven walk and the night of sleeping in my car. I breathed deeply and sighed.

"Nice, isn't it?" said Faeryn, snapping me out of my reverie and making me pull my fingers back out of the water. Once I did, the tiredness quickly seeped back into my muscles.

"Oh, you poor thing. You're so weakened and tired," said Arlee with a look of deep concern on her small, pretty face, "I can't often notice in humans, but you're so very much like my Faeryn."

It was true. After walking all morning on nothing but that latte, my hands were starting to shake and I didn't feel well. The faerie woman leaned down and drew a lovely carved crystal goblet through the stream above where Faeryn lay. She handed it to me, brimming with the cool sparkling water.

"Drink, dear."

Through the looking glass, Alice, I said to myself silently. I took the tiny, beautiful cup in my hands and drank deeply.

"Fiona."

My eyes were closed and the name floated by me as though in correction of my internal commentary. I felt the magic of the water suffuse throughout my body from the place it had touched my lips, trickling down my throat and flowing into each of my limbs and out to the tip of every finger and toe. The electric buzz of the magic seemed to chase the cobwebs of tiredness and soreness out of my muscles, leaving me refreshed and relaxed, with energy to spare.

I felt amazing. I felt as good as I had felt in Brandon's car after he had rescued me from the woods. As good as it felt to be clothed and safe and to be able to speak again, after being speechless and naked and scared for hours and hours. Better than that, even, maybe. But, this sensation did remind me an awful lot of the relief that I had felt that night, in Brandon's car, in particular.

"Fiona," the voice said again, and I opened my eyes. It was Faeryn, looking up at me, out of the pool.

"Yes," I responded automatically, amazed at how easy it was to identify that name as mine. It was truly a sound that my soul recognized, like the letter had said. But how had she known?

"How did you-" I started, and Faeryn smiled sadly again.

"The water," she answered, "it will tell me things when it knows them. Just now, it told me your name, and it told me that- well, it told me some things. Not as much as I expected, though." She gave me a look of intense curiosity and went on. "Your true given name is Fiona. I can see that clearly, and about your magical origins, I was right-"

"Of course," added Arlee, proudly.

Faeryn looked over her shoulder and smiled at the woman. "You and I do have an extraordinarily similar composition." Again, that glow of curiosity lit Faeryn's face, chasing away the aura of dolorousness that seemed to come over her whenever she was at rest. "I have an interest in the fae, like I mentioned. Especially in nearly perfect intermagicals, like us," she added. At this, Arlee gave a little gasp, bringing her small delicate hand to her mouth.

"I just think it's fascinating the way that the Fae Intermixing Declaration in the Americas ended up amplifying natural human magic like this. The fae didn't expect it, you know. Bit of a surprise when they realized what they'd done. And now! The things human technomagic is capable of, these days, or so I hear. Have you-"

She tripped over her words, speaking quickly in her excitement, the words flowing out of her in a stream, like the water coursing around her. "Have you really been living as a human? Have you seen it? The technology? The-" She gestured and a picture of a city skyline with great cranes building ever-taller monoliths appeared in the water. "The huge machines and the skyscrapers? I can loot at pictures in the spring, but it's something I long to truly experience." She gazed wistfully up at the city all around us, at its colorful, decorative faerie architecture.

"Uh huh," I said, nodding in answer to her last question, "Of course I have. I grew up in a big city with buildings like that. But, what do you mean by perfect intermagicals? Or the intra- intermix-" I pursed my lips and furrowed my brow, trying to remember the interesting new terms that she had just flashed by me.

"The Fae Intermixing Declaration, do you mean?" asked Faeryn with an apologetic smile, "Sorry. I get a little overexcited talking about this stuff. You really don't know about it? That's so interesting. I'll start at the beginning, then. Did you really grow up in a human city? Incredible. Are you hungry? I am."

"Uh, yeah," I said. An honest response to all of her questions.

At Faeryn's word, Arlee opened one of the nearby rocks like a cabinet and drew out an elegant tray of assorted delicacies. There were colorful little cakes and round white buns with pretty, delicate designs on the tops. Next, tiny finger sandwiches and a small, steaming teapot with delicate porcelain cups for tea. Arlee took out an ornate gold-trimmed plate and arranged a selection of items on it. Then she poured two cups of steaming tea and handed one to Faeryn and the other to me. Faeryn seized a pretty pink cake and bit into it ravenously.

"It is so good to see you hungry, my love," said Arlee affectionately, watching Faeryn eat.

I held my own teacup, which glinted mesmerizingly in the shifting light, and eyed the deliciously appointed tray speculatively. "I feel like I've heard stories where people eat faerie food and are never able to leave," I said. The buns looked delicious, though, and I was very hungry.

Faeryn threw back her head and laughed, making water droplets fly out onto the riverbank. "Oh, it would hardly do for a faerie to be trapped forever in Faerieland, would it? There are worse fates, after all." She shook her head, taking another bite of her own cake. "But even so, no. You can eat here without fear of reprisal. Those are old stories, anyway. Old country stories. And, not stories that tell the tale of the likes of you or I, being what we are. Please, eat, and let me tell you what I know. Or, at least what I think I know."

Chapter 18

Settled on my comfortable rock with a plate full of curious looking cakes to try, I nodded to Faeryn.

"About the American Faerie. Where to begin? Well, at the beginning, I suppose!" She beamed at me. "The first of us came over with some of the earliest European settlers. Faeries have always been curious, and the tales of a green land over the sea with wide seething rivers and towering trees appealed to some of the more open minded and adventurous of the Sidhe, so they stowed away on human boats traveling across the ocean."

"Easy enough, if the human's can't even see you," put in Arlee. Faeryn paused, an ornate yellow item covered in sparkling sprinkles halfway to her small mouth. "You know, I've been doing a little more research on that, darling, and I'm beginning to wonder if they mightn't have been better able to, then, than they can now, but- well, let's not digress."

Faeryn paused to bite her cake and take a long sip of tea before she continued. Each of our teacups was unique, and hers looked like a delicate porcelain violet with a pretty green curl of a stem for a handle. It didn't look particularly practical, but Faeryn seemed to be well practiced with it. "Now, the Sidhe who found themselves in the Americas were in for a surprise. A few surprises, actually. The first, that this land, described as 'largely uninhabited' by the report of storytelling sailors, was, in fact, quite densely inhabited by various nations of native humans and magical creatures alike."

She raised her eyebrows at me, animated in her storytelling and clearly enjoying herself. "The second surprise was that the Sidhe had not been the only ones with the clever idea to come explore this land of supposed milk and honey. Alongside these native magicals were assorted fair folk who had emigrated from here and there. Come by twos and threes, without any particular place to go, now that they had arrived, being without the hills and holes and shires they were used to. So, they found each other and they ganged together, for safety and for companionship." She ran her fingers through the water and painted the scene. A dockyard tavern lit by lamplight, full of the craggy and wizened, and the smooth and eerily beautiful of all different races and creeds, huddled together as though for warmth, in this wonderful but strange new land. "And so, though some of us may still know ourselves specifically to be faerie," she gestured to include the three of us gathered there, "that time was when we came to collectively call ourselves, 'The Fae' or 'The New World Fae,'"

I selected one of the delicate cakes from the plate, choosing a mottled confection in all different shades of pale blue. It was one of the simpler ones in my collection, and I eyed the other, more complex designs, suspiciously. "Yeah, that's what Godrin told me. That here, all the different magical creatures were just fae, or fair folk, even though there are lots of different types," I said, feeling like I was beginning to understand.

"Ah, so it is not quite true to say that you do not know anything," Faeryn mused, looking a bit put out.

"I think that might be the only thing I do know, really!" I implored her, wringing my hands, wanting her to go on and tell me everything she could, "Please, will you tell me about them?"

"Hmm, well," she continued, just a bit petulantly, "After a half hundred years or so, the magicals of the new world, these New World Fae noticed that the humans here were not behaving like the ones they had left behind. Humans had always changed things, made things, built things, putting them up and tearing them down again, but not like they were doing here. These humans were carving footholds out of the sheer rock faces of the earth with a shocking efficiency and speed. Making big, lasting changes. Powerful human magic, you know. Or, do you know?"

"Let's assume that I don't," I said, with a smile. I bit into the round little faerie cake I was holding. It tasted like blueberry, which made sense, considering its coloring.

"Well, let's put it this way. Humans can make changes that are real. They can cut a stone and build a wall and a thousand years later, that wall will be there because the world has been forever changed. But, humans are limited. They tire and sicken. They need to eat and rest. Their tools break. The humans of the harsher climates had to chisel and claw their existence out of the raw, bitter landscape. Their changes were real, but they took time. The magical creatures, like the faeries of Europe, developed their civilizations alongside the humans and when the humans changed the world, the fae adjusted where they felt they must. The old country faeries don't change if they don't have to, and old, ruined castles stay mostly the same, year to year, anyway."

Arlee chuckled and bent down to refill Faeryn's tea cup from the still-steaming pot. I couldn't see where the heat could be continuing to come from, but I figured I'd better just round things up to 'maybe it's magic' until I knew better. "But, as I was saying, these new world humans were a different kind. After a few score years' worth of nothing at all remaining the same, these same adventurous magicals who had come to explore the new world decided to gather and discuss the situation they were in. They talked long and wide, and they decided that in this new land, with these new types of humans, and this new type of New World Fae, it was time for a new plan."

"The intermixing declaration?'

Faeryn laughed. "I call it that, yes. I think I'm probably the pre-eminent researcher on the New World Fae, at this point. They don't really write anything down, or give things proper names. But yes, the Fae Intermixing Declaration."

"How were they planning to, er, intermix?" I asked, momentarily distracted by a tiny flying faerie that had glinted into view behind Faeryn's head, dust glittering in the light of the falls.

Faeryn laughed again, harder and longer than before. She seemed so happy to be talking with me now, especially compared to how glum she had been the rest of the time. "Well, some intermix in what might be considered the traditional way. Some African spirits can, I know. And, of course, we faeries have found that we can interbreed with humans through the, er, natural means. It's what has allowed us to build up our numbers in the Americas like we have, and create huge bustling cities like this one used to be. Though, we do find that often, crossbreeding directly with full humans creates unfortunate," she gestured to her chest, sadly, "consequences." She looked back up at me and a fiery expression lit her face. "But not," she said, fixing me with her intense gaze, "always."

"African spirits?" I asked, through another bite of cake, "You know, I met someone at the Fair Isle-"

Faeryn smiled. "The Gullah, yes. The very same. In fact, his own origin sounds quite similar to the faerie methods, although he says he doesn't think he's an African type of faerie, I've asked." Another tiny faerie had joined the first, and they started chasing each other, distractingly, as though playing tag. Arlee gave the pair a sharp look and they darted off, out of sight again.

"You call him the Gullah too?" I asked, "I thought, maybe someone who knew him, well, might have another name."

Faeryn looked at me with a half-grin that perfectly captured the dark man's humored expression, and answered, "Network security."

I laughed. Of course that would be the reason. "And the others? The ones who intermixed less," I searched for the word, "traditionally?" I eyed the enticing-looking plate of cakes again. If the blue one tasted like blueberries, what would the ornate white and gold confection taste like, I wondered.

"Well, there are any number of ways, for any number of types of fae. Gifting some of their magic to a particular human line, for example. Even being in proximity to them can do it, in some cases, through general osmosis."

"They could eat them," Arlee suggested, helpfully.

"Hmm," Faeryn said, looking as though she wished Arlee had not said that, "Anyway, It worked. By intermixing humans and magicals, we found that we could live amongst the humans, and alongside their changes more easily. Those who had more human than magic could live amongst the humans or the magicals or both. The magicals could gather in spaces created by part-humans, and enrich them with their magic."

"Like the Fair Isle," I said, understanding.

"Yes, like the Fair Isle, and like this," she gestured to the sparkling city around us.

"This city is Faeryn's" said Arlee, beaming with pride at the smaller woman, "her human side gives her such capacity to create."

Faeryn smiled, then sighed. "It will all fade away, in time. Once we leave this place for good, in a little while nothing will remain to even show that we were here. Just the falls and the caves and the mist." She smiled, sadly. "I can't do much human magic, at all, really. Not that I've had much chance to try, living here amongst the faeries. You're the most human person I've ever seen here."

"Apart from you?" I asked. I gave into temptation and seized the white and gold cake, nibbling the corner curiously. Lemon, and something floral. Elderflower? I took another taste. It was very nice.

"Not even me," answered Faeryn, "You are 42.7% fae, or 58.3% human. I, myself, am 48% fae, and 52% human, making you, for our purposes, significantly more human than me."

"Is that so?" I said, fascinated by the specificity, even if it didn't mean much to me yet.

"It is. It's an interesting combination, to be sure. 42.7% single-source high Sidhe. One of the faerie queens, if I'm not mistaken, although which one, I couldn't say. My mother's touch is upon you, shielding that information from view." She quirked her mouth up at my look of confusion. "From my view, and from others who could read it. It's my mother's idea of a protection for you, I'm sure."

"My mother is," I paused, uncertain, "The Queen of the Faeries?"

"No, not the Queen of the Faeries. That's my mother, and that would make us sisters. No," she said, answering my look, "that isn't physically possible. We are only a few months apart in age. You're just a bit older. That I can see, clearly. No, you simply come from the line of a faerie queen. It's more of a stature. An archetype. Matriarch might be the closest title that humans use. There are," she considered for a second, "maybe a hundred faerie queens, right now? In the New World, anyway."

"57% human, from the line of a faerie queen," said Arlee dreamily, gazing at me.

"Why?" I asked, "is that good?"

"It's-" Faeryn paused, still looking at me with that strange intensity, "powerful. You've been living amongst humans all these years? I can't imagine that someone as magical as you wouldn't have been doing human magic. Tell me, do you like to make things?"

"Make things? Like crafts? Yeah, all the time." One of the tiny faeries had re-emerged and peeked from behind a tree and pulled funny faces at me. I looked away, trying not to laugh and draw Arlee's razor sharp attention back to the pretty little creature.

"What kind?" Faeryn asked.

"Oh, I don't know, all sorts of things. Sewing, beading, woodwork, ceramics. Anything really. I like papercraft a lot, because of how quickly things come together."

Faeryn smiled, as though I were saying exactly what she expected me to. "And, what is it that you make?"

"Oh, practical things that I need. Gifts for my friends. Things I see and like, and think, 'I could make that.'" I laughed, thinking about my college roommate's face when she would come home and find me, yet again, surrounded by pattern pieces, tape, and scissors. "I only like to make things once, though, usually. Just to see if I can." More small, impish faces peeked from behind branches now, eyeing me curiously. "I always can," I added, quietly. It was true.

"Mmmhmm. So, you create things. Brand new things that have never existed before, out of elements of the natural world. You just take them, and create magic with them, with your own hands and mind."

"I don't know about the 'elements of the natural world' part," I said, skeptically, "I usually get my supplies from the craft store."

"Clay? Undeniable. Cloth? What sort? Cotton, the fiber of flowers. Wool, the hair of beasts. Paper, the pulp of trees. You take the natural world and you bend it to your human will. And quite powerfully, by the sound of it."

I noticed several more tiny faeries who seemed to be sneaking closer to listen, darting from tree to tree, laughing behind their tiny hands. "Okay, maybe so," I said, remembering what the Gullah had said about magic. His ideas were starting to make more and more sense.

"Now, tell me, in the human world, did you ever find that things tended to go your way?" Faeryn asked, sipping her still-hot tea.

Definitely magic, I thought, taking another sip of my own before answering, admiring the way my gilded teacup glinted in the light filtering through the windows. "I guess so," I said, "Whenever I wanted to sit next to a particular friend, in school, the assigned seats just sort of," I shrugged, "changed to what I wanted them to be."

"Why?" Faeryn asked, peering at me closely.

"I don't know," I answered honestly, "Are you saying that it happened because I wanted it to?"

"Maybe," said Faeryn, "I don't know. Did other things go right?"

"Yeah, I guess so. I usually get the jobs I apply for, and I win a lot of the contests I enter, for art and things. I guess I just thought I was good at that stuff," I shrugged.

"And so you are," said Faeryn, "talent is no small part of human magic."

"Oh," I said, thinking back over the events of my life with this new perspective.

"Last question," said Faeryn with a smile, "I've given you a lot to think about, I can see."

"Yes," I said, and meant it. Perhaps hearing the truth of it in my voice, Faeryn gave me a moment to digest before asking her final question, and I gazed off at the sparkling city, glittering in rainbows, in the distance, through the trees.

"Alright. Have you ever found that you could influence other people into doing the things you wanted them to do?"

"Oh, uh…" the question took me aback. That sounded like manipulation. "My mom always said that wasn't a nice thing to do, and that I should let people make their own decisions," I answered, defensively.

"And why would she tell you that?" asked Faeryn, smiling like a well fed cat, "Was it because you were good at it?"

"I guess it must have been," I said, thinking about the conversation when she had told me that. I had been telling my mom that I thought I could get my friend to go on the rollercoaster with me. "I can usually get people to do what I want," I had told her cheerfully, before she had scolded me. "Yeah, I think so."

"The three pillars of human magic," Arlee recited, "Creation, Manifestation, and Influence."

"Human magic?" I asked, "What does that even mean?"

"Why, the magic that humans can do, of course," said Faeryn, "Not all of them find themselves drawn to wield it, and fewer do it with intentionality, though all have the capability. Humans yearn for magic, and yet they cling to the short-sighted notion that, while others' skills may count as 'magic,' somehow their own abilities are miraculously excepted from being qualified," she shrugged, "Even though their capabilities are far greater than that of the common beast, and even those of many storybook wizards, humans tend to forget about their own prodigious skill when thinking about magical abilities. That doesn't make a human's magic any less impressive or less magical than the fae kind, though. "

"Oh," I said, my mind reeling, "Is that so?"

"It is," said Faeryn, grinning that cat's grin, again. "And," she said, resuming her lecturer's air, "the increase, and unexpected overflow of human magic has been an extremely interesting and unintended consequence of the last four hundred years of this intentional intermixing."

"What do you mean?" I asked, watching the little pixies advancing sneakily, giggling behind their hands as they crept closer and closer to Faeryn in the spring.

"The explosion of human industry. Science, medicine, and technology," she said, "the advancements of human society over the last few centuries. No one has proved it, of course, but I'm fairly certain. The combination of the fae ability to see and interact with the inherent magic in the world, and the human ability to enact real and lasting change has created an exponential increase in the overall effectiveness of human magic. And why wouldn't that be a powerful symbiosis?"

"It might create quite the crisis," Arlee said, with a giggle.

"A crisis? You don't mean… The Crisis?? You think that the Crisis Control Council's crisis is the fact that fae are mixing with humans?"

"In a way. More so that the human-fae intermagicals are becoming too powerful and too aware of their own power for the comfort of those that would control them. But again, this is pure speculation, if well researched," said Faeryn, drawing a hand through the water lovingly again. This time the vision showed pages and pages of papers flipping one after another, in a cascade.

"What can you see in that thing?" I asked, as images of papers continued to flip by.

"Anything that the waters have seen," Faeryn said, with a sad little sigh, "and it's been flowing around this world for a long time. It's the next best thing to being able to live outside this spring." At this, she started to cry, and silently sank below the surface of the water, again, leaving me alone with Arlee. The tiny faeries who had crept close during Faeryn's lecture darted away, at her change of mood, leaving trails of glowing motes behind them.

"Oh no," I said to the small, stately woman, "did I say something wrong?"

"No," said Arlee, sadly, "You said everything right. She's been crying under there for weeks now. Your visit is the most she's spoken since we heard the news. And the first she's eaten." She looked wistfully at Faeryn's plate of half-finished cakes.

"Really?" I asked, selecting a third cake, the most decadent of them all. This one was a tiny multi-layered extravagance, decorated with sugarspun lace. "If I could have food like this all the time I don't know if I'd ever stop eating." I took another bite of the delicious, delicate cake. Light and moist, it tasted divine.

"Oh, they're mostly tofu and she knows that," said Arlee, poking a cake which turned white and cubic for a moment before resuming its pleasing shape and hue, "but her body is delicate and her diet is particular. She has to eat something to keep her human body strong."

"Oh," I said, continuing to chew. Now that she mentioned it, the texture was reminiscent of a cold block of uncooked tofu. My chewing slowed. The cakes were not quite as appetizing now. "Since she heard the news? What do you mean, what news?"

"Why, the spring, of course," Arlee said, "The reason why all the faeries have evacuated." She took in my look of confusion and continued.
"Some ill-intended humans have discovered a place where these waters emerge from the earth."

Behind her, I saw Faeryn's fiery head rise slowly back out of the water. "What are they going to do?" I asked.

"Some human nonsense. Something about… what do they call it? Capital?"

"Money," corrected Faeryn, "They're going to thrust their nasty pump into the ground and rip the water out, with enough force to flood this cavern and slice through my heart like a knife, if I were to try to stay here. They'll destroy our city and the ecosystem both, just for a little bit of filthy money."

"They're doing what, now? Stealing your water? That's insane! Hasn't anyone tried to stop them?" I asked, incredulously.

"What can we do? Humans make changes, and we adapt. It is the way of the world," said Arlee, sadly.

"But, why?" I asked, "It doesn't have to be that way, does it? Wasn't that the whole point of the intermixing plan? So that intermagicals could impact human events and help the fae folk?"

"Well…" Arlee hedged, but to my surprise, Faeryn smiled.

"Maybe so," Faeryn said, looking thoughtful. "I'll admit it crossed my mind, when I realized who you are, or rather, *what* you are."

"What I am?" I asked, "why does it matter what I am?"

"Because a healthy, female, nearly 50/50 first-generation intermagical faerie is incredibly rare, Fiona," said Faeryn, as though explaining something very simple to someone very dense. "And for good reason, too. They just don't happen, half-faerie children. The child doesn't take. Or, when they do, they end up like me. Broken beyond repair. Maybe once in a hundred years, does one come out whole. Brimming with magic, and with a healthy human body to bring that magic out into the world. Most humans, most intermagicals even, wouldn't begin to contemplate creating an impact like that. Trying to change a known outcome, when the humans' course is already set. They just wouldn't." Arlee nodded in agreement.

"They would see it one of two ways. Like the fae, who know that this pump is evil, but are powerless to stop it. Or, like the humans, and either not see it our way, or feel themselves too constrained by human ideas about what is possible. Bound by the unwritten rules of human society. But, someone with your amount of inherent magic, your ability to create real change, and your human capacity to influence others' minds and the physical world around us…" Faeryn breathed deeply, her chest expanding with the possibilities she was bringing forth. "You might be able to change things, if you tried, I think. You might be able to save me. To save us."

"Me? Really?"

"I think so," she said, with a deeply hopeful look in her large, sad eyes. Then, abruptly, the look on her face changed, replaced by one of childlike excitement. "Say, do you play cards?"

Chapter 19

I turned the key to start the van. The clock blinked to life and I was surprised to see that it was still only early afternoon. It felt like a lifetime ago that I had tramped hopefully around and around that funny little building. My brain was buzzing with all the fascinating new thoughts fighting for front billing in my mind, and from the effects of a second dose of that incredible spring water. Faeries were real. Really, actually real! And apparently I was one of them, and a powerful one, too, by the sound of it.

I pictured the glittering spires of the faerie city, and felt an incredible sense of belonging and pride for a moment before a heavy sadness rolled over me like a dark wave. Faeryn's beautiful city, created from her imagination and powered by her will, would just fade away like the waterfall's mist in a few short weeks, after the pump turned on and she had to flee with the rest of the city's faeries. I had gotten more information about the city's other inhabitants over one of our many hands of Hearts.

Faeryn loved games, she told me, but rarely had the company to play them. Hearts, Faeryn explained, was a bit of a personal favorite. "Naturally," she had said, gesturing to her chest. In particular, she confessed, she perversely enjoyed the point in each game where hearts had to be broken. While we played, we talked. Or, mostly she talked, and I listened, occasionally asking questions. Arlee joined in the conversation periodically, and the tiny faerie who played the fourth hand didn't say anything at all. She didn't play particularly skillfully, either.

"I've taught a few of them the rules. They follow them, but they don't play well." Faeryn looked critically down at the tiny faerie holding the comparatively giant-sized cards. She laid down an unnecessarily high card, and snatched the worthless center pile with glee. "But, they do technically play."

"The little ones like the rules," added Arlee, "But," she smiled ruefully, "Even at my size, we mostly-magicals have trouble grasping the importance of things like points and winning."

"She understands the mechanics of the game," Faeryn elaborated, "but she doesn't quite grasp the 'why' of it all. Little ones like this are the last to leave the city. They're faerie, yes, but not exactly bright." With a little 'humph' the tiny woman launched herself into the air and flew in three piercingly bright circles. I laughed, surprised, and Arlee and Faeryn joined me, tittering prettily. "What I meant to say was that you aren't particularly smart," Faeryn clarified, addressing the tiny woman. The tiny faerie nodded curtly and returned to the ground, satisfied.

"We explained what was happening, and told them to pack up and head south like everyone else, but they just kept on dusting about the place like normal. Even if the city fades, though, they'll be able to live in the cracks of the mountain, or out in the woods, easily enough."

"Pack up and move south? Is that where everyone else has gone?" I asked, gesturing to the silent spires.

"Yes," said Faeryn, looking even sadder, "they've all fled south to the country home."

"The country home?" I prodded, when she did not continue.

"The country home," she repeated, sadly, "it's our home in the country. I told you that faeries weren't much for names. If I want something to have a name, I have to give it one myself." She gave me a wry look, and I got the feeling that she might name quite a few things for the faeries. "It's a gathering place for the fair folk. A market of sorts, in the summer. One of our more successful collaborations with the mostly-human intermagicals, in fact. They built us a marvelous little fae village, way out in the country, south of the valley. Humans come and use it for a few weeks a year, but otherwise, they leave it for the fae. It's quite charming really," she said, running her hands dreamily through the water. A scene of a narrow passageway overhung with charmingly crooked wooden buildings swam into view.

"Oh, how sweet," I said, leaning closer to admire the little marketplace, "Humans really built this?"

"Intermagicals," Arlee corrected, using Faeryn's aptly coined term, "They call it something, don't they, darling? The Fair Folk's Country, maybe."

"The Country Fair," Faeryn corrected, gazing at the image fondly. "It won't look like this now, though, I suppose," she said, looking at the moving picture wistfully. We watched as the painted wooden signs creaked in the breeze, and a single wizened fae stumped down the alley, hung his lantern over his door and headed into one of the narrow two-story shops. "The streets will be overrun with faeries now, with everyone packed in, taking refuge from the city. It'll be like the height of the festival season."

"So, uh, why haven't you joined them?" I asked hesitantly, guessing that the answer wasn't a happy one.

"I should. I will. Any day now." She reached out a hand and Arlee took it, holding it in both of her own. "Arlee, can you tell her, please?" she asked, her eyes beginning to well up with tears. At the small woman's nod, Faeryn sank back down into the water, hand still clasped in her companions'.

I wondered at the mechanics of this for a second, then realized that Arlee's seat had sunk lower along with her lady's, keeping them level even as the girl retreated underwater again. Magic certainly has its benefits, I thought, impressed yet again by this unusual place.

"Faeryn says that with the pump at full power, the pressure will be enough to flood this entire cavern. Even if she weren't washed away by the current, that much magic would be too much for her. She couldn't survive it. It would rip her apart. She says she's done…" she wrinkled her brow, searching for a word, then finished, triumphantly, "…the math."

I smiled, remembering. That concept had been hard for her as a faerie, but then I sobered immediately. Poor Faeryn!

"What will she do? How long…" I asked Arlee, trailing off.

"We're not certain, of course. If she's well rested, she can be out of the spring for a month of festivities in the summer. She pays for it afterward, of course, but it is what she lives for, the revels and the dancing. And the mischief," she added, smiling at the girl whose large eyes stared, eerily open, under the water.

"Mischief?" I asked, incredulous. The sad girl had been academically excited, certainly, but she did not give the impression of being mischievous.

"Oh," said Arlee, with an expression I couldn't quite read, "No, Faeryn doesn't seem the type, does she? They have many sides, though. You'd be surprised." Leaving me with that enigmatic thought, she continued. "The Queen is searching for a new place where we can start to build again. She has not had luck, though. Few places are nearly as magic-rich as this part of the world. That's why they call it Portal Land, of course."

"Wait, why do they call it Portal Land?" I asked, glad for the opportunity to inquire about this peculiarity.

"For all the portals, of course. Places where natural magic spills into the world, like it does here," she said, touching the water reverently, "There are so very many, right here at the foot of the great mountain and the confluence of the two rivers that some fae, including my Lady, believe that there must be a powerful source of magic in this region. It has been a major topic of her research. But, even though the portals are plentiful, there are none nearby, save this one, that would be acceptable for Faeryn. At least none that remain unclaimed. That is why the Queen is venturing into the far north, to search for a new, suitable home for us, in the unclaimed wilderness."

At this, Faeryn sat up out of the stream again, her little girls' mouth petulant in a pink moue of dislike. Not actually a little girl, I reminded myself. She had said she was almost exactly my age, but she was so small and youthful, it was hard to remember that, sometimes. I wondered if it was her broken heart, or her life in the water, or something else entirely that caused her to give off such a youthful impression.

"The far north," she said, pouting, 'I don't even know why she's bothering! It's so cold I would die just from that, I swear I would. I don't know what would be worse, a frozen Canadian river, or the soul-searing dread of sleeping for eternity in the stream at the country home." With a little wail of despair she disappeared back into the stream.

Arlee looked after her, with a sad, loving expression that made my heart swell, remembering it. "With her heart wide open in the spring like that, the emotions do just flow right out of it sometimes. She does truly dread enchanted sleep though."

"Enchanted sleep?"

"Yes. What will happen if we can not find a place for her to live. There is some magic in the other streams and rivers of this valley. Not like this though, just a trickle. Enough to keep her alive, but she would be," again, she searched for a difficult word. I was beginning to see what Godrin meant about the fae's attention and memory, "comatose," she finished, "And, in her dreams she is always so very, very cold."

Faeryn had slowly raised herself to peer out of the water again, as Arlee spoke. "Bitterly cold," she moaned, wrapping her arms around herself, "Cold awake or cold asleep. I don't know what would be worse." She looked beseechingly up at Arlee, and raised her arms, beckoning the other woman.

Without hesitation, Arlee, skirts and all, waded into the river behind the girl, gathered her long red hair expertly to one side, and settled herself so that Faeryn now nestled against the small woman's chest. They fit like puzzle pieces, snug there in the river, clearly having entwined like this many times before. Faeryn had looked so small and young, curled up against her. And so very vulnerable.

Now, alone in the car, where she couldn't see me do it, I let hot tears run down my face and sobbed, overwhelmed with the emotion I had held back. I wanted so badly to help that poor, broken hearted girl. *And, so that's what I'm doing,* I said to myself with conviction, as I turned off the winding mountain roads and onto the highway, heading back toward Portal Land.

Recalling the scene in the spring, I wondered again at the relationship between the two women. Certainly close friends, and that of a caretaker and beloved charge, but, remembering how they had looked, snuggled together, and the way that magical Arlee pushed so tenaciously to keep up with Faeryn's intermagical intellect, I wondered if it was more than that. I hoped so. Hoped that she could seize whatever bits of joy and warmth and love that she could, from a world that was, for her, so painful and cold and limited. Next to the highway, the tree line parted and the wide river sparkled. Not so limited though, I thought, remembering Faeryn's glittering creations. An entire city, born out of the symbiosis of her human imagination and her faerie nature. She had created a paradise of her own, and not just for herself. As Arlee's presence clearly showed, others could and did live inside her fantasy as well. For the fae, I reminded myself, illusions were real. Or, as real as they needed to be, I thought, remembering the delicate faerie cakes that had turned out to actually be blocks of raw, unflavored tofu. Filling, though.

I drove on, my mind spinning with all the new things I had to think about. Faeries and fae folk. Sparkling cities and magical springs. And pumps, I thought, my face darkening again, as I got closer to the city and tall construction cranes loomed into view. A reminder of human infrastructure and the problems it was causing my new friends. Faeryn had told me more about the pump when she had calmed down enough to talk about it. The faeries had been warned, she explained, by another powerful intermagical like us. A distant cousin of Faeryn's called Melodie Cristalline. Another lyrical fae name. She was blind, Faeryn had told me, seeing only indistinct shapes of light and dark, but she was gifted with a second sight, and the ability to see things yet-to-come. She had warned the Queen, and had been able to tell them enough that when Faeryn felt the first vibrations of the great pump, she knew exactly what she was looking for.

"The spring showed me their boxy little buildings, and their big, ugly machines," she said, as the water displayed an image of familiar-looking portable structures surrounded by close-knit evergreens.

'Wait," I said, peering closer, "I think I know that place. Can you-" I leaned in squinting, "Can you zoom in? How does that work, anyway?" Faeryn showed me, with her painterly gestures, how she could call up any image from her own memory, and, she demonstrated proudly, how she could see and hear anything happening within view of the spring, and any of the bodies of water it flowed into, all the way out to the ocean.

"But not in the ocean?" I had asked, clarifying. It was, after all, water too.

"No," she said with a grimace, "I've tried, but it's too fuzzy. It just gives me a headache. I think, at that point, the magic is just too diffuse, but it might also be the salt. I've tried some different things to try to make it clearer, but-"

"Darling, the pump?" murmured Arlee, quietly.

"Oh, yes, right" said Faeryn, snapping back from her tangent. She wiped away a blurry image of fish and ocean kelp, and put back the picture of the squat boxy buildings. Now, there were tiny people outside, walking toward the ugly black machine that marred the natural beauty of the scene. Faeryn spread her hands, making the image as wide as the stream itself, and the men's faces came into clear view.

I gasped. "I know that place. I know them!" It was Brandon, of course, and his father, the Deacon. In that moment of connection, the truth came crashing down on me. He had told me he was extracting water. This pump must be his project. It all made sense!

Now, in the car, I felt hot blood flush my cheeks as I thought about them. The Deacon, self-righteous and holier-than-thou, sure that I was a weak female in need of *shepherding*. And Brandon, his son! My stomach lurched again at the memory of finding out their connection. Brandon who had intervened to pull me out of harm's way not once, but twice! I Imagined the smug, self-satisfied expression that the Deacon must have made when Brandon had told him about how he had found me, lost and naked in the woods. And of course he would have told him all about it by now. The thought of it made me see red, anger flaring. Those two men talking about me, judging me, with their backwards opinions and their sanctimonious... My knuckles were white on the steering wheel, and I reminded myself to calm down. This wasn't safe. I was driving. I took a few slow, deep breaths and felt a little better.

After my initial exclamation to Faeryn and Arlee, I told them about how I had met Brandon and his father, and then Faeryn shared what she knew about the two men and their operation. The temporary buildings, the ones I had seen, had gone up after the leaves had started to change. The first tests of the pump had alerted Faeryn to the location of the Christian Springs operation, and since that time, Faeryn had been listening to their every word, aided by the magical properties of the springwater.

She listened as they discussed the results of their first round of testing, and the callous jokes they made about the effects that the incremental pressure increases would have on the surrounding ecosystem and environment, including the system of caves in which Faeryn had built her magnificent city. She heard, too, when they concluded that, due to the near-freezing temperature of the ground-water in winter, they would have to wait until springtime, and warmer weather, for the next phase of their plan. The faeries didn't know exactly when the tests would resume, so the Queen had ordered evacuation of the city at the Lamb's Milk Cross-Quarter Day. I had no idea what that was supposed to mean, but it sounded like it had been several weeks at least since the denizens of the city had traveled south to the country home, leaving Arlee and Faeryn alone.

Not all of the city's inhabitants had made the journey south, though. Most of the largest and most powerful members of the Queen's court had joined their liege in searching for a new home, ranging far and wide. Arlee and Faeryn were to stay in the silent city until the last possible moment, to allow Faeryn as much time as possible to seep in the magic of the spring before the time came to figure out how to survive without it. As we watched in the stream, the watery images of Brandon and the Deacon approached the pump and started cleaning off the debris of the winter. Whenever they spoke, Faeryn repeated their words aloud for me, since I couldn't hear them from outside of the spring, but they said little as they worked.

"This is it. This is it," said Faeryn, repeating herself morosely as we watched, "I knew it was coming, but it's actually today. I can't believe it's today. Why does it have to be today?"

"It's my fault," I said, apologetically.

"What?" Faeryn asked incredulously, "How could it possibly be your fault?"

"Just that it's today, I mean. It would have been sometime next week, I think, but when I told Brandon I wouldn't go to his church with him, he got really upset and he said he was going straight home and getting to work, instead of going camping with his friends,"

"Oh," said Faeryn, considering for a long moment, "Well, I suppose I'm glad you came here anyway. I would rather have someone like you on our side, and have it be happening now, than to have a week longer and have no hope at all."

"But, what can I do?" I asked, desperate to save these new, wonderful friends, but with no idea how to help.

"Human magic!" Arlee exclaimed, enthusiastically.

Faeryn smiled kindly at the excited faerie. "And fae magic," she said, then added, "You're an incredibly powerful intermagical, Fiona."

"But, I don't know how to do any magic at all!" I said, exasperated.

That was the crux of it, I thought, fingers drumming on the steering wheel as I followed signs to the intersection of the highway with the interstate. I just didn't know enough to do anything to help anyone. Not even to help myself, if the last few days were any indication, I thought, wryly.

If only I could have had a few years to learn and study first. At least a few months, or even a few days! But, no. This was all happening right now, and Faeryn believed that I was the only one with a hope to save her... If only I could manage to figure out how!

Faeryn and Arlee had tried to show me how to do faerie magic. They created beautiful sprays of flowers and crystals on their palms and transformed plain white cubes of tofu from a small underwater larder into exquisite delicacies before my eyes. They explained how to reach inside and draw the magic out from their energetic core. How to relax and allow it to refill slowly from the earth, or faster, from the abundant natural magic of the spring. I could see the magic easily enough, and I could picture what they were describing as they explained it. But, when I tried it, nothing happened. Not even a glimmer.

"What am I doing wrong?" I asked, raising my plain, unsparkling hand out of the spring again and again, trying to draw the magic to me, like Faeryn did.

"I don't know," said Faeryn, sadly, "I've just," she raised her hand, dripping with magical motes, "you know, done it, for as long as I can remember. I don't think Arlee even had to learn, being what she is." But I hadn't grown up seeped in the magic like they had. I could see it and touch it, and, having tried several of the delicate new faerie cakes that Arlee had created in demonstration for me, I could certainly taste it. I just couldn't seem to use my intention to influence it. "You'll just have to go south," Faeryn concluded, "It's the only thing for it. You'll find better teachers there. Ones that can show you in ways that I can't."

"Go south, to the country home?" I asked, and she confirmed. The faeries at the country home would help me, and I should go there as soon as possible. As soon as I could, that was the idea, I thought, as I waited at the stoplight. I should take the ramp heading south, straight to the faeries. But, I wondered, eyeing the sign back to Portland, what would be the harm in a short detour?

After everything I had seen and heard last night, I just had to take one more look at the Fair Isle. It had been the most immediately comfortable and welcoming place I had ever been, I thought, saddened again. If it really had been destroyed, like it had sounded last night, with the explosions and gunfire, at least I could see the front of it once, whatever was left of it, just to have one last memory of the magical place.

Chapter 20

I drove back to the Gardener Market, and traced my route back to the Fair Isle. It wasn't hard to find the little neighborhood center, a street filled with florists and pet food stores, and cafes with umbrellas and outdoor seating, and I wandered a little as I looked for the front door rather than the back entrance, driving up the street, then back down again, searching for an unnamed pub.

There! That must be it. In between an artisanal cheese shop and a high end barber was a thick brown door between a couple of dusty lead-glass windows. I could have sworn there were several more windows lining the wide front wall of the Fair Isle I remembered from yesterday, but the diamond pattern of the glass was just the same. The windows weren't broken. That was something, at least.

Finding parking on the street, I approached tentatively, nervous about what I would find. The antique oil lantern by the door was lit, with a flickering flame burning in its soot-stained reservoir. *Maybe that means it's open,* I thought hopefully, and pushed open the door. The crack of light cut a bright slice into the dim room. Motion near the shadowy bar caught my eye as my vision adjusted from the brightness outside. As the dark shape came closer, I saw it was the Gullah coming to greet me. The dark tones of his skin and clothing made him fade even deeper into the shadows, but his bright smile cut through the dimness like a knife.

"Fiona," he called in greeting, and I moved toward him. I was relieved to see that the bar seemed visibly unaffected by the chaos last night, and now I was even more curious about what had happened after I had left. "Did you find them?" he asked.

"Um, what?" I asked, confused, "What happened last night?"

"What? Nothing," he answered, mirroring my confusion, "The faeries, did you find them?"

"Oh," I answered, "Kind of, yeah. And what do you mean nothing? The raid? The gunshots? I thought I was going to find a burned-out hole in the wall instead of a pub, but here you are, just sitting at the bar drinking-" I looked down at the funny little teardrop-shaped cup he was cradling.

"Er, what are you drinking?"

He laughed, a rich low sound. "Oh, that. I guess that would have sounded pretty alarming from your side of things," he said, and offered me the cup, "Yerba mate. Here, try some, it's nice. And anyway, it's traditional to share."

I took the tear-shaped cup, a dried gourd, I realized, once I was holding it. The vessel felt warm in my hands, and I sipped the herbal brew from a wide metal straw. The taste was grassy and fresh, and sent a pleasurable buzz through my tired muscles. As we traded sips of the energizing drink, we exchanged our stories.

Right as I left, he told me, a crew of CCC lackeys, "filthy Corpsos," he spat, shaking his head, had pulled up outside the bar, acting on the tip they'd gotten from that idiot bigfoot blogger who had been talking all about the Fair Isle at one of the other local watering holes, telling everyone how interesting the people were, in here, and how much less crowded it was. The Gullah laughed, "And he wondered why."

As it happened, only two of the Corpsos had enough magic in them to make their way through the front door. The others, eight or nine in all, the Gullah thought, had smashed their way into the cheesemonger next door, busting through the deadbolt and ruining several nice blocks of aged cheddar. Of the two who found themselves inside, one of them had a gun. He had fired the first shot. The one that I had heard before I left.

"Right there," the barman said, and pointed up to a small hole in the dark wood of the wall, "We could fix it, certainly, but the truth is, that's the closest things have gotten to going wrong around here in a long, long time, and we would do well to remember it." The other sounds? The breaking of glass, the chaos and destruction. All illusion. With a few seconds warning, the fae folk of the Fair Isle had sprung into action, blasting the erstwhile attackers with every bit of discombobulating chaos they could muster. The barmaid Isla flounced by, and the Gullah nodded to her, deeply. "Isla here makes beautiful flowers, certainly," he said, with a charming smile, "but her real talents lie in the creation of spectacular serpents."

"Really?" I asked, incredulous.

"Oh sure. Love snakes. Adders, vipers, serpents of any kind, really," she said, giggling playfully and whirling toward me. Her arm shot out, and for a moment, it was not an arm, but a thick black snake that bared its long wet fangs at me, before curling back into a limb again.

"Eep!" I exclaimed, jumping in surprise, "Yeah, I can see how that might work to scare someone off."

"Oh, I had 'em draped from the rafters, and wrapped around the taps. One of those Corpsos didn't care for serpents, I don't think. He was white as a sheet, and ran like the wind," Isla said, and laughed her tinkling laugh again.

"And with the vantage from my window up above, I was able to take care of the ones outside," said the Gullah with a maniacal gleam in his dark eyes. I suspected that he might have enjoyed this opportunity to test his defenses. After he had satisfied my curiosity, I told him about my day in the faerie city. "Half-magical with a near-perfect split? Well…" he let his breath out in a long sigh, "that sure is something, isn't it? Explains that feeling when we touched, though. I'd been wondering if maybe we were," he trailed off, "but, anyway. That explains it." I went on, telling him more about the situation, the empty city, and the imminent threat of the pump. "I'd heard that they'd headed south. Keeping tight as to why, though. It's good to know what they're up to. Queen Viv does like to play it close to the chest,"

Queen Viv, I noted mentally. How familiar of him. "That's where I'm headed now," I said, regretful, but realizing that I had to go. I had only meant to stop in for a moment, to see how things stood here. Now I'd been here for the better part of an hour. The Gullah was certainly easy to talk to.

"Well, take my number," he said, handing me a black business card, "Call me if there's anything I can do to help." The card was covered in a complex pattern of numbers, letters and esoteric symbols printed in blocky white type. I goggled at it until he took it back from me and pointed, indicating a row of ten numbers on the bottom corner. "That's the phone number there," he said, with a smile.

"Oh, okay, thanks," I said, pocketing it. I'd have to think of a reason to call, I decided, as I got up to leave, this time through the front door.

Part 5 - Country Faeries

"Curses!" Velia shouted, fists balled and feet stamping tracks into the grass beneath her feet. The blasted girl was coming right this way, headed straight for the valley. Why would she come back here? Why so soon? It's barely been a day since she left. Someone must have told her. Someone must have known who she was.

As she paced, her eyes flicked busily, looking for inspiration. Velia spotted a single fluffy cloud drifting across the clear, blue sky, and seeing it, she smiled. She drummed her long fingers on her chin speculatively. There was no reason she had to make it easy for the girl, was there?

Chapter 21

Welcome to the Willamette Valley, I read from the sign by the roadside as the first clouds rolled in. With the valley spread open before me, and green hills on either side, I had a wide view of the sky as thick gray rain clouds roiled and grew into monstrous billows out of the clear blue sky. "We don't get weather like this in California," I said into the empty car, driving headlong into the gathering storm. Within a minute, I could hardly see anything at all, as rain pelted the windshield. My wipers sluiced the water violently from side to side, but the rain replaced it before I could get a clear view ahead of me. "How can rain be this loud?" I wondered aloud, white knuckles gripping the steering wheel. But, as soon as I asked the question I realized that the rain bouncing off the windshield wasn't rain at all. It was hail, and getting larger by the minute!

I pulled off to the side of the road as the hailstones grew from peas to marbles and then to golf balls. The wind rattled the car as I hunkered down and waited for the storm to pass, jumping at each crack of collision and hoping that the wind-whipped ice balls wouldn't crack my windshield. Suddenly, my vision was seared with bright white light and my ears rang with the deafening roar of thunder. A moment later, a big piece of flaming debris, dislodged by the lightning strike, hit my windshield hard, and, in a terrified reaction, I hit the gas and peeled off, away from the flaming wreckage and back onto the road. I barreled forward on the empty highway, hailstones the size of ping pong balls bouncing off my windshield, and didn't see the hulking animals in the roadway until I was almost on top of them.

"Oh My Gaaaah!" I yelled, wrenching the wheel and swerving out of the way of the shadowy bovine shapes. My van skidded and stopped abruptly, one back tire lodged in the shallow ditch on the side of the road. I clutched the steering wheel, panting. The hail let up, replaced by sheets of rain and I sighed with relief at the reprieve from the sensory onslaught. "I hate this valley," I said, as I turned my wipers back on and got a good look through my windshield, realizing that this was not the time or place to catch my breath, "I hate it, I hate it."

Large tongues of fire licked their way along the roadside toward me, undeterred by the rain, and I revved my engine, gravel spitting as I gained purchase and swung back onto the road. "Ack! Wrong way!" I exclaimed, as the wipers gave me a momentary glimpse at my surroundings. I flipped the car into reverse, starting the three-point maneuver that would turn the van back around.

Skreeeee!

A terrible, high-pitched caw cut through the thundering of the rain, and I looked up through my watery windshield, catching the maniacal eye of a diving hawk, plummeting toward me. With a sickening crash, it made contact, and I wrenched the wheel in my surprise, sending the car in a stomach-dropping 360° spin on the slick road. The heavy van skidded to a stop, engine dying. I'd managed to skid off the highway and onto the median, so at least I was out of the way. I clutched the steering wheel, knuckles white, breathing heavily.

Skreeee!

The hawk cried again as it circled above, preparing for another dive. I could barely see it through the heavy rain. How, then… I started to wonder, but the thought was interrupted as the bird dove again. It hurled itself at the van and hit the roof with a bang. The heavy car rocked with the impact. To my left, the shadowy shapes of the dark four-legged animals, cows, I assumed, but it was hard to see through the rain, lumbered across the roadway, blocking my forward progress. They must have been scared onto the road by the lightning, I guessed, but where had they come from? Turning to my right, I could see sunbeams lighting the hills and the fields, back the way I had come. This horrible storm had come up so suddenly. If I had actually just driven into it, maybe I could drive back out of it, and wait for the whole thing to blow over.

As I peered back down the highway, another car came into sight over the shallow hill behind me, driving toward the storm. If they're from here, maybe they're used to this, I thought, as the car barreled forward. It didn't change speed at all as it hit the wet pavement, and was buffeted by sheet after sheet of heavy rain. The sedan drove right past the wreckage of the lightning strike and the tongues of fire lapping the roadway. "This guy is a madman," I said, wonderingly, as the car winged by me, unaffected, and charged forward, heading straight for the line of dark, heavy shapes blocking the roadway. "Watch out!" I cried, although I knew he couldn't hear me.

I held my breath.

The car didn't swerve. It drove straight into the herd. Straight through, and off down the road. I blinked twice, then let out my held breath, slowly. The car had passed right through those dark, menacing shapes, as though…

I released my grip on the steering wheel to cover my open mouth. The car had passed through those cows as though they were not there. Right through the entire storm, in fact, as though it was not there. As though it was not actually real. As though it was an illusion.

The giant bird cried again. That unlikely hawk, flying in this terrible weather. And for what? To dive bomb its delicate body into my huge, metal van? That wasn't very hawk-like of it, was it? And the fire from that conveniently timed lightning strike that was burning so fiercely, in this heavy rain. That wasn't quite right either. Those road barriers were made of concrete. What was it burning?

"Fae illusion," I spoke aloud, into the deafening noise. As I said the words, the sound of the storm lessened its pounding on my eardrums. Had it actually, I wondered, or had it just become somehow less… important? "This rain is an illusion," I said, again, turning the key and starting the engine.

The hail started up again as I eased my way back onto the highway. Starting small, it grew back to marble size, then onward, until ping-pong-sized balls of ice ricocheted off the windshield and roof, threatening to break through it with each crash. Determinedly, I drove onward. Fake hail couldn't break a windshield. It had started again as soon as I started driving forward. Just more proof that this storm was reacting specifically to me and my actions. "And real storms don't do that," I said, with grim satisfaction.

I drove slowly, sight still limited by the storm's visual noise. As I got to the line of cows, I faltered. "Now is not the moment to lose faith in your own convictions," I said to myself, girding my loins. I took a deep breath, and pressed down the gas, heading straight for the nearest bovine. Not cows, I saw, now that I was almost close enough to touch one. These were something much larger, and much older. These were plains buffalo. Huge, brown and shaggy, with big, soulful eyes. These great beasts must have roamed these hills and valleys for thousands of years. Maybe a few of them still did, I thought as I barreled toward one, headlong, but I was willing to bet, bet my life on it in fact, I thought, nervously, that the ones that I was looking at were not actually standing in front of me, here, today.

I took a deep breath and pressed harder on the gas.

In a moment, I was through. Eyes glued on the reflective lane-markers of the highway ahead of me, I turned on my hazard lights and stayed in the slow lane. This was not going to be a relaxing trip but now that I knew that this storm couldn't really hurt me or the car, all I had to do was keep driving forward and get through it.

Chapter 22

By the time I reached the turnoff for the country home, it was nearly dark. In the faded blues of evening the faerie-style instructions Faeryn had given me about following the colorful flags and turning at the pointed red roof were useless. I started to panic, in the growing darkness, remembering my dead cell phone.

Oregon Country Fair read a sign pointing to the left. The country home of the faeries. Wasn't that what Faeryn had said humans called it? I sighed with relief and followed the arrow. *Closed, See You Next Fair!* read a sign hung on a chain between two tall pines. I tucked my van into the trees by the road, far enough that I didn't think anyone would bother it.

"Of course there wouldn't be anything helpful like fairy lights," I grumbled, pulling on a thick sweater. Eyeing the damp-looking trees, I added another waterproof layer. I wouldn't be sleeping outside unprepared again. In my thick wool hat and raincoat, I was as well-provisioned as I could be, I thought, staring out at the empty blackness ahead of me.

What are you waiting for? Mom's voice asked acerbically, in my mind.

"Nothing," I said, into the night. I didn't have a good reason to delay. With a deep breath, I stepped into the deep, dark woods, hunting faeries.

I ducked under the chain and waved my flashlight around, hoping to see the place from Faeryn's vision. At my best guess, though, I had found a parking lot.

"Hello?" I called.

I tried again on the other side of the field. "Hello?"

Nothing. No signs of life at all.

Beyond this field was another one, larger still. Just how many people came to this gathering of the fair folk every summer? Surely there couldn't be this many intermagicals living among the humans, could there? Enough to need two big parking lots like this? I wandered on, hoping I was going the right way, and paused at a fork in the path. In the darkness, the thin beam of light from my flashlight didn't show me anything useful. I flicked it off in frustration. Better just to let my eyes adjust to the night.

In the sudden blackness, the first thing I saw were the stars. Bright and intense, they cut through the scattered clouds like pinpricks in the velvet sky. As I looked up at the night sky, the clouds shifted and the light of the moon shone through. A shaft of cool white moonbeam lit the left-hand path, invitingly.

"Well, if that's not a sign, I'm not a faerie," I joked to myself, smiling wryly. I was equally as convinced by the moonlight as I was that I was really a half-faerie. Not very much at all, really. The further I got from Faeryn's glittering city, the less real it all seemed, and the more like something I might have made up, as if the cave had toxic gas bubbles that had made me hallucinate, or something. That seemed more likely than my having actually met real, live faeries, although how I could rationally explain the magic storm I had just driven through, I wasn't sure. But, there was no point arguing with myself, and nothing better to do than to go onward, I thought, resolutely. So, I plunged down that dark left-hand path, and hoped that my 'sign' would lead me right.

It did. Around the corner sat an empty booth with a sign reading 'Tickets' next to a wide gate guarded by a long toothed, rusty metal dragon.

Now, I thought with relief, I must be inside the fair. Narrowing pathways split and curved in two different directions, winding deeper inside. I chose one, and wandered slowly, looking left and right at the curious, dark alcoves and empty shops hung with the same type of old painted signs that I had seen in the images in Faeryn's spring. She had told me that the fair would be full of the faeries escaping the city. I expected this place to be noisy and crowded with the fae, but it was as silent as the city had been. There was absolutely no one here.

I wandered down the twisting narrow corridors and over a sweetly arching bridge with sunbeam spokes. A short, round stage at the center of a clearing caught my eye in another beam of moonlight. Following the moonbeam hadn't led me astray the first time. I climbed up the steps and took center stage. My bundled little body felt warm and somewhat inelegant, as I looked out over the empty audience.

"Hello," I tried again. It was exactly as effective as it had been before. In the moonlight, though, up on stage like a performer, I felt like maybe I should go on.

"Hi, um, my name's Fiona," I started, grateful yet again, for this simple yet powerful truth about myself. What else should I say? I decided to try honesty. "I want to help," I said, my arms outstretched, "I'm an..." I reached for the unfamiliar term, "an intermagical." The new word felt awkward and unfamiliar in my mouth.

"A big one, I guess. Um, a lot?" I trailed off lamely. I wasn't ready to use the words "powerful" or "nearly perfect" to describe myself, like Faeryn and Arlee had. Silence, except for the rustling of the circle of trees. Reminded of the two faerie women, I tried another tactic.

"Faeryn sent me," I said, resolutely, "from the city. She says she thinks I might be able to do something."

Blink.

A single mote of light appeared in front of me, halfway across the empty space.

Blink, blink.

Two more tiny lights winked on, drawing my eye in the darkness. They looked like lightning bugs, I thought, wonderingly, as I watched the glowing points appear out of thin air. I whirled, feeling a change in the darkness beside me. The stage was perfectly empty, until the oldest fae woman I had ever seen stepped into view, just a few feet away from me, as though she had been hiding behind an invisible tree.

"Is that right, child? Faeryn sent you? Well, what took you so long to say so?"

The wizened old woman's appearance had been the signal, and tiny faeries began to appear from everywhere. After the tiny ones, little faeries, like the one I had played cards with, blinked into existence. Then, larger and larger still. Knee high faeries and waist high. A scattered few standing nearly chest high. Within a few moments, the empty moonlit glade was full to bursting with the fae. Their faint glow lit the night so that I could see each curious, hopeful, upturned face.

"Faeryn sent you?" the ancient woman prompted, again.

I turned back to her, wrenching my eyes away from the fascinating tableau spread before me. "Uh huh," I agreed, "She said that, because of how I'm a," I braced myself and spit it out, "near-perfect faerie intermagical, she thought that there might be something I could do." The woman stared at me, eyes wide and mouth open. "You know," I went on, trying to explain, "Uh, because of the spring? Um, and the pump? I don't know what I'm supposed to do about it, but..." I trailed off and finished awkwardly, "I'd like to try to help if I can?"

"I see. Well, in that case," she said, smiling widely and gesturing for me to follow, "I think you'd better come with me." I followed her to a collection of open-faced buildings that formed a sort of courtyard, lit with hanging lamps that illuminated warm natural wood and glowed in colorful stained glass windows. She turned to address me, smiling kindly. "It's far too late to do anything useful this evening. Eat, rest, enjoy the moonlit night." She patted my hand. "We will speak of all of this tomorrow, in the light."

With that, she was gone, disappearing into the dark of the night. All around me were tiny floating creatures, lighting up the night with their faint opalescent glow that mixed with the warm light of the lanterns to form a shifting, hypnotizing sea of color. It made me a little dizzy. A tap on my shoulder surprised me and made me jump, lost as I had been in the shifting lights of the fae.

Chapter 23

"A nearly perfect faerie intermagical, hmm?" said a resonant voice from behind me. I turned to see a narrow older man, who tipped his tall, crooked cap to me. The hat and the long, knobbly nose that hooked over his wispy white beard made him look like a storybook wizard.

"I guess," I said, with a little shrug, "at least, that's what Faeryn told me. Just er-" I searched my over-tired memory, "wow, this morning, I guess. Did all of that really happen just today?"

The old man gave me a kindly smile. "It sounds like you've had a long day of it. Would you sit and rest with me for a while?"

I nodded, and he led me to a wide bench covered with deep cushions. I sank into them gratefully. The colors and patterns of the pillows reminded me of the pretty dress I had been wearing at the Fair Isle. The pattern's vining flowers curved and its leaves twisted, repeating organically across the cotton cloth. I loved the way it looked. If I saw these pillows in a store, I would definitely peer curiously at the price tag.

How much of this is fae illusion, I wondered, snuggling comfortably into the cozy nook, and how much is reality? Was I actually sitting on a cold, damp rock, or leaned up against a tree in the woods? I consulted my own senses and logic and decided that the bench, at least, was physically here. The cushion, too, I thought, although the softness might be somewhat exaggerated, as well as the charmingly eclectic decoration on every surface. The wizened gentleman settled into an elaborately carved tall backed chair and looked thoughtful and wise.

"Why is everybody so excited about a 'perfect intermagical'?" I asked him, "What does that even mean, anyway?"

He chuckled warmly and steepled his fingers together. "If I knew the ins and outs of that, well, I would know more than I do. More than anyone does, maybe." I frowned. That didn't seem like an answer that was going anywhere productive. But with a twinkle in his wrinkled old eye, he went on.

"But, I've lived amongst the fae lo these many years, so perhaps I know a few things that you might like to hear."

"Amongst the fae? Aren't you-" I waved my hands in questioning circles.

He laughed again, a friendly warm sound. "Not a faerie. Not like these folk," he answered, shaking his head, "I was raised as a human. Found my way to the magic in my own time and of my own accord. Seeking, you know. I helped build this place, actually," he said, and gestured around, encompassing our cozy alcove and the rest of the fairground around us, "when I was younger."

"Really? So you're an intermagical too?" I asked, interested.

"Aye," he said, and then smiled, "I mean, Yes. Yes, I am. I've been around the fae so much lately I'm starting to sound like them." He extended a gnarled, spotted hand to me. "Alaric Schmitt, at your service." I shook the proffered hand, feeling the gentle tingle of magic between us. He grabbed his hand back quickly, shaking it as though he had been shocked. "You really are quite a powerful intermagical. How about that?"

I shrugged. "I guess so. I'm still getting used to the idea, honestly. If it's even true. Wouldn't I have noticed if I was particularly magical, this whole time?"

He shook his head, kindly. "You mean to say that you never noticed anything? Never felt strange or different? Like you were something apart from everybody else? Like they had an," he paused, and laid a bony finger along his long, hooked nose," instruction manual for life that no one ever gave you?"

I stared at him, mouth ajar. "Well, now that you mention it…" I said, wonderingly.

"You wouldn't be the first one," he said, "It's the nature of the hidden folk to be hidden."

"The hidden folk?" I asked, knowing basically what he meant but curious about this new phrase.

"Oh, Ask Nona about that one. She would know. You know, I wonder sometimes if she isn't old enough to have seen it happen, herself," he added, with a twinkle of his hooded eye, "Aye, the hidden folk will stay hidden. But that doesn't keep the intermagicals away."

"It doesn't? But how can they know," I asked, gesturing at my surroundings, at the hundred or so beautiful creatures that flitted and glided through the busy little clearing, magic evident in every mote and gleam, "if they don't know?"

"Oh, they *know*, they just don't know," he said, enigmatically, "Why do you think people flock here every year?"

I shrugged, "I don't know."

"They come for the magic, of course. They come to dance and revel with their kin, the fae. They come because, for some reason that they can't explain, it feels like family. It feels like home."

"Oh," I said, beginning to understand. That sounded like how I had felt at the River House, that night in the valley, and again, at the Fair Isle.

"They might not see very much, depending on how much magic they've got. Or," he smiled at me again, "they might be like you, and see it all too clearly."

"What about you?" I asked, wondering if the world around us looked significantly different to Alaric's world-worn eyes.

"Oh, I've got a fair bit," Alaric said, humbly, "Like I said, I helped build this place. Tapped into my creative side too, Wasn't all just manly tree clearing. But," his gaze spread out over the open space around us, and then focused back on me, "the changes that I will make to this world, they've mostly all been made at this point, I'd wager. Young folk like yourself, though, you have limitless potential. Overflowing with youth," his smile widened, becoming a touch maniacal, "and power."

"Power," I echoed, "People keep saying that. But, what is this power? How am I supposed to use it?"

"Interact with the world as a human," he said, simply, "and change it. Humans and intermagicals, unlike pure fae, can truly change the world, for everyone, not just themselves, and change it for good. Permanently, I mean."

"You mean because humans can, um, build a wall, and then the wall stays built?" I asked, remembering Faeryn's example, "Do the faeries need a lot of walls built?" I eyed the wooden framework surrounding us.

"Sometimes," he laughed, "but it's a bit more than that, isn't it? Humans can build a wall, or pave a road, or make a law, or write a book. Humans can change their physical world, and their society, both. They can advance. The fae," he smiled, apologetically, "the fae are wonderful, but their nature is largely static. Humans are constantly in flux."

"So, the fae want what the humans have got. Wouldn't that make a hundred percent human the most powerful?"

"It would, by that logic," he agreed, "But, we humans have our limitations, too. We have a tendency to be limited by the human way of thinking. The urge to keep to the status quo. So, while humans do have the ability to make big changes, generally they won't. They'll build a wall or a house or a church in the same place their great grandfather built it, and when it falls down, they'll build it again."

"I guess so," I shrugged, "maybe a hundred years ago, but we're in America, the land of progress. Things are exploding with change here all the time."

"Interesting you should mention that," he said with a grin, and continued, "Quite the fascinating side effect of these first several generations of intentional intermagicals, isn't it?"

"Huh?"

"All these changes. Think about it. The unprecedented technological advancements of the past few hundred years, around the world, but here in America especially. Humanity, spiraling rapidly upward and upward, toward the stars." He raised his hands, gesturing to the sparkling night sky above us. "That's the product of powerful intermagicals at work."

"It is?"

"It is," he said, nodding deeply, "When you take that human ability to create and destroy this world and mix it with enough intrinsic magic to make someone see things differently, a powerful catalyst for change is born. A person with the ability to look out at the world and experience its magic and wonder for themselves, and to carve their own personal path into the real, tangible substance of reality. One that hasn't ever been imagined before." He gestured enthusiastically, for emphasis. "The union of a uniquely human ability to create change and the inspiration of the fae. The impulse to be divergent."

"Divergent," I echoed him again, "You mean like, neurodivergent? Autistic, stuff like that?"

"Funny you should say that," he answered, "You're not wrong, though. It's true that it's the unusuals that carry the magic inside of them. The odd ones. The divergents, as I said. And, humans do love to pathologize the fae and give our uniqueness interesting names like autism and bipolar disorder. Perhaps even," he glanced at two pretty young men kissing in a dark corner, "homosexuality?"

I watched the eerily beautiful couple for a moment, then looked away, trying not to stare. "Alaric, um, how many intermagical people are there? Because if you're saying what it sounds like you're saying…"

"Oh, it's impossible to say, at this point. We've mostly gathered in the cities, though, along the coasts. There might be more of us in the big cities than there are pure humans, anymore." He shrugged nonchalantly as he turned my entire world view upside down.

There were more intermagicals living in the city than regular humans? I had figured there must be quite a few, but this was on an entirely different scale than I had imagined.

"And," Alaric continued, absorbed in his own telling, "most of them will never know. Can never know. Who would tell them? But, they'll be drawn to congregate in the cities with others of their kind, or to spend their time on pursuits of magical interest, in one way or another. And, of course many are drawn to places like this. Gatherings where we can dance and revel with the fair folk, and experience the magic, to whatever extent that we're able." He chucked to himself. "You know, occasionally I'll see an intermagical that's dragged a pure human friend along to the fair with them. It's a funny thing to watch. They always have such a dull time. Just can't see what everyone else sees in it. And, of course, it's because they literally can't. Without any magic at all, they just won't see about half the fair, or even half the people standing right in front of them."

"So, the intermagicals come here because they're drawn to the magic. I guess I can understand that. But, what about the faeries and the other fae? Why do they come?"

"Oh, for the party," he answered with a grin, "There just aren't enough fully-magical or even mostly-magical folks to have a properly big festivity all by themselves, and the fae do love a good revel."

I laughed at that. The faeries swirling around in the clearing in front of us certainly seemed to be having a good time.

Chapter 24

"I just didn't realize there were quite so many of them. Of us," I corrected myself, "I guess intermagicals just look more like, uh, normal people than I would have thought. I mean, I can't figure out how I, out of anybody, would end up being a half-faerie." I gestured at my round little belly, pooched forward as I sat curled around myself on the bench.

He eyed me, understanding what I meant. "Faeries are typically small," he agreed, "but not necessarily slender. That's a myth based on little faerie girls. We of the fae mindset tend to think that the older one gets, the more beautiful," he said, turning a winning smile on a wrinkled old woman walking past us, "Haven't you ever heard the phrase lovely, wizened, and wise?" The old woman's returning smile lit the room, and, now that he mentioned it, she was strikingly beautiful in her aged visage. It was the same lady who had greeted me on the stage, who had promised that we would speak tomorrow.

"My mom spent a lot of time trying to make me thinner," I said, shoulders rounding defensively as I remembered my childhood of tasteless health food and disapproving comments. I had created some space from her rhetoric, while away at college, but my larger body still made me wince with shame when a stray reflection caught me by surprise.

"Humans do love to try to control things," he said kindly, "Even things they should not. Maybe even especially things they should not," he added, with a wry chuckle, "The fae will simply be. They understand the magic and the beauty of existing exactly as we are. Humans will forever find fault in things and try to change them, though. It's in their nature, I suppose, even if their efforts do sometimes leave them looking a little bit stretched and pinched."

"I guess so," I said, then poked at the round of my stomach under my sweater, "I feel like maybe I'm getting a little, er, stretched."

He laughed, richly. "I think not, my dear. As a powerful intermagical, you may simply need a sizable body to contain your larger than ordinary amount of magic. Some do, you know."

"Not all of them," I said, thinking of Faeryn, enviously, who had looked so slim and tiny in her pool. She looked like a proper faerie, unlike me. I wrinkled my nose, distastefully. Why was I even thinking that? Those old insecurities were rearing their ugly heads again. But, I realized, it wasn't just my mom's voice in my head this time. Hadn't somebody said…

I thought back to the night at the River House, when I had first learned about the fae, and remembered. It had been that woman, that Lady Velia. She had said that I didn't look anything like a faerie, and then speculated that I might be a dwarf or something. That thought had been niggling at the back of my mind ever since then, when she had planted that seed of doubt. Could someone who looked like me truly be a faerie?

"Not all of them," Alaric agreed, after a thoughtful pause, drawing my attention back to our conversation. "Fae come in all different shapes and sizes. Each individual is, of course, unique. Now, Faeryn, our powerful intermagical princess, who lives up north in the faerie city," he said, with a look of pride in his wise, aged eyes, "her body is quite a bit smaller than the average human. The water that flows over her just washes away nearly every morsel of food that she can manage to keep down. How much stronger she might be, if she were able to grow to her proper size, like you are doing." He gazed at me, speculatively. "I wouldn't be surprised if your body became larger yet, as you continue to grow into your full power."

Larger! My first reaction was to feel horrified on my mom's behalf, but as the kindly fae man looked at me with his level, accepting gaze, I pushed through the discomfort and really tried to see myself as he saw me. It helped. "Growing into my full power, huh?" I asked, the idea making me a little nervous.

He smiled, and nodded, stretching and standing slowly. "You look hungry," he observed. I looked where he indicated, at the large, well stocked banquet table across the courtyard from where we sat. When I turned back, the place where my companion sat was empty. He had faded away into the crowd and the darkness of the night.

He had been right, though. I was, in fact, very hungry, and as I stood up, my vision blurred and my knees wobbled, causing me to lurch into the path of a pair of twirling faeries who leapt gracefully out of the way. I caught my balance and sidestepped another waist high fae, doing my best to stay out of everyone's way. The dancers seemed to be moving to the music of the swaying trees in the breeze, and as I turned and glided in between them, I realized that I was dancing, too, and that by moving through their dance, I had become part of it, like a twig in the river, bobbing along with the flow of the stream.

Faeries, small and smaller, flitted around the banquet table, some dancers lighting on top of it as we drifted nearby. I stepped out of the flow of the dance and admired the heavily ornamented buffet. The centerpiece was fantastically elaborate, with cascading sprays of flowers, and blooms of colorful confections that I assumed must be edible, but didn't look like any food I recognized. And why would I expect to recognize anything at a faerie banquet, I asked myself, marveling at the wide selection. I wondered what, if anything, on this table, was actually going to taste like food, or fill my grumbling stomach. Well, who better to ask than a faerie?

I leaned down and got the attention of one medium-sized grazer. Her dark, curly head was level with mine as she perched daintily on the centerpiece, putting us effectively eye to eye. Smaller faeries hovered around us, fluttering like butterflies. "Excuse me, but, um, what do faeries like to eat?"

She tittered, a musical little sound. "Oh, we eat any number of things." Leaning down, she selected a pretty yellow flower and nibbled a petal delicately. "We love to eat flowers, naturally. Elderflower, certainly. And honeysuckle."

Other little faeries gathered around, blocking the lantern light but illuminating the table with their gentle ethereal glow. They chimed in with answers, their tiny ringing voices like pure silver bells, "Dandelion!" "Clover!" "Pansies!" "Chrysanthemum!"

The curly haired faerie gave them a withering look. "Ahem," she said, stamping her tiny foot bringing my attention back to her, "although I understand intermagicals like yourself often prize strawberries and artichokes, being both a flower and a human food."

"Some berries would be great, yeah," I said, and took the curious confection she indicated. It looked like a delicacy made by a master chocolatier with something to prove. I bit into it, not knowing what to expect. "Strawberry!" I exclaimed, tasting the pure, sweet flavor of the fruit.

"Mushrooms, as well," said my new little friend, presenting me with a charming spray of caps along a mossy log.

"I just…?"

She nodded, so I plucked one off, and bit it. The rich, earthy umami filled my mouth, fresh and perfectly crisp. It tasted like the forest. Next, I was shown a decorative soup pot with a lid like a toadstool that was filled with a warming vegetable broth, and beside that, a pitcher of sweet, fresh cream. By now, a crowd of small faeries had gathered around to watch me eat. They pointed out more faerie delicacies for me to try, and, in their high-pitched overlapping voices, continued to describe the eating habits of the fae.

"And of course, there are the Water Spirits that eat mostly shrimp and fish," said one.

"There's a certain nomadic type of fae that live up in the highest mountains who use the entire yak for everything they eat, drink, and wear," added another.

"And we Ground Fae prefer to dine on bugs and grubs," said a little one, landing on my shoulder. She leaned in, conspiratorially. "Have you ever heard of a human food called a 'gummy worm'?"

I assured her that I had, and that I even might have eaten one or two. Next time I came here, I promised that I would stop at a gas station and bring her a whole pack. She flew around my head in several brilliantly bright circles of delight, at that.

"Most fae have a traditional diet," said the curly headed faerie, "But there is tradition, and then there is what is done." She raised an eyebrow at the little fae who had requested the gummy worms. "These days, fae folk, especially the intermagicals, eat whatever appeals to them. Though," she cautioned, looking extraordinarily serious for one so small, "there are things it is wiser not to eat."

"Oh?" I questioned, curious.

"Eating things that are complex enough to have their own intention unsettles the digestion, we find. Especially over time," she said. At my look of confusion, she continued, listing, "Octopuses, elephants, dolphins, pigs, cats-" she looked meaningfully up at me through her tiny lashes, "Humans." Behind her, the ancient fae woman appeared once again. When she started to speak, all of the overlapping voices fell silent out of respect.

"Yes, it is true that most of the fae do not choose to consume human flesh," she agreed, reassuringly, I thought. Some of these little smiling faeries had wickedly sharp-looking teeth. "Although certain magical creatures do find the tradition and the cultural significance of eating humans to be important enough to their identity that they carry on, despite the ill effects. The stomach upset does tend to twist them into something quite ugly, to my eyes, though, after a few centuries. But, we all know that arguing with a devotee about the value of their tradition and their old ways isn't ever particularly effective, so we typically don't bother." She smiled at me. "Intermagicals like you can eat whatever they like, among the human foods and the fae foods alike. Although, you'll find that without human food your human body will weaken and tire, in time."

"Speaking of being tired…" I said, wistfully. The weight of the good food in my stomach and the lateness of the hour had me longing for the chance to lie down. She led me to a sleeping place, beautifully appointed, and deliciously soft and comfortable. Just the kind of bed I would have expected, from the faeries.

"Sleep now," she said, touching my forehead gently, "Tomorrow, we will talk."

Part 6 - The Nature of Magic

"What is happening? I felt her near me, growing closer and closer. And now, she draws farther away again. How can this be?" The tiny woman's eyes flashed daggers, her temper flaring. "You are my agent, Velia. Much as it irks me, I must rely on you to be my eyes and ears in this matter." The tiny woman stamped her foot imperiously. "Now, tell me! What has become of my daughter! Where has she gone? Where is she now?"

"I know nothing that I have not shared with you, my lady," Velia lied, coldly and levelly. Faeries like her Lady couldn't lie like that, but Velia was not a faerie, and though that knowledge stung for some reason she had never quite been able to pinpoint, the fact of it certainly came in handy sometimes. "But, half-magicals are unpredictable. They never do quite what you expect them to do, do they?" she added.

Certainly, Velia had been surprised that the girl had returned from Portal Land so soon, and had chosen to press so doggedly into the magical storm, through every obstacle that Velia's devious mind could think to throw at her. But, she had been truly shocked when the girl had driven off down the highway, past the valley and away from them.

Velia spun a jewel hung in the window, sending sparks of sunlight whirling hypnotically around the plant-filled room. "Sometimes they just change their mind and do the unexpected. It's the human in them, I suppose."

Chapter 25

The bright shafts of morning sunlight stung my eyes and I blinked sleepily. "Whuh?" I said, making an interrogative noise as the tiny creature who had awoken me buzzed in front of my nose. The little faerie was wearing an iridescent pouf of a dress that complimented the sheen of her ever-moving wings.

"Good morrow!" she tweeted before darting out of sight.

I let my eyes drift closed again. The nest of pillows was comfortable and warm, and I wasn't at all sure that I was ready to wake up yet, after all. Through the filter of my eyelids the morning sunlight glowed golden red and the birds in the trees twittered noisily. I twitched, as something many-legged tickled my arm. Giving the limb a quick shake, I opened my eyes again, squinting in the morning light. When my vision cleared, I realized that the old woman from last night was standing above me.

She looked tall from my vantage on the ground, and her long, translucent white hair was gathered over one shoulder in a braid, with loose tendrils framing her round, deeply lined face with feathery wisps. With the morning sun behind her, it looked like she was glowing. When she caught my freshly opened eye, her face twisted into the deep lines of a broad, well-practiced smile.

"Good morning, child," she said, then indicated the tiny faerie, "This little one just let me know that you were awake." The tiny faerie lighted on the woman's shoulder and smiled cheerily at me, fluttering her wings prettily.

"My name is Anonaziata," continued the ancient woman, "I am the Elder of the Country Fae."

"Good morning Ano-," I tried, "...nzi, uh…"

"Anonaziata," she said, with a lilting cadence I wasn't at all sure that I could replicate before a cup of coffee. I took a deep breath to try again, but before I did, she added, kindly, "But many here simply call me Nona."

"Nona," I agreed, gratefully. The faerie who had woken me, no taller than a deck of cards, landed on my head and leaned to peer down at me.
I looked back up at her, through my lashes and we blinked at each other.

"What's your name?" I asked the lovely young lady perched on top of me.

"Oh? Her?" asked Anonaziata, turning her gaze to the tiny faerie who had stepped nearly onto my forehead, and was bent nearly in half, to get a closer look at me, "She doesn't have one, I wouldn't think. Little pixies like that don't have enough intention to hold on to a whole name all by themselves. Do you?"

The pixie grinned and shook her tiny head, sending a spray of pollen-like dust into my eyes. I sent a quick puff of air upward from my lips. My breath blew away the dust, but also the faerie, who launched herself off my face with a surprisingly powerful kick. She flew in a tight loop in front of my face, then darted off into the woods.

"Not enough intention?" I asked, confused, "I didn't realize that you needed to have anything to have a name."

"Oh certainly," said Nona calmly, "In order for someone to truly possess a name, they must be able to remember that name and respond to it, hour after hour, and day after day. It requires a certain amount of attention and dedication." I could already tell that she was going to be a good teacher. She turned to another similar sized faerie that was darting and cavorting around the little clearing. "Would you want to make that kind of commitment?"

The faerie shook her pretty head so vigorously that her wispy hair flew in front of her face, making a bright white blur. Suddenly she stopped, hanging still in midair. She looked me right in the eye and smiled mischievously. Then, in a bright flash of light, she was gone.

"What?" I exclaimed, bewildered, and shook my head, trying to clear it of the unreality of what I had just witnessed. "Um, Nona? What did she, er- How did she just…?" I gestured at the empty space in front of me.

Anonaziata smiled at my look of startlement. "There are many things for me to teach you, today. That can certainly be one of them." She reached down with one craggy hand to where I sat on the ground. The joints of her knuckles protruded between thin, bony fingers and her skin felt papery and dry like bark. Her soft, thick veins were like roots under her skin and they rolled under my fingers as we shifted together. I was surprised by the strength of her grip as she levered me up from the ground.

Anonaziata settled us into a stained-glass alcove that I had admired last night. She handed me a lumpy earthenware mug filled with a spicy-smelling yellow drink that gently warmed my hands as I sipped the creamy ginger tonic. As I drank I felt its warmth spread from the crown of my head down to the tips of my toes. I woke up slowly, watching the faeries and other small fae folk ambling across the clearing, going about their business on this sunny spring morning.

In a flash of light, a tiny faerie appeared, flew a few feet and blinked away again. I blinked, too, startled, again, by this evidence of real magic right in front of my eyes. I turned to the old woman, face full of questions. She smiled back at me, and with a decisive little nod, began her lesson.

"So," she said, and sipped her warm drink slowly, "let us discuss the Nature of Magic." I took a sip as well, and nodded, eyes wide over my steaming mug. "Magic is, as I'm sure we can agree, the singular animating and intentional force of everything in our universe," she said, as though stating the obvious.

"It is?" I asked, eyes opening even wider, positive that this 'fact' had never been mentioned in even the most esoteric of my liberal studies courses in college.

Anonaziata looked over her mug at me, assessing. "Hmm, well. Let us take a step back, then. You called yourself an intermagical, so I assumed that you would have a certain level of understanding. You mentioned that Faeryn thought you might be able to help?" I nodded in agreement. "Well, my own Melodie Cristalline foretold your coming as well. But, of course, it is no surprise that an assumption about a prophecy would be incorrect. That is the nature of such predictions, isn't it?" She laughed. "So, with that, let me release all my preconceived notions about you." She tossed her head as though to shake those thoughts off, and smiled broadly at me. "Please, tell me about yourself, and how exactly it is that you came to find yourself here."

She asked, so I told her. I told her everything. At least, everything that had happened since I had nearly crashed my car into a tree, only four short days ago. I counted the days out twice on my fingers, just to be sure. I told her about the letter in the faerie book that had gotten ruined, and how I'd met that funny old man at the library. About finding the River House, and what Godrin had told me about the fae, there next to the fire. I told her about running lost, naked through the woods, and being leered at by all those men, then being rescued by Brandon, my hero… And then, I told her about finding out that his father was the Deacon and how they were connected to the spring and the threat of the pump. Which, naturally, brought me back to Faeryn, and the matter of the spring.

"Godrin sent you to the city, then?" Anonaziata asked, when I paused to sip my drink, "I'd have thought he might have sent you to the faeries on the Hill. It would have been closer."

"No, although, now that you mention it, I think Godrin did mention something about some faeries and a hill. But, I guess I forgot to mention-" I told her about my decision to go to Portal Land, and about meeting the Gullah and finding the Fair Isle. About the trouble with the CCC, the truck full of Corpsos and their attack on the bar, later on that night. I told her about Isla and her serpents, and then about her flowers, and, finally, about what those brothers Eudo and Odo had told me about magic. "And that's it," I said. I paused to really think about it, then nodded. "Yep, I think that's everything."

"What an incredible journey you are on," she said, eyes shining, "To have come so far down this path in such a short time. From completely uninitiated humanity to the heart of faerieland in a matter of mere days. No wonder Melodie Cristalline urged me to teach you. There is so much that you do not know that you must know, for you to be able to reach your potential and step into your full power."

The recounting of my adventures reminded me of just how much I had been doing lately, and how little good sleep I had gotten. "Yeah, it's been an eventful few days," I said, sinking deeper into the soft pillows with an exhausted sigh.

Anonaziata nodded and smiled kindly at me, folding her gnarled hands in her lap. "Indeed, and your journey is not over yet. If you're ready, I think we will go ahead and start at the beginning."

"Please," I agreed.

Chapter 26

"As I was saying, we understand magic to be the animating and intentional force of everything in the universe."

"Okay," I said, nodding. I could accept that idea, for the sake of argument, even if I wasn't entirely sure what she meant by it.

"Humanity has named many of the natural elements and the laws that govern our reality, like force, gravity and magnetism." As Anonaziata talked, she traced illustrative circles in the air with her hands. "And there are many things that humanity has not yet named, things that exist within us and beyond the edges of our perception, such as the very spark of life itself. Let us consider this." As she spoke, an illusory galaxy appeared between us, spun by her hands, rotating slowly and hypnotically. "Imagine, for a moment, the incredible complexity within each living organism. The collaboration of the myriad tiny factories inside each of us, all working toward a single common goal. Existence. Life, itself." She continued, and the galaxy changed, morphing with her words into something new. "The immeasurably large cycles of the heavens are reflected in miniature in every tiny atom, making up each particle of elemental matter, fractal upon fractal spiraling outward. Is it reasonable to imagine, then, that our universe itself might be but a single atom? A single part of an unimaginably complex whole?" She threw her arms wide, expansively. "We can not begin to comprehend these things, and nor should we try! The known, the unknown. The knowable and the unknowable. All of this is the inherent magic of existence."

"Magic?" I echoed, unconvinced.

"You would not call that magic?" she asked, calmly, "What would you call it, then?"

"I don't know," I answered, honestly, "I guess I've never really thought about it."

She nodded, solemnly. "That is a bit broad to tackle as our first pass, perhaps. If it is too much to consider the infinity of the cosmos and the microcosmos, let us narrow our focus and consider only our own natural world. Would you say that it is inherently magic?"

"I think I see what you're getting at," I answered, remembering my conversation with the brothers at the Fair Isle, "Eudo said that part of being magic was seeing the magic in all things. Like when dandelions bloom in the spring, but," I shook my head, "nature is wonderful and all, but it's not magic. It's science, it's biology."

"Is it?" she asked, "What makes the flowers bloom, then?"

"They, uh," I thought back to science class, "the seed germinates, and grows leaves. Eventually it matures enough to flower, which gets pollinated to make more seeds that grow and make more plants," I said, feeling like I had done my teacher proud.

"Is that so?" asked Anonaziata, leaning forward, interested, "and why do you think they do that?"

"Because it's their life cycle."

"Why?"

"Uh, evolution, I guess. So that they can keep existing for another generation."

"Why?"

"What do you mean, why? Because they're alive."

"Yes, because they are alive. And why are they alive? Why do they do anything? Why not just behave like a rock and sit, inanimate forever, unmoving? Why, even, does a rock hold its shape and not disintegrate into cosmic dust?" She waved her hands about enthusiastically as she talked. "Why do things? Why are things?"

"I don't know," I answered again, "I guess they probably didn't choose to be."

"No, I can't imagine that they did choose to *be*. But, we can agree that they *are*, and that they *do*, can we not?"

"Okay, sure," I agreed hesitantly.

"Well, I would personally argue that it is because of each thing's innate, inherent magic that it is what it is, and does what it does."

"But-"

"And," she interrupted me with a single raised finger, "the uncovering and understanding of our world, what something is, and how it does what it does, that discovery process is what humans call science. The existence of the mysteries to be uncovered, that is what we, the fae, understand to be magic."

"The mysteries… What kind of mysteries?"

"Ah, an example. Well, some of the more useful and interesting mysteries of humanity are the discoveries surrounding the practice of medicine." The image in front of her became a bustling medical complex, like an ant farm full of white lab coats. "Why are the keys to curing human's illnesses and ailments hidden to the roots and barks of the earth? Why do chemical compounds have such remarkable effects on the human body? What more secrets will be uncovered as science continues to pick apart the spiraling building blocks of the very genetic code of humanity itself?" The stairs of the illusory hospital twined together, transforming into a double helix. "How were these complex systems created? How are they governed? Was it purely accidental good luck and happenstance? Perhaps, but it seems an unlikely possibility to me. Instead, let us consider it the innate, intentional magic of the universe. The interconnected force of every being and even everything in existence."

This had my head spinning, and I closed my eyes for a second, resting my forehead on my hands. "Okay," I agreed, "maybe."

"The other various branches of human science, such as physics, chemistry and mathematics," she continued. The air before us flashed with images of test tubes and complex equations. "Are all different schools of thought which are aligned in their ultimate mission. To discover the innate truths and practical applications of the natural world. Our natural, magical world." She was having fun, now, and the illusory image before us erupted with flashes like scenes from movies depicting the various impressive advances of humanity.

"Humans have achieved the miracle of flight after so many eons of imagining it, by harnessing the magic of air currents and propulsion, allowing man free access to the most remote corners of the globe." An old film clip of the Wright brothers transitioned into a sleek fighter jet before my eyes. "Consider too, humanity's ability to light the darkness. In only a few hundred years, the world has made such progress from the humble candle flame." A scene like Times Square billboards at New Years, as bright as a camera flashbulb, made me squint, even in the bright morning sunshine.

"These images," said Anonaziata, gesturing to the ever-changing scene she was generating before us, "like all art, are filtered by my own perception. This type of interpretation has its own intrinsic value, certainly, but," the image zoomed in on a surreal facsimile of an advertisement playing on a screen, "with technology, humans have harnessed the incredible ability to record and replay sights and sounds, for anyone, almost as though they were there."

This was starting to sound familiar again. Hadn't the Gullah said something similar, about his collection of magical artifacts, and the competitive power of cameras and computers? As Anonaziata continued describing humanity's various achievements, they did sound like something out of a fantasy story, like the description of a wondrous, special, and deeply magical place.

"And," she continued, "humanity has also made progress in its understanding of the interconnectedness of all things. The truths found at the edges of our perception, and at the core of our reality. What I would call mysticism."

"You mean like, religion?" I asked.

"Not as much like religion as you might think," she said, with a small smile, "Mysticism, unlike religion, is a profoundly personal experience. It is the logical, thoughtful and intentional pursuit of understanding the mysterious, miraculous nature of the world that we find ourselves in."

"Oh," I said, "That all sounds great and all, but," I eyed her skeptically, "that still seems like it would count as a religious experience, wouldn't it?"

She smiled kindly. "I can see that you are still unsure. Let me put it like this then. Each religious system has been developed by humans to explain and interpret the inherent magic of the universe." I nodded. That sounded right. "But, with this interpretation comes a certain amount of control on the part of the organizers, and a separation between the individual and a true, direct connection with the magic."

She shifted irritably and settled farther back into her seat. "Especially," she said, "when one's religion upholds a singular figurehead of a god and assigns all of the power and the magic of the universe entirely to Him." Her exasperated motion disturbed several listening faeries who had alighted on her chair back and the cushions surrounding her, who rose a few inches into the air before settling back down, listening raptly. "And," she continued, "since religious leaders are human, however influential or powerful they may be, they must always live in fear that their adherents will discover their true energetic potential, so they create rules that distance believers from their own power and magic."

"Huh," I said, "I never really thought about it that way."

"Control the individual to control society, and ultimately the world," she said, nodding solemnly, "Religions are one of humanity's most ingenious and problematic tendencies, as I have often said. They are such powerful forces of control. But, at what ultimate cosmic cost? How limiting religion has been to the growth of human potential!" She threw her hands up, and the tiny faeries fluttered back into the air at her motion. They circled once or twice before settling back down again. I looked at her quizzically, trying to make sense of what she was telling me. "But, humans do prize power above all else, and religion is such a spectacular conduit for power." The image between us coalesced into the shape of a glowing red cross that pulsed ominously like a heartbeat. "If you can convince someone else that you alone understand the truth behind the magic of the universe and that you can interpret it for them, why, there is almost nothing you can't convince them to believe, and, then, to do."

"Huh," I said, letting that last thought sink in. It was hard to be sure, without a religious upbringing to compare it to, but Anonaziata's words lined up with how I had felt the other night when Brandon had tried to get me to go to church with him. Like he and his father were trying to control my world and take my agency from me. Like they were trying to get me to give up my own personal power. "What do you mean by power, though?" I asked her, "Political power, or like, magical power?"

"Yes," she agreed, "Influence. The power to shape society, culture, and behavior. The ability to win hearts and change minds. Political magic, as you say."

"Uh, I didn't, I mean-"

"I know," she smiled at me, "but it is true. One of the three foundational pillars of human magic."

"Creation, Manifestation and Influence?" I recited, recalling my earlier lesson. The power of influence did seem like it would go hand in hand with politics. I remembered what Faeryn had said, about how I might actually be good at it, if I tried, and the thought gave me an involuntary little shiver.

"Yes," Anonaziata agreed, "Faeryn's teaching, surely?" At my nod, she smiled warmly. "That girl does have a mind for magical theory. The connections she makes, well…" She shook her head, wonderingly. "But, that's the mind of a nearly balanced intermagical for you."

Nearly balanced.

My whole body relaxed with a sigh of relief. That was a much easier term to live up to than 'Perfect' to describe what I had recently learned that I was. I mentally tucked the phrase in my pocket for the next time I needed to explain myself. My own intermagical mind was hard at work, too, going over what Anonaziata had said, and checking her logic.

Influential political power controlled along religious lines. Leaders exerting control over the people using religious ideology. People giving their personal power up to the church's governing bodies. Religious leaders were political figures, I knew that much. I happened to see a little of the spectacle around the election of the last Pope in Rome on TV and it had made an impression. But, something Anonaziata had said…

"Nona, what you said about power being lost, because of religion. Did you mean social power, or," I raised my eyebrows, "other power?"

"It is all power," she agreed.

"But how does it get lost?" I pressed.

"Because the truth that these believers are being sold by these religions is not their own truth to believe. They are devoting their real, earnest faith, and spending their life's energy, on an interpretation of someone else's interpretation. A shadow of the real magic of the universe. A reflection of a reflection. And like any copy of a copy of a copy, it eventually loses its integrity and cohesion." She illustrated by making illusory photocopies that fluttered down to the ground in front of us. "Human religions, especially the dominant ones of the day, are," she sighed, tiredly, "quite significantly removed from their initial source material, by many hundreds or even thousands of years. They have become extraordinarily," she paused, searching for the appropriate word, "distorted, wouldn't you agree?"

I remembered the TV evangelicals I had occasionally seen on late-night infomercials, who sold religion to desperate people searching for anything to save them. Those greasy shysters were happy to sell it to them, for only however many dollars, ninety-five. I was sure there wasn't much magic to be found in that interpretation. There were better churches, though, I knew. Churches with a real heart that wanted to do the right thing, who believed that they were doing what Jesus would have done. My grandma had taken me to a church like that several times, growing up. I'd even done their weeknight youth program for a while.

Going to that church was what had made me ask my mom that question about God, the one that had gotten me shut down with a swift, '*Well,* some *people believe that.*' That church had been pretty nice, actually. The people there had been kind and welcoming. They had even had a gay pastor speak once. But then I thought about the types of stories we had read there. Simple bible studies aimed at children. Lessons about life and morality, set in antiquity, interpreted into coloring book pages. Where were those lessons actually coming from?

The bible has been translated and retranslated into countless different versions over the centuries, I knew. It wouldn't surprise me at all if the titular King James of the King James Bible had at least as much influence over the lives of certain church-goers as the historical figure of Jesus, who hadn't, if I remembered right, ever even taken the opportunity to write his own thoughts down. And, if religious leaders in our modern era were taking it upon themselves to interpret those translations of translations into something relevant to modern times, well, they'd be the ones doing most of the influencing, wouldn't they?

Distorted, she had said. "Yeah, I guess I would," I agreed, "The religions I've seen close-up seem to be pretty far from where they started."

"Far from where they started," she repeated, smiling, "and where would you say that was?"

Seriously? These questions were overwhelming. This whole conversation had been, actually. I brought my hands up to my face, letting my forehead rest on my fingertips. The pressure on my temples and the way my hands shadowed my eyes from the light helped with my feeling of sensory overload.

"My dear, you look tired," the sweet older woman said, standing up and walking to stand behind me where I sat. She laid her long fingers on my tired shoulders and pressed firmly into them. My muscles ached painfully, then relaxed, at her touch. "Come, let's get up. All of these new thoughts and ideas tend to get all caught up and tangled when we sit stagnant like this. We'll take a walk and let them straighten themselves out."

Chapter 27

I stood up, shaking out my stiff limbs and rolling my neck, disturbing tiny faeries. I watched one disappear and appear again a few feet away, then, another one did it. The faeries giggled and blipped playfully from here to there, all around us. "How are they doing that?" I asked, remembering that Anonaziata had said she would tell me later.

"Hmm? Oh, the little ones, there? 'Flitting,' is the term I've heard Faeryn use, when the Queen does it. It's a very handy little bit of faerie magic."

"Flitting? When they-" I pantomimed a bubble popping with my hands, "And you said that the Queen can do it, too?"

"Yes, she can and does," Anonaziata agreed, "I've been told that the method is simply to close one's eyes and believe oneself to be elsewhere." She demonstrated, squinting and making her eyes into tiny wrinkled starbursts. "And, when you open them," she stretched her eyes open wide, "there you are."

I followed Anonaziata out of the clearing and onto a wooded path, just wide enough for the two of us to walk side by side. We ambled slowly as the dappled green sunshine filtered through the leaves. I was feeling better already, the movement helping me to digest the information that I had been given, my brain moving faster now that my body was warming up. As we walked, I watched the faeries flit along the path beside me. Anonaziata had told me how, why not try? I gave a subterranean shrug, then closed my eyes and wrinkled my face in concentration.

I'm… over there!

Unsurprisingly, nothing happened. "Well, that didn't work," I said, good-naturedly to Anonaziata.

"Oh, the flitting? Did you…?" she laughed, "Oh, no it wouldn't have. That is not magic for the likes of you, or for me, either. It is true faerie magic. Only purely magical faeries can blink themselves from place to place. Or, at least, we are certain that humans and part-humans can not," she smiled at me apologetically. "Faeries are not tied to the physical reality of the Earth in the way that humans are. We might be able to do it, technically, but the significant part of us that is human would, of course, be left," she shrugged, and looked over her left shoulder, "behind."

"Oh," I said, giving an involuntary little shiver, "That sounds painful."

"Quite," she agreed, with a grim smile, "I've never heard a sound quite like the one that Queen Vivienne made when she completed the ritual divesting her from her humanity. All three and a half percent of it. Not a decision she took lightly. No, not at all."

I wondered about that for a horrified moment. What parts had been left behind? And then, remembering what I had just attempted, I felt a tingle run down my spine. "Could I actually have-" I started to ask, in horrified curiosity.

"Oh, no, child. You could not. You are far too human for your body to allow you to do that. Even I, with perhaps a quarter-tie to humanity at the most, would not have the strength to override my body's instincts. Just as you can not choose to die simply by holding your breath. Humanity's sense of self-preservation will hold out."

"Oh," I said. That made sense. I continued to watch the pretty little faerie girls flit all around us. And boys I noted to myself, as I looked more closely and realized that the fluttering poufs of iridescent fabric were dressing a spectrum of faeries of all different gender presentations. "How far can they go?" I asked Anonaziata.

"As far as they can focus," she replied, enigmatically.

I caught the eye of a little boy with tight black curls hovering near my shoulder. His wings were awkwardly large, as though he hadn't quite grown into them, and they shimmered golden in the sun. He smiled a bright, charming smile at me and tucked a little white field daisy into my hair.

"How far can you go?" I asked the little faerie boy. He screwed up his tiny face in concentration and wiggled his tiny round nose.
A bright flash and he was gone. I turned my head, looking all around for him. Out of the corner of my eye, I noticed the daisy, still perfectly placed, which surprised me. Whenever I tried to tuck flowers in my hair, they always fell out right away. It seemed like it could almost be magic. I exhaled in a silent chuckle. Right, because it was magic.

Another flash lit the dappled shadows about ten yards in front of us and a tiny voice shouted back at us. "This far!"

I laughed, and so did Anonaziata. The little boy made charming loops and spins as he zoomed back to us, pleased with his obvious success. Anonaziata took my arm and we walked on.

"The Queen can move herself several miles. Further, if she takes the time to meditate and focus, or when her destination is well-known to her," Anonaziata explained, smiling and nodding her approval to the curly-haired boy, "It's all a matter of focus. Intention. Will." I nodded, feeling like I almost understood what she meant. The little faeries dropped away as we walked farther from the fairgrounds.

Finally, we reached the top of a hill where Anonaziata pointed out a patch of early wild strawberries growing between the trees, and we stopped to rest and enjoy the sweet fruit in the mid-morning sun. Beside me, Anonaziata pointed a berry-juice-stained finger at the clear blue sky. From the high vantage point, I could see miles of wide grassy fields, and the rolling green hills beyond them. After a moment, I realized what she was pointing at. It was a pinprick of light that I hadn't immediately noticed in the bright morning sunlight.

"Nona, what is that thing?" I asked, shading my eyes to peer at the shining object hurtling toward us. It was growing larger and brighter by the second, and I scrambled to my feet. My heart started to pound in my chest as I looked up at the rapidly expanding point of fire in the sky. "What is that thing?" I asked, leaning into the small old woman nervously. I considered turning and running back into the woods, the way we had come, but Anonaziata placed her hand on my arm, stilling me. I stood by her side, watching as the great glowing ball grew, filling the noon-day sky with bright white light.

The birds continued twittering in the trees, and this, coupled with the calm presence of the woman beside me, made me realize that what I was seeing must be an illusion. Even so, I jumped at the sonic boom made by the illusory meteor, and again when it struck the ground before us, and the sensation of impact knocked me back on my heels.

Anonaziata took my hand, steadying me as a great wave of fire encompassed us, the illusion of heat pricking my skin but not burning me. As we watched, great storm clouds gathered out of the clear blue sky and opened, rain pouring down on the crater made by the incredible impact we had just witnessed. Where the rain hit the space rock, it hissed, creating a cloud of steam above the ruined field, and as the sun returned from behind the clouds, the scene before us lit with the spectral glow of a rainbow in the mist. Admiring the beauty of the light refracting in an otherworldly rainbow halo before us, I was thoroughly impressed by the creativity of the scene Anonaziata had constructed for me and told her so.

She smiled. "Do you have any further thoughts or insights about where religious ideas might have originated from?"

"From, uh, the awesome power of nature?" I guessed, looking out at the scene in front of us

"Yes, child. The origins of all human religious experience are found in the awesome and intrinsically magical power of the natural world where humanity resides. From the divinity of our world, and the divinity within us." Anonaziata leaned forward, off the hill and with a deep breath, she blew away the scene below us. It disintegrated, and she turned her back on it, clearly finished with the exercise. "All religions take their deepest inspiration from the same essential forces of the world and the universe. They take that elemental magic and make their own interpretation, and then they do their best, or their worst, to pass that inspiration along to others." She sighed, sadly. "But when you try to learn by copying from someone else's homework, you will find you have missed much of the important teachings of the lesson, won't you?"

"From their homework?" I repeated, confused. What would a faerie know about copying homework?

"Or so my Melodie Cristalline tells me," Anonaziata clarified, "My daughter takes a particular interest in the ways and practices of humans, being what she is." At my look of confusion, she clarified. "She is like you, nearly half-human and half-faerie, but she is unable to live amongst her human kin, due to her," she waved a hand in small circles, "idiosyncrasies."

"Huh, okay," I said, returning to the lesson at hand, "So, you're saying that humans created religion after experiencing huge natural disasters? I don't-"

"Not disasters, dear. Wonder. Experiencing natural wonder." She turned back toward the field and gestured at the tableau spread out before us, encompassing the wide, green field, restored after the fantastically disastrous illusory scene that had just played out, and the blue sky above, with one single fluffy cloud that moved swiftly on the spring breeze. The cloud passed in front of the sun, sending the valley into shadow, until a single sunbeam cut through it, creating a beam of pure yellow light that touched the ground like a gentle ethereal finger.

"Oh," I breathed, "I see."

She waved and the cloud disappeared, replaced by a clear blue sky. Another illusion! This time she had really managed to trick me, and that fact bothered me. Anonaziata must have seen the cloudy expression cross my face. "I am sorry, my dear. I mean only to illustrate my point. I certainly don't mean to stand between you and your true personal experience of the world and its magic. But," she chucked quietly, "it is quite frustrating to be shown falsities and be told that they are true natural magic, isn't it?" I nodded in agreement. It was incredibly frustrating.

She smiled. "I can not call up a real golden sunbeam on cue, only an illusory one." She pointed a knobbled finger at two birds dipping and weaving together in the warm breeze. "But that, there, is pure, natural beauty. I promise." I watched the two birds floating and weaving together. I didn't know much about birds, but it looked to me like they were having a lot of fun, spinning, dipping, and diving like that.

Anonaziata moved to stand behind me and placed a hand on my shoulder. We watched the birds together for a long moment before she spoke. "What is the character of their magic, do you think? What can they teach us about the world?"

"Joy," I answered, "Freedom."

"Yes," she replied, "Why?"

I didn't think, just let the words flow out of me. "They just are," I said, watching them dance, "So joyful and free. So completely themselves. Seeing them like that makes me feel happy. So, I guess it perpetuates itself, huh? Joy making more joy?"

"Has anyone ever told you that birds represent happiness? Or freedom?"

"Well, yeah, I guess so. I mean, the bald eagle is the official bird of the Land of the Free for a reason, right?"

"I suppose so," she agreed, "And how meaningful has that been to you, having the American eagle as an icon of your freedom? Do you think of it often?"

"Um, I don't think I've ever thought about it before at all, actually," I answered honestly. "It's just something that people say."

"Until now, when you personally experienced it," she said, nodding, "And, what did you feel today?"

"I felt-" I sank back into my body, trying to remember the experience of watching the birds play. "I felt warm and happy. Relaxed. Like my heart was light, like it was dancing with them on the breeze." I paused, considering. "I felt really, really good."

"The power of personal experience which is lost by filtering through another's interpretation."

"Yeah," I agreed, "I guess personal experience gives it a whole different scale of," I hesitated, "of power."

We walked back along the winding forest path, next to fluttering butterflies and bumbling bees, over burbling brooks and through dappled glades. The farther we walked the more I felt I was beginning to understand. Magic is everywhere and in everything. It is all around me.

I considered this as I walked, and found that I was smiling from ear to ear, looking at all the wonderful, natural things surrounding me. It reminded me of a make-believe game that I hadn't thought about since I was a kid, and I began to play. I pretended I was an adventurer exploring a new, magical world filled with curiosities and wonders, unlike my boring, mundane home.

There was a bug with bright orange stripes. What a fascinating specimen! And look at that unusual yellow flower, peeking out at me from behind a tree. I've never seen a flower quite like that in boring old Mundania, where I used to live, where nothing is magic or special at all, I said to myself, pretending.

In Mundania, if I ate that flower…

Well, in Mundania nobody eats flowers, but here in this world, maybe it cures diseases or is an ingredient in a powerful potion, or…

I turned to Anonaziata. "Nona, what is that flower? Does it do anything special, do you know?"

"Oh, these little trumpets? Taste!" She pulled out a long stamen and ran it across my lips.

"Sweet! Like honey," I said, wonderingly.

"Yes," she agreed, "it's native Oregon honeysuckle. Early this season." We walked on.

Now that I had expressed interest, she pointed out other plants and fungi as we passed them. She told me about their medicinal properties as well as their flavors and culinary preparations, sharing the particulars of the small, but nonetheless incredible, natural magic all around us. As we grew closer to the fair, the tiny faeries rejoined us in groups of twos and threes. Eventually, the air was so thick with them that it was hard to see through the flurry of glimmering wings.

"They're excited that you're here," Anonaziata said, as the curly-haired boy from earlier buzzed up to me.

He had a large bouquet of white field daisies which he held out to me with a charming smile. I thanked him and he flushed a dark pink before darting off in a streak of bright light. I held up the daisies and examined them. The bouquet was round and perfectly even, with each stem bent to meet at the center in an improbably neat little cluster, each petal straight, and pure, snowy white. Too perfect, I concluded. It had to be an illusion.

"Nona? How can I tell if something is real or if it's an illusion?" I had been thinking about this question quite a bit, ever since I had met Faeryn, and even before that, at the Fair Isle.

"Just like you did just now," she said, gesturing to the daisies.

"What do you mean? How did you-"

"I saw you look at them, study them. Sense them. Judge them. This is the only way. To find truth and defeat illusion, like with all lies, you must rely on your own senses, and your logical intuition to tell you whether you should believe, or whether you should be skeptical."

"Just look?"

"Just look, and when you look, see," she answered, "See the magic that is there. See the reality of what is in front of you. Use your own logical mind to interpret your senses, and come to your conclusions for yourself. This is the way to truly experience the logically mystical reality of the world beneath your feet." She handed the bouquet back to me. "Or, at your fingertips."

In my hand were five bedraggled little daisies. Their stems were bent and crooked, drooping weakly from the warmth of long handling. One battered head, petals askew and mostly missing, looked almost ready to fall off entirely. The actual bouquet wasn't perfect like the illusion had been, but it was real, and I loved the little fae boy for the tender honest truth of the real bouquet, and for the sweet, thoughtful intention that had crafted the other.

Ahead of us, birds squawked and fluttered, taking to the air as something crashed toward us through the underbrush, snapping tree limbs clumsily as they cut a direct path in our direction, regardless of the well-trodden path.

"Mama! Mama!" cried a child's voice, in a sweet, high soprano.

"Melodie!" Anonaziata cried, rushing forward with outstretched arms toward a girl who was beating her way toward us with a large, knobbled walking stick, "Melodie Cristalline, what are you doing out here in the woods?"

The girl looked young, no older than 8 or 9, with straight brown hair framing a thin, childlike face. "Mama! You have to come, now. We need to get underground right away," she called.

I rushed after Anonaziata, picking up the child's sense of urgency. As I got closer, I saw that her eyes were strange. They were milky and unfocused, and I wondered whether she was able to see at all.

"They're coming, Mama!" The girl's face panned side to side, her unusual eyes never quite orienting on me. "They're coming for Fiona."

Chapter 28

"For me? What? Why would they-" I said, tripping over my words and the uneven rocks of the path as we traveled quickly through the forest. I trailed behind, following the two fae women underneath, behind and between, and then down a long, dark hallway before ending up in a small underground room with smooth earthen walls, where bunches of onions and carrots hung from low wooden beams and dark oak barrels sat in dim corners. It was possible to reach the high cellar windows by standing on a crate on the floor, and Anonaziata promptly dragged a wooden box into place, perching on her tiptoes on the makeshift stool, peering out.

"Now, Melodie, tell us. What have you seen?" she asked, eyes never leaving the window.

Leaning against one of the tall barrels for balance, and facing no one in particular, Melodie Cristalline told us about her vision, in a seer's eerie sing-song.

"Corpsos, chests emblazoned with their hateful flag, making chummy conversation with the local constabulary, discussing a new out-of-town license plate they were looking to find... A stranger's van parked a little off the road, easy enough to see in the light of day... Clothing strewn about as the men searched it for evidence. Of what, they didn't say... A truck full of armed tough guys out to search for a lost girl... Their mission, to find her and bring her back with them by any means necessary..."

That must be me, I thought and shivered. I wasn't actually lost, though, of course. And I had no desire to be found by the likes of them, in any case. Why were they targeting me, anyway? I wondered. Because I'm a powerful intermagical, maybe, I speculated. But, how could they possibly know that?

I climbed up to peer out the still-empty window and wondered when they had gotten my license plate. With this thought, though, I realized the answer to both questions at once. The Fair Isle. The folks I had met there had known who and what I was. And, yesterday, I had pulled up and parked my van right in front, hadn't I? I had headed straight in the front door and stayed there for most of an hour. Anyone watching the place could have spotted me easily. Even if they didn't know who I was specifically, I was sure that the CCC would be staking out the neighborhood, after the disastrous raid attempt the night before. A stranger with out-of-town plates who had walked right into the front door of the Fair Isle? Of course, they had been suspicious.

I chastised myself, mentally. How could I have been so careless? I told my companions my thoughts, and they agreed that it was likely.

"I don't know whether they know who or what you are," Melodie Cristalline said, in her ordinary high soprano, without the eerie quality it had, earlier, "but, I would hazard likely not. Simply being unknown and connected to the Fair Isle would be enough to arouse their suspicions."

A small faerie buzzed in through the crack of the cellar door and whispered something to Anonaziata. "Dogs?" she asked the tiny flying fae, and he nodded before buzzing off. "He says that the men have brought dogs, as well as some of your clothing. Melodie did say that they had apprehended your vehicle and your belongings."

"The dogs will lead them right to us," said Melodie worriedly, picking at one of the loose ribbons of her dress.

With a strike of inspiration, I stripped off my woolen hat and my thick sweater, then my socks and shoes. "Can you ask them to fly around and scatter these things around the grounds?" I asked, "Take them far away from here. That should help confuse the dogs."

"Human magic! Yes!" exclaimed Anonaziata. She made a trilling little whistle that called several of the flying fae to her side and took the items of clothing from me, handing them out to the gathered faeries with hushed instructions.

"Human magic?" I asked Melodie Cristalline, confused.

Her mouth turned up in a smile, face pointed vacantly toward the corner. "Human magic," she confirmed, nodding, "Ingenuity, problem-solving. Thinking outside," she gestured to the four walls around us, "the root cellar."

"Oh. Okay." I considered that. I had always been a fast problem solver, that was true. Quick on my feet. Not literally, or physically, but certainly mentally. Human magic, though? Really? Problem-solving was hardly magic. But, I reasoned, can any other creature, magical or otherwise, solve problems like humans can? Not according to Melodie Cristalline, and as I ran the idea through my own logic filter, I decided she was right. "What else can you tell me about human magic?" I asked the childlike Melodie.

"Oh, lots," she answered, "I've been fascinated by it since I was a little girl, and human magic has made extraordinary changes in the world since 1917."

"Since-?" I asked, confused.

"Since 1917. The year I was born," Melodie Cristalline clarified, as though this were the most natural thing.

"But, but-" I stammered, looking at the girl, or, I corrected myself, the young-seeming woman, "that would make you almost a hundred years old!"

"Yes," she agreed, smiling, "That celebration will surely be a fine revel. Oh, my appearance, you mean?" she gestured, encompassing her small stature and the lank, childlike hair framing her thin, youthful face. I nodded, although I didn't think she could see me. "All part of my intermagical peculiarity. We often don't come out quite," she gestured to herself, "normal, by human standards. For me, it's my childlike appearance and my frail little body, as well as my limited physical sight. I can see some shapes in bright light," she clarified, gesturing vaguely out in front of herself, "And my extended sight, also. Awareness of things to come and insights into things I have no cause to know."

"So, it's just your appearance that's childlike?" I asked her.

She smiled, kindly if somewhat eerily. "Not just my appearance. There are a number of ways in which I am like a child. It is good to have my mother with me," she said and moved to stand by Anonaziata, who drew the girl, *the woman*, I corrected myself mentally, close in beside her, tucking her snugly where she seemed to fit best.

A small faerie buzzed in, and alighted on Anonaziata's shoulder, whispering to her. "It's working," she reported, "Only two of the groups were able to find their way into the fair at all, and one group, the men with the dogs, are now following the scent of your sock. Human magic at work. Ingenious!"

I smiled, glad that my notion had been a good one. We settled back down to wait, and while we waited, we talked.

"Human magic is, by my observation, of two basic types, and often aligns with the two human genders," said Melodie Cristalline, speaking with the academic authority of long study, "the feminine aspect is primarily concerned with creation and manifestation, and the masculine aspect prefers investigation and destruction. Most humans have a balance of both types of energy in some measure or another.

189

Your human magic of leading the dogs astray would be creative feminine magic, although it might also have been investigative, if, perhaps you had heard of that solution and wanted to test the theory?"

"Huh," I said, "I'm not sure. I feel like the idea just came to me when you said dogs, but I might have heard it somewhere, I guess."

"Creative, then," said Melodie, nodding and continuing her lesson.

"Humans are unique in that they can affect the world, permanently, in a way that no other creature, fae or animal, has ever been able to accomplish, although some insects make a good try of it. The cities they build can be impressive, and long-lasting."

"That sounds like what Faeryn was telling me," I said, "about how humans can change things, permanently, in reality. Like, how we build a wall and it stays built."

"Yes," she agreed, "but humans and intermagicals can impact more than just their physical world."

Humans, Melodie explained, learn to affect ourselves, first. From the time that we are tiny babies, we learn to control our limbs, voices, and behavior. As we grow older, our powers increase, and some even achieve a mastery where they can take full control of their own bodies and minds, through physical exercise and mental techniques like meditation. With enough motivation and effort, a human can change quite a bit about their internal and external realities.

"Unlike faeries," Melodie said, as one buzzed loudly in the window with a sound like a giant bumble bee.

"Faeries don't change?" I asked, surprised.

"Not typically. Nor do most of the fae. They are as they are. A nervous faerie will always be nervous. A native land spirit who always takes the long, scenic route would be vanishingly unlikely to decide, suddenly, to hurry up and get there faster." She shrugged. "The idea of self-development wouldn't, generally speaking, even occur to a fully-magical fae." I considered that, watching some of the smallest of the faeries dip in and out of the open doorway, making their reports to Anonaziata.

"Human minds," she went on, "are much more elastic. Sometimes just the experience of learning something new can be enough to fundamentally restructure a human brain, and change how one exists in the world." I nodded, feeling as though I had been fundamentally changed by what I had learned in the past few days. "And," she continued, "it's that same capability for flexibility that gives human magic its power to influence others. To rally humans together to achieve a common goal. I tend to think that the human ability to form groups and collaborate may be," she leaned on the words, "the single most powerful force on the planet."

"Wow," I said. It was a bold statement.

"Fae tend to go their own way," she went on, "They band together sometimes, around the oldest or the most powerful, like my mother, or the Queen, especially in times of uncertainty, but ultimately the fae will do what they have always done, according to their nature."

"Huh," I said, watching the little faeries flit in and out of the window with renewed interest.

"And, then there's the human ability to control the natural world, but you mentioned that Faeryn had already covered that," said Melodie with a respectful nod to me.

"Can you explain again, anyway?" I asked, feeling like I was still missing something, "I get that we can build walls, but…"

"Walls," she clarified, "which turn into houses, which turn into marvelous, towering cities. Walls around cultivated fields growing human-modified vegetables to an unnatural size. Walls around clinics that treat humans with rare natural diseases and let them live far longer and better lives than nature would dictate." She gestured to her own body. "Human healers have applied their magic to me many times, as their investigations into the nature of the world have uncovered new, helpful compounds, and as human doctors have invented ingenious and novel procedures to help-" She gestured at her vacant, unusual face.

"What have they been able to do for you?" I asked, curious.

"Improvements to my eyes, for one. Now, I can see light and some shapes, when it is bright enough. A welcome change from darkness. Perhaps one day, with enough human ingenuity, I will be able to see as you do." Her sad smile made me blink back tears. I was glad that she was probably not able to see them, and that Anonaziata was turned away, still peering out the high-set window.

Ourselves, mind and body. Other humans. Our natural world. I repeated the list to Melodie, "Those are the things that humans can control with their magic? Just those?"

"Hardly just," Melodie qualified, looking a bit put out at how unimpressed I sounded, "Within those spheres, they wield the powers of creation, to build and construct. The power of destruction, to unmake the physical components of reality, and even life itself. To deform or destroy it. To cause it to cease to be, as it is." From what the tiny fae were reporting to Anonaziata, it sounded as though the men searching for me were using their powers of destruction liberally, as they bashed their way through the fairgrounds. "The power of investigation," Melodie continued, "to seek specific knowledge, and to understand the nature of things well enough to be able to bend them to your will." The search party was certainly using their powers of investigation, too, I thought. Hopefully not very skillfully. "And, manifestation. The ability to change one's circumstances. To harness and bend the as-yet undirected energy of the world to your will and influence your own life," she concluded.

"Wait," I said, "you lost me there. Humans can do what, now?"

"Can manifest," she said, as though this were obvious, "Can align the chaotic forces of the universe to their energy, to assert control over the outcome. Humans like to call it luck, or chance, but it's quite a bit more directed than that, in actuality." She eyed me skeptically. "Mama says you were raised among the humans. Are you truly unfamiliar with the human good luck charm?"

"Uh, well, yeah, sure," I said, "My grandma liked to give me lucky rabbit's feet, sometimes." The tiny brightly dyed things had been incredibly soft, but I liked them less once I realized what they were, and where they must come from. "But stuff like that isn't real, is it? It's just superstition."

"Not real?" Melodie asked, incredulous, "Humans across the globe have always attempted to influence luck and circumstance, in one way or another. Why would they continue to do so, without a significant outcome?"

"I don't know," I said, "but those rabbit's feet never seemed to make me particularly lucky."

Anonaziata turned, joining the conversation for the first time. "Was this charm extraordinarily special to you? Was it imbued with the spirit of your strongest intention? Was it the specific earthly item that felt, personally and specifically, luckiest, to you?"

192

"No, Nona, it was just some tchotchke that my grandma bought me at a store," I answered.

"Exactly," she said with finality, turning back to peer out the window.

The power to impact the undirected, chaotic energy of the universe. Now that, for one, sounded like it might be actual magic and something I would like to try. But, the thought raised some other questions. "Okay, if that's human magic, what is fae magic, then? If I'm almost half-fae, what is it that I can actually do? I know I can't," I made an explosive gesture with my fingers, "from place to place."

"True," said Melodie Cristalline, "We can not flit as the faeries do. Nor can we fly." She nodded to one of the tiny faeries hovering nearby. "Except by using powerful human-made artifacts." I nodded. I had always thought airplanes seemed a little like magic. "And, one must consider that we three, here, are of the faerie folk. There are as many types of magic as there are types of fae. One particular magical up north in Portal Land has shown me artifacts of his people that accomplish things that the faeries would never dream of doing. But, the circumstances and the needs of the peoples of Africa will naturally be different than those of Europe, and so the natural abilities and proclivities of the fae of those regions will differ accordingly."

"Of Africa... You're not talking about the Gullah, are you?" I asked. That guy must really get around!

"Oh, you know him already? That's good. He is one of the more influential partly-magicals in the area, and one that we might call upon to aid us, now that we have a creative force of our own to act with. His prodigious destructive and investigative powers may prove helpful, depending on the nature of your plan."

"A creative force- Wait, do you mean me?" I asked, trying to follow her quick mental leaps.

"Yes, of course. A powerful faerie intermagical, imbued with, we hope, the natural powers of creation and manifestation, as female humans tend to be?" she raised her pitch, making the statement a question. I raised my eyebrows unconvinced, and she continued. "As opposed to the naturally masculine human forces of destruction, and the dogged pursuit of knowledge and the secrets of the universe?" she continued.

I shrugged noncommittally. "I guess so."

"Tell Fiona more about the faerie magic, darling," said Anonaziata to her daughter, turning to look over her shoulder, "It should give her personal experience more context."

"Ah, yes mother, of course," said Melodie, continuing her lecture. I settled on a wooden crate to listen. "Faerie magic centers the ideals of beauty, imagination, creativity, and inspiration," Melody explained, "It has many facets including the power of intuition and foresight. A sense of knowing, if you will. I have more than the average amount of that kind of knowing," she said with a sad smile, "but most faerie folk have at least a little, I've found. Faeries are also masters of illusion and the artistry of unreality. Pure faeries are not entirely anchored to this plane of reality at all." She gestured to a tiny faerie who had just blinked across the room in a flash, seemingly just for the fun of it.

"Can you show me?" I asked. She nodded and began with a prickly physical illusion that tickled me and made me giggle. Melodie tended toward non-visual illusions, she explained.

We turned as a tiny winged faerie dived in through the open doorway and grabbed hold of Anonaziata's ear, whispering fiercely. Many of the faeries spoke so that we all could hear, but some of them were quite shy. "They are? Truly?" Anonaziata asked, horrified, then turned to Melodie and me. "Those CCC brutes!," Anonaziata spat, "One of the groups of invaders have taken metal pipes and they're using them to break apart the fair."

"Our beautiful fair!" Melodie gasped, horrified, gripping my arm in agitation, "What should we do, Mother?"

"What we do best, dear," replied Anonaziata, grimly, then turned to me and said, "You wanted to see some faerie magic, Fiona? Well, this will be an excellent opportunity."

More faeries poured in, flying in through the open doorway or simply popping into existence in our midst, giving second-by-second updates on the men's savage actions. The troublemakers were drunk, the faeries reported, noting the scent of alcohol on their breath, and the jocular nature with which they were throwing beer bottles through windows. Luckily, Anonaziata knew the fairgrounds so well that she could picture every nook and cranny in her mind's eye. So could Melodie, although 'mind's eye' might not be the right analogy in her case. Since I couldn't imagine it, Anonaziata showed me, painting an illusion of what the faeries reported on the wall beside us. It didn't look very much like the photo-clear images in Faeryn's pool. More like a rough storybook illustration, animated by Anonaziata's evolving understanding.

"We'll have to make them leave, that's all," said Anonaziata resolutely, "From where they are, we'll want to drive them down the Moon Path, then up the Left Lane, and out."

"Through the Dragon Plaza, Mama?" asked Melodie.

"Quite," answered her mother grimly.

A faerie buzzed in and reported that the men, who had continued breaking windows, were now approaching some particularly pretty stained glass.

"They won't be nearly as dangerous without those nasty pipes," said Melodie Cristalline, scrunching her face in concentration, then, relaxing and adding, "See how they like that!"

In a moment, we got the report that they had shouted and thrown their weapons deep into the underbrush. Melodie nodded, satisfied. The windows, at least, were safe.

"What did you do?" I asked, confused.

"Made the metal feel red-hot to their touch," she told me, looking pleased with herself. Melodie's illusions, I reminded myself, tended to focus on senses other than sight.

I watched Anonaziata's moving illustration with interest as the men continued their winding progress down the path, kicking down the flimsy wooden walls of the fair's apparently-empty stalls and generally wreaking havoc. Anonaziata made motions with her hands as she crafted fake walls where there were none so that the men would kick thin air and stumble, and disguising real walls so that the men would trip over them. I remembered what I had learned at the Fair Isle. If people didn't have any magic, they couldn't be affected by it. In fact, I didn't think they could be here at the Country Fair, at all. The men, stumbling over fake walls, had been affected by Melodie's heat illusion, too, so they must be.

"These guys are intermagicals too, huh?" I asked.

"Yes," agreed Anonaziata, "not particularly magical, I wouldn't think, but certainly a bit." She shook her head and sighed. "But they are also quite drunk. Mostly-humans have much more ability to access magic when they are intoxicated. It's one of the reasons they enjoy it so much. Just look at how many creative ideas these fools are coming up with tonight. Human magic abounds!"

"Really? Drunk people doing stupid, crazy stuff is... human magic?" I asked, skeptically.

"It's not particularly good magic," Melodie replied, shrugging.

Speaking of bad ideas, I thought to myself, as another faerie lookout reported that the men had pulled more bottles out of their many-pocketed fatigues and were preparing to climb a ladder into the loft above a stall to drink them. Melodie tried her best, sending them physical and auditory illusions that made the ladder creak and sway alarmingly, but it was not enough to deter the drunken exuberance of the troublemakers.

"They really shouldn't be doing that," said Melodie, sounding worried, right before the largest wave of faeries we had seen yet swooped through the low doorway and began chattering over one another. The floor of the stall had collapsed, dumping all three men into a groaning pile on the ground. This had been enough to wipe the smiles off their faces, and the reporting faeries did wonderfully animated impressions of the men groaning and complaining on the floor, making us all laugh heartily. "I'm tired of these men in my fair," said Melodie, frowning, "Can we just chase them out now, Mother?" Anonaziata agreed.

As the men stood up and dusted themselves off, spectral shapes rose with them, reaching ghostly arms toward the men and moaning *Get ooouutt...* in blood-curdling wails. Tree branches reached and grasped for the feckless troublemakers. The images that Anonaziata made to illustrate this looked very much like the scary tree outside the window of the bathroom at the River House. The men fled in terror, tripping and scrambling in the precise direction Anonaziata and Melody intended. As they reached the giant dragon's head that guarded the main entrance to the fair, the fae women ignited the courtyard in an illusory plume of fire that chased the invaders out the front gate and off into the night.

Melodie and I whooped and cheered as several excited faeries gave humorous and overlapping descriptions of the men's final retreat. Anonaziata stayed quiet, although a large, lined smile split her wrinkled old face.

"We mustn't draw attention to ourselves," the old woman admonished, returning to her post at the window, "The other group of searchers is still about, and they are the ones with the dogs." She shook her head, answering my unspoken question. "No, we won't chase the others out in that same fashion. These men were out of their minds with drink. The others are uninebriated. It would not be wise to give them cause to think that the fair is haunted. That never ends well." Returning to her post by the window, she urged Melodie to continue with the lesson.

"Humans have done some significant theorizing on the existence of faerie and the fae. One such study is the philosophical field of Theosophy. They make some interesting assertions about faerie. Some that resonate with me," her face twisted into what I thought a wry expression must look like, on someone who had never seen one, "as well as several that do not." I settled back onto one of the barrels to listen. It sounded like I was in for quite the lecture. "Theosophists imagine that faeries translate the natural energy of sunlight, which they call *PRANA*, into the energetic material of flowers, essentially helping them to bloom and grow." Out of the corner of my eye, I said Anonaziata, turned away from us at the window, twitching her chin dismissively. "It's one theory," said Melodie with a shrug, "and I see how they might have come to it, but personally, I believe that the purpose of faeries' magic is to imbue flowers, and other such things, with their natural beauty."

"Faeries make the flowers beautiful?" I asked, then added, joking, "Do they paint the roses red, or something?"

"No," she answered with a smile, "Nothing like that. Simply, faeries have a particular magical capability to find the beauty in things. To discover it, or to uncover it, and to enhance the beauty that is there with their attention."

"So, um, humans think that flowers are beautiful because faeries made them beautiful?" I asked, trying to make sense of what she had just told me. It didn't seem quite right. "I don't know. I feel like, when I look at a flower, I can just see that it's beautiful, you know? I don't need a faerie to create its beauty for me. It's already there, looking back at me."

"Of course," Melodie answered with a patient smile, "You are faerie. That magical capability is within you."

"Oh," I said. I hadn't thought of it like that.

"You have an ability to find beauty in all things. That is part of your particular fae nature. Your magical side, not your human side. Your creativity and your imagination, too. Your inspiration. Your ability to look outside the ordinary and the expected. These are all manifestations of your faerie magic." Her face lit up at this. Clearly, this was a topic she was quite passionate about.

I felt my own forehead furrow, though. "I don't know. It seems to me like pretty much everybody agrees that flowers are beautiful, don't they?"

"Yes, indeed they do. But, do remember that faeries have been at work in the world for a long time, and flowers are a thoroughly end-stage project. They are, by all accounts, very beautiful. Nowadays, faeries here are more focused on the more esoteric beauties of the world, such as the curiosities of Oregon's myriad fungi."

"Oh," I said, "Well, some fungi are better looking than others, I guess."I paused and digested, deciding that something still didn't sit quite right. "I guess what's bugging me is that I feel like I don't see the beauty in natural things more than most people," I told Melodie about my college roommate who used to take me hiking in the woods. She would stop and moon over all sorts of plain little sprouts and bugs that she found. They didn't seem particularly special to me, but she knew everything about them. She was studying bees, now, out in the field all day with the plants and the insects. "I feel like," I said, taking a deep breath, preparing to unburden myself of something I had been carrying all day, "I feel like if anyone was going to turn out to be a faerie, if anybody was actually magic…" I trailed off, but Melodie waited, patiently, "I'd have thought it would have been her."

Melodie Cristalline nodded, considering, then took several steps in, nudging uncomfortably into my personal space. I resisted the urge to step back from her, in the small room.

"Will you give me your hand?" she asked, extending her own small palm, face up. I placed my hand in her narrow one, nervous. "Think of her, please. In fact, if you'd like, think of all of the important people that you have known and loved."

I did as she asked, thinking first about my sweet college roommate, the one who knit hats and loved plants and bees. Next, I thought about the couple who lived next door, who played board games in our apartment's tiny kitchen in the evenings. Then, farther back, my particular friend from when I was a kid. Creative and bright, like me, sporting multi-colored hair before it was popular. The one who hand convinced me that being weird was actually cool. Energy flowed between our clasped hands, warm and electric.

Well, your intuition is strong. That's why," she said, dropping my hand and looking satisfied, "But, it stands to reason. Someone as deeply magical as you are would be drawn to similarly magical companions, and so you have been."

"They're all magical?" I asked, wonderingly, "All of my friends?" I felt my heart well with emotion at the thought. "Because… I don't know. I guess my being so special just didn't make much sense to me. I'm no more special than her, or him, or anybody," I said, "but, if you're saying that they're special, too. If they're magical, too…" I trailed off, thinking more about my special, creative, unusual particular friends. How different they had seemed from the other kids at school. Other people in town, in my neighborhood. "How, er, magical are they?" I asked, "can you tell?"

Some, more than others, Melodie Cristalline thought, although it would be easier for her to tell if they were standing in front of her. Easier still, if she could touch them, too. Bits and pieces of this sort of fae and that. But, they were certainly magical, she said. She could tell. My college roommate did have more than the usual amount of faerie, Melodie thought, as well as some other assorted land and nature spirits. That must have been why she seemed so like me, and so unlike me at the same time, I thought, speculatively. And why she had such an affinity for the great outdoors. Melodie repeated the list again.

Imagination.
Attraction to the unusual.
Fascination with art and beauty.
Creative thought.
Inspiration.

These were just a few of the highly heritable aspects of fae magic, Melodie said. And, even those with a little magic, or more than a little, but from different, distant fae ancestors across the generations, could tap into these powerful forces in a way that pure humans could not. But, Melodie Cristalline clarified, these traits would manifest to different degrees based on the type and the amount of inherent magic one possessed, and upon one's personality and particular, innate humanity.

"And they don't know? They never find out?" I asked, appalled, "Just go through life feeling unusual and different like that and nobody ever tells them?"

"Who would tell them? Who could? It is the nature of the hidden people to stay hidden. Even when we speak out loud, even when we hold whole Faerie festivals, like they do up in Portal Land, the humans don't see us. They don't believe in us. Or they do, some of them, but they can't admit it out loud, or even sometimes to themselves."

"That's so sad," I said, considering it, "I wish I could tell them. All these things that I'm learning. All these things that I know, now, that I didn't know last week. Yesterday!"

"Quiet," hissed Anonaziata, "they're coming."

Part 7 - The Key to the Door

"Father told me that he's pleased I picked a nice, good, obedient woman like you. One who likes homemaking and decorating and stuff. This place sure could use it."

Velia bestowed a thin-lipped smile on the puppy as he continued laboriously hanging thick, ornate velvet curtains in her signature style. If she was going to be spending quite so much time in the young buck's austere student accommodations, she could at least make the place a little less dreary. Stepping around the corner, out of sight, she crafted another illusory bundle of fabric and handed it to Brandon to hang. It was quite convenient that he had enough innate magic to be able to interact with the illusions she crafted.

"Some women don't know their place in the world. They don't know how to act..." Brandon continued, tugging at the curtain roughly.

He was thinking about that girl again, clearly. Well, he wasn't the only one thinking about her, Velia mused. Where had she been headed, after she had pressed so doggedly through Velia's magical storm and onward, beyond the reach of magical sight? Well, there was no point in worrying about it now, with so much work to do, here.

Velia moved to stand behind the young man. She ran her sharp, dark nails down the length of his arm, making him shiver. There were ways of making him forget.

Chapter 29

I climbed on a crate next to Anonaziata and peered out the high window. Two large dogs led three men in combat black down the narrow path toward us. The dogs snuffled and sniffed, noses pressed to the ground, advancing slowly. A sweater dangled from the hand of the man without a dog. My sweater, of course. The one that had been wadded up on my passenger's seat. It made me angry, thinking of them inside my van, rifling through my things.

Deep breath, Fiona, I told myself. Focus. I had just called myself Fiona, I realized. I hadn't ever done that before. It felt nice. Correct.

"Mama, the dogs won't sense our illusions, will they?" Melodie asked, nervous.

Beside me, Anonaziata shook her head, eyes never leaving the window. Outside, I saw one of the dog's ears perk up. Its eyes darted in my direction. My heart started pounding faster in my chest. They would be on us any second.

"Melodie," I whispered, "I have an idea. Can you make a scent illusion, right now?" She nodded.

A second later, the first dog barked, then both hounds bounded toward us, growling and scrabbling at the loose gravel near our hiding place, trying to dig their way to us. We cowered away from the windows, into the shadows at the back of the cellar. I hoped that the midday glare reflecting off the windows would hide us, but then I noticed a slight shimmer in front of my vision and realized that Anonaziata was surely hiding us from view with an illusion as well.

"Melodie, the smell," I hissed into her ear, as we huddled together, "Are you doing it? Can you make it stronger?" In the close space, I felt her nod again. The dogs barked fiercely, spittle flying and spattering the window, as the men hauled on their leashes, straining to keep them under control.

"Ugh, yuck!" said one of the men, a moment later. His footsteps crunched on the rocky path as he reeled back a few steps.

"Do you smell that? The dogs want it, whatever it is," said another, yanking the leash even harder and making the dog skitter back.

"Hotdogs," said the third, "that smells like old nasty hotdogs." The men pulled the still barking dogs off down the row and away from us. I let out a sigh of relief and felt Anonaziata and Melodie Cristalline did the same.

"Hot dogs?" asked the older woman, raising one white eyebrow, "What are hot dogs?"

"Um, a human food, Nona," I offered, apologetically, "It was all I could think of, in the moment. I'm sure glad you knew what I was talking about, Melodie."

"It was a close thing," she admitted, "but I take an interest in human experiences, and I did attend a baseball game once."

"And you tried a hotdog?" I asked, curious how she had liked it.

"I caught a whiff of the ballpark trash can," she admitted.

"Which does explain the quality of the smell," added her mother, "I found myself becoming rather concerned when you said that it was food, Fiona." I shrugged. It smelled just like the school cafeteria on hotdog day, to me. We settled back on the low crates to wait until the tiny faeries gave us the all-clear. We wouldn't emerge until the men had completely left the fair.

"Such creative ingenuity," said Anonaziata proudly, patting my arm, "The kind of power that makes self-aware intermagicals so effective and feared that the CCC will go to such lengths to track one down. Look at how smoothly you were able to combine your human innovation with fae magic, and to such great effect!"

"But I still can't do it by myself," I said, with a sigh. I had tried to create my own images, following Melodie and her mother's calm and helpful instructions, but I just couldn't get the illusions to appear for me.

"You can do magic," said Anonaziata, squeezing my arm comfortingly, "and you are doing it all the time. Human magic is no less real than fae magic, for all that the ones in power would wish to convince you that it is not. The CCC obfuscates this truth only because of how much they fear its discovery."

"Alright, I'm confused," I said, holding up a hand to forestall her, "The Gullah told me some stuff about The CCC. About how it's a lot bigger and older than I thought it was. How I'm not getting the real story by listening to the news. He told me how they're not controlling *for* the calamity, they're actually the ones

204

manufacturing it, I guess, with their governmental policies, and whatever else it is they do. But, what you said right then made it sound like you think they're controlling," I spread my hands wide, encompassing the whole human experience, "like, everything, everywhere, across time. This is the multi-governmental agency we're talking about, right? The Calamity Control Council?"

The room was silent for a moment. Then, Anonaziata started to laugh. "The Calamity Control Council?" she hooted, shoulders shaking, "This is how they have presented themselves, as they emerge from the shadows? As an agency positioned to control a calamity? Oh, that is entirely too funny," she said, taking in great wheezing breaths as she laughed, "They must be quite pleased with themselves, for that one."

"Nona, what's so funny? I don't get it. Can you catch me up?" I asked, eyeing the wheezing woman worriedly.

Melodie spoke instead, and in her lilting way, she explained it so that I understood. The name 'The CCC' originated shortly after the Fae Intermixing Declaration, when the newly formed society of mixed fae and human folk had gathered together for community and safety. Intermagicals born to human parents were, by necessity, integrated into human society, for better or for worse, often never realizing their magical origins, but those born into the magical world strengthened this new community in the Americas.

Utilizing the gifts of these newly minted intermagicals to create and to change reality to suit themselves, these early fae communities in the Americas created magical safehouses, like the River House and the Fair Isle, all up and down the Eastern coast of the continent, and, later, inland, beside the cross-continental waterways and along the Western coast as well, mingling and intermixing with the native land spirits that were already congregated around these naturally bountiful locations. The fae preferred to live near running water, prizing locations of particular natural majesty. So did the new human settlers, and so it came to pass that fae and human cities both sprung up at the same natural nexuses.

After a few years of hard work clawing a foothold into this strange new land, the magicals, and intermagicals found that they needed some language to speak about a particular phenomenon and common experience that stood out more starkly here in this American mixing pot than it had done in the more stagnant old world. They gave name to the forces of darkness they observed insinuating into and spreading through the human communities around them. The insidious forces holding humanity back from its natural forward progress and ultimate success. The acronym,

The CCC, had been coined by an intermagical gifted with the power of naming, like Faeryn, as an attempt to capture the amorphous force's essence.

The three C's, in no particular order, stood for Capitalism, the personification of human greed and disconnection, and the root of so much of humanity's darkness, Climate Corruption, the theft, defilement, and disregard of our world's natural spaces and precious resources, and Conformity, the pressure to adhere to a singular Anglo-Saxon standard of rightness and religious belief.

"Which is almost invariably, at least in this part of the world, some form of Christianity," interjected Anonaziata, picking up the thread from her daughter, "The notion of the Christ figure is, at this point, quite ironic, to me, for how poorly his ideals reflect the reality of what Christianity has wrought on this world."

Giving this force a name gave the fae folk the power to keep an eye on it, explained Melodie. It allowed the fae to observe as it slipped tendrils of discord into the formation of a new country on already-inhabited land. It let them watch as these forces routed and destroyed so much of the land's native culture, and the balance they had achieved with the land spirits they had been living alongside so harmoniously, for so long.

"But," Melodie shook her head sadly, "it did not allow them to do anything more than watch."

And watch they did, as more and more of this new world fell prey to this insidious darkness. Having given it a name, the fae were more easily able to see that this mysterious force was not unknowing or uncaring. Instead, it seemed that its actions were specific and directed, set on holding humanity back from its highest potential, working tirelessly to trip up forward progress at every possible turn.

"Why?" I asked, attention held rapt by Melodie's explanation.

"Why does this force want humanity to fail?" Melodie asked. I nodded. "I don't know, even after having applied my gift of prescience, which is," she shrugged modestly, "not inconsiderable."

A gross under-exaggeration, I guessed. Anonaziata's expression, mouth held tight in a proud line, confirmed this supposition. "What do you think it could be?" I asked, pressing for an answer.

"I think," she frowned, brow furrowed in thought, "that this all might be a game. Perhaps there is a great cosmic contest of some sort, in which human history is the playing field. Perhaps there is some future goal marker or score to be counted, at which point, humanity will either succeed or lose, to its detriment, having been played as pawns." I frowned. That perspective made life seem pretty shallow and pointless.

"I've wondered," she went on, "for some time, about this mysterious figurehead of God that appears at first so openly and then disappears so entirely, in the stories of the Bible. I've wondered if he mightn't have been the player. Or, perhaps merely an early one. They have clearly gotten more skilled in the art of subtle manipulation since the examples set in the stories of Noah's Ark and the Tower of Babel," she twirled her long hair around her finger in a child-like way, thinking for a moment, before adding, "But, not good enough to maintain control, I think, if too many of their pawns were to suddenly become self-aware."

"But, who would want the worst for humans?" I asked, "Who would want to see humanity fail when we could flourish and everybody could be happy?"

"I don't imagine they see it that way. For something at the scale of the CCC, whether an organization or a single entity, human life must seem utterly insignificant. Completely without value or meaning in this game that they are playing on a global, or perhaps even cosmic scale."

"Just a game? You really think that the entire history of human suffering is just some kind of cosmic entertainment?"

"Perhaps, but then again, perhaps not. It could be this force, whatever it is, is gifted with the power of foresight, as I am. I have seen humanity competing in a contest, but perhaps it is not merely a game. Perhaps humanity's trial is yet to come, sometime in the future. Maybe this entity or organization wishes us to be caught unprepared, and unable to meet this important challenge and succeed."

"I like that better," I said, not really knowing why it mattered to me why this mysterious force was interfering in humanity's affairs, but finding that it did.

"So, the CCC is the fae's term, but now it's the name of a governmental group, too? You don't think that's a coincidence?" I asked.

"I do not," answered Melodie, "Unlike my mother, I have been paying close attention to the actions and the movements of the CCC, both as an ephemeral force and as an international governmental body. It is my conclusion that these two entities are in fact one, under the same name." She smiled and gave a small chuckle."I certainly see the humor in it that Mama did. It is quite brazen and a bit ironic that this many-headed evil has now taken our name as its own. But, names do have power."

"So, what do the fae do about it then, other than keep an eye on it?" I asked, curious and all too aware that I was being drafted onto the front lines of this ancient fight.

"For one, we continue to intermix," said Anonaziata with a smile, "Intermixing creates powerful actors within humanity who are not bound by the status quo and ordinary thinking. They are less likely to be swept up into human religion, and to be able to escape it when they are. And, they are less inclined to bend to social rules that contradict their own magical understanding of the world." She reached over and squeezed my shoulder with her bony fingers. "Occasionally, they even find their way back to us, like you have done, making our community stronger. More often, though, they simply use their innovative thoughts and ideas to move humanity forward, farther and faster than it would be doing on its own."

"What do you mean? Wouldn't humans have noticed intermagicals making big changes in the world?"

"Not if they perceive them to be ordinary humans. After all, they perceived you to be a normal human, didn't they?"

"Well…" I hedged. Many people growing up seemed to think that I might not have been particularly normal, and had taken it upon themselves to make my life harder, accordingly. And, here it turned out they had been right all along, just not in the way anyone had expected.

"And this powerful forward progress," continued Melodie, "is exactly the opposite of what the CCC tries to foster, but as we can see from the human magic explosion in the last few centuries, intermagicals are gaining in influence and in numbers."

"The human magic explosion?"

"Beginning with the period immediately following the Intermixing Declaration," Melodie clarified, "when our newly mixed children had grown up into adults and the first generation of intermagicals began to take power, here in the Americas. Human history books call this era the 'Industrial Revolution.'" I felt my eyes widen. "It continues onward from there," she said, "with the invention of the automobile and the airplane. Modern medicine and science, and now computers and technology. All invented by divergent humans, magical humans, thinking outside the box, and expanding humanity beyond its previous capabilities."

"So the intermagicals are winning then, against the CCC?" I asked, feeling the puzzle slowly coming together.

"Do you think so?" Melodie replied, cocking her head to one side, "I'm not so sure. The world has advanced, yes. But, at what cost? The cost of much of the environment and the world's natural resources, for one. The CCC has blocked cleaner, more effective, technologies, forcing humanity to retain its reliance on outdated fuel sources, while viscously looting and polluting the land even further." Her sightless eyes narrowed, and she clenched her small fists with feeling as she spoke. "Resources blossom forth from humanity's great forward progress, yet so many are left hungry and wanting, not from lack of supply, but simply from capitalist greed. Conformity to Christianity is essentially a cultural requirement in much of the world, and its two major competitors are a fallacy of real theological competition. One is an earlier version of the same monolithic concept, using the self-same text, or at least a part of it. The other, a near-complete copy of the book in a different language where the dogma, the control, and the separation from personal power all remain essentially the same."

"Well, when you put it that way…" I sighed.

A bright flash lit the room as a faerie popped in with news. The men had left, and the fair was safe, once again. However, the faerie reported, the men had driven away towing my van, so I was stuck here until further notice, without a change of clothes or any of my things.

"Just my luck," I griped, standing and stretching, glad to be getting out of this dark, dirt-walled den.

"Come now, dear, eat and rest," said the old woman, taking my arm and leading me down a new path.

"Thanks, Nona," I answered, gratefully.

She led me to a different lavishly adorned table in another part of the fair that was just as cozy and charming as the area I had been in last night, and I accepted the wooden bowl of soup and the soft warm bread she offered me.I watched the faeries drift all around the clearing, letting my eyes lose focus until they were just multi-colored motes of light drifting across my vision. I thought about what I had learned, and then I thought about nothing, letting my brain rest and digest the information. The adrenaline of the close encounter with those CCC men and their barking dogs had sapped my remaining energy. I was so very, very tired.

At some point, Melodie Cristalline came and sat down next to me. She didn't speak, and neither did I, lost in my meditative contemplation. Eventually, words rose to the surface of my quiet mind, and I spoke. "Do you really think all religions are the same?" I asked. The question hung for a long moment in the space between us.

"No," she answered. "Most, but not all. There were more religions before. Ones that were closer to the magic. Closer to nature, and to the truth, though still interpretations, of course. There are some parts of Asia that were never fully conquered by the CCC's monotheistic evangelism. Places that still practice such spiritualities even today."

"Buddhism?" I guessed.

"Certainly has its points," she agreed, "but once again, it has reduced itself to the worship of a single Christ-like male figurehead. Did you know that the Buddha himself was a Hindu?"

Hinduism, said Melodie Cristalline, was, she thought, humanity's most logical attempt to codify the mystical. She appreciated their description of a multi-faceted divinity, with a wide pantheon, not of truly eternal or infallible gods, but instead of relatable characters, whose experiences of success, failure, joy, and despair mirror humanity's. Overarching all of this is a divine trinity representing the turning of the great cosmic wheel, from creation, through existence and finally to destruction. They believe that human life follows this cycle as well, returning, as the wheel does, again and again, from birth, through life, and finally to death, before beginning anew.

"Why," she asked, "would something as powerful and vital as a human's own life force be the only energy in the universe that is truly lost, when it leaves this earthly plane at the moment of ego death?" She spoke also of Karma, the idea that each person's actions create his own future reality, and of Dharma, the duty to fulfill one's earthly role and to live each of life's stages in its proper time.

"For folk like you and I, with a mortal existence, rather than these fully-magical little ones, or pure faeries like the Queen," she clarified, "it is important to be mindful of our use of time and to do our best not to squander it," she paused and turned her face up, catching the golden rays of the fading evening sun on it, "to follow our own Dharma, and plant and harvest, each in its own season, don't you think?" I nodded noncommittally and stared out into the darkening sky. I hadn't thought about my mortality very much, and now didn't really seem like the time to start, considering how much else I had going on.

Hinduism is an interpretation, like every other religion, admitted Melodie Cristalline. But compared to so many other beliefs, Hindus put relatively little importance on whether or not their specific interpretation is, in fact, the truth, and that distance, she explained, makes it possible to see through the loose weave of the rhetoric to the reality behind it, if one takes the time to look closely. And Hinduism encourages that looking, Melodie went on, clearly speaking on a subject she was passionate about.

In fact, she told me, according to the Dharma, the notion of right action, and of doing the proper things at the proper time, the final stage of a human's life is set aside for spiritual growth and deep contemplation. Perhaps, Melodie added with the glint of firelight in her smokey eye, one might even attempt to achieve Moksha, the state of enlightenment where one escapes the cosmic cycle and joins with the universal oneness of everything.

"Can such a thing truly be possible?" Melodie Cristalline wondered, "It sounds so incredible as to be almost unbelievable, to me, but so must faerie magic to those who were not raised steeped in it, as I was."

I didn't know which sounded more fantastical, honestly. An eternal universal oneness, or any of the other myriad mind-boggling things I had experienced and learned in the past few days. At this point, anything seemed possible.

"I find it interesting," said Melodie Cristalline, "how strikingly similar faerie art is to the art of Southeast Asia. I tend to wonder if it doesn't reflect the similarities in our mystical beliefs."

Faerie art was pure decadence. Fantastical swooping swirls and twining, blossoming flowers. Ornate, gilded decoration, ornamented with sparkling gems and jewels. Now that she mentioned it, Indian design, with its rich colors and lavish pattern, did give me a very similar magical feeling. Maybe that was why I had always been drawn to those particular types of patterns when I shopped for scarves at second-hand stores.

Melodie's fingertips traced the swirling pattern carved into the post she leaned against, and I realized that her experience with both types of art must be largely tactile. Even as I thought this, Melodie's fingers danced away from the carving, extending and expanding the hypnotic design with an illusion that glowed faintly in the gathering twilight. Entranced by this demonstration I asked her to explain to me, again, how to tap into that internal fire of creation and draw it out with my will, allowing me to shape unreality to my own design.

She did as I asked, and I followed her instructions, trying again and again.

Nothing worked. No glowing designs burst forth from my fingertips. No flowers blossomed to life on my palm. Not a single magical mote or spark. By the time I had tired of trying, it was well past dark. My shoulders sagged, and I yawned, sleepily. I noticed Anonaziata as she walked purposefully across the clearing in front of us, not seeing me.

"Nona?" I asked, through another large yawn.

"Are you still awake, child?" she said, surprised to see me, "Come, come. Let's find you somewhere to sleep."

"It didn't work," I said, "the magic. The faerie magic." I trundled sleepily along behind her.

"Did it not? Well, don't worry about that. Alaric had some trouble getting in touch with his own magic, once upon a time. I'll let him know you'd like some help. He'll take you on a walk tomorrow. See if you can't find a key to unlock that particular door."

"Okay," I agreed, already half asleep. I crawled into the cushion-lined nook she indicated and was fast asleep before my head hit the pillow.

Chapter 30

I woke up wet.

Plink.

A fat drop of water hit my forehead and rolled down my nose. It had been one of many, I realized. The cozy bed clothes were heavy with the rain that had managed to seep through the boards of the rough-hewn structure I had been given to sleep in.

Plop.

"Argh!" This time the drop had hit me squarely in the eye. I sat up, shedding the wet blankets, and assessed my situation. I was more wet than I wasn't, I thought, pulling my clinging dress away from my humid torso. When I let it go, it fell back against me with a wet smack. I was still warm from the blankets, but I wouldn't be for long. My extremities were already getting cold, and the wind cut through my damp clothing like a knife. And, I remembered, all of my extra clothing had driven away with my van, along with everything else I owned.

I climbed halfway out of the structure, sitting on the edge of the bed, feet planted on the damp, loamy soil. When I let my forehead fall forward into my hands, it brought my head outside the roof's protection as well. The rain beat down on the back of my uncovered skull. I got increasingly cold as I sat there, still drowsy with sleep, and before long I started to shiver.

Pathetic. Me, a powerful intermagical? Yeah right! I didn't know anything about anything. I didn't have any idea what to do. I couldn't even do proper magic!

I tried it again, there in the rain. "Reach deep within," said Melodie Cristalline in my memory, "Feel the fire burning inside of you and draw it out." I tried to do what she told me and reach inside myself. Was that what it was supposed to feel like? Or, I wondered, disheartened, was I only pretending to feel something because I wanted to so badly?

"Now… make a flower," I said into the space above my hand.

Nothing.

"Make a flower!" I repeated, gesturing wildly.

"Bloom!" I yelled, "Bloom!" I was standing now, shaking my fist in the rain. No flowers appeared before me. Of course they didn't.

I started to cry. The streaming tears hardly seemed to make a difference to my already rain-soaked face. Faeryn, Arlee, and all of these tiny faeries, they were looking to me to save their beautiful city. To save their home and their way of life.

Why me? What made any of them think that I could do anything? It was only the fate of my birth that made me a powerful, 'nearly balanced' or even 'perfect' intermagical. What did that really even mean, anyway? That I was going to be able to do something spectacular and save the day?

But, I wasn't, was I? I wasn't going to save the day. I was just going to fail and disappoint everyone.

"Because," I paused, then spit out the truth to an audience of rain-soaked trees, "because I'm just not special, okay? I'm not. You've got the wrong girl. Go find somebody else!" I picked up a rock and threw it, knocking a spray of silvery droplets out of a leafy shrub. The disturbance set a chorus of crows to cawing, and a second later they exploded out of a nearby tree.

I had just wanted to find my family, that was all. To meet some people who looked like me and share a meal with them, maybe. And where was I now? No closer to achieving that goal than I had been when I got here, but a whole lot more wet and pathetic. The supposed heroine to an entire city of magical creatures now, inexplicably, counting on me to save the day.

They didn't expect much, did they? They hadn't even had the courtesy to offer me a magical sword to slay this dragon with.No practical silver bullets for me, no way! Apparently, I had to figure out how to fix things with my innate human ingenuity. That was all! Just think about it and solve the problem. Not too hard, right?

"Yeah right," I shot back, into the rain, "Like I can actually change anything." I couldn't even make a fake flower.

I was just some normal college kid. No, I wasn't even that, at least not anymore. Just some normal nobody. Mom had made that abundantly clear, growing up. That I was not special, just ordinary. Ordinary and disorganized and lazy and forgetful. She didn't expect me to be anybody remarkable, so why should anyone else?

I sunk down to the ground, back against the rough wood wall. And now here I was, sitting in the dirt, getting my only outfit muddy on top of everything else. Rain still beat down on my head, running in rivulets down my face, mixing with my tears. I was done. I wanted out.

I didn't want to try to do this anymore, I just wanted to go home. But where was home? Not my parents' house, where I had grown up. That wasn't what I was looking for. That had never been it. Maybe it was my cozy college apartment, filled with baking and laughter and friends. But, that was gone, now. Cleared out, and boxed up. Moved on. It had never been meant to be permanent, to be forever.

That's what I was looking for, I thought. That's what I really wanted. A real home.

And what had I gotten instead? I had gotten mixed up with these strange creatures that ordinary people didn't even believe in. Creatures who had dragged me into the middle of a huge problem that wasn't any of my business to fix. Then I'd managed to get my car impounded, with all of my earthly possessions in it. And now I was incredibly, depressingly, wet. I closed my eyes and wished that everything could just stop. That I could just stop existing for a minute. The rain continued to drip unendingly on the back of my bowed head.

"Fiona?" A word drifted through the darkness. The sensation of someone grasping my shoulder brought me back to my body.

"Fiona?"

Oh right, that was me, now. It sounded exhausting.

The rain had stopped. Or, maybe it hadn't. I no longer felt the patter of raindrops on my head, at least, but opening my eyes to the dim, dripping forest, where big, heavy drops still fell, I realized that it was Melodie Cristalline standing beside me, holding a dainty lace parasol that shielded us both from the rain. The pretty thing didn't look like it ought to be waterproof, but it was doing the job. She gazed, sightless, into the woods, strange in her stillness. With her vacant clouded eyes and childlike appearance, in a little pink dress, she looked like a porcelain doll.

I wondered why she chose to dress the way she did, since she was an adult, and nearly a hundred years old. Likely, I answered myself, when you've lived that long, you've decided what it is that you like.

"Oh, hi Melodie. I, um…" I trailed off, not sure what to say. I was embarrassed that she had found me like this, but grateful for her company and for the cover she provided from the rain.

"It's alright," she said, comfortingly, "you know, you don't have to tell me out loud." She reached out a small hand. "May I?"

Oh, right. Magic.

I reached up and hesitantly took the proffered hand, and the warm energy flowed between us like it had before. This time, I didn't think of anything in particular. I just sat in the rain, feeling cold, although admittedly, a little less cold, and a little less alone than I had been, before. Melodie spoke. She intoned, really. Deep and low, not like her usual voice at all. It felt like she was speaking directly from my soul.

"I just can't accept it. Why me? How could it be me? How can it be true that I'm special and powerful, but still well and whole? How is it possible that I come from a single source of faerie magic, and didn't end up sick, like you and Faeryn did? It's not fair, and more than that, it doesn't follow the rules that you're telling me. I can't accept that I just happened to be the one who got lucky. I would think you were all lying if I couldn't always tell when people were lying to me. But, that doesn't mean you can't just be wrong. I'm not who you think I am. I can't be. I'm not special. I can't save the day. It just doesn't make sense."

She withdrew her hand. The tingling between our palms eased, leaving a residual warmth in the cool damp air. I felt lighter, unburdened by what Melodie had brought forth between us.

"There are two things that I have seen that you need to hear," Melodie said, in her own lilting soprano, "First, you must understand that you are sicker than you know. Sicker than anyone knows. I feel it, though, when I touch you." She turned toward me, concerned. "Fiona, the feeling you get when you're hungry. How would you describe it?"

"Um, I don't know. I just feel hungry."

"But, how does that feel, in your body? When I-" she forestalled herself, "Can you tell me how it feels for you?"

"I don't know," I answered, really considering it for the first time, "I guess I know that I'm getting really hungry when my fingers get tingly and my vision gets a little blurry. And then, when I stand up, I feel like I might fall over or faint, and my knees get weak and wobbly. And then I eat something and I feel better. Hungry."

"That's not hunger, Fiona. There's something wrong with your blood." Melodie put her finger to her temple as though forming the image into words. "Like a sweet civil war. Your body is eating itself, rather than the food you feed it." Her expression looked pained. "Go see a good human medical doctor, when all of this is done. As soon as you can. You'll be alright, though, I think. It's better that you know now, when you can act, rather than waiting until later when more damage has been done."

She squeezed my arm, comfortingly, in exactly the way her mother had done. "The fact that you have lived so long without the weakness and the ill effects of your disability leading to its discovery is a testament to your mother's prodigious intention and personal power."

"The mysterious and powerful hidden faerie," I sighed, frustrated.

"No, not your birth mother, your mother. The woman who raised you. The one you call Mom."

"My-" I spluttered, "Oh, no, I was raised by humans. I mean, if I had to guess, I'd think my dad might be a little bit intermagical. He's an artist, he's got an imagination. But my mom? No way. She's as human as they come. She would just roll her eyes if I tried to tell her about all this 'magical nonsense'."

"That may be," said Melodie, "but it's not necessary to believe in one's own magic to possess it or to wield it. But I'll admit, your mother is an interesting case." She smiled her strange, unfocused smile. "She saw through the smokescreen of Christian rhetoric so effectively that she shut down that religious programming channel entirely." She paused and cocked her head, considering. "So completely that barely any of the magic of life was able to sneak through at all. But, the CCC's programming is just too pervasive. Even without the laws of religion to reign in her experience of her own magic, the cultural need to conform to society's standards swept her up, and served to disconnect her from her magic, anyway."

"What are you talking about?" I asked. Melodie explained. There were some things about my mom that I needed to understand.

Mom was not as human as I had thought. She had, said Melodie, a significant magical lineage from an old wizened type of fae found in Northern Europe. Scotland or Sweden or somewhere like that. These magical beings were distant relatives to the faerie. Similar in many respects, but colder and wiser, living higher in the mountains. These reserved, irascible people might have been the inspiration for grumpy old Rumpelstiltskin, who spun straw into gold so famously.

"She's an intermagical in complete denial of herself," Melodie said, of my mom, "She really truly believes that she is like everyone else and that everyone experiences the world in the same way that she does."

My mom's intense devotion to 'the rules' of society, coupled with her own personal drive to do the right thing had given her an unquestioning focus that faeries and most other fae folk could not begin to imagine. Mom believed, deeply, at the core of her being, that as a woman, it was her purpose in life to be a mother to a child. Just one child would be enough, she thought.

"Now, I personally don't see it that way," said Melodie, "which is lucky for me, because I will never have children. But, I am also free from the CCC's conformity programming, which certainly makes a difference."

Some types of intermagical find it quite easy to reproduce, Melodie told me. Others much less so.

"Oh yeah," I said, interrupting Melodie's explanation, "there were adopted kids on my mom's side and my dad's side. Being adopted seemed totally normal to me, growing up. It seemed like almost everybody in the family was."

"Yes, I can imagine that adoption would be quite commonplace, for those particular folk. They would make the perfect family nest for little fae cuckoo birds to leave their refugee children," the faerie woman quipped, lightly.

When a deeply magical child such as myself had needed a home, the natural eddies and flow of the universe had placed me in the care of that deeply magical, emotionally cold, and extraordinarily focused woman. Melodie continued, her words taking on that strange intensity that told me she was not speaking in her own voice.

"She wanted a child, and with her unerring intention, she manifested that child.

A child worthy of her focus and attention.
A deeply and powerfully magical child.

She sent that child out into the world, and the child found certain things to be difficult.

She did not want things to be hard for the child.
It seemed better for them not to be hard.

And so she said to the child, with her unerring intention, 'You should not find that hard,'
And the child heard her and believed her and so, eventually, it was not hard.

And so too, when the child felt ill,
She did not want the child to be ill
So she said to the child, 'You should not feel ill.'
And the child heard her, and eventually the child did show sickness.

And when the child felt weak,
she said, 'You should not be weak'
and so the child did not show weakness.

And when she said, 'Run' the child ran,
and when she said 'Climb' the child climbed,
and when she said, 'Achieve' the child achieved.

And then she said, 'You should be fine,' and so the child told herself that she was fine.
Because to the child, these all seemed the right sort of things to do and to be.

But, by then the child had grown strong,
By ignoring when she was weak, by pressing through when she was ill.
By running and climbing and achieving, and then, after it all, by being fine.

So when she and the world said to the child,
'But you can't. That is impossible. You can not succeed,'
The child, now grown, looked back at all of the nearly impossible things she had already
overcome,
At what she had achieved by ignoring her illness and her weakness and by pressing through what
was difficult
At what she had done by force of will, simply because it had been expected
The child, hardened and grown strong, replied, 'Sure I can, you'll see'''

"What?" I asked, taken aback by the intensity of what Melodie had just brought forth, "Where did that come from?"

"From deep inside yourself," she answered, "I apologize for startling you. It's something you already knew, deep down. I just wanted you to understand." She clutched my arm with her strong, thin fingers. "It's important that you understand. There are reasons why you are the way you are, beyond simple luck of biology."

"I mean, yeah, When you put it that way," I said, "I guess it's true that when I was a kid, whenever I had a problem with something, I was given no quarter. Mom had high standards, and I just had to live up to them. That was that." I shrugged, remembering how my childhood had been. My mom cared about me so much and poured the whole of herself into taking care of me, but there was always something that took priority over the fact that I didn't feel good, or didn't like something. Pressing through and doing it anyway was more important than my own bad experiences.

"But it wasn't like that, though. My mom didn't do magic on me. I just-" I waved my hands around, not sure how to describe it, "I would do stuff because she expected me to, you know? She has this way about her. These high expectations. She would just sort of imperiously will me to do something, and I-"

Melodie touched my shoulder, interrupting. "She did what?"

"She willed me to," I said with a sigh, "Yeah, I heard it too. But, I don't know. She's just so…" I paused, thinking about my mom. "So strong. So upright and virtuous, I just couldn't disappoint her," I explained, then added, sadly, "I always did, though. It seems like I always managed to get one last little thing wrong. But, I tried so hard."

"You did," Melodie Cristalline said, in comforting confirmation, "You fought so hard against your faerie nature and your weaknesses and limitations because she willed it to be so, with her formidable strength of character."

I started crying again, emotions flowing up from a deep emotional well that I hadn't known was there. "Because she lived it," I sobbed, the truth of Melodie's words crashing down on me, "That's what made it so powerful. She lived it, herself. The rigid control. The strict adherence to duty and right action. Every breath of every day."

"Did she ever-" Melodie's words faltered and she gripped my shoulder in sympathy. "Did she ever praise you? Did she ever acknowledge your hard work? Your incredible efforts?"

"Did she? Oh, well, I mean," I considered. I hadn't ever thought about that before. "Well," I hedged, "I think that she-"

I thought back to my childhood. My mom had surely praised me, sometimes. I was certain she had. She had always signed off on my finished products, giving me a hearty 'good job' after school plays or art shows, making sure to note my accomplishments. But, had she ever praised my efforts or acknowledged my struggles? Had she recognized my real personal achievements and the things I had worked so hard to overcome?

Mom, who had been so constantly and unrelentingly critical of me, remarking on every mistake or misstep, with her imperious and unrelenting 'Why?'

Why had I forgotten the assignment? Why had I broken the glass? Why?

Because I wasn't good enough. Because I could never be good enough.

The truth of that knowledge pierced my heart. Had she ever praised me for being me? Had she ever truly seen me and found me to be adequate? Not for my accomplishments, but just for myself? I tried to remember a time and found that I could not.

"No," I answered, finally, "I don't think she ever did."

"She is," said Melodie Cristalline, with that ring of verisimilitude that told me something was true, "and, you are."

"I am?" I asked the word catching in my throat.

"You are enough. She is very proud of you. There is nothing you need to prove."

"I-" I started and stopped, not having words for the unresolved emotions that
bubbled out of me at Melodie's words.

She smiled an eerie but heartfelt smile. "It's just their way, those cold-blooded Northern Fae. Sometimes those of us with warmer blood can find ourselves with a touch of frostbite." I smiled wetly at her, tears streaming down my face. Frostbite indeed. Beside me, Melodie gave a little shiver. "Which reminds me. I am actually quite cold. Do you mind if we go inside now?"

I agreed enthusiastically, and stood up, following Melodie as she led me around, behind and down into a network of low earthen rooms that reminded me of the root cellar we had hidden in yesterday. I followed her, lost in thought, barely noticing where we were going, as I let this new and powerful understanding that Melodie had just given me settle around me like a warm cloak. I could feel it when things were true, and I had felt it, then. Mom really was proud of me. She really did think that I was good enough, even if she didn't say so out loud.

Past the first few alcoves, the pale light of the rainy day wasn't enough to permeate the dimness, but Melodie walked confidently on, not pausing. I reached out to hold her shoulder and followed her deeper underground in darkness. After some time, she turned abruptly, walked a few more paces, and stopped.

"Let's get you into some dry clothes," she said, stepping out of my grip and leaving me quite alone in the dark space. I hadn't minded the dark too much before, with the inner warmth of Melodie's earlier revelations glowing inside of me, and Melodie's solid shoulder to hold onto, but without that reassuring anchor I felt my heart begin to pound. She paused, then said, "Nothing you like? I'm not surprised. I find these all to be a bit uninspiring, myself, but you'll warm up faster in dry clothes."

"What? How can-" I sputtered. Did she not realize?

"Melodie, it's dark in here. I can't see anything!"

"What? Oh really? Oh no!" she exclaimed, calling up a mote of bright white light between her hands. She tossed it upward, and it hovered near the ceiling, right beside a pretty stained glass lantern that hung at the center of the roughly rounded earthen room. I smiled, relaxed by the return of my sight, and charmed by Melodie's near miss with the lantern. Even with her unusual expressions, it was easy to forget that she was blind. She seemed to move through her world quite easily. She must know these grounds so well, to be able to navigate them so confidently, I thought wonderingly.

Melodie's light illuminated long racks of soft clothes in earthy, natural colors decorated with little pops of lacework and sparkle. I couldn't resist stepping forward and running my hand along the row of smooth fabrics. The racks of clothing lined four of the five irregular walls of the odd little nook. On the fifth wall, a plain wooden plinth sat in front of a wide, gilded full-length mirror. A clean, simple, coiled

222

wool rug was overlapped at the edges with mismatched runners, keeping the pretty, soft things off of the hard-packed dirt of the floor.

"So many dresses!" I exclaimed, taking them all in.

"Yes, she does produce a startlingly large number of garments, doesn't she? There should be something here that will fit you. Although, unfortunately," Melodie flicked a shirtsleeve dismissively, "as you can see, they are quite plain"

I got the impression from Melodie that the two fae women might be somewhat contentious. Personally, I didn't find the garments plain at all. Perhaps, I thought, eyeing the soft, natural lines of the skillfully handmade pieces, in contrast to Melodie's own many-layered pink confection, the two women clashed in matters of personal style. I browsed through the collection, pausing to admire particularly beautiful or complex details of the creative, somewhat anachronistic gowns on display. They all looked like they would fit right in at a Renaissance festival, or, I supposed, the fair that they put on right here, every summer. I made sure to keep my admiration to myself, though, mindful of Melodie's sour expression.

In the end, I selected a richly green overdress with a laced bodice, and a soft, full skirt in a misty blue. It was one of the simpler garments in the collection and I hoped it wouldn't be too damaged by my general carelessness about clothing, and the fact that I would surely be spending much of today outside. I draped a soft silk shawl around my shoulders, with irregular edges that looked like curling leaves, and unbraided my hair, shaking out the plait into soft, natural-looking waves. I sighed and smoothed the soft layers of fabric over my hips contentedly.

"Did you find something that will work?" Melodie asked.

"Yes," I breathed, pleased with the way that the tight bodice of the overdress clung to my waist and then flowed artfully away, making my shape much more graceful and elegant than my jeans ever had. Admiring my reflection in the gilded frame, I thought that I could just begin to see it.
That I might almost be able to look at myself and think, *Yeah, that's a faerie.* "It's funny you know," I said to Melodie, "this mirror reminds me a little of Faeryn's city and the other fae things I've seen. The clothing does, too, but, the rest of this room..."

I trailed off. Melodie couldn't see it, of course. And what did I mean by that, anyway? That faeries couldn't have old, mismatched wool rugs?

"Oh," she said, turning toward the sound of my voice, "I hadn't realized. Here." Melodie made a small, unselfconscious grimace of focus, and the room swam in my vision. I blinked, trying to clear my eyes. When they refocused, almost everything about the little space had changed.

The gilded mirror was the same, as were the racks of clothing. The walls, though, were now a pure, glistening white, like marble. They arched, tall and elegant, meeting the ceiling with intricate crown molding. The ceiling, once low and speckled with basalt and dangling roots, now formed a graceful dome, culminating in a large stained glass chandelier. I could see how the illusionist had gotten the inspiration for this magnificent piece of art from the colorful diamond shapes of the little lantern that I had been so charmed by, in the unadorned room. The carpet under my feet was lush and thick, now, with an intricate labyrinthine spiral that replaced the previous coil of braid.

"What did you-" I started to ask Melodie, marveling at the sudden change.

"I just re-invoked the illusion. I hadn't noticed that it had faded, since it is almost entirely visual. But, of course, she has been out searching for several weeks now, and naturally, her focus and intention will be elsewhere. I can't imagine anyone else having had a reason to come in here in quite some time."

So this was what a faerie space looked like without its layer of illusion. Similar in function, but just a bit ragtag, I thought, remembering the rough, worn furnishings. The lantern had certainly been beautiful, though. I could see why a faerie might be inspired by something like that, as a basis for more grandiose illusions.

Melodie led me back up through the winding passages. I was glad that she brought the mote of light along with us to light the way. I peered into the other nooks and hidey-holes as we passed by. Many were filled with a mismatched hodgepodge of furniture, rugs, and tapestries, creating a cozy living space for some fae or another. Other places were dedicated to intriguing collections, their shelves filled with books, shining brass and glass trinkets, or pretty clusters of crystal and rock, some artfully displayed, and others packed so densely that it would be difficult to squirm in between the teetering piles of treasure. A few of the spaces were still colored with that unnatural perfection of fae illusion, but most seemed to have faded back to their natural state of imperfect, often chaotic, reality.

As I compared the two, side by side, I thought I was beginning to pick up on some of the subtle signs that told me something was an illusion. There was a too-perfect, too-balanced artistry to it. As though an illustrator had created the room with his imagination, rather than a builder with his hammer. And that was more or less the truth of it, I thought, considering what Melodie had taught me about illusions.

Eventually, Melodie guided us into one of these illusion-perfected spaces. It was a cozy kitchen, idyllic with shining copper kettles hanging over a warm, glowing stove. Anonaziata was there, bent low over a steaming cauldron from which rose the most delicious smell. Smelling it, I suddenly felt weak. I hadn't eaten anything since that light bowl of soup last night, and as I sank into a chair, the elevation change made my head swim and my vision momentarily darken. That feeling wasn't normal, I reminded myself, remembering what Melodie had said. I probably would have realized that my hunger cues were abnormal much sooner if Mom hadn't made hunger out to be so shameful. As it was, I had always just tried to ignore those sensations as much as possible. I would go see a doctor soon, as Melodie had suggested.

Gratefully, I accepted a mug of the same frothy yellow milk that I'd been served yesterday and a small ceramic crock filled with eggs, mushrooms, and cream. I dipped a piece of crusty bread into the egg yolk and chewed it beatifically, feeling the tingling in my fingers and toes subside as my body accepted the offering of food.

Having served me my breakfast on the thick slab of a table, Anonaziata returned to the pot on the stove. She lifted the lid and tasted the contents with a long wooden spoon. Frowning, she reached up and seized a bottle of some dried herb, and then a second, sprinkling a little in the pot before covering it again with the heavy iron lid. Whatever delectable-smelling thing she was stewing did not seem to be quite finished yet.

"I asked Alaric to take you walking today," she said without turning, "He knows these woods better than anyone. If there is a key to be found there, to unlock the magic inside of you, he will be able to find it." That sounded promising, I thought, as Alaric ducked through the low door, unfolding his lanky frame into the kitchen in a practiced way, as though he had been waiting offstage to make his entrance.

"Morning, ma'am, miss," he said, dipping his head respectfully.

"Something warm to drink, Alaric?" Anonaziata asked, gesturing to the cozy collection of ceramic mugs lined up in neat rows on the shelf above her head.

"No thanks, Nona, I'm alright," he said, and turned to me, leaning against an old walking stick. "The rain has stopped, for now. If you'd like, we can be on our way."

Chapter 31

We stepped out onto the trail that would lead us into the woods and I admired the way that the morning sun glittered off the beaded raindrops at the tips of the forest's leaves and branches. As we walked, I imagined, fancifully, that the faerie queen had seen fit to bejewel the forest for my enjoyment. The thought made me smile as I watched the forest sparkle.

Alaric let out a quiet breath of appreciation. "That's lovely, Fiona. Thank you."

"Huh?" I asked.

His weather-worn face was turned up toward the canopy. "The diamond leaves," he replied, "They're beautiful."

"How did- You can- You can see the leaves?" I spluttered in surprise.

"I can," he said, nodding and giving me a kindly, bemused look, down his long nose, "You didn't mean to cover the leaves in glittering gems, then? Anonaziata did mention that you were having some trouble with your faerie magic."

"I…" I faltered, "Well, no, I didn't mean to, exactly, but I guess that was what I was thinking about, a second ago. About how they looked like they could be covered in diamonds or something…"

"Yes," he said, nodding knowingly, "Quite. And how did you think it was that illusions were created?"

"Um, Melodie told me to draw the fire of my intention out of my, uh-" I gestured vaguely to my abdomen and trailed off, still not entirely sure what it was that I was supposed to be doing or feeling.

Alaric laughed. "Well, I'm sure that's true if Melodie said so. And I'm sure that one does have to do what you describe, at some fundamental level, but I don't think that you typically have to try particularly hard. When you have been making this great effort to draw forth your intention, what is it that you have been attempting to create?"

We walked on and I picked my way carefully along the tops of the jutting rocks and roots that cut across our path. "I don't know. Mostly, I've just been trying to make a flower bloom, like I saw Faeryn do."

"What sort of flower?" Alaric asked.

"I don't know, just a normal one, I guess?"

"Ah, well," he said, raising a long finger to point upward in revelation, "Therein, I think, lies the problem. Without inspiration, without a particular and precise vision to bring into being," he explained, "there is nothing for your intention to create. Nothing for the illusion to become."

"Huh," I said. I considered this and thought about flowers as we walked onward through the glistening trees. There were so many types of flowers, and, I realized, I had never been sure what kind of flower I expected to appear in front of me, all of those times that I had tried to create one. I felt a little silly, actually, now that Alaric had spelled it out for me. Of course, I would need to know what it was that I was creating.

So, choose a flower. One flower. Which flower? The image of a perfectly symmetrical, softly petaled, and intensely pink bloom formed in my mind's eye. One of my mom's camellias, blooming bright and bold, early in the spring and late into the fall, when less hardy flowers didn't dare show their pretty faces. I closed my eyes and pictured it, lifting my hand, palm upward. Feeling a cool, flexible weight on my palm, I opened my eyes slowly.

In my hand was the perfect round flower that I had envisioned, just as I had pictured it.

"Eep!" I exclaimed, throwing my hands up in surprise. The flower disappeared as my hand passed through the space it had occupied.

"Ah, see, just like that," Alaric said, nodding.

"Oh!" I said, startled, "It felt so solid. I didn't know if it would fall, or…" I looked down at my hand where the flower had been a moment before.

"Precisely. You didn't know what would happen, so it disappeared. If you had known that it was going to fall, it would have fallen, following your belief and intention," he paused to peer at me over his long nose, "Do you see?"

228

"I think so," I said, not entirely sure that I actually did, but thrilled that I would now have the opportunity to experiment. I turned and smiled brightly at him. "Thanks, Alaric! That really was fast. You certainly did have the key to unlocking my magic. Do we, uh, head back now, or…"

He smiled in a way that made me feel like I was missing something obvious. "Oh good. I am glad to hear that you feel confident and at home, in your magic. Have you finalized your plans to solve our problem with the spring, or do you need a little more time?"

"Oh, uh…" I said, flustered and a bit wrongfooted, as had clearly been his intention, "I thought, once I figured out the illusions I, uh…"

"They are quite pretty, yes, but those of us in Faerieland can all do this, and with," he smiled kindly, "somewhat more skill, born of long practice."

"Well, what do you all expect me to do, then?" I asked, exasperated.

"I don't know," he said, with a shrug of one bony shoulder, "I don't know if anyone knows. I think," he said, and paused, placing one long finger along his nose, "that you are likely the only one who will be able to tell us."

"But I don't know!" I exclaimed, exasperated.

"Yes, I can see that," he replied, not unkindly, "But, if there is an answer to be found, it is one that is locked somewhere deep inside of you, Fiona."

"Locked," I looked down at my chest, set off to good advantage in my new faerie clothes, "inside of me? How am I supposed to unlock it?"

"We find you a key," he replied simply, and with a cock of his head that invited me to follow, he set off down the path deeper into the mossy green forest.

We walked in silence for some time, following the winding trail through the trees, and every now and again, Alaric would nod deeply to one particular tree or another, although they all looked pretty much the same to me. Eventually, we reached a large clearing dotted with strange-looking boulders, and I followed the path as it curved around a large mossy rock. The craggy surface looked like nothing in particular, until I took one final step forward, and, like a picture coming into focus, the cracks and fissures of the stone resolved into a beautiful and deeply intelligent-looking face.

I gasped, and Alaric turned to see what had startled me. "It's a face!" I said, surprised, pointing at the thing.

"Yes," he agreed with good humor, as I walked around the craggy rock, examining it from every angle.

As I circled around it, the changing perspective made the face's expression distort and twist. "You know, I've been wondering why a lot of the fae folk are sort of, uh," I searched for the right word, "unusual looking most of the time, and then strikingly beautiful from certain angles like that rock is." I looked up at Alaric. "Do you know?"

"Hmm," he said, stroking his long chin, "I would imagine it's for the same reason that natural crystals grow in spiky clusters, full of inclusions, and only glint and sparkle from certain angles. Fae folk, too, are creations of natural wonder."

Natural wonder. That was the same phrase that Melodie had kept using when she had been talking about how the faeries make the flowers beautiful. There were wildflowers dotting the grass all around us now, and I pointed one out to Alaric, repeating what Melodie had told me.

"I just don't get how that's supposed to be special faerie magic. Doesn't everybody just see that flowers are beautiful when they look at them?"

Alaric chucked in a friendly way. "The faeries do love to bring up the flowers, don't they? And rightly so. They're very proud of them. But, as you say, it's been a long time since the fair folk imbued the flowers with enough magic that they are full to bursting with the beauty of it. The same could be said of the magnificent spectrum of the noble bow."

"The, uh, noble bow?" I asked.

"The rainbow," he clarified, helpfully.

"Oh, okay."

"You are right," he continued, "Even the most mundane human will describe a flower as beautiful, at this point," he continued, "but there is still much more work to be done. In recent centuries, the fairies of Portal Land and the valley have been focusing their attention on the beauty of mushrooms and of the gnarled trees and the lichen of the forest."

"Huh," I said, remembering that Melodie had mentioned something similar and realizing that I had just been admiring the beauty of the soft, creeping moss on the side of the craggy rock, myself.

But, I reminded myself, I was partially faerie, and that was part of my inherent magic, too.

"So, if a human looks at moss or lichen, or old gnarled trees, what is it that they see, then?"

"I'm not sure," he said as he turned to walk on, "I've never asked one."

The mysterious face in the rock looked so natural that I had wondered for a fleeting second if it might be a lucky accident of nature, but as we continued on through the grove, I saw that each of the specially placed boulders and rocks had been carved into a different figure or design.

"Alaric, what are all these statues?"

"Oh these? Well, the fae's strength does not lie in their memory, but the fair folk live a long time. These monuments help us remember our history. Look, see this one here?" He indicated the rock next to us, carved in the shape of a tall, elegant woman with a beatifically calm expression. "This statue was of Lithia, the great Faerie Queene of legend, who had ruled the land of the ash trees, some ways to the south. Her powerfully calming aura had sunk into the very rocky strata of her realm and imbued the magical spring that ran through her domain with a calming essence that affected the local flora and fauna, and even the nearby settlements of humans. She had been so still in her placidness that eventually, she turned into stone herself. You can find her there still, deep in the mountains. A beautiful stone faerie made entirely of lithium, which continues even now to imbue Lithia's spring with her preternatural serenity.

"This-" I reached out and touched the statue, wonderingly.

"No, this is just a rendering of her likeness," Alaric clarified, "not the queen herself."

"Who are these little ones?" I asked as we turned another bend in the path. Tiny stone children with wide, curious eyes peeked out from behind the skirts of a beautiful woman, eyes turned upward, cowering in fear.

"Ah, yes, the hidden children. The origin of the hidden folk."

"The hidden folk!" I exclaimed, "You said to ask Nona about them, but I haven't had the chance." I peered at the scared, curious young faces. "Is she really one of these children?"

He laughed. "No," he said, "That's just a little joke that I find amusing. She would shake her walking stick at me if she heard me say it. Our Anonaziata is old. Very old. Some days she thinks she may even remember the decision to intermix." He stroked his chin thoughtfully. "But I am certain that she is not as old as our lady Eve, here, or her unwashed children."

"Eve? Like, Adam and Eve?" I asked.

"Eve, the all-mother," said Alaric, nodding his agreement. I gazed up at the unusually familiar-looking face of the woman shielding the strange little children behind her skirts. "It's an old folktale, which, by the bye, tends to be a good place to look for information about our history and our magic. It's a way of knowing that has been passed down when other, more scholarly sources have been hidden or destroyed. But, I digress."

He turned and genuflected respectfully to the stone woman before us. "In the story of the origin of the hidden folk, we are told that our all-mother Eve was halfway done with washing her young children in a creek. After the great expulsion," he noted, with a pointed look, "And God chose to visit her, unexpectedly. When she saw Him, Eve took fright and hid the children she had not yet washed behind her skirts. God was angry at her reaction, and as a punishment, he declared that those children that she hid from Him would forever be hidden from the eyes of man."

Alaric bowed, genuflecting to the stone lady respectfully. "And so, that's why the fae folk don't have to do much work to stay hidden," he explained, "It's just the way it is. Humans don't see us, even when we're right in front of them. They'll see you, or I," he clarified, "but they won't see the magic. If they notice anything unusual about us at all, they'll likely just think that we're a bit strange." He waggled his eyebrows and I chuckled agreeably. "Or," he continued, gesturing to some tall sculptures of curious-looking creatures with curved horns and large wide-set eyes, "they might simply fold us into their lore. As demons, perhaps?"

I looked up into the clever, mischievous face of the statue of the goat-legged young man that Alaric indicated. His expression made him look like he knew a secret that I didn't. I frowned at his stoney, impish grin tiredly and sank down onto a low rock that didn't appear to be carved into anyone in particular. The idea of sitting on one of the representations of the fae felt a little rude.

My head was swimming with all the new thoughts that this conversation with Alaric had given me, intermingling with all the other things I had learned in the past few days. There was just so much to sort through. I sighed, exhausted mentally and physically after the long, uneven walk.

"I just feel like I still don't quite get it, what it is that I'm supposed to be learning here. How to, uh-" I waved my hands in circles in the air, "really do magic, you know? I mean, if it's not the illusions, I guess I don't really know what, um…" I trailed off, looking down at my legs. A mischievous stone face stared back at me, and I realized that my seat was a statue after all, as a little somersaulting creature grinned impishly up at me from between my knees.

"Yes," answered Alaric patiently, "And that is precisely why we are here, looking for the key to unlock your magic. And, how about that?" He pointed, then stooped low at the base of a pale pillar carved into the shape of three women, arms intertwined. "I believe I may have just found the very key that we are looking for."

He bent nearly in half, face close to the ground, peering at something. I came to see what he was looking at. It was an irregular ring of creamy-colored mushrooms growing at the base of the statue. Alaric inspected them carefully, squinting in concentration, then nodded, confidently. He seized one by the stem and plucked it with a practiced motion. Unfolding languidly, he rose and presented the little fungus to me in the palm of his dry, weatherworn hand.

"A key," he announced.

"Um, really?" I asked, not knowing what it was that I had expected we would find out here, but certain it wasn't this. "What, uh, should I do with it?"

"Unlock your magic," he answered, ambiguously, "Unlock your understanding." He bent again and picked a few more of the spindly things. One of these, he raised and reverently placed into his own mouth, closing his eyes and chewing beatifically before swallowing and opening his eyes again. "The lock," he said, smiling and running his tongue over his large, white teeth, "to the door," he said, touching his finger to his temple, and then finally bringing his hand to rest on his chest, palm over his heart.

Oh. Well, then.

At least it's natural, I thought trepidatiously, as I reached out to take the little collection of pale fungus that Alaric offered in his outstretched palm. "Do I eat all of these?"

"I think so," he answered, nodding, "You are perfectly safe here, and you have been tasked with quite the puzzle to unravel within yourself. We are hoping that you will be able to find something that will save an entire city, after all. That is no small feat to expect of anyone, by any means."

My heart rate went up, at that, and I froze, hand halfway to my mouth. Just save them, huh? That was all they wanted. No problem, right?

"Not that we truly expect you to, of course," he said, answering my expression. He patted my arm kindly. "That would be extraordinary in the extreme. Exceptionally unlikely. More probably, it will be the Queen or one of her court who will return to tell us of the opportune new location they have found for our dear Faeryn. Maybe even a space to hold the whole court, like the city of the falls. Such a feat that place is, but-" he paused his reminiscing, "Anyway, as I say, no one truly expects anything of you, really. It's just that the universe often sends us fae folk precisely what we need, exactly when we need it, as though by chance, and so, being as you're you, and you're here, we've just got to try, haven't we? It just wouldn't be, would it, not to have a proper go at it, just to see if it mightn't be that you can?"

"Oh," I answered, relieved but also just a little put out by Alaric's pragmatic style of comfort. They didn't think I was really going to do it, huh? Was that right? I felt a spark of indignant fire ignite deep in my chest. Well, maybe I was the chosen one, or maybe I wasn't and I was just somebody, but if there was really something inside of me to unlock that could help save Faeryn and her wonderful city, well then by God, or, well… by something anyway, I was going to give it my best shot.

"Here goes nothing!" I said. Screwing my eyes tight shut, I popped the small handful of mushrooms into my mouth and chewed. The spongy fungi unleashed a surprisingly juicy burst of rich, earthy flavor, and I ground the stringy things between my teeth several times before steeling myself and swallowing hard. Opening my eyes, I saw Alaric bent over, peering at the other side of the statue.

"Come, look," he said, gesturing to me to come bend down beside him. More of the same little spindly fungus grew in circles, here. "Now, see here. This is another type of mushroom. Similar, but distinctly different, as you can tell by looking closely."

"Different?" I asked, uncertainly. I bent closer trying to see any distinctions between these caps and the ones that I had just eaten, but the little domes and narrow stems looked exactly the same to me.

"Quite." Alaric smiled humorlessly, pursing his lips. "Those," he said, gesturing to the area at the front of the rock from which he had carefully selected my snack, "are a key to help unlock hidden doors in the mind. But these," he gestured to the extraordinarily similar little caps at the backside of the rock, "unlock a different door entirely. A powerfully permanent door. The door of death." My mouth dropped open, still tasting the rich umami of the forest. "An important door, and sometimes a necessary one," said Alaric, "but certainly not the door we seek to open today."

"Yeah," I agreed, earnestly, "I sure hope not." I eyed the row of disconcertingly similar-looking deadly mushrooms suspiciously. "So, what's going to happen now? What should I do next?"

"My dear, that is completely up to you. My role was simply to be your guide and help you find the key. The rest of the journey will be yours alone to travel. To begin with, perhaps you might like to head a little deeper into the forest and have a look around. Get out into nature, get some…" Again, he laid a bony finger along his long nose, peering down at me, "…perspective."

"By myself? In there?" I asked nervously, eyeing the thick dense green of the forest that lay out past the edges of the sunny glade. It looked astonishingly easy to get lost in.

"There are many entities that make their home in these woods," he said, giving the trees a long look, "Faeries certainly, and other things as well. You will not need to worry about becoming lost, here. The forest will know exactly where you are, at all times, and in a few hours, we will come and find you. You are safe to explore. I promise." At this, he gave a little wink and a half bow, and turned on his leather-booted heel, striding purposefully off in a different direction than we had come.

I picked up my foot to follow him but stopped myself, and in a moment he was hidden by a bend in the path. I was all alone. A little flash of light caught my eye, and in the corner of my vision I caught the blur of tiny faerie wings. Well, nearly alone, anyway.

There was no clear path forward from where I stood. Deer tracks crisscrossed the meadow, winding around the rough-chiseled rocks and occasional finer sculptures. I turned around slowly, looking in every direction. Where was I supposed to go? What was I supposed to be doing? Without direction, I wandered aimlessly, staying within the open clearing.

Birds twittered in the surrounding trees, and the occasional bee or butterfly drifted by on the breeze. I tracked the flight of one bright-winged creature with my eyes, watching as it landed on the curving horn of a tall statue, facing away from me, near the edge of the clearing. Not having anything better to do, I followed it, wandering closer.

The statue was of a seated humanoid in a large, ornate chair. He was as large as a man or just a little larger, with two curving horns framing a long, serious face, one of which now sported a jaunty yellow butterfly. His beard was pointed, and wide-set eyes gave him an animalistic look, like the sculpture that Alaric had pointed out earlier, of the other fuzzy-haunched goat-man. Carved into the edges of the seat were the first words I had seen in the glade. *Magic is the Devil's Work*

"Is that so?" I asked aloud, speculatively. Why did that phrase sound so familiar?

"Oh!" I exclaimed, remembering. It had been on my first day in Oregon when the Deacon had been lecturing me about the dangers of the world. Hadn't he specifically told me not to get caught up in the Devil's Work? The thought made my mouth quirk up in a grin that didn't quite reach my eyes. And now what was I doing? Actively working to unlock my own magic. What would he think, if he could see me now? This scene would confirm his worst fears, no doubt.

Running around with the fae, expanding my mind, I smiled again, and this time it did reach my eyes. I was actively working against him and trying to figure out a way to foil his plans. Now that I really thought about it, maybe he was right to fear people getting involved with all of this stuff, after all.

"Speak of the devil," I said, looking up at the stoic face of the statue in acknowledgment of the irony. At the base of the statue's stone seat, I noticed more of the spindly little caps. They looked just like the ones Alaric had handed me, or, a shiver of fear ran down my spine, maybe these were keys to the other door. The permanent door, he had called it. The door of death. Alaric had seemed sure that the ones he had given me were the right kind, I thought, leaning in for a closer look, careful not to touch the delicate things. I didn't want to doubt him as my guide, but as far as I could tell, the two kinds of mushroom looked exactly the same.

Could I really trust him? Had he truly known? Or, was there a deadly poison bubbling up in my stomach right now? Was I about to just keel over and die, all alone in the woods where no one would look for me? My heart started to beat faster, thumping in my chest. Maybe I was starting to feel a little queasy, I thought, clutching nervously at my gurgling stomach. A blur of motion startled me, on the ground near my feet.

"Aah!" I yelped and reeled back a few paces as a little black snake whipped away, into the tall grass of the field. I clutched my chest, heart pounding from the surge of adrenaline at the surprise appearance of the tiny serpent. "I don't like snakes," I said between breaths, grimacing up at the solemn stone figure. *No offense*, I thought, eyeing the two stone snakes intertwined in the seated statue's lap. I was glad I had managed to stop the words before they came out of my mouth, not wanting to risk hearing an answer 'None taken'.

I looked off, walking in the direction that the little snake had slithered. I was not a fan of snakes, that was true. I would even go so far as to say that I was afraid of them. And, I recollected, smiling with wry humor at the memory, it was a fear that I had created entirely for myself. Once, when I was maybe 9 or 10 years old, I went to a carnival with some friends. There had been a reptile exhibit there, and I remember thinking that it would be cute and girlishly becoming of me to be afraid of snakes and to shriek and carry on like I had seen some of my other, more feminine friends do. And, so I did, and, I was. When I shrieked and cowered, and acted like I was afraid, the sensation of fear that I created in myself felt real, even though I'd never been afraid of snakes before, and after that, it just kept coming. I had created it, I knew, but that didn't stop the fear from welling up inside me whenever I encountered something slithery and scaly.

And, I thought, stepping forward to peer again at the strange little mushroom caps in the grass, here I was creating fear for myself, again. No, I couldn't see the differences between them. In fact, I didn't even really know what it was that I had eaten, or what it was going to do to me, to unlock these supposed 'doors' of my mind. What I did know was that I trusted Alaric. I've always had a good sense about people and can tell when they're lying or trying to take advantage of me. Alaric, Nona and Melodie, and all the little fae of the country home, they all felt safe. I trusted them. This was a journey I wanted to be on. There was no point in creating unnecessary fear for myself, was there?

I looked up at the bright blue sky dotted with high, fluffy cotton clouds. The intensity of the color burned cool against the bright green of the backlit spring leaves. It was beautiful, and I stared for a long moment, enjoying the sight. My eyes drifted out of focus, and the leaves silhouetted against the sky swam in my vision, making swirling eddies like the watery magic of Faeryn's pool. With a twitch of my head, I cleared my vision like an etch-a-sketch, and the leaves reformed.

That had been an interesting and unusual sensation. It hadn't been unpleasant, though. Not at all. This was not the time to let anxiety rule me, I decided. And, I decided, smiling widely with the release of my fear and the return of my good mood, it was high time to get out of this glade. There was plenty of daylight left and an incredibly beautiful forest for me to explore. I turned toward the trees and followed a winding deer track, curious to see what I would find behind the next bend.

Part 8 - The Little Queen's Hill

Velia nestled deeper into the crisp white sheets of the puppy's bed. Illuminated by a single shaft of morning sunlight that sliced through the thick curtains, the young man tossed and turned in his sleep, disturbed in his dreams.

Unconcerned, Velia smiled. It had been two days since the girl had driven away from the valley, taking a large portion of Velia's worries with her. She was far away by now, surely. Returned back to wherever she had come from.

For the first time in ages, Velia felt as though she was able to relax. That matter, at least, seemed to be settled. Her place in the court was secure. The threat had removed herself. Yes, she thought, glancing at the agitated man sleeping beside her, all of her plans were coming along swimmingly.

Chapter 32

It was dusk by the time I noticed the little faerie lights blinking on, all around me. First one, then another. Little pops of brightness that lit the dim of the darkening forest, and reflected off the little stream where I had settled myself some time ago, to gaze up at the shifting, breathing canopy of trees above me and down into the flowing, changing water at my fingertips. I blinked, and the tendrils that had been curling out of the shadows of the leaves retreated.

A small faerie zipped up to hover right in front of me, and my eyes followed the motes of golden light that trailed behind her distractedly, refocusing on the faerie's tiny face only when she spoke. "It is getting dark, miss. Please, will you follow us back now? We can lead the way."

Feeling as though I was mostly floating, I glided across the roots and rocks, through the forest, back to the fair. I followed the weaving faeries intuitively as though we were dancing, and used their dips and dives to help me sway out of the way of gnarled trees' reaching branches, nearly invisible in the deepening twilight.

Before long, I was back in Anonaziata's comfortable kitchen, and while the cool evening air hadn't been unpleasant, I found that the heat radiating from the cozy fireplace in the corner was quite welcome. The kindly old woman filled a wooden bowl from the pot on the stove and Alaric brought it to me, seated at the table. I inhaled deeply, enjoying the delicious aroma, and watching the steam that rose from the bowl in curious whorls that took the shape of a tiny, nebulous imp. It reminded me very much of the creatures that had laughed and pulled faces at me in the bath at the River House. That seemed so long ago, now. I blew and the steam dissipated, taking the form of the imp with it.

Even just this morning, I might have seen this dissolution as evidence that the imp had not truly been real, but now, with my mind laid open, watching the tiny faeries that darted in and out of the small open window, I was able to sit comfortably in the acceptance that there are many different ways for a thing to be real, and that each type of reality has its own value. And, I thought, as I watched the steam begin to curl back out of the bowl, that each individual piece of reality has a spirit that is both unique and special and, at the same time, universal and infinite.

That was the crux of it, really. What I had learned, out there in the woods. Or, at least as deep as I could penetrate toward that truth, here in this warm kitchen, surrounded by the order and structure of civilization, disconnected from the chaotic logic of nature.

Anonaziata bustled across the kitchen and handed me the spoon Alaric had forgotten. I hadn't realized, too lost in my own thoughts to have gotten around to trying to eat the soup yet. I looked into the older woman's kindly, wrinkled old face and felt an incredible sense of connection in her gaze. Connection to her, in this space, and to this community that I had been welcomed into. Connected simply as…

My brain stuck on the phrase, wanting to say, 'human beings' but recognizing that Anonaziata was not actually human, at least not mostly. As *beings*, then, I decided. We are all connected as beings, simply because we happen to be.

The doorway darkened, and I looked up to see Melodie Cristalline's small frame silhouetted there, festooned from head to toe in ribbons and bows. Her dress positively dripped with them, hanging as fringe, and twisted into enormous, sweeping cascades. Her hair, too, was intricate and complex, interwoven with a multitude of colors, piled high and braided into something towering and artistic. In my current state, the complexity of the pattern was mesmerizing and I stared unabashedly, taking it all in. A tiny faerie darted into view from behind the massive hairdo, trailing yet another ribbon that she wove expertly through the ornate design. Melodie reached out a small hand and waved it away somewhat irritably.

"Enough, I said. Yes, yes, it's very pretty. Thank you." She turned nearly but not exactly toward Anonaziata, at the stove. "Mama, I hear that Fiona has returned. How did she fare on her journey?"

"I was just about to ask that myself," said Alaric, puffing away at something long and fragrant, as he sat by the fire.

"Yes, dear. She is at the table, and Alaric is on the stool," said Anonaziata helpfully. Melodie made her practiced way across the room and perched on a bench under the small, high window.

"So, how are you feeling, Fiona?" Alaric asked, turning to me, "Would you like to talk? Are you ready for that? It's alright if you're not. These journeys move at their own pace, and we want to respect that process."

It was an interesting thought. Was I ready to talk? I thought, in fact, that I was. All this time alone with my thoughts had given me a lot to process, and speaking these new understandings aloud would be a helpful way to sort through them.

"I'm feeling good. I'm-" I paused, assessing, "Yeah, I'm feeling good. Really good."

'That's good," Alaric said, reassuringly, "Would you like to tell us anything about what happened? You certainly don't have to. It is an incredibly personal experience."

"Yeah," I answered, "I think I do. Do you want to hear about it?"

"Very much," he answered.

So I talked. I told them about wandering in the glade and being scared by the little snake, before setting off on my own into the woods. I told them about how I had found a gnarled old tree with an interesting-looking knot, and how I had gazed into that knot, and seen an extremely familiar face looking back at me.

"Thank you," I said to Melodie, "for what you said about my mom. About her being proud of me, even if she doesn't say it. I really thought about it, and I think you're right. It's the only thing that makes sense." The realizations had been so clear, there in the woods, as I spoke to the tree that had my mom's face on it. "Her coldness, her criticism, it's just who she is. I don't even think she realizes how it sounds."

Had I really been convinced that she was a human? I mused, wonderingly. It hardly seemed possible that I hadn't noticed before. It seemed so obvious now. But, of course, I had assumed everyone was human, until a few days ago. I said as much, to the folks assembled, and Melodie Cristalline nodded, knowingly.

"Her own belief in her identity will also help to color others' perception of her. If she believes so deeply that she is ordinary, who would dare to believe anything different?"

That made a lot of sense, actually. "She didn't want anyone to think that stuff about me either," I said, "She taught me a lot, and, um," I remembered the unyielding force that my mother had been, in my childhood, "she made me get used to a lot so that I would fit in. So that no one would think that I was weird or different," I continued, processing as I talked, "but I am different, and I'm not scared of that." I smiled at the people gathered around me. "I want to lean into it. I want to be myself, as wholly and completely as I can."

"To step into your full power," Anonaziata said, nodding.

"To step- uh, yeah. I guess so," I agreed, hesitantly, and then with more conviction, "Yes. To be wholly myself. To step into my full power." Something deep inside me rumbled in agreement. I felt a sensation in the pit of my stomach, which happened to be quite empty still, the steaming bowl of soup still sitting, untouched, in front of me. My insides burbled, like a pot over a fire, warming me from my core, and rising, like the steam imp, twisting and twining out from my center, filling the space between my ribs and encircling my beating heart with a glowing warmth.

I breathed as I stood up, and felt this new energy shift inside me, moved by my breath. As I breathed out, I could almost see it, sparkling out of me like the motes of Faeryn's stream.

"Oh, Fiona," Melodie exclaimed, "that's extraordinary!" She had turned to face me, full-on, clouded eyes precisely focused.

"But, how…?"

Melodie smiled. She could see magic, she explained. My outline was now glowing brightly golden, which made it easy for her to see me. It seemed to be true, I thought, as I watched her track my movements easily with her face. Talking to her felt much more natural now.

Anonaziata stood with Alaric by the fire, and I turned to the pair of them for confirmation. Gesturing to my chest, I asked, "Is what I'm feeling… is it magic, truly? Inside of me?"

Nona smiled and Alaric chuckled and nodded. "Magic is a human word for a human experience."

Magic is a human word for a human experience.

That made so much sense. Thoughts and realizations collided, and I sat down, my head spinning.

Was that the big secret that the great nemesis, the CCC perhaps, was trying to keep from humanity? Was trying to hide behind the smokescreen of religion? That the magic that humans long for, that they write about in storybooks and pretend to wield in video games is, in actuality, a facet of their own reality? Something that they experience every hour of every day if only they would open their eyes to the undeniable reality of it?

244

It must be. Why would humanity create a word for something that doesn't actually exist? Why would we yearn for and crave something that is beyond our experience? The magic that we seek is all around us.

The energy inside me pulsed happily at that thought, resonating with it. Magic is what powers each being's every thought and action. Magic is everywhere, all around us, animating and vitalizing our world, and only our world. Our deeply and wonderfully magical world. Still feeling spacious and expanded, I felt that glittering haze of magic trickle up my spine and twist itself deep into the strata of my cerebral cortex, etching those words in a glowing golden script.

Magic is a human word for a human experience.

"That's what they're trying to keep from us, isn't it? I started to understand earlier, I think, but it's all coming together now that I'm talking to you." After I had parted ways with the tree knot that was my mother, I had followed the sound of water to a pretty little brook trickling over some mossy green rocks. The flowing water looked like liquid silver. Pure magic, I thought, running a finger through it, and creating new patterns in the stream. But not real magic, I reminded myself. Just water. Plain, ordinary water. But what is water? What are its properties?

I considered this, settling myself down by the bank. We need it to survive, for one thing. Without it, we'll die, and, incredibly quickly too. Within just a few days. What else do people say about water? That it's the universal solvent and will dissolve almost anything into itself, eventually.

I reached out and touched the river rocks, worn smooth by the flow of the stream. Rocks like these are nearly unchangeable save by this unending and inexorable force. A curved little leaf floated along the stream, bobbling along like a little boat. We use water for shipping and to power waterwheels. We use it as ice, and we use it as steam. I raised my wet hands and traced some wavy lines on the dry rock next to me. And, it can make art, I thought, smiling. Water has so many applications and so much potential that humans tap into.

Why isn't water considered magical? Because it's natural? But, everything that exists is natural. How does that discount it from being magical?

"I've been wondering," I said to the group gathered in the kitchen, "is it true that someone or something is really hiding the truth from humans? Hiding the fact that the world is magical? Because-" I paused, considering how to phrase it, "now that

I'm looking right at it, it just seems kind of obvious that we live in a magical world. I mean, human stories are full of magic. Where did we get that idea, except by looking all around us?"

Alaric nodded but said nothing, encouraging me to continue.

"I feel like maybe people used to know, used to look around at the magic all around them, and find it in the trees and the streams, like I did today." I looked out the window at the stars starting to peek through in the darkening night sky. "I feel like people used to actually experience the magic in the transition from day to night, and in the changing of the seasons, didn't they? What happened to us?"

"The great darkness," intoned a low voice from over my shoulder. I turned to look at Anonaziata, drying a freshly washed pot with a soft rag and looking grim. "The forces we have been calling the CCC," she said, continuing, "They have been incredibly successful in their mission to convert most of the world to Christianity, and, in doing so, to one very specific, and limited definition of magic and wonder. Their capitalist rhetoric has been extraordinarily successful as well. When we assign a value to the planet's resources based solely on the price they will fetch in the marketplace, we lose so much of our ability to understand the magic of nature," she sighed, sadly.

"And as this for-profit perversion of our environment destroys more and more places of natural wonder, it makes it all that much harder for the unenlightened to ever discover the magic of the world," she said, shaking her head, sadly, "I can see that you truly felt the power of it, there by that stream today, surrounded by the majesty of our forest. What if the only place available to you to open your mind had been a parking lot? What then? Would you have seen the magic in the blades of grass that shoot up through the cracks of the asphalt? There is magic there, too, but it is not as easy to access."

I nodded, letting this sink in, allowing it to color this new understanding of the world that was unfolding before me. "So it really is intentional, then. Pretending the world isn't magical?"

"Who can say?" answered Alaric, standing up and beginning to pace, "although with this new organization, this Crisis Control Council, they certainly do seem to be coming out into the open, don't they? But, if you doubt the intentionality of it all, then tell me how else we are to explain the Crusades? The Inquisition? Why has there been this great push to infect the entire world with these Christian ideals, unless there was something powerful to fear from those who dissent? Why the great effort to disempower those who seek to understand, and personally connect with the magic?"

"Why? They would say it was to save our immortal souls," Melodie answered, and laughed humorlessly, "which is certainly a mighty claim, especially given the example they have set with their own conduct, in this life."

"No, it is something larger," said Anonaziata, resonant in her conviction. "Something organized. Something other."

"Something 'other'?" I asked, "What do you mean by that, Nona?"

"I am not certain, of course," she answered, "but I have lived a very long time," she paused and scowled at Alaric, who looked sheepish but did not make any comment, "Not infinitely long, but long enough to see the world change once and change again. And, always there has been an inexorable darkness surrounding humanity, driving it, and penetrating it, perverting its successes away from peace and prosperity and always toward limitation, discord, and pain." Her wrinkled face was agitated, and she continued to rub at the same dry pot fretfully. "Now, some of that is human, certainly. Greed is naturally a powerful motivator for humans and fae alike, but this is something else. Something greater and more sinister than the sum of its parts, something perhaps even from outside of this world."

"Like what Melodie said about forces preparing for some great cosmic contest or something," I said, "making sure that humanity won't be ready. That it will lose. That Earth will lose."

"Perhaps," said Melodie, "The intended outcome is not clear to me, but such a contest would align with the visions that I see of the future, and answer for some of the enemies' more inexplicable behaviors. It would make some sense of the senseless pain and violence that has resulted from their actions, as well as the limitations of human progress."

"It would," Alaric agreed.

We sat in silence for a long moment, letting that thought hang between us. Eventually, I spoke again. "I've been thinking a lot about human magic. Trying to understand it. How to use it. How to amplify it." Alaric nodded along, stroking his long chin. "I understand that we can change physical things, like walls and buildings, and springs," I added, acknowledging the problem at hand, "and I get that we can take control of ourselves and our circumstances-" I took a deep breath. "And that we can influence other people in our society and the culture of our community."

I had come to a realization, I told them, as I sat there by the stream, watching the light sparkle like magic in the shifting waters. I had been thinking about old magic, the kind that humans used to do, before the invention of words like biology and pseudoscience, and the push to separate the notions of science and magic from each other.

The first thing that came to mind, when I thought about old human magic, was the iconic image of the witch in her pointed black hat, brewing potions in her bubbling cauldron. Was whatever she brewed up really more otherworldly than the giant vats of chemicals that create plastics that exist eternally and never degrade? Are chemical formulae really any less magical than a potion made from "eye of newt"? I wondered aloud why those Shakespearean witches had felt the need to add newt to their brew, anyway.

To my surprise, Anonaziata had an actual answer at hand, for my idle musing. "Likely for the antimicrobial properties. Although it might have been a source of selenium. Or phosphorus."

"Or for the calcium," suggested Melodie cheerfully.

"Of newts?" I asked, incredulous.

"Of mustard seed," clarified Anonaziata. She reached up and handed me a jar from a high shelf. It was full of small black seeds, just the right size to have come out of the head of a small amphibian.

"Oooh, that makes more sense. It's representational, which-" I paused, searching for the right words. "Nona, what do you think about rituals?"

"Rituals? What about them?"

"I don't know, that's just the other thing that came to mind when I thought about human magic. The idea of rituals. Dancing around a fire, chanting and all that. I feel like, if that kind of thing didn't work, people wouldn't have done it. But, if it did work, then why did people stop doing it, unless-" I paused again, getting ahead of myself. "Sorry, I'm getting all scrambled. Everything was so clear, out there in the woods, but now that I'm trying to say it out loud, it's hard to find the words."

"It's alright," Alaric said, coming to stand behind me, and putting a comforting hand on my shoulder, "you're doing well. It is hard to condense such expansive thoughts into something as limited as words, sometimes."

I nodded gratefully and went on. "Here's what I realized. I think we're still doing rituals. That they just look so normal to us, that we don't even notice that we're still doing that same kind of old magic, and using the same strategies to influence and manifest our reality, except it just looks a little different, now."

At this, Alaric's expression was quizzical, but Melodie nodded vigorously in agreement from her seat across the room. "So many human interactions are ritual in nature," she said, enthusiastically, "The social exchanges and greetings, the way humans put on funny little costumes to go do their business rituals. I especially enjoy how they dress up in their special suits to ring their bells and dance their money dances on their walled streets."

"Wall Street," I corrected, gathering her meaning.

"That's the kind of thing I was thinking about, yeah," I said, and added, "Organizations, too, like governments and city councils and things like that. It's all ritual magic, isn't it, how they're all vying for power? This Deacon and his son must be cooking up some pretty powerful stuff, to get this little operation of theirs off the ground."

"And you know what," I said, picking up my spoon and admiring my strange reflection in its shining convex surface. I dipped it into the warm soup, and tasted the thick broth that clung to the metallic surface. It was richly herbed and tasted at least as good as it had smelled, this morning. "I actually happened to remember something interesting that Brandon let slip about their plans for the spring when I was out there thinking in the woods today." The feeling in the room shifted, as though all of the air had suddenly become perfectly still.

"You have an idea," Anonaziata said. A statement, not a question.

"You know what, Nona, I think I just might."

Chapter 33

I bumped down the rocky dirt track away from the fair in Alaric's bulky old truck. Glancing down at the clock on the dash I noticed that it was nearly ten in the morning. It was the first time I had known what time it was in days, I realized.

The curious charm Melodie Cristalline had given me was swinging to and fro on the windshield. It was a pretty, but strange-looking little bundle that reminded me of Melodie's ornate hair-do, woven through with all of those ribbons. This was not faerie magic, Melodie had told me, when I had asked about it.

"It's some proper human witchcraft," she said proudly, fingering her handiwork, "taking some inspiration from tradition, and a bit more from my own intuition and magical style. The little ones help me to weave it so cleverly. To my particular specifications, of course," One of the little ones in question, the curly-haired little boy faerie, had lighted on her shoulder and preened, pleased by the attention. This charm was intended to shield me from the evil eye, she said, as I headed back into the valley.

After I had shared my ideas, there in Anonaziata's kitchen, the decision had been unanimous that I should head straight for the House on the Hill, to the faeries of the valley, and pay a visit to the Little Queen.

"She holds court in her house on the hill, and reigns over the fae folk of the town and the valley spread below it," explained Alaric.

"No," Melodie corrected him swiftly, "Not the town, not the valley. Queen Vivienne has been quite specific. Our Queen rules over Portal Land and the Twin River Valleys both. Her sister is queen of her own hill, only. Thus," she gestured at a height near her knees, "the Little Queen."

Reminded by this geography discussion, I had taken the opportunity to tell them about my experiences in the valley. The strange things that kept happening and those instances of unusual bad luck that had been my first clues that magic might be more than just stories and make believe. I looked from one expressive face to another, taking in their looks of concern. I had been right to be worried, then. The ill luck was real.

Melodie had handed me this charm in the morning before I left. I hoped that she was right that it would let me fly under the radar and reach the house on the hill without any more unfortunate incidents. I held my breath as I passed the road sign welcoming me back to the valley. Nothing happened, this time. No lightning clouds gathered and no suspiciously anachronous buffalo threatened my forward progress.

The uneventful drive gave me plenty of time to think, and my mind wandered back to the cozy kitchen and the plan that we had cooked up there, last night. It was just an outline, a skeleton of an idea, but it was a place to start. Anonaziata and Melodie Cristalline were heading up to the city, to Faeryn, so that she could use the properties of her spring to learn all she could about the Christian Springs bottling plant, in the hope that some of it might help us. As for me, I was driving straight to the faeries of the hill, to let them know what was going on, and ask for their help. The Little Queen's dominion was the closest to the spring, but Melodie said that she wasn't sure whether or not the Little Queen knew about their plight.

"Of course, she may have heard," Anonaziata clarified, "with all the faeries evacuating the city and fleeing south. Word of their movement would have been hard to miss, but those two do not communicate overmuch, and I do happen to know that the Queen has not sought her sister's assistance in this matter."

I took the next exit off the highway, following the instructions that Alaric had scrawled out for me this morning. "Oh!" I exclaimed, surprised. I recognized this intersection. It was the place where I had hopped out of the Deacon's car on my first day in town. I rolled down my window and welcomed the scent of the fresh spring breeze. There was the tire shop, open sign blinking and door ajar. Now that I didn't need it, of course. And, down the street was the coffee shop where I had found the letter from Queen Vivienne that had set me on this path of discovery.

That letter, and the rest of the documents I had lost, had been the best clues to finding my family. They were the reason I had come to this particular part of Oregon in the first place, and I hadn't really made any significant progress toward my goal since losing them. In fact, I realized, I had hardly thought about my birth family at all since I had left this town the first time. But, I reminded myself, I'd only been in Oregon for a week.

Today was Thursday, and the plan to save Faeryn's spring was going to have to come together in just four days, on Sunday morning. After that, this business with the faeries would be out of my hands and there would be plenty of time to look for my family. I drove on through the town and beyond it, following the directions I had been given.

A quick rain shower made me fumble with the truck's old-fashioned wipers, but before too long, I had driven through it, and was snaking up the side of a small hill toward the address Alaric had given me. The first thing I noticed about the house was its unusual shape. It looked like a two-layer birthday cake, perched on the top of the hill. Was it actually completely round? It was, I concluded, as I reached the top of the steep gravel drive and the backside of the house came into view. As I turned off the noisy engine and the clunky truck settled into silence, I admired the scene out the window

"Yeah," I said, breathing a quiet sigh of appreciation, "faeries could live here."

The strange round house was cut into the hillside. A lush garden sloped downward in front of it, lined by vines on artful trellises. Winding paths disappeared into the greenery invitingly, and butterflies lighted on flowers that bloomed in the bright sun of the early spring morning. Dew drops sparkled on the tips of fresh green leaves, and, as I opened the door and stepped down from the tall truck, I caught the scent of jasmine and honeysuckle on the breeze. I turned as I shut the door to the truck behind me, and the sight made me catch my breath.

A wide, clear view of the valley spread before me, the expanse of blue sky dotted with fluffy clouds over acres of waving grass spotted with occasional puffs of green tree. The sky met the land at some scrubby hills off in the distance, and a picturesque little graveyard nestled cozily in the corner, completing the scene. As the sun moved behind the clouds, the light shifted, and the fractal of an iridescent rainbow appeared, arcing across the sky. The domain of the Little Queen, I thought, breath taken by the majesty of the scene. I wondered, idly, how far that dominion spread. Melodie had told me that she was queen of her own hill only, but as I looked out across these empty rolling fields, somehow I felt sure that everything within her sight belonged to her.

"All that the light touches," I said to myself, with a little chuckle, turning back to the house. The porch was artfully cluttered with all manner of hanging chimes, trinkets and baskets of flowers. Something caught my eye, in the small window beside the door. It was a pair of wide, dark eyes. As we locked gazes, the eyes widened still further, then blinked once and disappeared from view.

"Oh!" I exclaimed, startled, then shrugged, "Well, I guess the folks of the house will know I'm here, now."

As I waited, I watched the chimes spin and twist in the breeze with their tinkling faerie bells. A noise from the garden to my left made me turn. From around the bend stepped a small woman with a gauzy halo of long, golden hair. After her hair, the first thing I noticed were her eyes. They looked right into mine, piercing me, filled with an intense emotion that I couldn't quite identify. She looked incredibly familiar.

"You're here," she said quietly, stopping to stand in front of me, our eyes still locked.

The intensity of her gaze made the hairs of my arms stand on end, like the air around us was charged with electricity. In the silence of the long, still moment, a pretty, short-haired child, eyes nearly as wide as they had been in the window, peered out from behind the woman's wide skirts. The child's appearance broke the tension, and I felt the rising energy dissipate into the bright, sunny morning. As the small woman reached down to grasp the child's shoulder, I suddenly realized where I recognized her from. She was the captivating woman I had seen dancing with her hula hoop at the park on my first morning in town.

"Um, yeah. Were you expecting me? Melodie told me she didn't have a way of letting you know that I was coming here, so…" I trailed off, flustered by the intensity of her gaze.

"I've been expecting you for weeks," she said, eyes staring straight into me, "For years, maybe."

"Um, what? You…" I paused, and looked at her again.

She was beautiful, that was true, and she was strange in the way of the fae, but she was also very familiar. Not just because I had seen her that one time, though, I realized. The familiarity was in the shape of her face and the curve of her chin, and in the way her pleased smile cut round apples into cheeks. In the gentle slope of her neck and shoulder, and in the distinctive wave of her long hair. I looked back up at her face, and into those eyes that I recognized so profoundly. Because, of course, I realized, they were my eyes. My exact eyes.

As that realization overtook me, I felt tears well up in my own eyes, mirrored by the pair across from me. Then we were hugging, holding each other and sobbing, shaking with emotion. As we cried and embraced, the energy that I had felt between us before, rose up again, surrounding me and warming me like the radiant glow of a roaring fire after a long, dark, cold night.

"Mama?" asked a voice from near my elbow, "who is that?"

She pulled back and we stepped apart, her hands still on my shoulders. Then, she smiled and looked up into my face. "This is your sister, love. Your sister Fiona."

Chapter 34

Having been welcomed inside and offered tea, I perched on a tall stool in the kitchen and admired the interesting way that the cabinets and counters joined, to form the curving walls of the unusual building's interior. I wondered why someone had bothered to create such a complicated structure. For the pure, artistic joy of it, if I had to guess. A fitting home for a faerie queen, indeed.

Admittedly, I might have been inspecting the architectural details of the place, like the thick center column with its impressive helix of stairs, to avoid the uncomfortably powerful swells of feeling that welled up whenever I looked at my newly found family. I snuck quick glances at the two of them, little Zelai and my mother, the Faerie Queen, letting the emotion out in short bursts, like venting extra fizz from a soda bottle. Evita served us brightly pink tea from a teapot shaped like a strawberry, then sat by the window and listened as I described my plan, and the reason I had been sent here, to her, today.

"So you'll be using primarily human magic, then? Interesting," the little queen mused.

I had launched into telling her about the plan as soon as we had sat down, both because it was so time sensitive, and because it seemed easiest. At least, talking about that, I knew what to say. "That's the idea, yeah, since humans can make changes, like the Deacon and his friends are doing. The fae can't really do anything about it, but I'm pretty sure that other humans could, you know? If they knew what was going on, and if they cared enough." I lifted my mismatched paisley mug and inhaled the floral steam.

Across from me, Evita leaned her small pointed chin on her hand, thoughtfully. The gesture was strikingly familiar, and I recalled catching myself in mirrors in exactly that pose. I forced myself to look out the window and away from her, trying not to stare.

"I suppose it could work," the little queen opined, "although it might be a little too human for me to understand it entirely. And I will certainly help you in any way I can, especially since it is you who asks it of me." She smiled at me, brilliant in her joy at our reunion. "And for sweet Faeryn's sake, if not for my sister's. I remember her from when she was young, and so very small." With this memory her expression fell slightly. "It has been a long time." She paused and I watched as her face flicked through a series of emotions before settling on indignation. "It is just like my impudent sister to have sent for you in her time of need like this. Taking what she wants from me and mine, yet again."

"Oh, no," I said, waving away the idea, "Queen Vivienne didn't send for me. Not at all. I came here looking for you." A glint from a prism hanging in the window caught my eye and reminded me of those odd flashes of bad luck. "You know, I actually got into town last Friday, but as soon as I did, all of these terrible things started happening. Well, not all of them were terrible. Some were just annoying. Little accidents and things. After a couple of days of it, I just wanted to get out of here, and I remembered how this woman Velia that I met, and this guy Godrin, they told me that the best place to find out about the fae would be up in Portal Land at the Fair Isle, so when I got my car back I just-"

The loud crash of something shattering made me whip my head around. My mother, the little queen, stood perfectly still, face white as a sheet, her mug smashed to pieces in the center of a pink pool of tea. She began to pace, muttering quietly and intensely, ignoring the shattered pottery.

"Velia," she hissed, her tight voice no louder than a whisper, "You met Velia a week ago. A week!" She grew more agitated, the ends of her hair beginning to float as though with static electricity. "I've been feeling your energy all this time, and I told her. I told her! She said, but… She knew! An entire week ago!" She threw her hands into the air and strode out of the kitchen and out of sight.

From around the corner came Evita's voice, piercingly high and imperious. "*Velia!*" she shrieked, then again, furiously, twice more, "*Velia! Velia!*" A bright flash like a bright camera bulb shone from around the corner, and I peered around it, seeing a startled Velia, who had apparently just materialized in the strange round house's plant-filled living room. Behind her, in the room's wide windows which showcased the house's impressive view, I could see dark, heavy storm clouds beginning to roll in. That might be a coincidence, I thought, but as I saw the stormy mood echoed in the little queen's face, I suspected that it was not.

"Evita, my dear," simpered tall, elegant Velia, eyes flicking between the smaller women's furious expression and the gathering storm out the window, "to what do I owe the-"

"Don't you 'Evita dear' me, you snake-tongued deceiver," interrupted Evita acerbically, "Just last night you sat here drinking my mead, belaboring me with your endless complaints, and" she added scathingly, "regaling me tales of the extraordinary efforts you were making toward finding my daughter." She clenched her fists, body rigid with fury. "A week!" Evita spat, "A week! You've known that she was here for a week!" The last word became a shriek that pained my eardrums and made me flinch back a step. Little she might be, but this queen's rage was certainly royally intense. "You, with whom I entrust my most delicate personal operations, have chosen to break that trust and betray me?"

The feeling of a touch on my shoulder startled me, and I jumped, turning to look. A young man, or maybe even a teenager, with deep, dark eyes and a long calm face stood close behind me. He must have come from around the corner and all the way across the kitchen without my having heard him at all. "This is court business," he said with a stern expression and gestured for me to follow him.

I did so without hesitation, responding to his serious, businesslike attitude, following him out into the garden. I could still hear the shrieks of Evita's displeasure emanating from the house behind us as I watched his long braid of black hair swing to and fro at the level of his fingertips, as he walked in front of me. Bees bumbled by as we strolled through the charmingly chaotic faerie garden, bursting with bright sprays of flowers.

With enchanting tableaus tucked into each bend of the winding path, I found myself wondering how much of this beauty was real and how much was enhanced by illusion. A fair bit of it was emphasized for effect, by my guess. We reached a woodsy back corner of the yard and the long-haired young man gestured for me to sit. I did so, settling on one of a ring of low stumps, as he took the seat across from me.

"So I guess you're my sister then, huh?" he asked, with an easygoing simplicity that took me aback.

I was?

"I'm Egan," he continued, rising halfway and extending a hand for me to shake, across an empty fire ring.

"Oh, um, really?" I asked, surprised, then added, "I'm Fiona."

I shook the proffered hand and felt a warm tingle of sensation at his touch. It didn't feel very much like the zing of energy I had felt at the Gullah's touch, or the overwhelming warmth I had felt in my mother's embrace. This was a different kind of energy, grounding, and comfortable.

"Yeah," he said, "I know. We've been waiting for you to show up for a while now. The whole court has since Mom felt you orient on us, or whatever. But I've known about you for longer than that. You're why Mom and Aunt Viv have been going at it for so long. You're the child the Queen sent away. Mom never forgave her for that, you know."

"Huh," I said, absorbing all of this new information.

Egan knelt down beside the stone circle that lay between us and started building a fire. My brother, I thought, with amazement, as I watched his hands moving quickly and confidently. "And now apparently Velia's betrayed us," he continued. He shot a weary look in the direction of the house, which still emanated with the faint sound of feminine screeching. "Again."

He rolled his eyes. "You know, on my dad's side, we have long memories. But faeries?" he shrugged, "not so much. Did I hear that you've been here for a week already? And nobody's brought you here till now? No wonder Mom's in such a state."

At that moment, the volume of the yelling increased dramatically, as an exterior door opened and then slammed shut. "Go run back to your new Lord then," Evita's shrill voice rang out, "and don't come back!" This was followed by the loud crack and signature bright flash that I had become so familiar with on my first visit to this valley, then, a moment later, by the sound of heavy, wracking sobs.

Egan stood, leaving behind his half-built structure of neatly stacked sticks, and headed for his mother. Our mother. I followed after him, and when I came upon them, he was kneeling beside her, one long hand resting comfortingly on her back as she spoke, seemingly to herself.

"I trust too much, I know I do. I'm too naive. But I've known Velia for so long, and she's done so much for me. I don't want to believe that she really- that she could- I just-" She stammered, her voice catching. "But, it's not the first time, and I know it's not right, the way it is with Velia, but with my memory… After a while I forget, and she just keeps coming back!" Her small face was cradled in her hands, and her long hair fell in front of it, shielding it from my view.

At the sound of my shoe scuffing the garden gravel, she looked up and saw me standing there. "But," she said, as she broke into a wide smile, her demeanor shifting like the sun emerging from behind a cloud, "you are here now, and that is what matters." Behind her head, I saw the gathering storm clouds begin to dissipate.

The big-eyed child slipped into view, as though from thin air, perhaps summoned by their mother's change in attitude. He had been introduced to me as Zelai, my other little brother, although apparently if I had arrived a few months sooner, I would have been introduced to my little sister Zalina instead. At a fae coming-of-age ritual, the details of which sounded intriguingly complex, the powers of the universe had made it known that my sibling was not herself and was, in fact, himself. Zelai had confirmed that this was true, and blushed handsomely at the retelling of it.

"It's good to meet you, little brother," I said and grinned at him warmly. He returned the look with a small, shy smile of his own, before ducking back out of perceptible reality again.

We spent that night around the fire. Egan built it into a blazing roar, and the four of us sat around it, sharing interesting tidbits and details about our lives. I told them all about my adventures since arriving in Oregon, and they agreed that Velia had been the source of my mysterious ill luck. It hadn't been only the coincidences that I had noticed, either, like the time I was nearly splashed by the puddle. Velia had been manipulating the area's ambient energy and stirring the men of the town into an aggressive frenzy.

"I just couldn't figure out what was causing it, but I'm certain that's what it must be. I can hardly believe it! So many women with stories of rowdy, aggressive men last week, and she did it on purpose, just to make trouble for you?"

Evita glowered, incensed. "The nerve of Velia, really."

Egan threw his head back and guffawed laughing when I relayed the story of my towel disappearing in the woods. "Yeah, she can push and pull reality a little, since she's not exactly bound by it anymore," he explained, helpfully. He made a motion with his hands like a candy maker pulling taffy. "The little faeries can do it too, but they mostly just use it to move from here to there. The bigger fae can get real creative with it, sometimes, though," he said, shaking his head.

"Speaking of little ones," I said, looking around at the garden. It was empty, except for the tiny curly-haired faerie boy, who had apparently stowed away in the truck with me. He now buzzed around our heads happily, occasionally alighting on our shoulders. "I would think a faerie queen would have a few more subjects around."

"Well," Evita answered smugly, "I had a special feeling about today and sent them all away. They'll be back tomorrow, with the sun, but I thought it would be nice to have one evening to ourselves, alone. Just family."

Early morning birds chirped outside the window of the curious little pie slice of a room that I had been given to sleep in. I woke up slowly, nestled deeply into the kind of plush goose-down duvet that my mom never bought because they made her sneeze. It felt like sleeping in a cloud.

A sunbeam sliced across my pillow. Likely what had woken me, I thought, drowsily. The sensation of my feet hitting the cool wood floor woke me up even more. Little wisps of smoke were curling under the door and, curious, I opened it. I found my brother Egan standing there, brandishing a smoking bundle of herbs. He paused whatever it was that he had been doing and turned to me.

"Uh, g'morning," I said, sleepily, "Whatcha doing?"

"Smudging," he answered, then resumed his walk around the circular book-lined chamber that enclosed the house's central pillar and spiraling helix staircase, adding, "It clears out the negative energy, like that whole mess yesterday."

"Oh," I said, inhaling the rich herbal scent of the smoke. "My Mom never let me burn incense, or anything like that," I said, gesturing to his bundle of herbs, "she hates the way it smells. I remember, one time, she gagged and left a store that smelled like that."

"Sounds like it was doing its job then," he said with a chuckle. He had heard quite a few stories about my mom, last night around the fire.

I laughed, too. "Maybe so!" As I reached the second story, the scent of smoke was replaced by a delicious aroma coming from the kitchen.

"Good morning," said my mother, the Queen, who stood at the stovetop, frying mushrooms and eggs in butter. Several colorful little faeries swarmed around her, iridescent wings fluttering prettily. Evita's long hair was, for once, not flowing around her shoulders. It was twisted, instead, into a high bun, and as I watched, one of the flying faeries dipped and snagged a loose strand, winding it lovingly back into her Queen's coif. Another dived to snag a mushroom from the pan, and Evita flicked him away with her spatula with an easy ferocity.

"Good morning, uh-" I stalled, not sure what to call her and landing somewhat awkwardly on, "Your Majesty?"

She laughed, another tinkle of faerie bells. "I'm sure that won't be necessary. I am your mother after all, but," she nodded, acknowledging my uncomfortable expression, "you have given someone that title already, and there is no need to create awkwardness between us." She touched her small chin, considering. "What if you were to call me by my name, Evita?"

"Evita," I said, trying out the sound of it.

"Yes," she said, nodding in satisfaction, "I like that. And it fits, too. Evita, the life bringer. The Little Eve."

I settled myself at the low kitchen table by the window and Evita brought me a plate piled with mushrooms and eggs, and a thick slice of sourdough toast, dripping with butter. It smelled delicious. She watched me eat appreciatively and then cocked her head speculatively.

"First, perhaps we ought to find you some new clothes," she mused, looking me up and down. I still wore the dress that I had borrowed from Melodie's friend, not having had anything else to change into.

"That would be good," I said. I gestured to the outfit, which, in addition to looking like a fantasy costume, was also pretty dingy-looking after two nights' sleep, and quite so much time spent outdoors. "If I'm going to try to convince the humans of this town that they should listen to me, I might not want to look like this."

"Quite," Evita agreed, looking me up and down. I would have withered if my mom had looked at me like that, but when Evita did it, I could tell that she was finding fault with the clothing, and not with the person inside of it. "I've always found that a little bit of glamor magic goes a long way toward convincing humans too," she pursed her lips and raised her eyebrows meaningfully, "see things in a particular light."

"Oh, um, okay. Sure," I agreed, hesitantly, not at all sure what glamor magic would entail, but curious to find out.

She nodded, pleased. "I know just the spot."

Chapter 35

We walked down the backside of the hill together, through the streets of Evita's neighborhood, where pink petals dusted the tree-lined sidewalk. "What is this place?" I asked, admiring the quaint little street dotted with shops and restaurants, "I thought the town was on the other side of the hill, over there."

"It is," Evita agreed, then raised her finger to her lips conspiratorially, "but this is my little town."

"Wait, what? You, uh, you made your own town?"

"Oh, no, no, I just found it, that's all. Tucked away back here, all by itself. My sister is quite particular about the fact that the entirety of the twin river valleys is her dominion, but no one ever bothered to account for this little town." She gestured to the small line of shops that formed a quaint main street. "And I've just been," she bent, and pulled a yellowed, dying leaf off of a plant as we walked by, "tending to it," she smiled at me and wiggled the little leaf before tossing it back into the yard, "and helping it to bloom." We turned the corner. "Here we are," Evita said, cutting across a small parking lot to a door underneath a red awning.

"Thrift Store," I read from the sign, "This is the spot, huh?"

Evita smiled and waved familiarly to the two women behind the counter. I followed behind her, like a shadow. "Yes, of course. Where else?"

"Um, a normal store?" I offered, skeptically.

She strolled by shelves piled with home goods, occasionally reaching out to touch something or other as she passed. "As a faerie queen, I could hardly walk into an ordinary human store and expect to have them serve me and sell me their wares with a-" She made a sweeping motion with her hand, and I gathered that she likely meant 'credit card.' "And anyway, the things that humans craft for themselves aren't meant for us. They're meant for humans. But the things that humans use and discard, well, those are once again a part of nature, are they not?"

"Are they?" I asked.

"They are," she said, with a smart little nod of finality, "We faeries may have the things that humans cast off. Their discards have been thrown back into the world for harvesting." She walked on, fingering various used items contemplatively. "And so, we find what we require in the bounty we are given by the natural world. But, humans are the dominant species, are they not? So we also find it in their trash pile and recycling heap. And, from the sales they hold in their garages and from the estates of their recently dead, as well as from places like this one, which are much more pleasantly organized than the average trash heap, wouldn't you agree?"

"I guess so when you put it that way," I said, still unsure. When I needed clothes growing up, my mom would just take me to the mall.

"Oh!" she exclaimed, making a half-turn back toward me and reaching up onto a high shelf. She felt around behind a display of trinkets and drew out a clever brass owl figurine with wide round eyes. I had no idea how she had seen it way up there on the top shelf, behind the souvenir shot glasses and other tawdry baubles. Magic, probably. I asked her about it, curious. "One of my particular magics," she said, confirming, then stopped to adjust her long hair in a mirror hung for sale, preening proudly as she explained. Evita could, she said, pick out the things that she, or her family, or particular folks in town, needed at any particular moment, simply by following the guiding light of her intuition. "They just have a bit of a," she outlined the little owl with her hands, "glow about them, I suppose."

"Who is the owl for?" I asked, admiring it.

"Well," she said, considering and turning the item over in her hands, "the owl has always been a special talisman for me and for the women of our family. She is wisdom, and she brings that which is unknown into knowledge." Evita looked up at me with that intense gaze of hers. "Considering the journey you are on and the attempt you are making, I wonder if she mightn't be for you?" She held the owl out to me, and I took it, startled by the unexpected weight of the thing. "Yes," she said, nodding, "That is just what we need. It will hold our enchantment well."

Hold enchantment well? What a curious thought.

Deeper inside the store, we browsed through long racks of interesting garments, some so old that they had come back around into style again. Evita parsed through the racks expertly, finding more beautiful and curious items than I would have expected. She held things up to me, nodding or shaking her head confidently, and soon, ushered me into a curtained cubicle, my arms laden with promising options. It felt good to peel off the tight bodice and long skirts. The faerie garments had fit me wonderfully, laced snugly to hug my figure, and I hadn't felt uncomfortable wearing them, but now that I was released from the constraints, my body ached and I took a long moment to stretch before reaching for the pile. As I bent forward, the Gullah's card, tucked into my top, detached from my sticky skin and fluttered to the floor, and I picked it back up, pleased to be reminded that I had it. Choosing an item from the top of the stack, I draped a delicate floral garment over my shoulders.

What's the point of that, though? I heard in my mom's acerbic echo.

It was true that the gauzy item wouldn't provide much warmth, or much coverage, since it didn't even close in the front, but, twirling in front of the mirror, I admired the way it moved around me and smiled at my reflection. *The point is to feel beautiful, Mom,* I thought to myself, and I did feel that way in this lovely, frivolous faerie clothing. I rejoined Evita, arms laden with my new treasures, and followed as she wandered down each aisle, seizing the most unusual things from the most unlikely places. It seemed like she was finding something for nearly everyone in town.

"Who is that for?" I asked, eyeing the particularly esoteric bit of old-fashioned machinery that she was examining.

"No idea," she said with a shrug, "I'm not even sure what it is. A windle maybe? Some sort of mill." She turned the heavy brass crank in demonstration, and the old gears ground against each other. "But, I'm sure its purpose and destination will make itself known within a week or two. It always seems to."

By the time Evita was ready to leave, we had several bulging bags, and I eyed the cars in the parking lot longingly, not looking forward to balancing my awkward load on the long walk back up the hill. As my eyes scanned the half-full lot, I was surprised when they lit on a familiar face.

It was my friend from the library, the charming old man who had given me the address of the River House. He stood leaning against an old vintage sedan, as though he were waiting for something. Then, seeing us, he smiled widely and doffed his crumpled little black hat.

"My queen," he said, genuflecting respectfully to Evita, "would you happen to be in need of a ride?"

"Luck is an important part of faerie magic," Evita explained, as we relaxed luxuriously in the wide back seat of the antique automobile, hands dangling out the window and fingers dancing on the breeze, "I put my trust in my faerie nature, believe that things will work themselves out, and let the magic find its own way."

I had assumed we'd be going back to the hill, but we turned the other way, heading down a winding country road. I started to open my mouth to ask where we were going, but then shut again. After the week I had been having, I thought I would hardly be surprised by anything, so I let our destination remain a mystery and sat back to enjoy the ride.

Eventually, we turned off the main road and onto a gravel drive that ran along the edge of a wide, grassy field. The car trundled slowly along the dusty track toward a row of trees at the edge of a wildflower-spotted meadow. Once the big old car had rumbled to a stop, Evita hopped out and grabbed one of the bags from the thrift store, thanked our friend, who agreed to wait for us, and headed purposefully off toward the treeline.

"So, uh, where are we?" I asked, finally giving in to my curiosity as I followed after her.

"Just somewhere I know," she answered, smiling over her shoulder at me, "A good spot for a bit of magic." She spread a fringed cotton blanket from the thrift store out on the grass, in the shade of a tall oak tree. It was the perfect picnic blanket, I realized, as I looked at it. The thrift store had given her exactly what she needed when she needed it. I wondered what else she was going to pull out of the bag.

She satisfied my curiosity momentarily, pulling out several other items and placing them on the edge of the blanket. A well-burned candle, a small crystal dish, my new faerie wardrobe, and the noble brass owl. Motioning for me to stay put, Evita bustled off through a crooked little gate and over a small bridge, into the trees. I waited, perched on a log near the blanket, unsure what to do with myself.

The bridge she had crossed spanned a mossy little creek. On either side of the bridge, a single stripe of whitewashed boards formed a fence, marking the line where the field met the forest. Something was written on the fence in a looping cursive script, and I walked closer to read it.

October 4th, 1582, the Gregorian Calendar is implemented

"Interesting," I said to myself, then took two steps to my left to read the next board.

1582, Pope Gregory XIII invents the modern Gregorian Calendar

It was a historical timeline, and, not having anything else to do, I wandered along it in reverse chronological order, reading the entries as I passed, until one, in particular, made me pause.

June 24th, 1559, the Book of Common Prayer, a Protestant Prayer book, becomes the only legal form of worship.

That reminded me of something Melodie or maybe Faeryn had mentioned, about conformity and Christianity. The idea of outlawing different types of worship made a shiver run down my spine, and I turned away from the timeline feeling a little unsettled. What a curious place this was, that Evita had brought me to. I paced between the fence and the picnic blanket, to pass the time, while I waited.

Being with Evita didn't feel awkward, exactly, but finding myself alone here with this lovely, captivating woman who was, apparently, my family, certainly wasn't entirely relaxing either. It had been a major shock, finding Evita, Egan, and Zelai so unexpectedly, when my mind already felt full to bursting with all of the new things I had been discovering, and with my plan to save Faeryn and her spring.

Now, I had a whole set of new thoughts and ideas to contend with, on top of everything else. What did it really mean to be the daughter of a faerie queen, anyway? This felt like an entirely new game with entirely new rules, and yet again, I found myself without the rulebook. Soon enough, Evita returned, arms laden with lichen-covered sticks, mossy rocks, and all manner of green things. She unloaded her bounty onto the blanket and beckoned me to come sit with her.

"There are many things that must be said, by me to you, and you to me," she told me, not looking up as she arranged the items on the center of the blanket, "but there will be time for all of that, after. For now, let us focus our energies on your plan to save my poor, sweet, sick niece" Her soft expression hardened. "And my insufferable sister." What we would be doing here, she explained, was simple ritual magic. It wasn't specifically faerie magic, Evita explained, it was simply a method that we could use to help us channel the undirected forces of energy in the universe toward our particular desired outcome.

First, she marked the four cardinal directions, giving each direction its own elemental symbolism. Our fire, flickering and hot, burned deep in the recess of the lumpy old candle, and she filled the crystal dish with water that she dipped out of the little creek. For air, Evita brought forth a dandelion head, dried, white, and ready to puff, and for earth she used the dandelion's thick root, covered in dark brown soil.

After these four items were in place, she moved on to the rest of her collection, touching and considering each item before placing it deliberately into the artful arrangement of leaves and bits of bark that took the form of a radial sun on the blanket between us. She talked as she worked, explaining the meanings behind the various components of the design and describing the steps that we would take next, once everything was in place. Finally, she took the brass owl from where it sat at the side of the blanket and placed it reverently, right at the center.

"Any questions before we begin?" she asked, holding out the purple flower that would be my prop for this pantomime.

"Um, I guess not," I answered, holding the proffered flower by its long stem like a wand, then said, "But, do you really think it's okay for us to use magic to control people's minds, like this, though? To make them side with us about the spring, I mean? It's getting me what I want, sure, but it does feel kind of wrong, you know?" She laughed loudly, the tinkling noise ringing out over the nearly empty field. The old man waiting by the car turned his head toward us, roused by the eruption of sound.

"I don't think we need to worry over much about this sort of magic overpowering anyone's free will," she said, "although it is wise of you to consider those sorts of things. But no, the human mind is not so changeable that we would be able to control them, in mass, with a bit of herbs and stone, and ritual." She shook her head. "What we do today will orient our own energies toward our own success. Toward effective and influential persuasion, and," she added with a twinkle of her bright eyes, "toward charm."

That seemed safe enough, I thought and told Evita so. She agreed and so we began. "How did you learn how to do all this?" I asked, when the candle had burned low, and the ember of the old man's long pipe was the only thing I could see in the vast darkness in front of us.

"Learn how? Oh, well," Evita answered, reverently removing the leaves and sticks from the blanket in front of us, "some of it is learned, I suppose, the herb lore and such, but most of the work of building a ritual is intuitive."

"What do you mean?"

"Well, each ritual is different, with a few basic universalities," she said, indicating the four elements she had started with, "and when I want to make magic, I ask the spirit of the land and my own inner divinity to give me what I need, and to show me what I should do, to accomplish my goals." She smiled at me. "The women in our line have a tendency toward this particular talent. Have you ever done anything like that?"

I nodded. I had always loved the idea of doing magic, even if, as Mom insisted, it was all make-believe. That did sound like something I had done a few times when I was a kid. My attempts had certainly been less elaborate and intentional than today had been. But, that had been the magic of a child and not of a queen. Now that I knew what I was doing, though, I might just want to try it again.

Chapter 36

That night I went back to the Raven, this time with Evita by my side. It felt very different to step through the front door of the bar in my lovely new faerie clothing, brimming with the aura of confidence and charm generated by our ritual. Last time, I stood in the entrance like a deer in headlights.

This time, we walked into the room like everyone had been waiting for us to arrive. I had a mission to accomplish, and I knew what I was here to do.

"Your abilities are a gift," Evita had told me, during the ritual, as she anointed my face and shoulders with the juices of some sweet-smelling leaves, "Do not fear the attention that you can manifest with your talents. Wield your power with intention."

I strode over to the karaoke booth. Tonight, I wanted everyone's eyes on me.

"Welcome back, darlin'!" said the friendly mountain of a man behind the booth. His sporadically-toothed grin widened as he looked over my shoulder and saw Evita behind me. "Oh, girl, wait! Are you really-? Stars above, if you're not just the spitting image…!" He reached out and grabbed me by both shoulders, shaking me enthusiastically. "We've been waiting for you, girl! Looking all over for ya. Should'a realized, when I first saw you, I guess…"

"Yes, perhaps you should have done," came a coldly imperious voice from over my shoulder. I turned and saw Evita wearing a witheringly fierce expression that I wouldn't have expected from her. The man behind me froze, locked in place by her stare, and the air around us seemed to grow frosty. A moment later, though, Evita smiled, and with it, the sensation of gathering cold shattered and dissipated. "But, she is found now, and what has passed is past," Evita continued, benevolently.

"My queen, what happened? How did-" asked the large man, eyes wide.

"Velia," Evita spat, looking fierce again.

"Vellia? Oh wow! Are you looking for her? She's here tonight, right over-" he turned and scanned the sea of bodies, "Well, I guess she must have slipped out the back."

"I would expect so," Evita said, smiling slowly in a way that did not break the gathering cold, this time.

"The missing daughter," the big man said, turning back to me with another wide grin, and I stepped back, startled, as he bent in two in a comical bow, adding, "Your humble servant, m'lady. What song may I queue up, on this fine eve?"

When I took the stage this time, I used the high position to my advantage and looked out over the sea of faces turned up toward me, trying to gauge their openness and receptiveness to what I was about to say. On my cue, I started to sing, pleased by the clever intentionality of the song that Evita had chosen, about the pain of seeing natural spaces paved over and tuned into parking lots.

I sang and saw many of the upturned faces brighten with enjoyment at the old song. Some, though, decidedly did not, and I made a mental note of which was which, deciding who I would talk to, first. "You don't know what you've got till it's gone," I told the audience, feeling the truth of the lyrics deep inside me. We would do what we had to, to protect it, this time, I thought fiercely, channeling my emotion into the music. By the time I stepped off the stage, Evita was already hard at work, enchanting a group of men by the bar. She flirted and laughed with them charmingly.

"Oh, really, you like to hike, too?" she asked, coquettish eyelashes working overtime, "Oh yes, there's nothing better than the unspoiled natural beauty of the Oregon wilderness. I completely agree."

"You have to find out what they care about," she had explained to me as we made our preparations for tonight, "and then you have to make the cause relevant to them, personally. If you can manage to hook them by their heartstrings, they'll follow you anywhere." I caught her eye and she arched her brow as if to say, "Get on with it, girl."

Right. Mask on. There's work to be done.

At first, it felt awkward, but after a while, I found my stride. I flitted confidently from group to group like the faerie I was beginning to believe that I was, discovering how the people of this town really felt about their natural world, and why it was important to them, personally, to protect it.

"I've never been mountain biking, but you make it sound amazing," I said, only somewhat insincerely, as I leaned in, captivating a tall, dark-haired Oregonian with an easy smile. He was more than willing to tell me more. "You sure seem like someone who really cares about nature," I told him, sometime later, "You know, I've been hearing about this thing that's going on. It's really terrible." I painted a beautiful picture of the idyllic woodland surrounding the spring, the beautiful, if damp, area that I had walked through when I had first crash-landed in Oregon. Then I described the disastrous impact that development would have on the natural spaces nearby, such as, I theorized, probably the best local mountain biking trails. "But we might have a chance to stop it if we all stand together. Is there any chance you're free Sunday morning?" I blinked beseechingly up at him, then smiled. As luck would have it, he was.

Buzzing with energy rather than alcohol, I floated out the door with Evita after last call, pleased with the impact we had made with our night's work. As we walked down the crowded sidewalk, I could hear that the chattering crowd around us was all a twitter about the trouble with the spring and the event that I was planning for Sunday. We had done all that we could, tonight. Tomorrow's plans were in place. Everything was as prepared as it could be. Or almost.

Feeling almost drunk on the night's success, I smiled, thinking of just one more thing I could do that might help. I borrowed a cell phone from one of my new friends in the crowd and made a call. "Hi, um, I could use your help. Tomorrow. With the little queen, yeah. Thanks. See you then." Positively floating on air, I followed Evita into a conveniently waiting car. It was time to head back up to the hill and get some sleep. I wouldn't be getting much rest tomorrow night.

Part 9 - The Plan

"How dare she!" Velia raged, stamping her prettily booted feet and clenching her fists as she marched to and fro across the small apartment's living room, "How dare she! That arrogant, self-aggrandizing potentate, hounding me out of the Raven like that." The overhead light flickered in response to her mood. Brandon turned his face up to eye it suspiciously. Seeing this, Velia stilled, attempting to quiet her chaotic energies. She must not blow her cover.

"I don't know what you're talking about," Brandon said as he dragged a chair from the table to the center of the room, "Nobody did anything to us last night. You saw, uh, whatever it was you saw and then you dragged me out the back." He rubbed his upper arm in memory and climbed up on the chair, reaching up toward the flickering light fixture.

Velia nodded, eyes narrowing. Perhaps the puppy was right. Perhaps she had acted too hastily in the face of the queen's rage. After all, Evita had no power over her now. Velia was the little queen's subject no more.

"You know, this light did that a few weeks ago, too, when this, uh, this lady came by. She wanted to talk about the Christian Springs project. She, uh..." he looked over his shoulder at Velia, "she didn't like it."

"Is that so?"

"Yeah, weird lady. Kept calling herself the Queen. Queen Veronica or Victoria or something,"

"Vivienne," Velia hissed, her eyes narrowing. The Queen herself had come here, had she? Fascinating. But, that was a good reminder. This town was not Evita's own, anyway. This was the Queen's realm, Velia recalled, smiling slowly. Though, with Velia's help, the balance of power shifted further away from the Queen and her family, day by day.

Velia would do well to remember that there was nothing, truly, to fear from the Queen's littlest sister, now.

Chapter 37

"I saw you, actually, the first morning I was in town," I told Evita as I loaded an armload of brightly colored hula hoops into the back of Alaric's ancient pickup in the bright morning sunshine. "You were dancing. It was so beautiful." I sighed, remembering, "and I wanted to come over and meet you so badly, but I was so fixated on what I was supposed to do, and what I was supposed to be trying to find that I didn't realize that what I was looking for was right in front of me."

"And yet, you found me, even so," she said, squeezing my arm, comfortingly, "but it is certainly true that what we believe we ought to do often diverts us from the path of our intuition."

I drove us back down from the hill and into town for the Saturday morning market. According to Evita, it would be another great opportunity to spread the word. We dropped the hoops off at the top of the same grassy hill where I had first seen her dancing, and Evita led me down the rows of market stalls, piled high with leafy vegetables, bright, round fruits, local honey, cheeses, and wine. It seemed like she knew everyone, and she introduced me to each of the shopkeepers by name, effusive with a different but no less intense charm than she had displayed at the Raven last night.

"My daughter," she said, beaming with pride as she presented me. I smiled back, still buoyed by the confidence of yesterday's ritual, and the joy of my newfound family and sense of belonging. Evita lingered at some stalls longer than the others, talking in a hushed, conspiratorial tone, and telling the sordid tale of the pump and the damage it would do in vivid detail. "The gossips," she said with a wink as we walked away, "They'll have the whole town talking about it before noon." Others, she simply told the time of the gathering, accepting their various offers of baked goods and lawn chairs. "The helpers," she said in explanation, with a grateful nod to the old woman at the stall we had just departed, "Those people make the earth turn round, you know."

Once we had visited all the market stalls, Evita led us back to the hillock and the pile of brightly patterned hoops. Zelai was there on the hilltop already, spinning, then thrusting and parrying, wielding the hoop like a martial artist. Evita handed me one colorful hoop and showed me the basic steps of the twirling, hypnotic dance. It wasn't as difficult as I expected and after a few minutes of practice, I was able to relax into the fluidity of some of the simpler motions, closing my eyes and enjoying the feeling of the breeze as I spun.

"Cousin!"

A shout from right behind me made me jump, and I whirled, eyes flying open. I stumbled over the hoop and the flowy faerie clothing and tripped, tumbling down the backside of the little hillock. "Aaaaaaaaaaaaaaaaaaa! ...Ow" I rolled to a stop at the base of the hill, a tangle of clothes and limbs. Unfurling, I looked up and was surprised to see a familiar face staring down at me. "Faeryn?"

It certainly looked like Faeryn's translucently pale face, with long red hair peeking out from under a jaunty little cap, but the intensely masculine expression that it bore gave me pause. Arlee stepped forward and extended a hand to help me to my feet.

"This is Visc, actually. Faeryn isn't much for danger or savagery, but Visc and I are both here to help," she smiled, showing sharp white teeth, "however we can." Visc stepped past me to hail his other cousin Zelai, and the two small, delicate-featured boys greeted each other with curtly masculine nods. In moments Zelai was busy showing Visc the fighting moves he had been practicing with his hoop. "It's been quite some time since we last had the opportunity to visit our cousins here in the south. It is so nice to be with them again," said Arlee. We stood together, watching the two young men feint and parry. "Hmm," said Arlee speculatively, "I feel as though Evita's youngest was a little girl, last I noticed. Though, I suppose Faeryn is typically a girl when she isn't Visc, isn't she? Funny how those things change."

"Yeah," I agreed tentatively. I didn't think I had the mental space to unpack all of that, with everything else I had going on today, so I moved on.

"So, you guys are here to help us with tonight, huh? Melodie Cristalline got through to you?"

"Yes," Arlee confirmed, "And Faeryn, well, Visc- it doesn't matter really, they positively leapt at the chance to get out of the spring and do something real to try and help. She thought it was an absolutely brilliant idea, that you want to-" A sound from the other side of the grassy hill made Arlee pause and startled Visc and Zelai from their play-fighting. We all walked over the hill together to see what was causing the commotion.

"-TO DARE TO WALK THROUGH MY TOWN IN BROAD DAYLIGHT," Evita shrieked, enraged.

"But it isn't your town, as we both well know," said Velia, tall and disdainful. She looked down her nose at us, arm in arm with a fair-haired male companion. "And it'll be his Lord's town, soon enough. That's where the real power is. I'm sure even you can smell which way the winds are blowing, can't you, tiny queen?"

"Our Lord," corrected the man next to her. His voice was familiar, and I turned my attention to him for the first time.

It was Brandon! "With him?" I cried, the words erupting out of me, "Don't you know what he's doing?" All of the eyes of the crowd that had gathered around this altercation now turned their sights on me, but my stare was locked on Velia and her face told me everything I needed to know. "You do!" I yelled, pointing accusingly, "You know all about it, don't you?"

"You have no idea what you are talking about, you silly girl," replied Velia, looking down her sharp nose at me.

"How dare you speak to my daughter, after everything you put her through! Put the town through! Put me through!" Evita shrieked and lunged forward, making Velia feint backward, away from her. I expected her to flit away and disappear. I knew she could, I'd seen her do it, but for some reason, she did not. When I saw her shoot a nervous look at Brandon, on her arm, though, I realized why. Instead, Velia spat vitriol back at Evita, giving as good as she got.

While they fought, I watched Brandon. I had really liked him once, I thought, looking at the concern on his handsome young face.
He was someone I had felt a real connection with, at least for a moment. Someone that I could really talk to.

"Brandon," I said, and he turned toward me, away from the bickering women, "Did you know that your water pump is going to ruin the entire ecosystem of that part of the forest? There are lots of natural things that depend on that spring continuing to flow naturally. Do you think there's any way you could just-"

"If I could just what?" he interrupted, surprising me with his coldness, "just walk away and leave my Father's personal gift from God right on the ground where he found it? Come on. Grow up, Fiona. This world's gifts are ours to use."

"Yes!" I cried, exasperated, "They're ours! All of ours!"

"Not yours," he spat, "Ours. God's Children. Heathens like you have no place in the kingdom of God." This nonsense again. I tried another tactic.

"Brandon, Christians care about people, right? This pump will kill Faeryn, okay? She needs it to survive, she-"

He cut me off again, with a dismissive gesture. "You think my Father doesn't know that? You think that pathetic 'Fairy Queen' didn't come begging me to talk to him, 'Save my broken daughter! Save my magical city!' It's all heresy. They're not even really people anyway. Father says they'll get what they deserve at the hands of the Lord."

"But, Brandon, if you could see the Queen, and speak to her that means-" my mind was racing, putting things together, "that means you must be at least partly fae, too. If you weren't, you wouldn't have been able to talk with her at all! You're an intermagical like me and Faeryn, Brandon. We're all the same."

"How dare you say something so vile about me?" Brandon shouted, "I am nothing like them. I could never be like them, with their blasphemous magic and grand delusions, hiding in their sparkly little holes. Am I supposed to be impressed with that? Is that supposed to make me want to save their pitiful brats? Why? They don't matter to the Lord, Father says so. We are the true sons of God. This world is ours, and we will do what we please with it," he intoned, sounding just like the Deacon. Brandon didn't share much, physically, with his adopted father, but at this moment, the resemblance was uncanny. "Those faeries aren't any threat to me with their fakery and their illusions," Brandon said, turning to leave, "Their heresy and lies can't hurt me. I'd like to see them try." He grabbed Velia's hand and dragged her away from us, and she continued to retort imperiously to Evita's accusing screeches until she was out of sight, lost in the crowd.

Visc appeared silently next to me, watching the pair depart. "No," he said, voice low and cold, "It isn't Evita's city, but it is my mother's, and I will be sure to tell her all about this as soon as she gets back." He clenched his fists, staring daggers at Brandon's back. "Their pitiful brats can't threaten him with their illusions, hmm? Well, be careful what you wish for," Visc said with a menacing little grin, "I'll certainly enjoy it, if I do get the opportunity to try."

Chapter 38

With all five faeries piled into the single wide bench seat, Alaric's old truck was filled past capacity. As I glanced down the row of packed bodies, I thought how lucky it was that everyone apart from me was quite small. I eyed Evita and Arlee speculatively wondering if my eyes were deceiving me, or whether they really were even smaller than usual. It seemed as though they might have shrunk a bit so that we could all fit in. Even so, it was still uncomfortably cramped, and I looked forward to stretching out once we got back to the hill. To my surprise though, the hill was swarming with folk, and as I rolled up the gravel drive, I parted a sea of bodies nearly as tightly packed as we were, in the car.

"What's happening?" I asked Evita, "Who are all these people?" We reached the top of the drive, and I saw that the winding paths of the lush, overgrown garden were also filled with all manner of fae.

"Melodie must have gotten the word out," Evita answered with a pleased smile, "A goodly portion of the wild folk of the surrounding few counties appear to be here, ready to lend us their support tomorrow."

I opened the door and stepped down from the car, with Evita close behind me. Turning my head back at just the right moment, I saw her shift subtly back to her full size. She straightened her back and raised her chin high, and I took her raised hand, helping her alight gracefully from the seat of the high truck.

As we moved together toward the front door, the gathered fae parted and genuflected respectfully as we passed. At that moment she wasn't just Evita, she was the queen, and she bore her role with seriousness and dignity. She was a person to be reckoned with, I thought proudly, and I was her daughter.

"Seems like you called a few other friends for help, too, huh?" said a deep, resonant voice over my shoulder.

I turned with a small intake of breath and saw the Gullah's white smile widen at my startlement. "Oh! No, I didn't, they just, uh-" I sputtered in my surprise at his sudden appearance. I took a breath and gathered myself, turning to face him with a smile. "Hello," I said, trying again, "Thank you for coming." I spread my arms encompassing the overwhelming sea of fae surrounding us. "I don't know who any of these folk are, actually, but I'm sure ready to get inside. Would you please come in? I have some questions that I'm really hoping you can answer." He nodded and followed me inside. When the click of the front door separated us from the chaos outside, I let out an enormous sigh of relief.

Evita settled us in the broad, sunny front room of the strange, round house. The wide curving window that made up much of the front wall gave us a clear view of the misty blue hills in the distance and the sloping lawn and garden that positively swarmed with fae of all sorts. "Oh, they'll be happy enough in the garden tonight," answered Evita at my questioning, "These far-flung fae folk will take any excuse to gather, now that spring is in the air. I imagine most of them headed our way as soon as they received the invitation. Tonight will surely be quite the revel."

Evita's home was one of several in the neighborhood, and I looked out at all of the other houses dotting the hillside and wondered aloud what her other neighbors would think of that. She laughed, waving an airy hand in dismissal. "It won't be the first time or the last. The ones who are magical won't mind, and the ones who aren't can't see them, anyway. Though they find enough reasons to dislike me, regardless."

Once inside, she had dropped much of her air of queenly regality. Among family, she was simply caring, motherly Evita. Constantly in motion, she brought us cups of herbal tea, peppermint, and lemon balm for clarity and focus, and fussed with long, leafy green vines that draped artfully from the high-beamed ceiling above the panoramic window.

I looked around at the faces surrounding me. The Gullah perched, long-legged, over a tall stool in the corner, fingers wrapped evocatively spider-like around his steaming mug of tea. He saw me watching him and grinned, raising an expressive eyebrow. He reminded me of that eight-legged trickster from stories. The name was on the tip of my tongue, but, focus!

Arlee and Faeryn, or rather Visc, I corrected myself silently, sat cozily together on the couch. It was obvious, now, that they were romantically linked, as the more masculine Visc's slender arm rested protectively on Arlee's dainty shoulder. The sight of them, cozy on the couch, made me smile.
I was glad I had been right.

Little Zelai was there, too. He was as busy as his mother, fiddling with some project on the floor in the corner, and sneaking curious glances at his cousin Visc, whom he clearly admired. And so was Egan, my other brother. He stood at the window looking out at the gathering below us. Long-haired, and serious, he didn't seem nearly as relaxed as his mother about having all of these visitors in the yard.

Our war council was assembled.

"So, what's the plan?" asked Visc, leaning forward, steeped hands resting on his knees, "I knew I hated this Brandon guy already for what he's about to do to my spring and my city, but after what he said today…"

Interested, Egan turned away from the window, and the Gullah asked, "Wait, what happened today?"

We told the story of our encounter with Brandon and Velia at the Saturday market, rambling and overlapping each other pleasantly, and reinforcing the interwoven narrative in a way that was, apparently, quite natural for fae folk.

"So that's why she tried to keep us from finding Fiona," said Egan, nodding to himself. "She's with the church now. Aligned with the CCC. She probably thinks she'll get some of the power from exploiting the spring. Although, why she thinks she'd get more from them than she already gets from you, with all the stuff that you let her get away wi-" He cut himself off, seeing the storm brewing behind Evita's eyes.

"I don't think so," Evita said, coldly, "I think that it was our search for Fiona that drove her to them. Her jealousy at my having a daughter. Her obsession with our family. Her obsession," she spit the words fiercely, "with me." Obsession, she explained, could be a fatal flaw of the fae. Fae folk, Evita said, have a heightened ability to focus on the things that they are fascinated by. So heightened, in fact, that they can sometimes forget to eat or sleep, or lose the ability to speak about anything other than the subject of their obsession, at times when their hyper-focus is at its peak. Obsession, taken far enough could even become psychosis. "It can be a blessing," she said, continuing to preen her elaborate vines, "but it can sometimes be a curse."

Velia, she explained, had been obsessed with Evita for some time now. It was flattering, and it was helpful to have such a large and powerful fae at the beck and call of the court. Even more powerful since Velia was a fully magical fae, who had chosen to divest from her small store of humanity. Becoming fully magical in that way was a choice that was not taken lightly, and as a result of her decision, many of the folk would not trust her. Velia's association with the little queen's court had given her a helpful level of credibility among the larger community of the fae. She had never been able to become a true member of the court, though, as she was not a faerie herself, and she had never fully accepted this. The subject had spawned an uncounted number of heated arguments between Evita and herself.

"But, my sister has been excruciatingly clear," said Evita, with a knowing glance at Visc, which he returned. Given Velia's status as a powerful, fully-magical ally of the little queen, who also did not happen to be bound by the rules that Queen Vivienne had set for the subjects of her court, it had been Velia who Evita had tasked with the particularly sensitive and important job of finding her lost daughter. She was to keep watch, said Evita, beginning on the morning of my twenty-first birthday.

"Why then?" I asked.

That was the day that Queen Vivienne's edict had been lifted. She had decreed that no one of her court might take any action to communicate with or call back the changeling child. One perfect half-magical half-human changeling, her own daughter, would bring enough attention to the court and would have sufficient power to enact any human magic the court might desire.

"And we all know how well that plan worked out," interjected Visc wryly.

At twenty-one, I was inarguably an adult by any measure, and would not be bound by a decree made about a child. At that moment, Evita had set things into motion to send me the paperwork that had pointed me toward Oregon. And, she said, she had reached out with her magic and called out to my spirit to come home to my long-lost family. "I felt that," I said, placing a hand on my chest, "Nobody understood why I just packed my stuff and drove to Oregon like that, but I just felt like I had to go. I guess that's why." That special link between Evita and me, that stretched across distance, which had allowed Evita to call out to me, was something that she had been able to share, in part, with Velia, to allow her to help my mother in finding me. "Seems like she did that easily enough," I said with a chuckle, "running me off the road before I even got to town."

"What?" the Gullah asked. I told the story for those who hadn't heard it, about all the strange 'ill luck' I had experienced when I had first arrived in town, from the flash of light that ran me off the road, to the storm that had rolled in, the moment I had driven back into the valley. Evita was incensed again, stamping and glowering with rage.

Behind her, Egan rolled his eyes, as if to say, "That's Velia, for you."

"So she made the storm to stop you when you drove through the valley to visit the country fae," Visc said, putting the pieces together, "but what did she do when you came here to the hill to meet Evita?"

"Nothing," I said, puzzled, then remembered, "but, that's probably because of the charm Melodie gave me. I told her about what happened, and then she gave me something to, uh, hide me, I guess." Visc nodded, accepting the explanation.

"Ah," said Evita, "That must be why I couldn't feel you until you stepped out of the car. I had been wondering."

The Gullah leaned forward, interested. "Do all faerie changelings have this sort of tag-lock? How does it, er-" he sat back, collecting himself, "Sorry. That has some interesting implications for something I'm researching, but we can talk about that after all this is over with."

There was that word again. *Changeling.*

"Is that what I am?" I asked, curious, "A changeling? I've heard you guys say that a couple times now, but people also keep calling me an intermagical. Do they mean the same thing?"

Faeryn smiled broadly. No, not Faeryn, Visc. I reminded myself, looking at the sleek black outfit. She spoke, and I realized that I had been right the first time. Faeryn was wearing Visc's clothing, certainly, but the light behind the eyes had shifted to the air of academic excitement that belonged distinctly to Faeryn. It was interesting how easy it was to tell the difference.

"Intermagical is my word, actually. There wasn't really a word for what we are, in the broadest sense, so I coined one. But you're older than me, by a few months anyway, and when you were born, they had to have called you something. Cambion is another term for us, though a bit of a charged one, I'll admit. Changeling had been the accepted nomenclature for what we are for a long time, especially among faeries, but it has," she made a funny little snort, "fallen out of fashion in recent years."

Egan, too, seemed to be holding back laughter. "Who was it that the old hag was talking to, cousin? Was it you, truly?"

"It was," Faeryn said, now giggling openly.

"What?" I asked, "What happened?"

"Alright," said Faeryn, settling into a familiar story, "I met a woman at the Fair Isle, once, although I don't think she can really have known where she was, there couldn't have been more than the faintest spark of magic in her, and I mentioned a changeling like you, a baby that was sent off by the faeries to be raised among the humans. Well, she didn't like that, not one bit, and she corrected me, and sharply, too!" Faeryn raised an imperious finger in imitation of this unfortunate person. "According to the Fairy Faith of Ireland, *which was where it originated after all*, she told me, a Changeling could be either an aged, old fairy or some sort of stick, or log. She was insistent that a changeling must be one of those two things, and those two things only. Certainly not a baby, she said, and told me in no uncertain terms that as a *learned member* of the Fairy Faith, she would like to know what qualifications I had to tell her that I knew any better."

Faeryn's caricature of the hoity-toity woman with the audacity to question the bona fides of the reigning princess of the Queen's court, and the world's primary academic in the area of all things faerie, had us all laughing heartily. "I suppose she could be right," Faeryn continued with good humor, "We might be able to send an old faerie like Melodie Cristalline off to live as a human child, but to send a branch in place of a baby, can you imagine?"

"Wasn't her friend the mean old bat who told me she hoped I'd get eaten by a kelpie?" asked the Gullah.

"It was!" agreed Faeryn, "Those Fairy Faith folks did not like having their ideas challenged, did they?"

"Well!" said Evita, once we had all mostly quelled our giggling and jesting, "It does tend to make one think that it really is all religions, doesn't it? That sort of belief clouds the mind so thoroughly that someone can just completely miss what is right in front of them, even religions that take the name of Fairy."

"Speaking of religions and the damage they do," said Egan, "didn't we have a caper to plan?"

"Yes," I agreed, glad that he had the good sense to guide our meandering conversation back to the topic at hand, "we do." I turned to the Gullah. "So, if I were to ask you if it was possible to remotely disable a bunch of wireless security cameras pointed at a certain facility, if, say, our friend Visc here," I turned and looked at the couch to confirm, "could give you access to any information that anyone's typed into a keyboard at that hypothetical facility…"

Visc, who had assumed control again as soon as we were back to planning, waggled a little vial of spring water that sparkled in the afternoon sunlight streaming through the window.

"Hold on," said the Gullah, raising one long finger, "Remotely? Are you implying that you're going to break into a CCC-backed compound to steal their documents to expose them to the public and you think I'm not going to come?"

"Well, I mean," I hedged, "if you really want to come…"

He smiled, showing all of his teeth, then shrugged. "But, yeah, sure I could do it remotely."

Sometime later, I walked into the kitchen looking for some peace away from the chattering of Zelai, Arlee, and Visc who were reminiscing cheerfully about some particularly fine revels from summers' past. "Oh!" I blurted, startled from my racing thoughts by the presence of the Gullah, leaned over the sink, washing his mug methodically. The pale light coming in through the curtained window made a stark silhouette out of the already dark man, and the sharp point of his short beard gave him a wicked look, like one of those statues in the clearing. At my sound, he looked up, breaking the spell. I shook my head to clear it. "You startled me, there. I don't know why, though. I think I'm just buzzing around in my own head too much. Going through the plans for tonight, over and over again, trying to find holes in the logic and think of things we forgot."

The plans that we had made for the evening were quite thorough, with the benefit of our considerable resources. Visc brought with him a vast amount of first-hand information about the pump and the buildings around the spring. He poured his little vial of spring water into a shallow black dish that shined like glass, and through its energetic connection to the larger spring, Visc asked the water to show us reflections of everything interesting it had seen as it flowed in and around the pump, and inside the water dispenser of the office, as well. The spring water had seen a lot, and with the Gullah's tactical expertise and Egan's keen eye for detail, we were able to build the rough strategy that Melodie and I had come up with into something actionable and strategically sound.

The Gullah wiped his hands dry and turned to face me. "Buzzing sounds about right. Your energy is jumping around everywhere." He drew some jagged lines in the air with both hands. "Like, za'yow!"

He stepped toward me and reached out, as though to put his hands on my shoulders, but paused. I met his eyes and realized that he was waiting for my acknowledgment before he touched me. My gaze had given it, and he laid his water-cooled hands on me, sending a radiating calmness down my spine. I sighed, gratefully.

"You'll probably want to learn how to ground your energy before tonight," he said, releasing me. I wished he hadn't. "Do you want me to show you?"

Escaping the omnipresent fae outside the house, the Gullah led me down an alleyway and over a low stone wall into a grassy, tree-lined cemetery filled with old, worn stones covered in Oregon's particular type of damp, green moss. He took my hand to help me over the wall, and I liked the feel of it, long-fingered and strong in mine. I found that it was easy to communicate with the man without too many words. It seemed almost like he was reading my mind…

OH NO LOOK AT THAT!

I shouted loudly and suddenly, in my thoughts, hoping to catch him at it. Nope, no reaction at all. So, he wasn't literally intruding, then, probably. I chucked to myself and he smiled in response. I hadn't truly believed that he was reading my mind, but I wasn't used to anyone being that aware of me or so responsive to my body language, and it didn't hurt to check. We walked on the grass along the outside edge of the cemetery, near a mossy stone wall.

"My grandma always said not to whistle in a graveyard because you never know what might decide to follow," he said conversationally, as we walked, "and, I try to make sure I don't walk over anybody's head, out of respect, you know, but I've always liked walking in graveyards for the silence, and for the nice, old trees." He looked up thoughtfully at the old oak we had stopped beside. "They tend to have a particular point of view."

"Interesting," I said, looking up at the gnarled old oak, "Yeah, I guess I could see that."

This was a very expressive tree, with its thick trunk and lumpy knots, like a great-grandmother, beautiful, wizened, and wise. Under the shade of the oak, we took our shoes off and stood barefoot on the cool ground.

"Comfortable, about shoulder-width apart," he said, eyes closed, rolling his head back in a relaxed stretch.

He described the way that he cycles his own energy, sending it down into the earth, then back up into himself, refreshed and recharged, and without the chaotic, emotional buzz that my own energy currently rang with. There are any number of ways to do it, he said, but the way he liked best was to visualize all of the stagnant energy in his body, like red blood coursing through his veins, and to gather it all at the based of his spine, before releasing it down and into the earth underneath his feet. Then, he explained, you can pull fresh, recharged energy back up out of the earth, through the soles of your feet, into that taproot at the base of the spine, and out into all the cells and molecules of the body. The fresh energy could look like anything but, he noted with a shrug, he visualized it being blue.

"Some women feel like they're gathering energy in their womb, which is right there at that root, too." He arched his back, stretching, and patted his lower abdomen. "Which makes sense, it's the root of life. But for me," he said, raising his chin, and letting the sunbeams warm his face, "I like to gather it at my spine, then spread it all out, nice and even."

We walked back to the house, slowly, and I breathed in rhythm with my steps. I felt the clean, fresh energy pooled inside of me, full of potential, but calm and under my control. "You know," I said, turning my face up toward the Gullah walking beside me, "now that my energy isn't buzzing all over the place, I'm wondering if I might actually have the capacity to raise a little more. For, uh-" he looked down at me and I flushed, cheeks warming under his intense gaze, "for the ritual tomorrow, I mean. To help power it."

He nodded, thoughtfully. "I'm sure you do, but it would be better to try that after our mission tonight is successful, I think. Having that extra space inside of you to spool any excess energy could end up being key to being able to keep your head in a crisis. You aren't used to this kind of thing, are you?"

"No, I'm not. That makes sense," I agreed, regretful, but not quite sure of what.

As we walked on, the back of my hand brushed his with a rush of chaotic sensation like static electricity, but only at the spot where our hands had touched. A step or two later, he reached out and gripped my hand in his. The conductive sensation was stronger, but the constant pressure of his hand made the jumping static relax into a steady energetic link, a current that coursed between us with each breath. We walked back up the hill like that, breathing our energies back and forth through our linked hands. My mind felt open and clear, like how I imagined a yogi in meditation might feel.

He was a very good teacher.

Chapter 39

Eventually, the hour was upon us. We left the hill shortly after eleven, planning to reach the pump right before the witching hour, so that we could use that sweet spot right after midnight, when preternatural forces have extra power, to our advantage. Visc assured us that the buildings around the pump were always empty, shortly after dark. The Deacon was an early riser and he strongly encouraged those around him to be, also. The security cameras and motion-activated lights were all accounted for, and the large, territorial dog had been assigned to Arlee to soothe, with her particular talent for canines and some magically enhanced links of sausage.

"In and out," Egan repeated for the umpteenth time, from the third row of the large, dark SUV that Evita had materialized for the occasion. Velia had seen Alaric's truck already, and it was far too small to fit all of us, anyway. Reaching the lonely road marker that signaled our destination, we turned off onto the unpaved track that led toward the group of temporary buildings surrounding the small first pump. That sinister bit of machinery would be destructive enough in its own right, but its threat was minor when compared with the Deacon's future plans. As the tires shifted from smooth pavement to the crunch of loose gravel, the view out the window suddenly changed. The dark trees vanished, replaced by solid white as our world was blanketed in a thick white fog.

"Velia," hissed Evita, seated behind me, "She just loves her weather magic. This must be an illusion, though. She might be able to pull together a real fog this thick, but not nearly so fast," she said, shaking her head, "Yes, just a visual illusion. Triggered by our driving into it, likely. Not particularly difficult to do."

As she spoke, I noticed that she was rummaging in her large shoulder bag. The rest of us had packed light so that we could move quickly, and I had wondered what all she was bringing. Now, as she searched, I saw that the pack contained a number of odds and ends, including a long length of cord that she was using to tie together a little bundle of objects with a quiet, fierce energy. "There!" she said, holding out a small packet of sticks and herbs bound around a carved obsidian arrowhead. It looked a little like the clump of ribbon that Melodie had given me, which now hung from the rearview mirror. "Dangle it, like so," Evita said, showing me where to hold the pieces of dark cord, "and remember how it felt when you rode down this track before. It will follow your memory, and act as a compass, guiding us through."

"But, I don't remember how the track turns," I said, looking nervously out at the thick blanket of white.

"That's not what matters," Evita assured me, "Your energy will remember. Jus let it flow through you."

I closed my eyes and remembered how I had felt bumping along on that dirt track with the Deacon, worried about my car, clothes soaked through, with wet, stringy hair plastered to my face.

"Drive" urged Evita, and I heard the tires roll forward as the Gullah followed the direction of the magic compass. In just a few minutes, we reached the clearing, and as we passed the treeline, the unnatural fog faded away.

As we stepped out of the car, our presence did not trigger the motion-activated flood lights and the woods stayed dark. "They're cheap, high-tech ones," the Gullah had told us this afternoon, "I can blow those with a quick infrared pulse." He must have done it while simultaneously navigating blind through the fog, guided only by my energy on a string. Impressive!

The dark man strode purposefully off and was quickly swallowed by the night. He had his own job to do, something about cutting the power to the security station, I thought, recalling the details of our planning. But, my focus was on my own part of the assignment.

I had been tasked with retrieving the documents from the Deacon's private office, including the manila folder full of my own papers that had gone missing from my hotel room, as well as several other items of a personal and often incriminating nature that the Deacon had collected about key social and political figures in town. Knowing her community's local political scene as well as she did, Evita had been impressed.

"This has the makings of a passably competent city-wide takeover."

These were secrets that the Deacon had collected, in his guise as a religious leader, that he could use to pressure powerful people or to blackmail them if the inclination took him. Some items would be neutralized simply by removing the evidence. Others would lose their sinister power by being brought out into the open, into public view. If I could find everything I was supposed to be looking for, tonight would end up being a major blow to the Deacon's political machinations, as well as to the Christian Springs project.

I climbed the creaky metal steps to the landing of the Deacon's personal office, treading lightly. Coincidentally, It was the one building in the encampment that I had been inside before. Visc told us that they rarely bothered to lock this door, after the key had been misplaced one too many times, relying on their remoteness and their other security measures to keep the building secure. I tried the handle, nervously. As the door swung open, I let out a sigh of relief and stepped inside.

My relief didn't last, and my intake of breath turned into a shriek, as a lumpy shape near the floor lurched toward me. My heart leapt into my throat and I barely stifled a scream.

"Fiona?" said a familiar voice in the darkness, slurred with either drunkenness or sleep. It was Brandon! "See, I told Father you would try something like thizz." He hung onto the last sound in a way that convinced me that alcohol was at play. "But he never believes me. An' wouldya looka' tha', I'm right again." He managed to pull himself to his feet, the thick silhouette of his mummy sleeping bag falling and pooling on the floor, leaving him standing unsteadily in front of me. "You evil little heathen," he said with vitriol as he leaned toward me, breathing out the pungent scent of liquor, "What are you trying to do, anyway? Break the extractor?"

Well, if he really thought that was all we were up to, I certainly wasn't going to educate him. "You really won't see things our way?" I asked, trying for the third, and, I expected, final time, "You're really going to destroy the spring and this whole ecosystem, just for a little bit of money?"

"You really don' know, do you?" asked Brandon, brazen in his stupor, "this spring is miracle water, alright? Like, a real God-given miracle. And we can bottle it, and then we can sell it to people. We're not talking about a little money, okay? We're talking about lots and lots of-" He hiccuped, and lost his balance, catching himself on a wall. He was really very drunk.

I remembered an innocuous moment earlier, when Evita had been playing with her charming antique bar cart, pouring spirits back and forth from one little brass jigger to another, over and over again, and wondered if Brandon might not have gotten this intoxicated entirely on purpose. That, in turn, made me wonder about the rules and the ethics of faerie magic, because it seemed to suggest that they were not as strict as some magical rules might be. But, this was not the moment for philosophical musings.

"Visc," I called out the door, into the night. In a moment, he was there, summoned from lookout duty for this particularly savory task. "Would you distract him while I get what I need?" I asked my cousin, indicating the staggering man in front of me.

"Would I?" the little faerie asked savagely, stepping forward, "With pleasure. After all, he did dare me to." I moved off toward the desk in the corner, but I was still close enough to hear Visc whisper. "You'd like to see the puny brat try, huh? Well, let's grant your wish."

As I grabbed my own manila envelope and the other items that we had decided to take with us, I could hear Brandon whimpering with fear behind me. Heading back out the door, I passed Brandon, unseeing eyes open wide, stricken with terror as he dodged and swung at whatever illusory horrors Visc was throwing at him. "We need to head out in a minute," I warned Visc, who was grinning and wiggling his fingers in vicious glee.

"Just one more thing, then," he said, bringing one arm down with a sweeping motion. Brandon yelped, and dove for the floor. I headed back outside, not wanting to see more.

Arlee dashed out of the woods close behind me. "The dog," she said, panting, "He just started acting strange. We should leave."

The Gullah, coming from the other side, arrived at the car at the same moment we did. "There's chatter on the radio," he said, holding up a small black receiver, "Time to go!"

"Visc!" I yelled over my shoulder, followed by Arlee's high-pitched screech of "Faeryn," hot on its tail. To my surprise, it was Faeryn who streaked across the empty courtyard and flung herself, panting, into the waiting car.

"He didn't want to stop," she said, by way of explanation, and Arlee nodded, understanding. Visc's tough look overtook Faeryn's scared expression, and he looked around sheepishly, then grunted "Sorry."

The Gullah turned the engine over and headed back down the gravel drive. As soon as we hit the path, the illusory fog rolled in. I had hoped the magic would be one-directional, but it wasn't going to be that easy.

"Can I do it now that I've driven it once?" asked the Gullah, reaching for the compass bundle.

"No," said Evita from the back seat, "It has to be Fiona. It's locked onto her."

I took the talisman and tried to focus. My jangling energy was bouncing around everywhere. The compass swung to and fro, uselessly. The Gullah reached out and took my hand, and as that grounding energy flowed between our connected palms again, my breathing slowed and I was able to bring my thoughts into focus. As soon as I did, the little arrowhead stopped swinging and the Gullah peeled out of the drive with a spray of gravel.

Once we were out of the fog, I felt him relax, and his face split into a wide grin as he tapped the flash drive of confidential information that he had just downloaded on the steering wheel, making a syncopated beat. Having a vial of springwater that knew all of the network passwords had been unbelievably handy.

Visc rifled through the papers we had seized, enthusiastically confirming that we had gotten everything we were looking for. There were the blueprints of the water bottling facility, both the modest early iteration that Christian Springs had submitted to the city council and the sprawling, pollution-spewing production monstrosity that was their ultimate goal. We also had the environmental impact surveys, both versions. The copies they had submitted to the city, and the damning private research that showed the true scale of the ecological devastation, including the list of native animal species whose habitats would be threatened by the project.

"Are any of them cute?" I had asked, practically, during our afternoon discussions.

"This scrubby sort of vole, maybe?" offered Visc. He brought up an image of a tan little rodent and Evita and Arlee both purred, looking down at the beady-eyed thing.

"Oh yes," Evita had said, "I think we can make this little fellow plenty sympathetic."

The fact that none of those disastrous ecological impacts had made it into the official report submitted to the city, was the result of some pretty significant bribery and blackmail, evidence of which we were also planning to seize. "Blackmail, seriously?" I had interrupted to ask, as Visc described the lengths taken by the Deacon and his cronies.

"Oh yeah, there's a whole filing cabinet full of information on people in there. I've heard them laughing about it. They made a lot of jokes about the damage they're going to do to the ecosystem, too. It's not like these guys don't know exactly what they're doing," Visc spat, fists clenched around the mug of tea that Evita had brought him.

"But, how can they do all that stuff and still not realize that they're the bad guys?" Zelai asked, bewildered. I shrugged. I didn't understand it either. How could the Deacon stand up in front of his congregation every Sunday and preach about goodness, when this was what he was doing behind closed doors?

"Because they think everyone's doing it," the Gullah answered, expression grim, "They think that everybody is just as self-serving and twisted as they are. It's one of the reasons they turn to a religion that's so focused on sin, to give them a way to understand all the darkness they have inside. And they assume everybody else must be like that, too. It's one of the reasons people like that always tell on themselves. Listen closely to anybody accusing you of something ridiculous, and you can be just about sure that they're doing whatever it is they're raging about."

"You know, I heard what the Deacon was planning to preach about on Sunday," Visc interjected, "it's a real barn burner, 'How not to let our sin nature bespoil the kingdom of God'." Visc captured the Deacon's blustery inflection, and we all laughed.

"You're not kidding about them telling on themselves!" I said, turning to the Gullah, "'Bespoiling' is a great term for what they're trying to do."

We drove back to the hill, raucous with excitement at our success. The Gullah, to Visc and Arlee's confusion, pulled through a human-style drive-through for a late-night snack. The faerie woman enjoyed the curious bubbling of the sugar nectar that we handed back to her, and Visc commented wonderingly on the density of the energy stored in the cheeseburger, which Arlee declined to try.

"Love, if we used these instead of the tofu, I'm sure I would manage to eat a lot more."

"Hmm," said Arlee, eyeing the little puck suspiciously.

As we drove by darkly silent houses and storefronts on our way back to the hill, the party atmosphere inside the car was at odds with the silence of the sleeping town, but our destination was another story. As the road curved and the hill came into view, it was clear that the night's revel was still in full swing. Dots of light from many-colored lanterns and sprays of sparks from several bonfires lit the strange layer cake house, and the motion of countless bodies made flickering shadows dance before our eyes.

"They're still going?" I asked, wonderingly. The party had already been well underway when we had left.

"Of course," said Egan, resigned, "they'll go till daybreak. Lucky that you don't need most of them until almost noon."

I stepped out of the car and into the heart of the fae revel. It was overwhelming, as voices and various musical instruments overlapped, all of the different melodies swirling together. The smoke from a nearby bonfire made my eyes water. Another time, it might have looked enticing, but tonight, it was not.

I saw a harried expression on the Gullah's face that matched my own, and I gestured for him to come inside with me. Inside the house, it was dark and silent, with Evita and the other faeries still out at the revel, so I led him through the only door I knew, into the room where I had slept last night. I flipped on the light. The illumination centered on the softly pillowed bed, dominating the space.

"Your room?" asked the Gullah with an unreadable expression.

"Oh, um, hardly. I mean, I stayed here last night, but-" I said, flustered, and hurried over to the little loveseat under the window, dumping my small collection of thrifted faerie clothing off of it, so that we would have somewhere to sit.

"That all went well, tonight," he said, walking to stand at the window, through which the firelight still flickered.

"Yeah," I agreed, my voice tired, but my body still tingling with chaotic energy, "Now I've just gotta get through tomorrow."

"It's an ambitious plan," he said, moving to stand behind me and squeezing my tense shoulders in his large hands. The sound of his voice and the closeness of his body made me nervous, but my muscles relaxed under his touch and I leaned back into him, gratefully. "It won't be easy, but I'll be there to stand with you. We all will."

His touch on my back had the same calming effect as holding his hand, and I breathed with him, working to soothe my internal energetic chaos until my heartbeat slowed and my body relaxed. "Thanks. It's not quite as scary, knowing that I won't be doing it alone," I said, thinking about the close-knit crew of family and friends that had been with me tonight, and all the friendly faces of the townsfolk we had spoken to, that had said they would be there too, "but I still can't shake this feeling. Why me? What makes me think that I'm so special that I can really change things? That I can save the day?"

He chuckled, and tugged on my shoulder, spinning me around to face him. "Have you ever heard of imposter syndrome?" he asked, kindly.

We were close now, chest nearly touching chest, his hands still on my shoulders, channeling that calming, grounding energy. I looked straight ahead at his dark t-shirt, not wanting to risk the intensity of his eye contact. "No," I answered, "but that sounds like something I would have heard about in my psychology classes."

"Maybe, but it's more common to talk about it in the technical fields like computer science. Once you start learning about computers, the internet, and all the amazing things we can do with technology, and once you begin to really understand just how much there is to learn, it's easy to feel like you, and your knowledge, are too small and insignificant to matter, in comparison to all of that. But the truth is that nobody knows everything. Nobody, no single person, I mean, can ever really know very much at all, in the scope of things. We're all just learning what we can, in our specific little areas, and doing the best we can to deepen the knowledge that we have."

"In technology," I said, uncertainly.

"In technology," he agreed, "but once you start realizing that you're not an imposter in that world, or, at least that if you're an imposter, everyone else is too, at some level or another, it's pretty easy to sort of extend it out to," he lifted his hands from my shoulders, and spread them wide, "everything." The break of the energetic link between us hit me like an abrupt chill. Woah.

"So what you're saying is that if I'm not qualified to do it, well, at least nobody else is either?" I asked.

"Yeah," he said enthusiastically, grasping my shoulders again and giving them a squeeze. I got the impression that he had disliked the sensation of our disconnection at least as much as I had.

"You know, that's actually surprisingly comforting."

"Isn't it?" he agreed. I wasn't sure whether we were still talking about philosophy, or about the energy flowing between us at our point of physical connection, and I wasn't sure if it really mattered.

"So, um, about that energy, for the ritual, tomorrow. You said you could show me after we got back?"

"Oh, right," he answered slowly, looking at me with his deep, intense gaze, "Sure. Well, there are any number of ways to raise energy with our bodies. We can create friction and generate heat this way-" He demonstrated, taking my one hand in both of his and rubbing it vigorously. It did get warmer with his motion.

"Or?" I said, meeting his eyes and holding his gaze, chin lifted.

"Or," he bent his face down to meet mine.

At the point where our lips touched the energy intensified into a crackle like miniature lightning. All sensation narrowed into that isolated spot where our bodies connected, in a single mote of fire. Our lips parted, and I rocked back, nearly bowled over by the sensation, but not put off by the power that flowed between us. I felt my mouth quirk into a small smile, and looked at him, my gaze a challenge. "Or?" I asked, again.

"Well, when you invite the red-blooded son of a minor fertility god back to your room, so late at night..."

I met his level gaze with my own. I was too keyed up by what we had already done tonight, and what we were planning to do tomorrow, to have gotten any real sleep tonight anyway, and there was still plenty of time until daybreak.

Sometime later, the early morning sun streaked through the window and we lay entwined, talking languorously.

"I don't know why," he said, "but I guess they're probably just afraid of the energy that it has the potential to create. Afraid of anything so powerful being outside of their control. So, they call it immoral, and label it a sin."

"Mmm, probably," I agreed, snuggling deeper into the soft pillows. My body felt like it was glowing, both energized and relaxed. Ready to take on anything. Which was fortunate, considering what I had planned for the day ahead. "You know," I said, propping myself up on my elbows and looking at the man next to me, "it feels a little funny to keep thinking of you as The Gullah, I mean, considering. Is there maybe something else I can call you?"

He smiled, stretching lazily like a large cat. "That's fair enough. Alright, call me *Jaah*, then. It's one of my names."

"*Jah*," I said, trying it out.

"With two a's," he corrected, smiling, "*Jaah*. I can hear it if you don't pronounce the second one."

"*Jaah*," I tried, elongating the sound.

"Nope, now that's three a's. Try again." I shot him a look and saw from the sparkle in his eye that he was teasing me. We both laughed, and I boffed him with one of the fluffy down pillows.

"You want to be a funny man, huh?" I asked, brandishing the pillow again with mock ferocity, but the expression on his face made me lower it again.

"There's one more thing you should know, actually," he said, meeting my gaze with his deep brown eyes, "I don't exactly think of myself as a man. I'm not a woman either, I'm just-" He spread his arms wide, looking vulnerable and a little shy, "I'm just me."

"Like nonbinary?" I asked, and he nodded. "Okay, sure. No problem. I knew some nonbinary people in college. Do you use they/them pronouns, or…" I trailed off, not sure what to say next.

"No," he said, shaking his head, "I look like a man, and I don't need other people knowing my personal business." He met my eyes again and I nodded, understanding.

"Network security!" I said with a grin.

"Exactly!" He kissed me soundly, pressing me back down into the soft pillows. There was still a little time before we had to face the challenges of the day ahead.

Chapter 40

"I'd heard that the little lost faerie who didn't believe in magic had found her way home to her kin at last," said Godrin, clapping me heartily on the shoulder with one of his giant mitts. I greeted him warmly. It was good to see him again.

If only Velia hadn't intervened, Godrin would have sent me straight to Evita's hill the very first night I had found out about the fae. But, if he had done that, I wouldn't have met Faeryn like I had, and I wouldn't be here now, in the middle of this town square with a hundred helpers, setting up banners and signs, and carafes of donated coffee.

My little brother Zelai, sporting dark circles under his eyes, looked pleased with himself as he and two other small fae hoisted a large, detailed replica of the spring and its topography into place on a scaffold. I was impressed by the complexity and the size of the thing. He had only had one night to complete it, after all. Zelai hadn't been allowed to come with us on the raid, but he had managed to make an impressive contribution to the cause in his own way, after spending all afternoon hearing about the pump's potential for environmental atrocity.

Two stubbly little fae helpers stirred buckets of black sludge with knobbly sticks. I suspected I knew what Zelai had planned, and grinned, imagining the impact of the noxious ooze engulfing the enchanting diorama. I caught my brother's eye and saluted his artistic vision at work.

"Nice thinking, Zelai, that'll be really gross!" He waved back, with a shy, grim smile.

The signs were impressive, too. Poignant facts about habitats and pictures of impacted wildflowers were hand painted onto banners. They called out the most interesting and evocative facts we had uncovered, like the different types of native plants and animals this project had the potential to displace or even extinguish completely. Someone had even created an adorable cartoon out of the scrubby little vole.

Those fae hadn't just been singing and dancing around the fires last night, it seemed. They had been working with Zelai to make his impressive artistic visions a reality. I wasn't the only powerful faerie intermagical here, I reminded myself.

The details about the Christian Springs project, and more than a few rumors, had begun to spread around the town. More townspeople were arriving all the time, some holding their own protest signs, with details both factual and fantastical, some in handwriting, and others that had been printed and photocopied. We welcomed them all and pointed them toward the cookies and the paper cups of coffee.

I was curious to see how the townspeople mingled so closely with the unusual-looking fae folk. No one seemed alarmed, or even particularly surprised, as ordinary humans rubbed elbows with waist-high pixies. Were they all really just so integrated here in Oregon that regular people took the presence of the Fae for granted? I asked Godrin, who was standing nearby and who I knew to be good for explanations.

"Oh, they'll see what they expect to see," said Godrin, waving off my question, "We are the hidden folk, after all." That was what Alaric had said, too, when he had told me about Eve's hidden children.

As I thought about Alaric, I realized that he was standing in front of me, right across the street, helping Melodie Cristalline and her mother out of the back seat of an oversized vintage sedan. His taste ran toward the classics, it seemed. I waved to them, glad to see their familiar faces.

Jaah walked up to me. The Gullah, to Godrin, of course, I thought, a little smugly. The two men exchanged familiar nods. He really did seem to know everyone.

"Are you going to want a microphone?" Jaah asked me, holding out a wire and a small black box.

I considered but then shook my head, no. My voice was a big part of my magic, and I didn't think the distortion of a tinny PA sound system was the right choice. I wanted people to hear my message straight from the source.

It was almost time for this human magic ritual to begin. The big bell on the clock tower of the church across the street from us chimed noon. Everything was prepared, and a large crowd of townsfolk had already assembled. Many of the gossips and the friends they had spread the word to had gotten there early, so they could see and be seen, but there were still more trickling in now, fashionably late.

Newcomers took a lap around the spectacle before grabbing a coffee and stopping to chat with their neighbors.

This was a key step in powering the ritual with human magic, Evita explained. I might have preferred to get started and get right to the point, skipping past all the unnecessary small talk, but Evita insisted that humans need that time to create a proper energetic space for the magic, so I waited as people mingled. Conveniently, this also gave the local media trucks time to arrive. This was an event that nobody was going to want to miss.

Evita stood beside me, watching the crowd. Her eyes danced across the gathering, and the tip of her tongue flicked the air like a reptile, tasting the energy. Eventually, she nodded and squeezed my arm. "Now. It's time."

Queen Beauty Toilet Soap, I read, as I stepped up onto the wooden box that Evita had brought from the hill for this purpose.

A literal soap box. Clever faerie. I took a deep breath and hummed, preparing to use all my vocal training to project my voice out over the crowd.

"You all came here today because you care about nature. About Oregon's beauty and wildlife," I said to the assembly, whose boisterous chatter diminished, at least somewhat, "You're here because you care about our community and won't stand idly by and let our natural resources be exploited and destroyed for profit." My voice rang out to the people assembled. They heard me, and they agreed. The ritual went on in that manner for some time.

After me, Faeryn spoke, her tiny voice amplified by Jaah's impressive technology. Evita went next, sharing the stage with some scientists she knew from the local university, whom she had contacted and who had been happy to give their unbiased opinion on the research we had uncovered.

Zelai took the stage next, with a crew of fae helpers. His diorama had looked impressive this morning, but now it was magnificent, enhanced by faerie illusion so that the flowing water sparkled and the paper trees waved and danced in the breeze.

When Zelai dropped the giant scale model of the water extraction facility on top of that pristine backdrop, everyone gasped in horror. As the black sludge that represented the factory's potential pollution oozed evocatively down the scene, people covered their mouths and gagged, and not just because of the acrid stench that spread through the crowd.

"Euch!" said the woman standing next to me, looking at the cookie she had just picked up, and setting it back down, but she didn't make a move to leave, and neither did the others. They were too enthralled by the presentation. Zelai grinned, pleased with the effectiveness of his performance.

I glanced up at the church's clock tower. Any minute now.

It was Alaric who stepped forward next, and it was his speech that was interrupted when the big doors of the church across the street opened, and the Deacon's entire congregation poured out onto the large building's front steps. Alaric's oratory voice carried well, and just as I had planned, many of the church-goers looked curiously at the spectacle across from them and started to wander in our direction.

"And of course, we can see why this plan would be so attractive to the unconscionably greedy, but no amount of money could justify the harm this will do to our cherished natural spaces," Alaric intoned grandly, voice carrying across to the gathered churchgoers.

"WHAT IS ALL OF THIS?" boomed a voice to match Alaric's own from across the square. As one, like at a tennis match, the crowd turned to look at the red-faced Deacon, standing on the church's top step.

"This is a demonstration to raise public awareness about an urgent ecological risk facing our community," Alaric said, speaking to the Deacon, but also to the crowd of church-goers who had paused but had not yet walked across the street to the square to join us, "and to ask the City Council to step in and act to prevent the pollution and destruction of our beloved streams and forests." At this several people stepped toward us, interested in hearing more.

"Demonstration! Not allow-" said the Deacon, clearly flustered. He paused to collect himself. "Now, see here. The Christian Springs project will be a great boon to this church and to our community both." The Deacon waved his hands vaguely in the direction of the park, overplaying his dismissiveness. "All of this is baseless slander from godless troublemakers." He caught my eye and glowered. "Public announcements had been planned, following the, er- I mean to say, in the coming week, with details about just how beneficial and lucrative this gift from God will be to our church family," he said, then looked out at the sea of people gathered and added, "and to our community."

"Yes," agreed Alaric, "I'm sure the private stock portfolios and offshore bank accounts that are set up to receive the majority of the company's proceeds are all intended for altruistic, community-minded purposes." Alaric fanned himself conspicuously with the printout of the financial documents that we had photocopied and made available to the public after Jaah managed to extract them from a supposedly secure server, last night.

"Paperwork is complicated," intoned the Deacon, "and business even more so. I will not apologize for ensuring the future of our church family by making wise financial decisions." He cast a withering look across the street toward Alaric. "Naturally, someone who has never had enough money to bother managing properly wouldn't understand the fiscal complexities of the situation. This is clearly an underhanded attempt by the agents of the devil to thwart my divine purpose and steal what is rightfully mine."

"Steal what is rightfully yours?" Alaric repeated, "Can you really be so blind? That's exactly what we're trying to say here today, that these natural spaces and resources are rightfully ours. All of ours, to treasure and to protect. Don't you see that?"

"No Sir, I do not," roared the Deacon, "We made this discovery in the Lord's name and made our claim officially and legally. We are God's children, and it is our manifest destiny to conquer this land in the name and the glory of the Lord. You, Sir, are a spawn of Satan and the world owes you nothing. Your very existence is an abomination and a product of evil and heresy. Every word that leaves your lips is a lie. There is no truth and no righteousness outside of the word of the Lord, cambion." The Deacon spat this last word, fiercely.

Alaric seemed to taste the insult on the air, savoring it before he replied. "You dare to call me a cambion, do you? The child of a demon and a human. Perhaps you do see me that way. And by your own definition, truly, how can I stand before you and say that you are wrong?" Alaric let this thought hang in silence for a moment and the crowd began to mutter quietly amongst themselves. "You and your kind have been trying to stamp the magic out of this world for centuries, burning our temples and perverting our festivals, stealing them for your own, and, of course, giving our names and faces to your demons."

Alaric commanded the attention of the crowd like a master thespian, working the stage. "Do any of you happen to know the name of the first son of Earth to be called a cambion? Which great figure was the first fabled byproduct of man's union with the mystical? Alaric addressed his audience and paused for a response, but met nothing but attentive silence. "It was none other than the hero of the very first story, King Gilgamesh. You call our existence an abomination, but we are as old as history. As old as the oldest stories. And in those stories, we hold the roles of leaders and of sages."

"Begone, demon!" spat the Deacon

"You call me a cambion," Alarac continued, "A child created from preternatural dream conception, where an otherworldly figure approaches a human woman and causes her to bear a child." Alaric smiled impishly. He was clearly having fun. "Cambion, known as breakers of tradition, originators of new thought, and natural born leaders of men. Surely that description isn't familiar at all, is it, Deacon? Not reminiscent of any major characters from that book you're so fond of quoting? Or perhaps someone up there on that cross?" Alaric's eyes twinkled even as his face grew drawn and serious. "If we are abominations to you, my friend, I can only imagine what you must think of him!"

The courtyard hung in stunned silence for a long moment, as everyone pieced together what Alaric had just said. Eventually, the Deacon found his voice and it roared forth.

"How dare you speak this blasphemy on the Lord's day! I will not stand here and listen to such imprecation. This is a horde of heathens and liars. May the righteous hand of God strike you down!"

"You would ask your God to strike me down, would you Deacon? Well, pardon me if I say that I think it's highly unlikely," Alaric said with an irreverent smirk, "If this God you're calling upon is supposed to be benevolent, all-knowing, and all-powerful, his existence hasn't been a concern since Epicurio settled the matter with that clever little philosophical proof of his, back in 300 A.D."

Alaric turned to address the crowd. "If we want to know whether a benevolent, all-knowing, all-powerful God exists we must ask ourselves this." Alaric tipped his hat to the Deacon across the street, who continued to glower. "Since we do, in fact, recognize that there is evil in the world, is this God willing to prevent evil, but not able? Then he must not be omnipotent. Is he able, but not willing? Then he must be malevolent. And, of course, if he is both able and willing, we must ask ourselves, how is it that there is evil?" His smile widened, as he reached his conclusion. "And, if it is the case that he is neither able nor willing, I ask you, why should we call him God?" At the finish of his speech, Alaric swept his hat off his head with a flourish and took a sweeping bow.

The Deacon, body rigid and jowls quivering, raised his arm to point accusingly at Alaric. "I condemn you, heretic, in the name of the Lord," he shouted. Then he turned and stormed off through the open door of the church, with Brandon following in his shadow.

"Your Lord," Alaric called after him, "Not mine."

Some of the church folks left after the Deacon's final abnegation, but more of them stayed. More townsfolk wandered in too, drawn in by word of mouth and by the festive atmosphere of the gathering. People ate and talked amongst themselves, reading the painted signs and looking through copies of the collected evidence, displayed on folding tables for their perusal.

Evita came to stand beside me, nodding respectfully to the group of Native elders that she had just been speaking with, who were now headed toward the refreshments. She subtly indicated a short, balding man in an unassuming tan jacket who was peering at the stack of private ecological research documents that we had so recently made public. He was clearly deep in thought. "That man right there is on the City Council," she whispered excitedly, "He's the second member I've seen today. And I know humans. If these two have heard what we have to say, the whole Council surely will also." She squeezed me around the shoulders. "I couldn't be more proud. My own daughter, changing the very fabric of our reality with her human magic."

Across the street, a side door to the church opened and the Deacon and Brandon left quietly, driving away. Evita noticed, as well. "That young man, that Brandon. I haven't been able to stop thinking about it since we saw him at the market yesterday, trying to piece together why he looks so familiar. But, seeing him just now, skulking behind his father like that," she furrowed her brow, "he was the spitting image of my sister Enide."

"There's a third faerie queen?" I asked, curious to know more about my newfound family.

"Not anymore," answered Evita, "She was lost to the darkness ages ago."

"Lost to the-" I started, then paused, filling in the blank myself. Lost to the CCC. To the great nemesis. Thinking about that amorphous entity made me suddenly nervous. We had discussed the threat of the CCC yesterday, and I knew that Evita was making sure, in her own magical way, that they weren't going to crash our party today. She seemed confident. I just hoped that she knew what she was doing.

"Lost to the church, we believe," Evita clarified.

"Brandon told me that he was something called a 'Son of the Church'," I said, "that he was adopted by the Deacon."

"Hmm," said Evita speculatively, "I wonder…" Before she could say more, the Native elders, with cookies and paper cups of coffee, were back for her attention.

"Hello!" said a sprightly voice behind me.

I turned to see a round-faced girl holding the leash of a large lolling-tongued dog. She smiled brightly at me. "Hi, I'm Betty. I heard you speak earlier and I thought you were really great." Her words had a familiar bouncy excitement to them. "I just wanted to come over and invite you to a Social Club for Autistic Women that I'm running over at the university."

"Oh, um, I'm not-" I started, before she interrupted.

"Oops, I'm sorry. I thought you probably already knew. I have a habit of uh, randomly diagnosing people after hearing them talk for a few minutes. I could always be wrong, though?" she shrugged, honest if a little awkward.

"No, I mean, I'm not a student," I said, then added, "I just graduated from a college in California."

"Oh, that's okay!" she said, smiling widely, "It's for anybody in the community to join!"

I scribbled down my information in the notebook she handed me, wishing that there had been a group like that when I was in college, then wondering if there mightn't have been one available if I had ever thought to look. Looking at her bright, cherubic face, and listening to her excited, bouncy speech, I realized that she reminded me very much of my own newfound family and the fae folks I had met at the Fair Isle and the Country Faire. And, I smiled to myself, she reminded me of me. I wondered how many more kindred spirits I might find at that social club, and whether any of them had ever heard of the Fae Intermixing Declaration.

My speculations were interrupted by flashing blue and red lights that heralded the arrival of four large police vehicles. They screeched loudly to a halt, parking at jutting angles halfway onto the sidewalk in front of the gathering. Policemen piled out of the vans as most of the assembled crowd edged back toward the center of the square or off onto the adjacent streets and away from this alarming new development. The only exceptions were the news crews who kept their cameras rolling and nudged closer.

"There she is!" shouted one of the visored men, pointing directly at me.

Another uniformed officer, coming in from my left, grabbed me and wrenched my arms behind me. He wrapped a plastic band around my wrists and zipped it painfully tight.

"Youch!" I exclaimed as the man muscled me toward the waiting vans while muttering my Miranda rights.

Leaning against one of the transport vehicles stood the Deacon, arms folded. He tracked my progress toward the van with a smug expression. "I hope it was all worth it for this pathetic stunt, little girl," he said when I got close enough, "I've got eyewitness proof that you broke into my buildings and stole my private property. You're an evil little witch who ensorcelled my son and I'll make sure you go far, far away, for this. Somewhere where your sacrilege can't poison decent people."

"Father, she's not the one who-"

"Hush, Brandon." He waved the younger man off and focused his intense gaze on me, eyes blazing. "I told you to take care and stay on the right path, girl. To listen to good God-fearing men who know what's best for you. But you wouldn't listen and now look at you. You've gone and thrown your entire life away."

The policeman pushed my head down and the Deacon's sneering face was gone, replaced by the stark metal insides of the first police vehicle I had ever seen up close. I looked out over my shoulder through the van's grated window. My gaze met Evita's and I felt my heart drop. The intensity that I felt as her eyes met mine left me breathless.

As the engine turned over and the car rumbled to life, I saw her mouth form words. "*No daughter of mine.*"

No daughter of mine? "What's that supposed to mean?" I asked aloud.

"Quiet, back there," said a gruff voice from the front.

Whoops.

Part 10 - Human Magic

Velia poured the dark red wine and handed Brandon a carved crystal goblet, in the style she liked best. "To our victory," she simpered.

He clinked his glass with hers, reluctantly. "I don't know. I don't feel good about this," he said, not meeting her gaze.

"But why not, my dear? The heretic girl is gone. The day is yours. The world," she gestured effusively, "is yours."

"I just…" Brandon looked at her, eyes dark-rimmed, looking haunted, "Last night, I saw some things and they made me," he shrugged, "wonder about some stuff. Stuff I've never really wondered about before."

"My dear, what-"

BANG! BANG!

The loud knocking interrupted Velia mid-sentence. With a third, louder crash, the door busted free from its latch and swung inward. Three enormous creatures stooped to pass through the doorway, shoulders nearly brushing the sides, then straightened up, the bulk of their mottled blue-gray bodies completely blocking the light from the open door.

"Madame Velia le Vilaviti," intoned the largest, "you are hereby accused of high treason by the court of Queen Vivienne of Portal Land and the Twin River Valleys. You will now be punished and then banished, according to the laws of the realm." The formal words and tone were surprising and at odds with the troll's torpid expression.

"Treason?! Treason! You come here and presume to accuse me? Outrageous!" Velia flared, eyes flashing, "How dare you! On whose orders do you disturb my peace? The Queen herself is leagues away. Well, all know this to be true." As she raged, Brandon came up behind her, placing a hand on her shoulder and lending his steadying strength to her fiery indignation.

From behind the creature's bulk stepped a thin red-haired girl. "On my orders," she said, voice youthful yet authoritative. Brandon screamed, a high-pitched, terrified shriek, and dashed for the bedroom, slamming the door behind him.

Chapter 41

This is the start of the rest of my life, I thought morosely, careful to keep silent as I was led down another set of stairs into yet another stark white hallway. I stumbled in the clunky laceless shoes I had been given to wear.

"Sorry," I mumbled, eyes downcast.

The last hour had been the most demoralizing and humiliating experience of my life. I had been stripped naked and left to stand for far too long, chilly and exposed in the office-building air conditioning. Then I had been poked and prodded in places that I certainly would never have thought to hide a weapon, before being tossed some big white underthings and a set of scratchy gray sweats. And, of course, these infernal shoes, I thought, almost tripping again but catching myself in time.

A man behind a thick glass window looked up from his paperwork. "Cell 7," he said to the big man at my arm and gestured down the hall with a heavy square chin.

"Cell 7, Sir?"

"End of the hall."

"I know which one it is, Sir. I just, we don't usually..." the guard trailed off, voice concerned.

"Cell 7," the square-jawed man repeated, "Do you know who this girl is? That call from the Deacon about the big disturbance at church this morning?"

The guard's grip on my arm tightened. "I didn't realize, Sir. She's so young, I-"

"The Devil doesn't care how old they are, Son. Throw the godless bitch in with the ghosts and demons. By morning she'll be crying out to the Lord for forgiveness."

The man at my arm stiffened, gripping me roughly. "Watch it, girl," he said, tugging me further down the hallway. I hadn't realized that the guard was trying to be gentle until he wasn't. I scampered to keep myself from falling as he dragged me past several big metal doors. At the end of the hall, he swung the last door open wide and shoved me inside with a grimace of distaste. "Get cozy with your roommates, bitch. You're going to be here for a long time," he sneered, his large body filling the opening of the doorway.

Then he slammed the door shut with a resounding bang, and I was alone. I took stock of my surroundings. It was a narrow rectangular room with four metal cots. The lightbulb over my head was bright and unforgiving inside its protective metal cage, but the bulb on the back side of the room was burned out, leaving the furthest bunks in dim shadow. Even so, I could clearly see that there was no one else here. "Get cozy with my roommates?" I said into the empty space, "Huh?"

Throw her in with the ghosts and demons. Wasn't that what the other guard had said? "Well," I said to myself, quietly, "it's a good thing I don't believe in ghosts." A noise from somewhere outside startled me, and I jumped, alarmed. "Oh!" I exclaimed, heart pounding and breath coming fast. I sank down on the nearest cot, hand gripping my chest, and waited for my heartbeat to slow back down.

As my breathing returned to normal, I let out a small ironic chuckle. This time last week, I would have said I didn't believe in magic or in the fae folk, either. This might not be the time to be getting over-confident about what I believe about the inexistence of ghosts or demons, or anything else supernatural, for that matter. This time last week… I considered, was that actually true? No, it wasn't quite right.

This time last week, I had been at the Fair Isle, talking to Odo and Eudo and hearing about perfect intermagicals for the first time, and telling them that I didn't think I could probably have very much magic in me, at all. In fact, this time last week I had been experiencing real magic for the very first time, watching Isla make her flowers. Or at least, it had been the first time that I had actually realized what it was that I was looking at.

The actual first time I had seen real magic would have been, what? Well, it would probably have been right before I ran my car off the road, wouldn't it? Velia's first attempt to keep me away from town, and to prevent me from ever meeting Evita and the faeries. She had gotten so creative in her attempts to drive me off. Why had she gone to all of that extraordinary effort? Jealousy, Evita had said, and fear. Fear of who I might become, in Evita's life and in her court, and also, maybe, to the world.

Well, she didn't need to worry now, I thought, sighing heavily, since I was stuck in here where I couldn't do anything. I shivered, realizing for the first time how cold it was in this dank little room. Grabbing the thin gray blanket from the cot, I wrapped it around myself as tightly as I could and curled against a wall. Could this really be my fate? To be locked away, silenced, and forgotten? Me, a nearly-balanced, nearly-perfect intermagical. A being with more potential than, the fae had told me, almost anyone else on the entire planet-

Huh.

"Well, that's not true," I said, aloud. That internal sensation of veracity that I always felt when I believed something was startlingly and starkly absent. I sat up, letting the blanket fall away from my shoulders. My surprise startled me out of my upset, and my internal gears shifted from self-pity to inquisitive analysis.

I expect to feel a particular sensation inside my body when something is true, and I didn't feel it, just then. All week, as I had been expanding my understanding of the world and its mysteries, I'd been relying on that sensation, the visceral internal confirmation that I believe what I am hearing and saying, to allow me to keep accepting and integrating all of these new concepts into my evolving worldview. I'd gotten a lot of practice noticing that particular gut feeling lately. It was startlingly obvious when it was absent.

"Well, I guess I've got nothing but time to test the theory," I said aloud into the emptiness. I stood up, planting my feet and straightening my shoulders. "My intuition is a part of my magic, and I can trust it," I said, reassuring myself. When I said it, I felt my body rock forward slightly, responding to that inner pull that meant truth. It was comforting, too, to know that my intuitive gifts came from my powerful matriarchal line. Even when I was all alone, this was a tool that I had available for me to use. Well, let's put it to work!

"My name is Fiona," I said, resolutely. I felt the resonance of it deep in my body. True. So true.

"I am in a beautiful grassy meadow," I said, with the same confident tone. No. Those were just empty words.

"I am in jail." There it was again. That little tug of verisimilitude.

"I'm going to rot in here forever and ever, and never see the sky again," I said. This was, of course, not true. Small comfort, though. I was here, now, and that was bad enough. I sighed heavily. Back to the task at hand. What was it that I had been trying to learn? I had been after something specific, not just using my intuition like a child's magic eight ball. Oh right. That.

"I am a powerful intermagical," I said, confirming that it was so.

"The combination of fae and human magic gives me extraordinary power." It does.

"Healthy, nearly-balanced intermagicals like me are uncommon and rare," I said, echoing what Faeryn had told me. No, something about that statement wasn't quite correct. Well, if I went by what Melodie had told me, I wasn't as healthy as I thought I was. I sighed deeply and tried again.

"Balanced intermagicals are uncommon," I said. That was not the case either, apparently. But, all the fae folk I had met had told me…
I tried again.

"Nearly-balanced intermagicals are not particularly uncommon, at all?" There it was. As though the sensation had been lying in wait for me to ask the right question, the confirmation of my answer flooded through me like hot tea, warming my body from the inside out.

I continued to ask and answer my own questions until a metal grate in the door clanged open. A tray of something wet-looking slid under the door and I poked at it with a shoe-clad toe, not having any desire to investigate it more closely. Distracted by this unpleasant reminder of my current reality, I sat back on the cot to think about what I had learned.

"I don't think I'm actually all that special after all," I said, smiling, although that was certainly a matter of perspective.

What was rare, I had determined through my semi-scientific intuitive testing, was that I was a nearly balanced faerie intermagical with one primary source of fae magic. But, my intuition had confirmed that being a single-origin intermagical only really mattered to the fae, because, with my lineage, the faeries had a claim over me and a hope that I might be willing to intercede on their behalf with the humans. And so I had done, for better or for worse, I thought, looking around at my bleak surroundings.

What my single source of magic didn't do, though, was make me any more powerful than anyone else who had roughly half magic and half humanity from different sources or types of fae folk throughout the generations. I thought about all of the intermagicals I had been drawn to in my life. How many generations had there been, since the fae had made their Intermixing Declaration, for people with a little bit of magic to find each other and combine to create increasingly concentrated magical offspring? And sure, like single-source intermagicals, some of those children might have too much magic to be able to integrate and thrive in human society. I smiled again. But, some of them were out there changing the world.

I thought about the girl who had introduced herself to me this morning. Betty, who ran the Autistic women's club at the college. She's a powerful intermagical, I bet. With the thought came confirmation, and a real sense of belonging and community. I was finally finding my people. And, my family.

"No daughter of mine"

The words I had seen Evita form, silent and intense, as she stared me down, there in the back of the transport van, reminded me that I wasn't entirely sure where I stood with my newfound faerie family. What had she meant by that? Was she really so disappointed in me? What had she expected me to do, fight off the policemen and flee? There wasn't anything I could have done.

The sensation of powerlessness overwhelmed me, sweeping away any good thoughts or happy emotions I had managed to conjure. The idea of joy at my newfound community was transmuted into despair as I remembered that it might be ages, years even, before I would get the chance to see them again. This was supposed to be my beginning. My new start. I was fresh out of college, brimming with potential, the world at my fingertips. I had thought that I could do anything. I'd thought I could save Faeryn.

I wondered if I would even get to hear the outcome of the city council vote tomorrow. After my arrest and seeing how connected the Deacon was, I doubted anything I did could actually change anything. All I had truly accomplished was to get myself into this terrible situation.

I curled up on the hard mat of the cot and wrapped the blanket close around my shoulders. Shivering, I let out a quiet little warbling moan of despair. A single hot tear spilled out over my eye and ran down my cheek to fall onto the cold plasticine mattress. More tears followed the first and in moments I was heaving and shaking with the release of my pent-up emotion. "What am I going to do in jail?" I cried in desolation.

"Well, for one thing, you'll practice your attention span," came a raspy voice from the corner.

Chapter 42

I froze, instantly alert, silencing my sobs. I was all alone in this room, I knew that for sure. The door was heavy and noisy. No one could have come in or out.

"Better to be out there livin', o'course, especially when you're just a child like you are," said the voice from deep in the far corner of the cell, where the burned-out lightbulb made the shadows dark and long, "but it's a valuable thing to have time to practice the art of sitting still. A skill that the young often neglect. Now, when you're my age…"

Way back in the dark corner, something shifted with a sound like the rustling of dry leaves. At this suggestion of motion from my visitor, I shot up from where I lay, still clutching the blanket around me. Standing on the bed, I pressed my back against the cold stone wall, putting as much space as possible between myself and whatever had just spoken.

"Throw her in there with the ghosts and demons"

"Hey! Uh, what- wait, who- er," I stumbled over my words, not sure what to ask. I could hear my heartbeat pounding in my ears "How did you get in here?" I finished, finally. That was a place to start, at least.

"You'd think a body'd know what it had done, wouldn't you?" she muttered, almost as if she were talking to herself, "But, it doesn't. So much goes on in there that those living in em don't even realize. Couldn't control 'em if they did." The voice sounded like it might belong to an old woman, and the shadowy mass in the corner shifted as she talked. "Your mama asked me to look out for you tonight, child. Real insistent, about it, too. An' I heard 'er, so I crawled on up an' sat myself inside a tear and waited for you to go ahead and' cry me on out. Took your sweet time about it too."

"Cry you out?"

"Mmhmm," she said, "Better to have put myself in those powerful lungs of yours and ridden out on one of those heavy sighs you've been heaving all night though."

I blinked at the apparition in confusion. This was not how I expected an encounter with a ghost would go. If this was a ghost, I thought curiously, peering more deeply into the shadows. Well, the direct approach was serving me well so far.

"Are you a ghost?" I asked, trying my best to sound matter-of-fact, and not accusatory.

"Oh, well. That's one sort of way to look at it, but I suppose I would be. Remarkable, I've never been a ghost before."

"You haven't been-? But you're here, I thought-" I paused, and thought for a moment before continuing, "I guess I don't know anything about ghosts."

"Well, suffice it to say that I'm a copy of your ancestor that you carry inside yourself. The part of me that I passed down to you. But here I am standing in front of you, and it's surely true that I am long dead, so call me ghost if you must, or you could just call me Mama Jo." At that, the shifting lump unfurled, and a stout little woman with long white hair stepped forward into the light.

My first impression hit me like a wrecking ball to my gut. Her lined, aged face looked incredibly familiar. She looked an awful lot like Evita, and a little like Zelai and Egan, too. But, most of all, I realized, struck by the depth of my recognition, she looked like me.

"You're my ancestor," I said, mouth dropping open in awe.

"Yes, girl, I just said that, didn't I?"

"Yeah, you did, I just- you look so familiar, and I'm not used to seeing people that look like me. It took me by surprise." I came closer, peering at her round little face. "Evita sent you to me tonight? You look a lot like her."

"Eh well, like mother, like daughter, I suppose, but that's a compliment. She always was a pretty one," the old woman said, preening. The way she fussily tidied her thick, long hair made her look even more like my birth mother. If Evita was her daughter, then, I put the pieces together, that would make this woman my grandmother. "'Course she sent for me. Good little bit of spell-work she did to reach me, too. She's a powerful talented witch, your mother. Skills I never mastered. She could teach you, though, if you'll listen."

"I'd like that," I said, then pressed on, giving voice to the fears that had been plaguing me all night, "I guess if she sent you, she can't be that upset with me. She can't have actually meant that she doesn't want me as a daughter." I cast my eyes down, not meeting hers.

"My word child, you really have been worrying over that little turn of phrase in that busy mind of yours all night, haven't you? I don't know what she meant, child, but I know she didn't mean that. Family's not as fragile as that, is it?" I looked up and met her eyes just for a second and made a quick thin-lipped grimace before looking away again. "Oh, child, I know. I've been with you, in your life. It's hard to trust, after so much loneliness, but you'll get there." She patted, and I sat down on the edge of the cot, next to her. "It'll be alright. That feeling of being apart from everyone has just made you all that much stronger inside yourself, girl. And I can tell you, there's no escaping it. All the women of our line feel that way, at some level or another. It's our fate. I take comfort in thinking we're like Sarah in the Bible, the lonely foremothers of a culture that doesn't exist yet."

I laughed. "The last thing I expected was to be comforted by the Bible right now. After everything I've learned in the last week, that's the last place I'd think to go to for answers."

"Why?" she asked, "It has its own wisdom. It's not the truth, certainly, in the way it is regarded to be by," she glanced meaningfully at the door, "some people, but it's got history and important lessons. Nothing that's persisted for as long as that book has could be completely without value."

"Really?" I asked, "You think so? Even though it's wrong about-" I hesitated, "About God?"

"Of course!" she answered, her eyes twinkling with humor, "It's a human book, and humans will always be wrong about the nature of the divine. Every single one of 'em every single time, at least a little bit, and most of them, quite a bit more than that. But that doesn't mean that there aren't beings out there that are something beyond human or fae that take an interest in this world, and interact with it." She gave me a meaningful side-eyed look.

"There are?" I asked.

"I believed so, when I lived, and now that I am in the state I am, well…" She winked and smiled esoterically before continuing. "Humans just love to give names and faces to things. Always human faces, ironically enough," she said with a chuckle,

"Now, as I was saying, humans have always been at least a little bit wrong in their interpretations of the divine, but each individual's experience may well be genuine. Those beings may simply have the ability to appear to us as we would expect them to be, making our own personal relationship with them the only one that's truly relevant."

"They're real? The gods? Like, really real?" The idea took me aback. I had honestly never believed in a 'higher power' of any kind. "Should I, uh, worry about them? Like, obey them, or give them offerings? Worship them, or…" I trailed off.

She raised one expressive eyebrow and gave me a long look. "Do you yearn for subordination, child? Do you wander, lost, without a master to control you?"

I paused for a long moment before I answered. "No?"

"Then take no master, child!" she crowed, "You have no need of one, either in the Christian God or from the myriad pantheons that came before him."

"Okay," I said, "I guess I won't then. But, if I don't follow one human path or another, what, uh-" I hesitated, unsure of what I was really trying to ask, "What am I supposed to do?"

"Think," Mama Jo answered, simply. She tapped her own forehead, knowingly. "You've got a good brain on your shoulders, child. I've been in there, I know." She stood and walked to the wall where there hadn't been a window. Now, though, there was, and she opened it, letting in a cool breeze carrying the scent of the evening. I followed her and breathed deeply, looking out the open window at the darkening sky. "See that group of stars right there?" she asked, pointing at a cluster of glittering pinpricks in the sky, "the bright one's Aldebaran, and that little grouping there'll be the Pleiades. D'you know what we call that constellation?"

"No," I answered, staring out into the wide emptiness of the night.

"Taurus," she said, "The bull. And do you know when humans linked that particular group of stars with bovines?"

"No," I said, again.

"Well, neither do I, but I can tell you that they wrote it down some sixteen thousand years ago, so we can say for sure that it was at least some time before that."

"Sixteen hundred years, that's a long time," I said, still gazing out at the night sky. I realized that it must be an illusion but it was better than the alternative.

"No, child. It's not. But, I said sixteen *thousand* years. There are cave paintings of the ancient aurochs running wild across the plains, interposed with maps of these particular stars."

"Oh," I said, turning to look back at her, "Wow."

"And we still call those stars by the name of the bull today. If something sticks around that long, well, there's likely something to it. And," she went on, "if it pops up again and again, in all different parts of the world in different sorts of cultures, well, there's likely something to that, too."

"Yeah, I guess so," I agreed.

She reached out the window and plucked one of the stars from the sky, handing it to me. In my palm was a tiny clear crystal point that glinted in the illusory moonlight. I closed my hand around it and felt the cool geometric shape press into my palm. "Follow the logic, child. Take that little piece of earthly magic there as a reminder to be a mystical scientist. Learn everything you can from the natural world. Nature is your very best teacher, second maybe to that prodigious bit of intuition you're working with." She clicked her tongue and shook her head at me. "And learn from history. Learn from other people, magical and human ones alike. You've been doing well this past week, listening and questioning, and deciding for yourself what it is that you ought to believe."

"Logical mysticism," I said, "Looking with my own eyes and trying to understand the magic of the world, for myself."

"Yes, child. That's a fine name for what it is that we do. Logical Mysticism. I like that. Reminds me of something." She thought for a moment, hand resting on her chin, the same way I sometimes did. "Ah, yes, that's his name. Bertrand Russell, an old intermagical thinker. He said it just the same way, let me see now-" Mama Jo turned away from the window and without her attention, the night sky faded, leaving only the rough stone wall behind. She rifled in her layers of clothing and pulled out a thin paperback printed with the title 'Mysticism & Logic.' I sat down, opened the little tome, and read the first sentence.

Metaphysics, or the attempt to conceive the world as a whole by means of thought, has been developed, from the first, by the union and conflict of two very different human impulses, the one urging men towards mysticism, the other urging them towards science.

"The union and the conflict, yeah," I looked up from the book, "Mama Jo, that's exactly what I- uh, Mama Jo?"

"Yes, child?" came the suggestion of speech from inside me.

"Oh, you're back in, uh, in there, huh?" I asked, feeling awkward speaking aloud into the once-again empty room.

"Yes, child", came that same subterranean sensation.

The cell felt cold again, and I picked up the blanket from where it had fallen, wrapping it around myself like a cloak. I clutched the little crystal point in my fist until it hurt. All alone, I felt the weight of my situation crashing back down on me. The tears welled up in my eyes, threatening to overflow and I felt my breath catch.

"Oh child, this will be one long night. Read your book, now. Sleep when you can. It will be alright."

I delved into the text's description of the four characteristics of mysticism, trying to distract myself from my current circumstance. could see immediately why Mama Jo had given me this particular book to read.

Mystical philosophy, in all ages and in all parts of the world, is characterized by certain beliefs. The first and most direct outcome of the moment of illumination is belief in the possibility of a way of knowledge which may be called revelation or insight or intuition, as contrasted with sense, reason, and analysis…

I paused, closing the book with a finger tucked inside to mark my place. Intuition. Yeah, it's hard to deny it once you've experienced it, but it's hard to convince anyone else if they haven't.

The second characteristic of mysticism is its belief in unity, and its refusal to admit opposition or division anywhere.

Well, that's hard to swallow at a time like this. I'm feeling pretty opposed right now, actually. But, that wasn't what division and unity meant here, was it? I thought, remembering how Anonaziata had described magical energy, the single animating force of everything.

A third mark of almost all mystical metaphysics is the denial of the reality of Time. This is an outcome of the denial of division; if all is one, the distinction of past and future must be illusory.

I looked at the wall where the false window had once been and sighed. Time might be an illusion but it would be nice to know how much of it had passed, in here.

The last of the doctrines of mysticism which we have to consider is its belief that all evil is mere appearance, an illusion produced by the divisions and oppositions of the analytic intellect.

Well, I certainly appear evil to the Deacon and his cronies, I guess, and he sure seems evil to me.

"Evil, truly?" That sensation of speech from inside myself, again. Was Mama Jo speaking to me, or was that my own internal dialogue, I wondered, because the truth was that I had always talked to myself, all the time, and answered myself, too.

"What's the difference?" I heard, echoing in my chest.

"I don't know," I answered, contemplatively, "Maybe there isn't one."

Chapter 43

The scraping of my cell's metal door woke me and I jolted awake with a start. I must have fallen asleep at some point.

"Go on, out for processing," said a bulky guard, propping the door open with a heavy booted foot.

I scrambled up off the cot. The book, Mysticism & Logic, seemed to have disappeared but the crystal point lay where it had fallen on the bed. Not wanting to lose it, I popped the tiny thing into my cheek and followed the guard out. He led me up several flights of stairs to a small waiting room with stark white walls and hard metal chairs.

"You're up first this morning," the guard grunted, then shut the door, leaving me alone.

I paced back and forth in the small room, fidgeting with the crystal nervously. I was first, but first for what? A hearing, an arraignment? Words from law tv shows ran through my nervously racing mind. Shouldn't I have been offered a lawyer by now? I remembered the way the guards had spoken about the Deacon and got even more agitated. Maybe these cops weren't going by the book, in my case. Maybe they were taking the law into their own hands.

I glanced up at the clock on the wall. At least I could tell how long I had been in here. The time was 7:45 a.m. Still hours before the City Council's vote that would determine whether I had just thrown my entire life away to save Faeryn and her spring, or whether it had all just been for nothing. I kept pacing and fidgeting with the sharp stone in my hand until the door opened again.

A different guard led me down a hallway and into the side door of a large, old-fashioned courtroom with high ceilings and arched windows. As I entered the room, the faces of the gathered crowd turned toward me. I could see some faces that I recognized, Brandon and the Deacon standing near the front, and the Gullah in the shadows near the back, but many more that I didn't. There were more people here than I would have expected. Striding purposefully toward me came Evita, flanked by two long-haired native men, her eyes once again blazing. Reaching me, she leaned in and hissed into my ear, so that only I could hear her.

"No daughter of mine will bend the knee to human law for daring to act bravely and do what is right." I smiled, feeling tears well behind my eyes. The younger of the two men stepped forward, extending a hand to shake. "This is my friend, Mr. Yellowbird," Evita said, "he will be your lawyer." Mr. Yellowbird's handshake was firm and his eyes were intelligent and kind. The gentle pulse of energy that I felt at the touch of his hand was calm and reassuring.

"Hello Fiona, it is good to meet you," said the tall, stately-looking man. He clapped my shoulder comfortingly. "I want you to know that we have been able to recover your vehicle as well as your phone if you would like me to make any communications for you. It is my hope, however, that you will be walking out of here today and you will be able to make those calls yourself." I nodded, flooded with relief at knowing that I wasn't alone, that I had people on my side to help.

As other people in the courtroom milled about, I sat numbly under the watchful eye of the guard and looked around for anything to distract me.

Historic County Courthouse, read a cardboard sign propped on an easel at the edge of the gallery. *Haunted Oregon - Stop #8 Construction of this noted historical site was completed in 1889, and reports of ghosts and other supernatural happenings began to be reported almost immediately. After-*

"The honorable judge, presiding over case number …" the bailiff announced, pulling my attention away from the sign, and I scrambled to my feet with everyone else as the judge made his way to the dais and took his seat.

"You may be seated, court is now in session."

"Sir," said Mr. Yellowbird on my left, "as we discussed by phone, we intend to put a pretrial motion in limine, with regard to the jurisdiction of this case. Per the international regulations instated earlier this year, pertaining to tribal land rights, our verifiable historical claim on the land gives full legal jurisdiction of this matter to the Kalapuya Nation. Per statute C.C.C.359.11 we are asking for immediate dismissal of this case and remand of the accused to our custody."

The judge nodded, "Yes, thank you Mr. Yellowbird, with regard to your motion-"

"Now wait just a minute!" interrupted a loud male voice from across the court.

Another voice overlapped the first, saying, "Sir, if I may-"

The first interrupter was the Deacon. He barrelled on, fists balled. "You can't just release this dangerous person back out into the world, with the heinous things she's done and said, I'll-"

"Order!" came the voice from on high, along with a crack of the gavel. The judge gave the Deacon a withering look and the red-faced man quieted, looking cowed. Then, he turned to the other man who had spoken, the lawyer for the prosecution, and nodded his assent.

"Sir, the designation of the disputed area as a place of specific, historic spiritual significance is still up for debate. These-" he looked across the room toward Mr. Yellowbird and the gray-haired man seated on his other side, "people have been making spurious claims with no physical evidence to support them, and not to discount their very," he eyed the men again," creative claims, but this matter is far from settled, and we would like to recommend that this dangerous person be remanded without bail for the entirety of the discovery process, due to the nature of her crimes and our opinion of the likelihood of recidivism."

"Mr. Yellowbird, is that the case?"

"Your honor, this site's spiritual importance is clearly indicated in our oral tribal record, and while no specific pieces of physical evidence that support our historical claim has been unearthed, the nature of my people's relationship with the land means that lasting evidence of our residency would be vanishingly unlikely."

"He admits it, your honor. All evidence of their claim is hearsay,"

"Our oral traditions are not hearsay, Sir," said Mr. Yellowbird, turning to the opposing lawyer and drawing himself up to his full height.

"Order," said the judge, sans gavel, "I hear you, Mr. Yellowbird, but with due respect to the traditions of your people I can not dismiss this case on your word alone."

"Yes, Sir. That is why I have brought an elder of the Kalapuya tribe with me today, who has been recognized by the court as a certified expert in our people's history, to affirm-."

"Hearsay!" shouted the Deacon.

"Sir, one more time and you will be removed from this courtroom," said the judge, looking unamused at the Deacon's outburst, "But, until physical or written evidence of the tribal claim on the land can be produced-"

As the judge continued talking, my vision darkened and narrowed. My fists clenched so hard that the point of the crystal threatened to cut into my palm. I had dared to hope, for just a moment, that everything was going to turn out okay, but who knew how long it would take before the tribe would be able to prove their claim, if ever? How much of my life would I waste rotting in jail for this?

I cast my eyes down at the table in front of me. There was my phone, that Mr. Yellowbird told me he had gotten back. I wondered how many missed calls I had from my mom, and what she would think when she found out where I was. How had I gone from a college graduate, full of potential, to a condemned criminal in the course of a single week? The tears welled up in my eyes, and I wiped them away. If I'd never come to search for the faeries and discovered this hidden world of the fae, none of this would have happened, I thought bitterly. I should have just stayed at home and been a happy, normal girl, like everybody else.

Would I have been happy though? I'd never been normal, I'd always struggled to find my people and fit in. No, finding the fae had been a good thing, but there were so many paths I could have taken to avoid ending up here. If only I could have found Evita right away. I never would have met Faeryn and found out about her problems. Never would have tried to do more than I should have to try to save her, and gotten myself into this situation.

But, even if I had met Faeryn, it would have been alright if I had never met the Deacon. If I hadn't recognized him when Faeryn showed me his picture in the spring. If only I could have shrugged my shoulders and said, "That's terrible, but I don't know anything about it. Sure is a shame though." If only Velia hadn't been so obsessed with keeping me away from Evita and my family that she had ended up running me right into him, scaring me off the road, making me pop my tire, like that. If only she hadn't made my first introduction to Oregon that wet, soggy slog through the wet woods into-

My heart skipped a beat. I started to lean forward, but seeing the guard move his hand to his gun, I changed my mind and turned instead to the long-haired Native man seated next to me. He leaned down to listen to me, and as he did, his face split into a wide, fierce grin. He held my phone out to me to unlock, under the glowering gaze of the guard, and opened the photo album. There it was, at the top of my photo roll, blurry with rainwater, but distinct enough. The images I had taken of a big, mossy stone statue, three men, and a boxy moving van. He held the phone out to the Kalapuya elder next to him, who looked at it for a long moment, then nodded gravely.

"Your Honor," said Mr. Yellowbird, "We have new evidence to put before the court. May I approach the bench?" The two lawyers spoke to the judge in low tones, as the Deacon leaned forward over the banister, staring daggers through their backs as if by glaring hard enough he could see what was on the other side of the phone screen.

"Elder, can you please approach the bench?" asked the judge, and the gray-haired man joined them at the podium. The judge held my phone out for the elderly man and asked him a question quietly, once, and then a second time. On the third try, the judge's words were audible when he said, "Elder, can you confirm whether or not this statue is of spiritual significance to the historic Native peoples of this valley?

"Oh, oh," said the ancient man, in the extra-loud voice of the hard of hearing, "Yes, of course. This is a marker stone that would be placed to indicate something sacred to my people."

I saw the Deacon at the edge of my vision and watched his face fall into an expression of horror before he recovered himself and transformed it back into a beet-red sneer.

"Which," added Mr. Yellowbird, "is verified expert testimony documenting a physical claim of my people on this land, and one," he continued, turning and returning the Deacon's dagger stare with interest, "which was intentionally and willfully removed from its place of significance in an attempt to dispossess and defraud my people. Please know that we take this matter very seriously and will be pursuing this issue to the full extent allowed by law."

The judge thanked Mr. Yellowbird and turned to address the Deacon, whose vein was pulsing visibly in his forehead. This is you in the picture, isn't it, Sir? Were you aware of the significance of this artifact at the time you displaced it?"

"No," he spluttered, "That's ridiculous. It's a boulder. A big rock, that's all it is. We needed it out of the way. No way to know that it was anything more than that. They'll obviously say anything to get what they want and intercede for this lying harlot. She's bewitched them! She-" The Deacon grew redder and redder as he shouted, shaking his head violently, spittle flying. Some of it, I saw, flew, and landed on Brandon. In contrast to his father, Brandon looked solemn, eyes downcast. He raised his eyes slowly to look at the judge and nodded deeply.

"Enough," the judge pronounced, striking his gavel and silencing the irate man. "Son," said the judge to Brandon, who met his eyes nervously, "Do you have something to tell the court?"

Brandon straightened his shoulders and addressed the judge, not looking at his father next to him. "Yes, your honor, we knew. It was obvious it was something like that." I watched him quail a little under the glare his father gave him, but he swallowed hard and stood tall.

"Now, you aren't in this photo, son," said the judge, taking my phone and looking closely at it.

"No, I left early that night," said Brandon, "I didn't like it, what they were doing. I know where that rock thing ended up though. It's in a warehouse on 9th street," he said, nodding to the Kalapuya elder and Mr. Yellowbird who were still gathered around the judge's podium, "It's not right, what we did. I think they should have it back." The young man's expression firmed into something resolute, and I saw a flicker of that same light in his eyes that had made me so interested in getting to know him when I had first met him at the Raven. That must have been why he was at the bar before his friends and had been so conveniently able to rescue me.

At that moment, the significance of what Brandon had just done washed over me, bowling me over like an enormous ocean wave. The rush of emotions welled up, and my eyes overflowed, sending me into paroxysms of gasping sobs. He had just rescued me, again.

Brandon had been raised by the Deacon, steeped in the doctrine of that evangelical church all his life. A child of the church, he had told me. Of course, he would buy into their ideology, and their drive to convert and proselytize. It was all he had ever known. But, I realized, looking up through my tears at his tight-jawed face, standing there in opposition to his powerful father, at his core, he was a free-thinker, and his heart was in the right place.

"Thank you, son," said the judge to Brandon, then he addressed the court as a whole.

"I hereby dismiss this case on the grounds of the tribal claim of jurisdiction and order the prisoner to be immediately reprimanded to their custody. Mr. Yellowbird, is the tribe prepared to provide appropriate detainment facilities?"

"Yes, thank you," said Mr. Yellowbird, "Elder, how do you find, in this matter?"

"Not guilty," said the Elder to me, with a wide, lined grin, "She is free to go."

"Elder, under the Native Land Rights regulation C.C.C.359.14 pertaining to extended criminal penalties for the willful degradation of Native spiritual sites, do you wish to press charges at this time?"

"Yes, yes, I do," the wizened man said, his wide grin taking on a shark-like quality.

"Your honor, I would greatly appreciate your offer of detainment facilities, in this additional matter. We would like to request your assistance in the immediate remand of the confirmed suspect, pending trial at the tribe's convenience," said Mr. Yellowbird.

"We just had our annual council," said the Elder, speculatively, "it will be some time before the appropriate bodies are gathered again, to arbitrate such a case."

"What?" the Deacon shouted, face beet red and fists in tight balls, "How dare you take my son into-"

"Your son isn't in this picture, Deacon, but you are," said the judge, waving my phone, still held in his hand. The Deacon's tomato-red face seemed to swell, becoming somehow even redder than before.

The judge turned to the bailiff and said, "Remand him, please," and then, to me, "You are free to go, Miss." The bailiff unclipped his handcuffs and advanced on the Deacon, who started shouting and gesticulating angrily. "Order, order!" shouted the judge, banging his gavel, while the Deacon continued to rage, ignoring him. "Enough! One more word out of you, and I'll hold you in contempt of court," the judge bellowed. Finally, the Deacon quieted, his eyes still bulging angrily out of his beet-red face. "I'm taking a break," said the judge irritably, "Court is in recess."

Silence hung in the courtroom, after the departure of the judge. Mr. Yellowbird nodded with satisfaction and placed a reassuring hand on my shoulder and we stood together and watched the bailiff handcuff the Deacon.

"Religion has always been our biggest problem, since contact," the tall lawyer said to me in a deep, resonant voice that carried across the quiet courtroom. "Ever since the Pope's Doctrine of Discovery in 1493 when he authorized and asserted the rights to enslave, colonize and convert the indigenous peoples of America. It basically said if we weren't Christian we didn't have entitlement to land. It was either convert or else."

He took a step forward, turning to face the attentive crowd. "The Christians know that our power lies in our spiritual practices and Christians have always tried to sever our spiritual relationship with the land by outlawing and decrying our practices as evil, and here we still are today, watching people like this," he shot a disparaging look at the Deacon, who was silently struggling with the bailiff, "despoil our sacred spaces, disregard our artifacts and dispossess us of our land. What most people don't realize is that our spiritual practices were given to us by the Creator. They were given to us by the spirits that work for the light, the spirits that are part of creation."

Now he spoke directly to the Deacon, eyes blazing, "So who are you to tell us that we aren't praying to the Most High, the Great Mystery? It's not like a crossed telephone wire where everyone is dialing the wrong number except for you. It's arrogant and self-righteous. It's unconscionable."

"I see it like this," he said to his audience, "Christians believe in conquering the land. Indigenous peoples believe that we are one. We are connected. We are related to the land. Christians seek control and religious domination, we seek freedom. You have fences and borders, we have medicine lines. You have pets, we have relatives. You have human law, we have natural law, and you created hell to instill fear and control the people."

By now, the bailiff had succeeded in handcuffing the red-faced Deacon and was leading him across the room, toward the door where I had entered, the one that led down to the cells in the basement. "Some may even say that we had heaven on earth before contact with the churches, now you tell me what sounds more evil?" The Deacon passed in front of us, and Mr. Yellowbird acknowledged him with a deep nod, which he did not return.

"Now, don't get me wrong, there are many good Christians out there," Mr. Yellowbird said to the crowd, with a particular smile for Brandon, who didn't meet his gaze, "Ones that actually practice 'One shall not judge' and don't force their beliefs onto others. But just go ahead and take this as a reminder and leave our culture alone."

The Deacon had reached the door by now. He turned back to the room, as though to say something, but, perhaps remembering the judge's admonition, quickly shut his mouth again.

"I'll leave you with this," said Mr. Yellowbird as the door swung shut, "a quote from Mahatma Gandhi that I really like. He said, 'I like your Jesus because he was a beautiful man and a great teacher, but not so much the Christians.'"

Chapter 44

I may have officially been free to go, but nothing can happen without the appropriate paperwork, so I found myself sitting with Mr. Yellowbird in a cramped clerk's office, tapping my foot anxiously as the clock ticked closer and closer to 10 a.m. and crucial the city council vote, as we languished in the particularly frustrating magic of human bureaucracy that makes simple tasks take all day and feel like they took all year. Finally, the ancient fax machine coughed out its last ink-smeared page, and the clerk nodded to Mr. Yellowbird.

"She's all yours, Sir. Have a good one."

I looked up at the clock on the wall. Almost a quarter after. They might still be deliberating. If I ran, I might make it across the courtyard in time to see the vote. Mr. Yellowbird held the door open for me, motioning me through. I flashed him a bright smile of thanks, and dashed through the door, trailing the fluttering skirts of the colorful faerie dress that Evita had brought for me to change into.

As I flung open the heavy courthouse door, I saw that I was too late. People were already spilling out of the building across the courtyard, down the steps, and onto the lawn. Zelai, hand in hand with Evita, saw me first and pointed with a delighted shriek, drawing the crowd's attention to me. A roar rose up as overlapping voices shouted the news across to me.

"We won, we did it!"

"It was a landslide, never had a chance!"

"Only his cronies, on his side, seven to three! Seven to three!"

"We did? We won? Really?" I shouted back, picking up my skirts and running down the steps toward the throng. We won. We won! The joy of it welled up inside of me, filling me with radiant energy. I let it explode out of me in a shower of bright sparkles that hung in the air above and around us, as I met the throng and was swirled into the shouting, triumphant mass. Hands clapped my shoulders and smiling faces congratulated me, blending together in the chaos of celebration.

There was Alaric, tall and lanky. He waved his hat in one hand and winked when he caught my eye. Melody and Anonaziata were there too, looking glad but disoriented in the boisterous crowd. I saw Faeryn, next, riding on Arlee's back. The blonde faerie was taller than I remembered, which fit her stately bearing well, I thought. She seemed to carry the smaller Faeryn as comfortably as she would a backpack. Faeryn slipped down from Arlee's back and ran the last few steps to me. She flung her arms around me, crying, deep heaving sobs.

I joined her, letting hot tears of relief flow down my face and onto her thin, quivering shoulder, feeling all of the things that I had kept bottled up over these last few days and hours. Relief, like heaving off a heavy coat of anxiety and fear, for Faeryn, who would be safe now. Her city would shine on, and the spring would be protected by its Native land stewards. Relief for myself, too. I was free and whole, with my entire life ahead of me. And, a powerful feeling of joy. Joy at having this newfound family and community at my back, and nothing but time to get to know them, and for us all to get to know me, Fiona, powerful intermagical daughter of the littlest faerie queen. I felt that golden effervescence of internal power well up inside of me, blossoming with a sensation of radiant warmth, and I exhaled, letting it flow out into the universe with my breath.

Faeryn's arms unclasped from my neck, and she smiled up at me, her pale face shining with moisture from her tears. "Thank you," she said, meeting my gaze, and we shared a look of familial understanding that was all-encompassing. Arlee stepped forward, reaching to pick Faeryn back up. She had been out of the spring for a long time, and the intensity of the last few days had cost her in strength. To my surprise, Faeryn waved her off. "No, love, I'm alright now. Fiona just refreshed me."

I did? She smiled at me gratefully, before being drawn away by someone wanting the broken-hearted princess's attention.

My brother Egan walked by with a group of young fae men. My brother punched my arm lightly in congratulations. I smiled at him, then caught the eye of one of his friends and blushed deeply, pretty sure that I recognized him from that back garden patio at the River House. At that moment, I spied Eudo and Odo in the crowd and hailed them, glad for the distraction.

"Daughter o' the Little' Queen down in the valley, are ye? Well, isn't that the tale of it," said Odo gruffly.

"Isla sends her congratulations," said Eudo.

"Or condolences," grunted Odo, which made Eudo elbow his brother in the rib.

"An' she wishes she could be here, but someone has to mind the bar." Now that all this was over and done with, they said, I would have to come throw stones with them, at the Fair Isle. I agreed enthusiastically.

Next to catch my attention was the Kalapuya elder. "Evita reached out to me right away, after you told her about this outlet of the creek that had been found," he said, clasping my hand in his deeply wrinkled one, "So much of our land has been taken and the location of so many sites has been lost. We are glad to be able to start the official process of reclaiming this piece of sacred territory." His creased, old eyes twinkled. "It's incredible to see the creative ways that our young people are finding to subvert these international CCC regulations to help us reclaim the lost lands of America's native tribes. The power of brilliant young minds looking for innovative solutions using all the modern tools at their disposal."

Innovative solutions with modern tools was right, I thought, as I overheard the Gullah talking nearby with a young androgynous intermagical that we had met yesterday who was studying hydraulics engineering at the university. With the Christian Springs project proving just how much of the water's magic was retained even after it was bottled, the two technomages were deep in conversation about how to design a wearable, portable spring for Faeryn.

Zelai ran around in happy circles, arms outstretched like an airplane. He zoomed in for a landing, coming to a stop in front of me, with a big grin. "Hey big sis, I'm glad you're not in jail! Are you gonna come and live with us now?"

Evita, overhearing, turned toward us. "You know, you would be more than welcome, Fiona. You could have the room that you slept in the other night."

I thought about the other room, the one that the Gullah had mentioned was available for rent, up near the Fair Isle. From what he had told me, there was some interesting stuff going on up there that I might want to check out. "Thank you," I said, "Yeah, maybe! I'm still trying to figure out what I want to do, but I know I'll be at the hill a whole lot. There's so much for us all to catch up on, and there's so much for me to learn."

Mr. Yellowbird came down the stairs behind me. "You left this back there," he said, holding out my phone. It buzzed to life as soon as he handed it to me. *Home,* read the display, *27 missed calls.* I answered.

"Mom, hey. I know. I'm sorry. I'm okay, I'm safe. I'm really good, actually. Yeah, I did find them… and um… Mom? My name is Fiona, now. Really? I'm so glad.

Yeah, I like it too. It's been crazy actually. And, Mom, you're never going to believe this…"

Author's Note

This book is a work of fiction, but there are a number of parallels between our world and the world of the New World Fae and between my life and the life that Fiona leads in the book. I, too, was adopted, and my birth mother did name me before I was born, but unlike the Fiona of the book, I didn't take up that mantle until after I had my son, at age 30, at which point, I felt very much as though I stepped into my own magic, and connected with my powerful matriarchal lineage.

This book positively fell out of me in three months, while I layed next to my young son's bed as he fell asleep. I started writing Intermagical at the beginning and wrote it, essentially, straight through to the end, using a pretty basic outline, and with Deborah Chester's Fantasy Fiction Formula as a general roadmap. This was the first thing of any length that I had written since my funny little high school made me write a 75-page autobiography, which, as it turned out after I wrote it, wasn't actually all that long, or at least it didn't feel like it to me. This novel didn't feel very long either, and neither did the second book in the series, the first draft of which I completed in the calendar month of November 2022.

Without truly knowing what I mean by this, I feel as though I almost channeled this book and its sequel. As though, by opening myself up to writing a story about a girl like me, who moved to Oregon after college, to build a relationship with her birth family, and, also like me, though perhaps not as literally, found them to be faeries, I might have received a story from a world that parallels our own.

Many of the characters and locations in this story are based in reality. The family that Fiona finds in this novel mirrors the family that I have found here in Oregon, as I make my home in Portal Land, with my husband, a son of the Gullah Islands, and visit often with my faerie of a birth mother and the rest of my birth family.

Including my cousin Faeryn, who is a beautiful, wonderfully imaginative, and creative fae-identified person with a broken heart. She was born with a congenital heart defect and we are so lucky to continue to have her with us, as we continue on through our 30s together, but she is struggling, as our human society fails to take care of her and provide what she needs to be comfortable and happy. More than anything, I realized, as I continued to ask questions and receive answers, allowing this story to tell itself, through me, Intermagical is for Faeryn. Saving her, and using human magic to make real, meaningful change, is the heart, if you will, of the plot, and, by purchasing this book, you have made a real meaningful difference in saving the real, live, Faeryn, who desperately needs it.

If, in the way that human magic occasionally does, this story catches the cultural consciousness enough that Faeryn is well and truly saved, and I am able to provide her with the care and comfort she deserves, I'm planning to use anything additional to help other intermagicals and to create intermagical community here in the Pacific Northwest, and around the world.

So, if you were given this story by a friend, that's totally alright. Stories should be shared. I'm a faerie, not a capitalist. But, if, after reading, you are moved to take real action to help save Faeryn, or if you're looking to find more intermagical community, you can find us online at http://intermagical.com

Thanks so much to my friends and family for all of the encouragement and aid you've given me in getting this book finished and releasing it out into the world. Particular thanks to Joy Love, Holly Hedge, and Dante Ashby for their absolutely invaluable developmental feedback. Special thanks to Chris Yellowbird whose eloquent words I borrowed and loaned to our lawyer Mr. Yellowbird for the final courthouse scene and thanks also to those mean Fairy Folk ladies without whom I might have dared to use the word Changeling, and never have come across the term Intermagical. Your help, if unpleasant, was invaluable. And thanks to you for reading. I really hope you enjoyed it, and if you did, I hope you'll share it with your friends.

Wishing you all the best,

Fiona

Author's Note, PostScript

I wrote and recorded the above Author's Note on April 1st, 2023. On that same day, Faeryn was admitted to the hospital with an infection, the complications of which sent her to the ICU in critical condition.

On April 13th, she made a post saying, "I'm never getting out of here," and I felt that terrible ring of truth in her words, and on April 18th, 26 short days before this book was scheduled to be released, she passed, finally free of the body that had caused her such pain and anguish for 33 years. When we got the chance to speak, hours before her passing, she told me how much it meant to her that she would get to live on in fantasy, and in the hearts of all of you.

We're going to start a foundation with the proceeds of this novel, but there is no real need to donate. There is no urgency anymore. In fact, writing this, still in the depths of grief from our family's loss, the exercise of releasing this book at all feels a bit empty and shallow, but it helps to remember how much she loved it and to think of the good works that we will be able to do for our Intermagical community, in her name, and in her honor.

Now, more than ever, for Faeryn.

Acknowledgements

All my thanks and gratitude to the following people, without whom Intermagical would be a thought that I once had, and not a book that you can hold in your hands. It takes a village to create something like this, including beta readers, copy editors, financial supporters, inspiration for characters and someone to loan me their house for a long weekend of audiobook recording.

I appreciate each one of you more than I can say.

Andrew Frishman
Audreaanah Davis
Benjamin 'Jaaya Nansi' Davis
Chris Yellowbird
Conner Scott
Dana Swisher
Dante Ashby
Danielle Zandeki
Elijaah Davis
Eli VanDerPol
Holly Hedge
Joel Stinghen
Joy Lovegood
Kalliope LaBarre
Keenan Michelson
Linda Urquhart
Megg Lynne Hance
Melodie Cristalline De Callistelie
Rebecca Michelson
Rhett & Leslie Wilkins
Sarah Sharp
Seamus O'Quill
Susan Baima
Tara Gray
Tristan Meinke
Zaavanah Davis

About the Author

The author, who grew up with the uncomfortable initials 'TS' and now lives much more happily as Fiona, moved to Oregon after college to get to know her birth family. At that point, fiction and reality diverge, but much of this work of fiction was inspired by the real people and experiences of the author's magical life with her husband, young son, bonus children, polyamorous loves, and an ever-expanding neurodivergent community in the mystically beautiful Pacific Northwest.

Fiona never set out to be a writer, but she did live with one for most of her twenties, a highly intelligent and deeply magical bridge troll who inadvertently gifted her with the knack of turning expansive thought into storytelling. She started her career in the field of mental health to satisfy her desire to understand why people are the way they are and provided care to adults with severe mental illness for several years before burning out and transitioning to the field of technology.

After resigning from a highly anticipated, but ultimately ill-fated start-up for whom she had been the acting CTO, she decided to take an easy administrator role for a year, to give herself a much-needed break. Without the intensive technological problem-solving to take up her intellectual bandwidth, this novel flowed out of her like water from an underground spring, with a second installment following shortly after the first.

She looks forward to a long, green summer full of fun, festivals, and building a greater intermagical community.